BOOK TWO OF THE CATALYST SERIES

KINGDOMS OF SORROW

KINGDOMS OF SORROW

A NOVEL OF POST-APOCALYPTIC SURVIVAL

by JK Franks

Published by Red Leaf Press
Made in USA
2017

Kingdoms of Sorrow is a work of fiction. The characters, events, names, places and incidents are products of the author's imagination or are used fictitiously. Any resemblance to actual events, locales or persons, living or dead, is purely coincidental. Any references to historical events, real people or actual locales are also used fictitiously

Cover art: Mohammad Qureshi
Editor: Kate Juniper
ISBN: eBook: 978-0-9977289-3-4
Hardback: 978-0-9977289-5-8
Paperback: 978-0-9977289-4-1

v-8102-0422

For Milton,
The original storyteller.

"There are only nine meals between mankind and anarchy."
— Alfred Henry Lewis, 1906

PROLOGUE

Andes Mountains, Peru – *1550*

The young girl heard her mother's warning, but it was already too late. Moraikai knew she had offended the god, Supay. It was forbidden for females to venture into the cloud forest unaccompanied by a male. She had not meant to wander so far, but the tiny Andean spectacled bear she had spotted wandered into the trees, and she had followed. The village's ruling priest had already blamed Supay, the spirit god of death, ruler of the underworld, for the recent evils. Other Incan villages had already fallen prey to his wrath.

With the object of her attention now lost in the thick forest, she looked back to the beautiful city perched on the ridge. Her mother, Kalixil, stood a few-hundred steps down the hill, still calling anxiously to her. At barely twelve years old, Moraika was constantly breaking the rules, but as one of the many daughters of the Emperor, she knew she could get away with it. Whatever punishment was deemed appropriate would be passed on to one of the servant girls. That was their job.

She shuddered suddenly at the thought; some of the punishments were harsh, she knew that even with her limited knowledge of suffering. She pushed the thought from her mind, as she did all unpleasant thoughts.

It was time to head back. She pulled the colorful blanket around her shoulders and turned for home. She did not see the shadow, nor realize the man was standing behind her. What she heard first were faint mumblings, and she smelled an odor much like a wet dog.

Kalixil furiously ran the *quipu,* a knotted rope, through her hands, reciting the prayer for her daughter's forgiveness. Unfortunately, it would not be enough. She heard the scream and, looking far up the hill, watched in horror as a spray of blood blossomed from her daughter's tiny body just a moment before she was flung down the hillside. The god of unsavory death had taken its punishment directly this time, refusing to allow the priest to transfer judgment to a less important child. The sudden mass of soldiers running past her in the direction of the carnage surprised her.

They would not interfere with the god's judgment . . . unless it was not judgment, but something worse. She wanted to run to her daughter, but her fear was too great. As an Aclla—a Chosen Woman—her place in the royal court forbade her from mourning her child. If the darkness was already here, though, it might be too late for all of them. She would ask the Sinchi, the girl's father, for advice. She ran back into the city and away from the growing sounds of death on the hill above.

Deep inside the cloud city of Machu Picchu, Sinchi, the chieftain of the village, was facing his own crisis. He was watching the village medicine men perform yet another procedure to remove the evil from one of the tribal elders. This rage-inducing sickness had been responsible for wiping out all the villages in the valley. Machu Picchu had been built to keep the royal family above the sickness of the lowlands, and closer to their god. The healer, a priest known as QuiOlc, was using a hand drill to bore into the man's skull and free the demon. The elder was wide awake and bound tightly to the rock table. He was mumbling gibberish and attempting to thrash and bite. The healer gave a brief smile as he removed the drill and a spurt of liquid emerged from the hole in the skull, briefly clear, then white, then dark red. Sinchi could smell the fetid odor of disease, similar to rotting fish.

The elder stopped his thrashing and looked up at the healer, then at

Sinchi. Clearly relieved for the moment, from the torment of the disease, he weakly but clearly said a prayer of forgiveness and then died. Sinchi walked away. The elder's body would be dumped over the wall of the city to join the unclean mass of corpses that was growing far below. Sinchi heard the anxious tones of one of his wives as it echoed down the hall.

"Allow her to pass," he called to the guards.

Kyoto, Japan – 2003

Icco Yanamura's eyes were locked to the eyepiece as he examined the sample in his microscope. He had received the sample of SARS due to his research on chimeric viral diseases at the prestigious labs of his employer, the University of Tokyo. Icco was becoming convinced this was not a naturally occurring virus, but a mutant. His question now was, had it been engineered by humans, or through some other process? While new discoveries in his field were routine, a new class of unknown virus—particularly one capable of jumping hosts and causing a pandemic—was very rare.

He was intimately versed on the most ruthless of killers throughout history: Spanish flu; bubonic plague; dengue fever; cholera; down to the more minor players like HIV and the Ebola virus. While terrible, these were known to science, all heavily researched. What scared Icco was the unknown. Plagues that had been overlooked or misdiagnosed. Ancient bacteria and viruses that may have predated history, or even humans. What he was looking at now was reminiscent of something he had seen years ago, in a collection of disease fragments on file from a millennia earlier, when a pandemic that started in South America eventually wiped out ninety million people. The virus was attributed to the conquering invaders from Spain. The illness they brought with them, the so-called "Spanish Flu," was also a global epidemic at the time. The unnamed virus, though—the fragment he'd examined—had been killing for many years before then. It was much deadlier and had a very different set of symptoms. Its lethality was near 100 percent, and Icco thought it was likely the killer that in the sixteenth century had completely erased so many civilizations, particularly in Mexico and the Andes mountains in South America.

All he had had until now were ancient fragments of genetic material from the original virus; this was puzzling since the SARS virus he was looking at now was such a close match. The protein shell of the virus, called a capsid, as well as the enclosed genome could have been a twin of the older virus.

Khyber Province Pakistan – *six months ago*

The scientist spoke without leaning away from the binocular microscope. "Tell them—" he paused for a moment, deciding his next move, "—tell them I'll be there in a minute." He resumed his study of the SA1297 sample.

"But Doctor," the young man said in a pleading voice.

"What?" the older man snapped. The ferocity of his voice and its accompanying glare froze the timid assistant in place. He opened his mouth to respond, but a Klaxon began sounding throughout the level. It was not the containment breach siren; that would have been accompanied by doors shutting and locking and inert gas being pumped through tubes that lined the walls and ceiling filling every room and suffocating all lifeforms.

The scientist threw up his hands at the interruption, "What now?" he bellowed.

His assistant shouted above the din, persevering: "They said it was urgent. You need to come now!" He turned and walked briskly away.

This is ridiculous! Dr. Van Siedler fumed inwardly. He was more aware than anyone of the dangerous life-form he was working with, which was why he wanted to be left alone to his work. And yes, it *was* alive, no matter what any of his peers might say behind his back. It was alive and, in his eyes, a work of art. The fragment of the original tissue he'd started with had been frustratingly complex, even to a man of his skill and advanced degrees. It had defied rational understanding, like no disease or pathogen he had ever studied.

Finding the obscure Japanese scientist's twenty-year-old notes had helped more than he cared to admit. Until that point, he had been working on the assumption that this pathogen had evolved from something older, most likely the product of several diverse genetic lines combined, as its biological matrix contained a confusing array of genetic clues.

Dr. Yanamura had developed another hypothesis: a radical idea that this bioform was not a descendent, but instead the ancient ancestor. From this life-form, he drew extrapolations that tied it to numerous modern infectious agents. Yanamura's line of thought had been initially preposterous to Siedler, but over the years, he had explored and dismissed all other conclusions.

The basic question of whether the bioform was a virus, bacterium or something entirely different had still not yet been answered . . . but he had solved one of the more fundamental questions of epidemiology: Are viruses alive? Of that, he now had no doubt. In fact, his more recent breakthrough indicated that viruses might actually have created life.

They were a key to evolution, not just a biological oddity: they had a crude form of DNA; they could, in a way, reproduce; they could adapt to their surroundings, sometimes masterfully: the litmus test for life. What else would it take for his colleagues to qualify it as life?

The Klaxon rose in pitch and volume to yet a higher, angrier level. Protocols dictated that he put the sample back into cryo-containment. He knew how to use the remote manipulator arm, he just normally left that to one of his junior researchers. The task was difficult and time-consuming, and Dr. Siedler was frustrated. Doing so would also mean he would need to wait for hours for the sample to thaw again once whatever supposed crisis had passed. He was one of the oldest research scientists in the God forsaken complex! He also had a well-earned reputation for obstinacy.

While he had worked in labs all over, this place's isolation pleased him in many ways. Stuck down here, hundreds of feet below the scorching desert above, was normal for him after a lifetime of highly secure work in remote facilities.

Giving up for this session, he began the process of storing the sample slide back in the case. Using the black robotic arm, he closed the tiny case and initiated the sequence to place the sample back into cold storage. The overhead lights flickered, and a sudden power surge caused the manipulator arm not to line up correctly with the opening of the nitrogen-filled containment vessel by only a few millimeters. As the arm mistakenly released the grippers, the case, containing a single slide of SA1297, fell to the floor. The Klaxon was almost immediately replaced with a siren that caused Van Siedler's blood to run cold and sent panic through every person at the facility. The lighting overhead shifted to red, and every door on the level began to close, sealing itself forever. Then, everything went dark.

CHAPTER ONE

Present Day - Southern Arkansas, USA

People were dying. Good people had died. Sadly, his sweet wife would soon be among them. He held her hand, looking down at the tears that carved lines in her mud-caked face. Her lips trembled; she was trying to speak, but she could not. The wounds were too deep, and she had lost too much blood. At least she seemed to recognize him again. Or maybe it was just his hope that convinced him she did. It felt like they'd been on the run for hours, but it had not been long.

This was just so wrong! He should be the one in pain. She didn't deserve this.

In the distance, he heard the sounds of their pursuers: the men and the dogs that were hunting them. He felt a weak tug on his arm and saw her lips were moving. He leaned in, desperate to hear her soothing voice once more.

No sound came out, but he thought he knew the words she wanted to say. "Shhh, I love you, too. It will be okay. I wa—" he stopped. He knew what he had to say. But it wouldn't come out. *God, how has it come to this?* Their world had been torn away, and now he was losing her. Watching her suffering like this was breaking his heart. After everything they had been through, after all the time apart, for it to come to this . . . The arterial blood pumping from her wounds was lessening. That was not a good sign.

"I want you to let go now, hon. Just let go. It will be better." His voice wavered and broke; he struggled to continue. "It's better . . ." he struggled, "if you just go ahead. I'll join you soon." A distant dog bark caused her to flinch weakly; she was still aware. Perhaps they could still save her if they got to her soon. That would not do. That would be worse.

How had he ever been one of them? Cowardice, that was how. He could have chosen another route—any number, probably—but instead he agreed to be a part of their madness. It hadn't seemed like a choice at the time, but he realized now, too late, that it was. What drove them and their mindless savagery was beyond his understanding: they possessed a hunger to survive. One that forfeited all humanity, one that he could stay with no longer.

The world had ended with a flourish of color in the night sky; from that point on, civilization had collapsed, those in authority had vanished, gangs and thugs had come and gone. It had all come apart at the seams. What was once normal had disappeared forever in those rippling waves of colored light that lit up the night sky last summer.

The sounds came again, closer now. He raised his eyes from his dying wife. He couldn't leave her, but if he didn't move quickly, he would also die. *Those goddamn bastards.* He would find a way to unleash his rage, somehow, before he, too, gave in. *Before I give up.* She was all he had left, and soon she would be gone, too. He brushed her dark hair away from her face, the face that was still so beautiful as the fingers of his marked hand swept back the wispy strands.

He prayed for her to sleep. Begged God for her pain to stop. He watched the shadows and jittery beams of the flashlights approaching as the men worked their way through the trees toward their hiding place. He could not leave her, not after all he had done to find her, not while she still drew breath. He could not let those animals have her back. Leaning over her, he kissed her cracked, dry lips one last time. "I love you so much, I am so sorry for all this. I'll find her, I promise." Their eyes met, and he thought he saw a small nod of acceptance. Slowly, he slipped the knife from its sheath. It had to be done.

CHAPTER TWO

Harris Springs, Mississippi

Scott Montgomery could barely move in the confined space. While not normally claustrophobic, he knew he was getting close to losing his shit. "DeVonte!" he yelled for the third time. This time he heard a faint response. Looking back down the metallic cave to the entrance, he could just make out a small rectangle of light. "Try it again," he yelled in that direction. He was stuck here in the bowels of the silent cruise ship, attempting to bypass the useless control system in order to access the weather radar system.

"That got it," the response echoed back down the wiring conduit to a much-relieved Scott. There was only room in the narrow space to turn around at key junctions. He was currently curled up in one of them with a multimeter for checking voltage in one hand and a completely fucking useless radio in the other. He wondered again why he was doing this job—then he remembered. *Oh yeah . . . it was my freaking bright idea.*

He wrapped insulating tape around the connection and bound it back into the wiring bundle with a zip tie. "Coming out," he yelled to anyone who might still care that he was down here. Slowly, he twisted his body into a contortionist-worthy position that would allow him to begin inching back up the conduit to the opening on the ship's bridge. He felt a twinge that signaled the beginning of a leg cramp. *Not now*, he thought, trying to force the pain away with sheer willpower, at least until he was free of the confined space.

They had made it through the bulk of the previous year's hurricane season almost unscathed. Here on the Gulf of Mexico, having some advance warning would be very helpful. Inside the massive cruise ship that most of the former town of Harris Springs now called home, Scott had eyed the dead radar dish pensively until he came up with a plan to repair it. The radar system was state of the art Doppler technology, as with most things on the massive cruise liner. The *Aquatic Goddess*, as she was formerly known, had needed the weather radar during its normal routes to avoid frequent tropical storms. The ship no longer went to sea; Scott and his friends had moved into it and then moored it here in the Intracoastal canal behind the town of Harris Springs. It now served as both a refuge and a base camp for over two hundred people who lived in its staterooms as permanent guests. While the residents of the ship could easily withstand the frequent strong storms, others in the surrounding area might not be so lucky. The ship provided for many locals' needs, yet the residents still relied on and helped support countless fishermen, farmers, law enforcement and others living off-ship in the area. Advanced warning of a storm could allow those away from the ship, whether on land or on water, to seek shelter, move resources and do whatever else was necessary to prepare.

It had been five months since the solar flare had brought down the power grid and killed most of the planet's electrical devices. They were just now learning how to bypass some of the ship's control circuitry and adjust voltages from the roof-mounted solar array to get a few things working. The solar flare, or CME blast, had hit late last summer; it was now mid-January. In the months after the collapse, a lot of shit went down. Many died, and much of the town was destroyed, including Scott's house, which was burned down in a pretty dramatic gang attack . . ..

Harris Springs had had a population of nearly 700 people before; now it was around 240. The winter had been especially tough, so that the number of recent dead outweighed the living by a large margin. No family had been spared loss. The grim predictions Scott had learned of in the Catalyst documents his hacker friend had sent him had all proven quite accurate. If anything, the mortality rate, in reality, was even worse than the forecasts had conjectured.

DeVonte gave Scott a hand as he came out of the tiny hatch. Todd, who was the acting mayor of Harris Springs, or perhaps more accurately, Chief of the Boat, turned and winked at his friend. "We got peektures," he joked, drawing out the word to comical levels as he watched the recently animated screen in front of him. Scott could faintly hear the motor on the enclosed radar dish above the superstructure. If it was working correctly, it was turning the dish a full circle about every thirty seconds. "Looks like a storm up to the north, though that could just be terrain that's showing up," Todd continued. "We'll have to watch and see if it moves. May need to adjust the dish angle. The view over the ocean is clean, though. I've moved the view out to the max, which looks to be 250 miles."

"Power use looks preddy steady, and it's drawing a bit less than you projected," DeVonte chimed in, "We should be okay just using it a few times each day. Won't drain the batteries much."

Electrical power was an ongoing issue for the ship. They had a generator, and the big engines themselves also generated power. Occasionally, they ran the massive machines just to charge the batteries and cycle seawater through the onboard desalinization plant. Unfortunately, the amount of fuel needed to run the engines was obscene. While they had plenty of diesel, it was strictly rationed. In time, it would either run out or go bad. The council had to be prepared for that day.

Much of the last five months had been spent bypassing computer controls, fried circuit boards and the various built-in safety systems of the ship. The whole boat was now jury-rigged, but it was mostly working to their minimal requirements which meant it never moved; it was essentially a floating refugee camp. The biggest problem they were facing onboard was air circulation. Even now, in winter, the lower decks of the boat were uncomfortably hot, and most areas had little air movement. Even with access doors and hatchways open, the fresh air did not penetrate far enough into the bowels of the beautiful ship. In the warmer months ahead, they would be unbearable without running AC, but the ship's central HVAC air system would simply not come back to life, no matter how much coaxing they did. The team would be forced to look for other options. Thankfully, most of the current occupants could fit above deck level where most of the rooms had windows or balcony doors to the outside.

DeVonte began to shut the revived system down. "Oh, Kaylie was lookin' for you. I told her you was stuck in the plumbing like a big ol' giant turd. She's waiting for you down in the bar."

The bar was the forward galley several decks below. It had been one of the smaller restaurant/bars on the ship, but it suited the small community's needs for a common space these days.

Todd, Scott, Jack and Bartos had been the combined driving force that saved what was left of the town last summer, and they continued to play their roles on board. Todd and Scott had brought the abandoned cruise ship in from open ocean to its current mooring. Now it sat in the Intracoastal Waterway just down from the mostly abandoned town, their original home, Harris Springs. "Thanks guys, I'm beat. Let me go see what my niece needs . . . then I'm calling it a day."

Scott grabbed a towel off a maintenance cart and dried the sweat and dirt from his face and arms. His unkempt, dark blonde hair needed washing, but that would have to wait a few more days. He pulled on a t-shirt with the guitar-and-spaceship logo of the seventies band, Boston, on the front.

When he arrived at the entrance to the bar, he paused at the door to look at his niece. She was a smaller version of her mom and just as beautiful, although he had to admit she had gotten too skinny lately, a complaint he might apply to everyone he knew. Calories were increasingly hard to come by. Their food was heavily rationed, and frankly, most of what they had to survive on was not very appetizing. Scott had lost almost thirty pounds, and he had been pretty lean to start. "Hey, girl," he greeted her playfully, "what's up?"

Kaylie turned and smiled before she stood and hugged her uncle. She was always genuinely glad to see him, but this show of emotion was unusual, even for her. Scott held her close; something had happened, though he wasn't sure what. "They said Little Rock was judged," she said, nearly in a whisper.

"Who said?"

Tears filled her eyes. "The Messengers. They said Little Rock was judged and found wanting. That the Messengers of God have purged it of its sin and evil."

Scott took his niece by the hand and sat her down in one of the garishly-colored chairs in the Caribbean-themed space. Kaylie was from Little Rock, and the last anyone had heard, her parents were still there. He waited for the sobs to diminish before speaking.

"Your dad is a smart man, Kaylie. He told me they were bugging out the first week. Honey, they would not still be there. You have to stop listening to those preachers on the radio. The crusaders, or Messengers, or whatever they're calling themselves this week, are simply spreading panic and guilt. We don't have time for that. They want everyone to believe the Rapture happened, and God is using them to unleash the Four Horsemen on the Earth! I'm going to talk with Bartos. He's letting you spend too much time in the radio room . . . it isn't healthy."

"I want to find my mom, Uncle Scott! And I need to stay in touch with DJ," she said, a bitter edge to her voice. "Besides, the Messengers are on almost all the channels that are still broadcasting. It's hard to hear anything *but* them . . . Could they really have destroyed an entire city?"

Scott wasn't sure. The group seemed to have formed from a number of evangelical survivors and now appeared to be massing into more of a radicalized Christian gang. "I don't know, Bubbles. I doubt it. Most likely they found the city in ruins and are just taking credit for it."

"Well, shit, that makes me feel so much better," she said sarcastically.

Scott raised his eyebrows apologetically. "No lies, remember our deal? I'm not sugarcoating anything for you in this fun new world. We'll keep calling for your dad, you stay on schedule with DJ, and we'll let Bartos or the other listeners monitor those Bible-thumping crazies up the road."

DJ was Kaylie's boyfriend. She had left him behind in Tallahassee when Scott and Todd rescued her and DeVonte from the campus in the days just after the CME. DJ was doing bioresearch at FSU under pressure from a mysterious occupying task force called "Praetor." Scott still wasn't sure if they were good guys or not, but the viral research DJ performed seemed to be vitally important to them following the flare.

Scott had attempted to set up a way for the two sweethearts to talk by radio, but the distance had been too far. They had not been able to make contact at all, until a repeater was set up near Mobile, that is, by some US Navy guys that Scott and Todd were friends with. Now they were able to get semi-regular reports from DJ from the labs at the university. In turn, they passed any strategic information back to the surviving Navy. In truth, the Navy was probably monitoring it all; after all, they had the equipment and the frequencies, but Todd went through the motions of keeping them informed via a secure military link just to be sure.

So much had changed in just five months, since the massive solar flare had struck Earth and crippled the electrical grid, rendering most electronics useless. The power failed; transportation ground to a stop, effectively ending all food supplies; clean water became harder to get; medical care ceased. Then the economy collapsed, dollars became worthless, banks closed, and quickly, law enforcement and the government stopped functioning altogether. Survival was now a constant endeavor and death a frequent visitor.

He looked at the empty bar. The liquor bottles were all but gone at this point. *What I wouldn't give for a few fingers of good Scotch and a steak,* he thought. Scott kissed his niece on the forehead. "Nothing's changed since yesterday, Kay. Your mom and dad are not in little Rock. I'm heading to the bunks to get some rest."

"Not going home tonight?" she asked.

"Too tired," he said, wandering down the darkened corridor. "Love you," he called back.

"Love you, too," she whispered as he disappeared into the dark.

CHAPTER THREE

They had both decided to live in one of the nicer beach homes after the family cottage had been burned down. Quite often, though, they wound up staying on the *AG*, as it was starting to be known. Much of their work was there, and, especially with the shorter winter days, walking or riding bikes several miles home in the dark wasn't fun. Scott still wasn't comfortable being surrounded by people day and night, but it was certainly safer. He had once been something of a misanthrope, a loner hiding out after a ruined marriage, but his social anxiety had been pretty much pushed to a remote corner once every hour of every day became laser focused on surviving.

≈

Kaylie tried to sleep. She knew her uncle was probably right. Her dad was prepared; he would have gotten out of town quickly. Probably headed deep into the Ozark Mountains where the family had a small cabin. She was pretty sure he had a couple of caves in mind as backup locations, too. He was always a bit of a crazy prepper in her mind . . ..

He'd told Scott he didn't have a working vehicle, though, and the

Ozarks were almost 200 miles north of their home. Maybe they actually tried to come south toward where she, Scott, and the family's beach cottage was—*used to be*—she corrected herself. She knew in her heart that her dad would have multiple safe places to go. She just had a bad feeling, something she just couldn't shake. After Todd and her uncle had gotten her from Tallahassee, they'd been unable to reach her parents to let them know she was safe. She knew that not knowing whether she was safe would be driving them both crazy with worry.

She tossed and turned in the small bunk, listening to the snores echoing through the confines of the space. Kaylie was supposed to help in the clinic tomorrow, and she knew it would be a long day, it always was. But all she could think of were the horrible things she had heard about the Messengers and their terrifying spree. It wasn't fair. Surviving through everything so far had been hard enough: the soldiers, the gangs, the hunger. And now, after all that, she had to hear about these supposed Christians reining righteous vengeance on the living. She tossed the cover off, slipped into her sneakers, and grabbed a light by the bed. She headed down to the gym where she could practice her Keysi training and try to work off some of this anger.

Nearing the glass door of the gym, she was surprised to see a light coming from within. As she walked in, she noticed another woman working out on one of the machines. Kaylie had seen her several times, but they had never actually met. She gave a polite nod in greeting. Many of the workout machines wouldn't work without electricity; others had been modified to bypass the controls, so they functioned but without displays or timers. The other woman sighed as she finished up a set and appeared about to move over to some nearby weights. Walking over, Kaylie smiled and introduced herself.

The tall, African-American woman returned her smile and said, "I know who you are honey ... still, nice to meet you. I'm Angelique. Call me Angel."

Kaylie picked up on the woman's accent right away. "Angelique is an unusual name . . . and your accent . . . I'm guessing upper Midwest, maybe Minnesota?"

The woman chuckled. "Close, Wisconsin. Good guess, though."

"So why did you take this particular cruise?" Kaylie asked with a smile.

"Oh, you know, the food, the entertainment, exotic ports of call . . . it seemed to satisfy my need to explore, but with less sea sickness." They both laughed.

Kaylie and Angel, as she preferred to be called, talked as they worked out. "So, Angel, were you here on vacation?"

"Yes, I was with some friends. We were staying in one of the condos. The day the flare hit we were all lying out on the beach. No one really noticed anything about it, except for the fact that most of our cell phones were dead. Then, we got back to the condo, and the power was off. Man, that room was hot! I don't know how you guys ever made it here before air conditioning."

Kaylie smiled. "You get used to it." Sweat was dripping from both women in torrents.

"No," Angel laughed, "No, you don't. Anyway, here we all were, with no family around, no friends in the area and no way to get home. I didn't even have a way of getting money or calling anyone for help. Took me a while to figure out I was stranded. Honestly, girl, I was scared to death.

"We all stayed in the condo, but before long it started to stink, people was getting crazy . . . I started helping the preacher in one of the volunteer tents just so I could get some food and bottled water. I didn't know what else to do. When your uncle and Todd came back, I mean, after the battle downtown . . ." A faraway look crossed her face for a few seconds, " . . . I decided I was safer here than trying to get home. I just try and help out where they need me, do odd jobs, survive."

"What happened to your friends?"

Angel's face stirred briefly with emotion before she cleared her throat and said, "It's late." She stepped off the treadmill, "I gotta help in the cafeteria for breakfast. It was nice meeting you, Kaylie."

She raised a hand in goodbye as she left the gym for the dark beyond.

Puzzled, Kaylie replied, "Likewise . . . see you around," and resumed her late-night workout.

CHAPTER FOUR

August, the previous year

Pakistan - Undisclosed Location

The wind blew fiercely but gave no relief from the oppressive heat. Instead, the sand cut and burned the hands holding the binoculars. "Shit," he said as he dropped them back to his side. *What a clusterfuck this assignment was becoming.*

Two days before it all went to shit, he was standing above the River Liffey in Dublin, Ireland. He had been watching a group of teens harass a pretty girl. Hooligans, his grandpa would have called them. He was trying to decide whether to get involved or not. That was the moment he got the call. The call from a special phone, the same phone that even now was in his pocket.

He had been in Ireland to help teach counter-terrorism tactics to a small group of French, British, Irish and Belgian soldiers and police, all of them, spec-ops members. Even in August, Ireland had been so cool, just wonderful compared to this nightmarish heat. He was on loan to the Army when the phone rang. When the higher-ups called, you did what they said. In this case, what they had said in a nutshell was, "Get to Pakistan immediately." The tasking instructions sent later added that he was not to travel by air nor take any of the European high-speed trains that were so efficient. *So, he was to rush but not take anything fast. Military intelligence was indeed an oxymoron.*

Puzzling as the instructions were, he went to his loft apartment and collected all military insignia and papers that identified him, even though none were in his actual name. He placed them in a burn bag, which he would drop in the furnace chute when he left. Packing his gray-and-beige-patterned battle fatigues, he pulled on his rarely used civilian travel clothes, geared up in as covert a manner as possible, then checked the ferry schedule to England. Once again, his identity to them was just the combat call sign and a number. He was on permanent assignment to Praetor, full name Praetor Paramilitary Battlegroup 9. No one used a real name or rank. He was simply Skybox-5: five for his rank, something close to a captain in the Army, though any comparison to the normal military was irrelevant. Praetor Battlegroups had a ground-up command structure: soldiers in the field made the decisions, and since every fighting member of Praetor was an elite soldier of command rank, those decisions were generally the correct ones.

The trip had been exhausting and eventful to say the least. He had almost made it through Austria on his way toward Turkey when the solar flare hit. He had been on a regular passenger train, but even that ground slowly to a halt. While most passengers stayed put, he had hit the door and immediately started off on foot. In the distance, he saw the large steel support towers with dozens of electrical lines. Random electrical discharges were arcing up and down the wires. He felt sure someone must have dropped a nuke or an EMP bomb somewhere on the continent. This close to good old Mother Russia, anything was possible.

It soon became evident that the problem had not just been with the train and the electric lines. While most of the old cars on the road were still working, most newer vehicles had been abandoned. Some seemed to have gone out of control and wrecked or drove off into ditches. Every single one of the small towns he walked through was dark.

He walked for three hours before his phone chirped. He knew it was hardened against EMP blasts but was still relieved to see it was working. He had to admit, P-Group always had the best toys. The ID documents they provided got him through every checkpoint without incident, and his compact go-bag included almost anything he could possibly need to move across both hostile and friendly territory with ease.

The text message contained his tasking instructions and acknowledgment that electricity worldwide had been affected by a massive, X-class CME (a coronal mass ejection to civilians). He was to continue on his original orders by making his way to a seaport on the east coast of Italy. Suitable transportation would be waiting.

Yeah, I'm fine, thanks for asking, he thought. They knew he was alive; they tracked his every movement on the phone. That was all they needed to know. The instructions also contained a time limit. He had to reach the Italian port of Ancona in twelve hours. That didn't give him much time.

At a small farm near the Austrian city of Graz, he reluctantly "borrowed" an old Fiat sitting outside a ramshackle barn. He left two gold coins on the steps of the barn as a very healthy rental fee.

The car was older than he was, and none of the instruments worked. He didn't imagine the car—let alone whatever fuel remained—would get him all the way, but it beat walking. His priority, as always, was to fulfill the mission. Never did he waver from that objective.

As he crossed into Italy a couple of hours later, he had to fight the urge to stop and help when he saw the unmistakable wreckage of a sleek, bullet train. He guessed the train had left the track traveling near its top speed: over 400 kilometers per hour. The kinetic energy would have been like a bomb going off. It had demolished most of the idyllic village with which it collided. The unmistakable sounds of people in agony came from across the wreck site, the carnage partially masked by billowing black smoke that came from the ruined buildings and the twisted wreckage.

While he was a hardened soldier, he was not heartless. Far from it, in fact. Staying focused on getting to the port instead of rendering aid to these poor people took a great deal of effort. His many years of training and experience in the field forced him constantly to compartmentalize and prioritize. His assumption was whatever the mission he was on must be vital. Another thought that kept creeping in was that someone at command had known the CME was imminent. The original instructions on the call had said as much by its specific travel instructions.

Whatever the reason, his new mission took precedence over everything else.

It had taken five more days just to cross the Mediterranean on a smelly fishing boat, then navigate down through Saudi Arabia. A suffocating, hot train ride and yet another fishing boat across the Gulf of Oman got him at last to Pakistan. Finally, thirty-six hours after crossing the border, he reached the site outside Peshawar in the Khyber Province.

He had been frustrated at how long it had taken, but he was still the first of his group to arrive. Now they were all here in this hot, miserable sandbox. One of his senior leaders, a man he had only ever known by the call sign Reaper-3, reported that the patrols were back.

"Very good. Did they confirm our intel?"

"Yes, sir, all occupants of the university as well as the village are dead."

"Anything on the PBS?" The portable biohazard sampler was one of their nifty gizmos from Praetor command.

"No, sir. Genghis doesn't think it's working. He said the sunspots probably took it out. I ordered the patrol to wear the bio-battle suits, but they're all suffering from the heat and dehydration now because of them. Those damn things are just too hot to use here."

Well, shit, Skybox thought. Genghis was the group's lead tech, and he would know if the PBS were on the fritz. Apparently not all the cool tech they had was hardened sufficiently. "Reaper, verify that everyone got both rounds of immunizations. Whatever the hell got out of that lab down there could wipe us out, too. We take no chances."

Nodding, Reaper turned and walked away. Command had said the vaccines they supplied yesterday would offer protection from the pathogen that had been released from the level 4 facility. The medical university nearby had provided abundant talent for the secret facility. Skybox wasn't sure if it was one of theirs or someone else's, but the fact the vaccine arrived so quickly made him think this was their problem. Black sites like these would not be put on domestic soil: usually the more remote the location the better. *And this is pretty damn remote.* The small village ahead and this large university were all there was for hundreds of kilometers.

Pulling up the schematics on the tablet, he still could not grasp how a failure could have occurred. *When the power failed, there were backup generators, and other fail-safes, and multiple levels of redundancies to make sure the facility was self-contained . . . No circulation of air, water or people would leave the building in such a circumstance. Everything went into lock-down. The damn thing's designed with failure in mind.* He dropped the device back to the table and dropped heavily into the hard chair beside it.

Darkness was settling in, but he had to come up with a plan. Looking over the valley, he could almost see it in his mind's eye. Closing his eyes, he went over the intel. From the surface, the small building looked like any other structure on the campus. The actual labs were many stories below the non-descript stone-and-brick building. He knew that the most dangerous labs lay in the very bottom levels, buried deep here in the desert. *Nothing should have ever gotten out of that building when the power failed.*

Yet something did, and it was killing everything within miles already. Not just killing, either. What it did to the victims before death was unspeakable.

CHAPTER FIVE

Long before he was Skybox-5, he had been a somewhat reckless teenager living near Chicago. He had a different name then, not that it mattered now. Only one person from that life still existed, and he was trapped in a body with a damaged brain. That man, his friend, would never be able to speak his or any other name again.

Skybox believed in the mission of P-Guard, or just the 'Guard' as they often referred to themselves now. What kept him loyal, though, was the brotherhood, the love for his teammates. It was the only brotherhood he had.

He had convinced Tommy to join the Army with him when they turned eighteen. They went through basic together and early on had been assigned to the same unit. Skybox had made it up the ranks to become a Ranger and was eventually picked by the CIA to join the Jawbreaker team that went into Afghanistan after 9/11. Tommy had his own unique set of skills and later was also recruited into the paramilitary branch. Once more, he was deployed to the same Area of Operations as his best friend. The two met up as often as possible, and Skybox eventually got Tommy reassigned to his division.

Skybox had been the one driving the Humvee when they hit the IED outside Fallujah in 2004. While he had come out with only a few cuts, a jagged piece of the passenger-side floorboard had blasted up and through the side of Tommy's helmet. His friend would never be the same again, and he could never stop blaming himself for it.

It was around then that the CIA had officially stepped out of Iraq, although not very far. When the unit came under new leadership and started referring to itself as Praetor, they offered him a command level position, an upgrade from P5 to P9. The one other inducement they had offered was to give Tommy the best care possible. His friend had no family, and Skybox couldn't stand the thought of him being in a VA hospital for the rest of his life. He had signed on, and command had kept their word. Even with whatever was going on out in the world right now, he knew Tommy would be safe and cared for.

That didn't mean he understood or agreed with everything P-Group was up to. He hoped to hell they didn't have anything to do with this lab being here. That would not sit well with him or his men. But why else would his deployment orders have brought him here before shit even went down?

His eyes were heavy, and the reports were starting to blur when a thin man with vague Asian features walked into the tent. Genghis was command level 2, but right now their tech guy was the one really in charge of figuring out how to fight this microscopic enemy. "Tell me you have an answer," was Skybox's greeting.

"You aren't going to like it, Sky. We have to pull back and do it now. This pathogen is unlike anything on record. It's scaring the shit out of all of us."

"We're protected, we have suits and the vaccines. All we need—"

"No!" the ferocity of the man's voice surprised them both. "You don't understand. What we have isn't working. The men that went on patrol are showing symptoms. They're not allowed outside the Q-hut."

The impact of Genghis' words hit with the force of a heavyweight boxer. His was not a large squad; he had handpicked everyone in Talon

Battlegroup. He had sent those men down there. "Neither the suits nor the vaccines are working?" he asked.

"The suits didn't work. Whatever these crazy bastards cooked up down there can get through our filters. It's probably how it escaped containment when the power failed." Genghis leaned heavily on the table, looking exhausted. He wiped a stream of sweat from his forehead. "Our research suggests that the vaccines we all took are slowing the pathogen, but they aren't stopping it. This shit is worse than the Aral Sea incident."

Skybox wasn't familiar with the reference, though he knew the Aral Sea was a mostly landlocked lake in Kazakhstan that had shrunk considerably over the last thirty-plus years. Genghis filled in the blanks. Vozrozhdeniya Island was a speck of an island in the vast Aral Sea—back when it *was* a sea. The Russians did bioweapon research there as it was thought to be ideally isolated. In 1971, they accidentally released a weaponized version of smallpox into the air. The first person infected was on a ship, nine miles away. The release was later attributed to maintenance personnel failing to change filters in the air scrubbers as needed. The facility also housed samples of modified anthrax spores and bubonic plague. While the number of deaths from the release was unclear, the genie was out of the bottle. And with the shrinking of the Aral Sea, Vozrozhdeniya was no longer an island; it was a peninsula. "Although the labs were closed shortly thereafter, it remains a biological hot zone—one wholly unprotected, so anyone can walk up to the front door. Just like here," Genghis concluded.

Skybox yelled for Reaper. Already he could feel his chest tighten and his breathing become shallower. Reaper poked his head in the tent flap. "Yes, sir?"

"Time to move us back. We need to put a buffer between us and the hot zone. Relocate the base back twenty klicks."

"Roger that, sir. Gladly!"

CHAPTER SIX

September, the previous year

Khyber Province, Pakistan

It had been a month since the solar flare had hit. Skybox had never faced an enemy like this; he felt sure no one had. Military solutions in this situation simply would not work. Yes, they could do a reasonable job of keeping any locals stupid enough to wander into the hot zone from ever leaving again, but the contagion was still spreading.

He sat on the cot staring through an open tent flap at a beautiful sunset over a distant mountain peak. *You did this. You are the enemy.* A strange thought. He considered his options. *Containment is failing, treatment and research is progressing too slow . . . Communication with the rest of the world is almost nonexistent.* Normally, the Guard would have brought in top experts from around the globe. Now, they were cut off. They were on their own.

The solidly built quarantine rooms, or Q-hut, had been moved just outside the camp's perimeter. That was not so much for safety but in order to lessen the sounds of agony and torment that were coming from the infected. Talon was losing several men a week to the infection. If they became symptomatic, Genghis' team separated them out. Everyone knew no one survived once they went into quarantine. Several of his team had taken matters into their own hands: opted for a faster way out. One had wandered into the desert and pulled the pins on several grenades clipped to his battle vest. No one wanted to go through those final stages of the infection.

Even now, Skybox could hear the growls coming from the direction of Q-hut. This entire assignment was sliding sideways. To make matters worse, P-Group was requesting tissue samples and bodies. His men were not stupid; they felt like lab rats. Dying a stupid death in this miserable place only to wind up as a body in a research lab was not what any of them had signed up for. That, combined with the rumors of the rest of the world going to shit, had made keeping anyone focused on the mission nearly impossible.

Skybox knew that he was a good soldier, maybe even one of the best. He followed orders, never failed on a mission and above all, was very adaptable. No plan survives contact with the enemy; every soldier knew that. But this mission was tossing everything out the window. Everything had been reactionary, and nothing had been remotely effective. He needed answers. P-Guard Command wanted a military option. If he didn't give them one, they would make the decision for him. Right now it was, at best, a war of attrition for his Talon squad. If he kept losing men and pulling back, it was just a matter of time before the end. The virus would be out, and all would be lost.

"That would be a big mistake," an aggravated soldier said as he looked out over a terrain filled primarily with sand and misery.

"Diesel, would you care to elaborate?"

"Sorry, sir. It's just that dropping an incendiary bomb on the target would likely just disperse the agent even more. Sure, you can kill whatever is still in that building, but this little bugger is out. It's breeding, multiplying and actively searching for new hosts. It's a fucking plague, sir."

"Is that your professional opinion?"

"It's the truth. It's a fact, and no one studying this pathogen will tell you anything differently."

His second-in-command was being insubordinate, but that did not mean he was incorrect. Skybox's piercing gray eyes held the man's glare. "Diesel, I need answers. The containment failed, the protective suits failed, the vaccine failed." He swallowed down the thick taste of bile and stared out across the barren wasteland. "You make a good case not to carpet-bomb the place back into the Stone Age. But shit . . . the hot zone keeps expanding, and our job is *not* to just keep backing up. We're almost fifty klicks from the lab now. Give me some options."

"Sir, I don't have any. We've tried to sterilize everything from here to the labs. The only things living that we can see are those damn vultures that keep going in after the bodies. Our gunners are killing them off, but . . . well, I'm sure some have gotten past us. Birds, rats, fleas, who knows what else, they're all getting out. The plague is not contained. The hot zone is expanding beyond our sights whether we know it or not. It's a matter of days until we start hearing of other infected zones outside of here. Genghis has cooked, bleached, irradiated, exposed the test samples to everything we have. Nothing kills it completely. I'm not even sure we could kill it all with a nuke. Whatever these guys cooked up down there is one vicious motherfucker. Sir, I would suggest you talk to Genghis again, see if he has any new ideas."

～

Genghis was not much more helpful. The man was obviously exhausted and irritated at being summoned from his lab to brief his commander. He sat awkwardly on the uncomfortable stool.

"Chief, I don't know what else to tell you, we're not even sure if it's viral or bacterial. HQ thinks the closest thing we have to it resembles Mycobacterium tuberculosis, but to me it seems much more primitive, ancient even. The way it behaves is more like a prion . . . it affects the protein structures in the spinal cord and brain."

This man was one of the most distinguished scientists in his field. Back in the States, he would be running his own research lab. A medical doctor with advanced degrees in biology and chemical engineering and state of the art field equipment, Genghis was pretty much unquestionably - the best they had. It amazed Skybox that he worked for P-Group when he could easily be getting rich in a biotech company back home. "Doc, what's a prion?"

Genghis pulled the shemagh tactical scarf away from his neck, wiped the grit from his face and chin and tossed it on the table. "Think — mad cow disease."

Skybox looked at him, puzzled. "Our men are dying from mad cow disease?"

"No . . ." Genghis sighed, clearly frustrated and exhausted. "No, mad cow disease is one of the better known neurodegenerative disorders which is caused by a prion. While viruses or bacteria are the more common infectious agents, prions are a third. We don't understand much about them, but they are always fatal, typically causing a form of encephalitis—inflammation of the brain. Prions literally fold and reshape proteins in the brain, with unpredictable results."

Skybox nodded his head, only partially understanding. Genghis paused and helped himself to a bottle of water from the cooler before sitting back down. He might as well take his time; what else was there left for him to try in the lab?

"Maybe a little history would help. The lethality of this pathogen appears to be over ninety percent, which makes this an incredibly hot disease. By *hot* we're referring to how fast it spreads and how quickly it kills. Those two parameters are usually in opposition. If a disease kills

too fast, then normally, that limits how far and how fast it can spread .
. ..

"Most global pandemics we know of are much less lethal than this. Bubonic plague or the Spanish flu were, at best, thirty to fifty percent lethal. See, a disease which quickly kills off all the potential hosts leaves it with nowhere else to go, so a hot infection's zone is normally a small, well-contained one. This doesn't seem to be the case here, however, because this thing is adapting, mutating. The newer victims are showing very different symptoms to those first infected. And the original samples we took three weeks ago are different to what we see now. That's why Command keeps asking for new samples. What's more, the survivors—the ten percent—appear to be completely asymptomatic. And I have no idea why."

Skybox flinched at the mention of samples. Genghis was referring to bodies, both alive and dead. Already, a number of his men had been sealed in vacuum sleeves to be frozen and airlifted back to the States in portable self-contained level-5 containment vessels. They looked like a stainless steel coffin to him. He looked up at Genghis. "Look, I know you're doing your best, but if we can't stop this, we're all going to be samples. Give me the specifics. How can it be spread, what options do we have to slow or stop it?"

Genghis stood with what seemed to be all the energy he had and went to the board hanging on the wall of the tent. "It seems to be communicable by multiple pathways. The initial method appeared to be airborne, but thankfully, that supposition was proved false. Primarily, it was transferred by direct contact. We've tested it, and now it is also transmitted via blood and saliva, like rabies. It can live in a state of dormancy outside the host for long periods. We see very little degradation, so hard to say how long, but trust me, this thing was meant to survive. Also, although unlikely around here, it could be water-borne. This thing has an outer shell the viral equivalent of Kevlar." He looked at Skybox to confirm he was following before he turned back to the board and continued.

"Inside the body, something about it changes. What we see indicates that the main infection vector is bacterial. Only that's not completely accurate. My feeling is that this is something else. Something more closely related to an Archaea domain." Looking over his shoulder, he saw he was losing his commander again. "Sorry, sir. Archaea are a relatively new classification of life on our planet. Single-celled microbes with no nucleus or other attributes that would classify a living organism as plant or animal—the two categories all life has been organized into 'til their discovery in the seventies. Normally, we think of them as extremophiles, living in very harsh conditions . . . think underwater volcanoes or caves that have been sealed for eons. They don't belong to either of the other two kingdoms of life, yet they are ancient. All life may have come from them, or something like them."

"So, these Archaea are deadly to humans?"

"Not necessarily, which is why no one seemed to be considering it. On their own, they would not be, but they possess the ability to use and manipulate other life-forms, sometimes changing those life-forms in strange ways. For instance, the tiny shrimp that live in the extreme heat of those underwater volcanoes, the black smokers deep down on the ocean floor—how are they not cooked instantly? My personal theory is that it may likely be thanks to a form of Archaea at work."

"Okay, Genghis, but we're not shrimp, and these Archaea aren't assisting our survival, they're denying it."

"True enough, Commander, but keep in mind, this thing was engineered. If the Archaea is as ancient as we think, it may predate nearly all other life-forms. Which could also mean it's an ancestor to other life—even all life! It may be the genetic key to the backdoor of all life! How else could it have survived so long, in such obscure places and hostile environments?

"That key—its ability to adapt and control—was likely the most intriguing factor to whatever scientist was investigating the type of bioweapon they could turn it into.

"Well, he or she has combined it with the mother of all viruses. If I'm right, the Archaea is the thing that is constantly readjusting the viral agent, something the original research scientist may not have realized in their controlled environment. The virus portion is mutating and replicating while the Archaea is looking to expand into new hosts and new environments. One of the good things about viruses has always been that they don't often jump species. But this one can. It's a chimera, something that should never have existed outside of nightmares.

"Sir, most infections are bacterial, viral, parasitic or fungal. This bitch is none of that, and yet it's some parts of all of them—one mean fucking killer in a league all its own. As I said, the ancient part—the original part—could have been around for millions of years. It could be what wiped out the dinosaurs! Whoever re-engineered it, though, didn't think that was enough. They went ahead and gave it Ironman-like super powers."

The scientist leaned against the table and took a drink of water before he looked his commander directly in the eye. "Sir, what we have here is a nearly perfect bioweapon. Easily transferable, with a slow incubation, so enemy combatants can carry it back to villages or camps, at which point, it ramps up quickly and drives the hosts insane along with all the other crazy shit. As I mentioned, it has a near ninety-one percent lethality as we speak. It's been designed to be super-aggressive, kill large groups relatively quickly, then die out completely."

Skybox watched as Genghis wrote all these facts on the board. "So why is it not dying out?" he asked.

Genghis thought for a moment. "Consider this possibility, sir, and admittedly it's only a hypothesis. Life—really all life anywhere—has one real function: to survive. Typically, it does this through reproduction. Many life-forms simply die once they replicate—even human physiology begins to decline after childbearing. An ancient life-form would have to be super-effective at survival in order to expand and escape the primordial soup. It would have to replicate, fill an ecosystem, expand into new territory and evolve into more and more advanced permutations. Life wants to exist, and it's engineered to find a way. Viruses, or possibly this even more ancient Archaea, could have started it all."

"So, all life started from an ancient virus?"

"It's possible, yes. Not that we would necessarily identify its ancestors today as viruses, but in light of the clues, many other scientists and I say, yes, life likely evolved from a virus. Or Archaea. In other words, it's fucking resilient."

Skybox let out a long exhalation. His face drained of color as he considered this. "Holy shit. So, the disease is adapting, but the victims are dying. They are mutating, but they don't survive it. If what you're saying is accurate, shouldn't some of them have shown signs of mutation? Shouldn't there be an increasing survival rate?"

"Yes," Genghis nodded, "and that's the problem with my theory. The mortality rate and symptoms have changed very little. But we have no idea how long an Archaea might take to actually modify a host life-form. It would probably come down to the creature's makeup. A simpler life-form might be changed in a few thousand to a few hundred-thousand years . . . more complex creatures could take millions of years. The original weaponized version...the engineered pathogen was designed with a limit to how long it could survive outside the host body. This would have been done to increase lethality, but limit spread of infection. They likely did this by tinkering with the genetic code, splicing in fragments of other DNA and RNA.

"We think it also originally had a problem replicating in colder climates. If it is indeed as old as we suppose, then the Ice Age would likely have made it go dormant or nearly extinct. In monkeying around with the code to make it withstand cooler climates, we think . . . I think they incorporated the Archaea and inadvertently gave it a hidden ability to adapt its replication process. This isn't some computer program that will simply perform its task then shut off. It's a living thing. To be honest, I doubt whatever mad scientist dreamt this nasty bugger up would even recognize it anymore. Anyway, it changed, morphed, grew a super suit—in short, it's out, and it wants us dead."

Skybox looked pained. "Okay. I actually understand a lot of what you just said. I just can't believe those idiots would have created something so deadly." He felt anger rising and took a moment to control it. "How do we stop it? And what the fuck is it doing? To the . . .victims?"

"You've seen it, heard it. It's damn sure not natural. Our best answer is little more than a guess at this point. Since we can't find any sedation that works reliably on the victims, we can't get close enough to study them until they're near death. From what we've witnessed, it mirrors some symptoms of rabies such as mania and hyper-excitability, followed by a persistent low-grade fever. Then something starts happening at the cellular level.

"My guess is that it is epigenetic—the victim's base genome is being rewritten, manipulated, and with that comes unbelievable pain and . . ." he sighed heavily, "the initial onset of rage. That stage lasts several days before the bodies begin releasing shocking amounts of epinephrine into their systems, preventing them from feeling all pain. As the encephalitic symptoms begin, there is swelling in the brain as its proteins fold. The victims are only partially aware of themselves and their surroundings at this point. They appear to lack all ethical judgment and become filled with the desire to attack prey—an effective short-term method of spreading. The subjects experience acute rage, they attack violently . . . at times they kill, though more often it is simply to wound. Whatever, or whomever they attack are almost always infected in the process."

Skybox rubbed his forehead in disbelief and groaned. "This sounds like sci-fi zombie shit."

"Not zombies, sir," Genghis replied. "They're not brainless. They're not slow. And they're not trying to eat us, although they certainly bite. If you shoot them, they will die. You need to shoot them someplace vital, but they will die. The agent that's driving them is primitive and efficient. It wants to grow, reproduce and survive like any form of life. Think of it more like rabies, but amped-up a hundred times. Given enough time, I think it may find a better way for replication . . . and that will be worse."

The soldier-cum-scientist wrote two more words on the board then dropped the marker back into the tray. "Sky . . . in my opinion, while the CME might have started this, the global blackout is likely the least of our worries. This pathogen may well mean the end of the human race. Extinction, sir." He waited a moment for a response, and when none came, he turned and walked slowly out of the tent.

Skybox heard another rage-filled scream from the Q-hut as he stared at the final words scrawled on the whiteboard: *The End.*

CHAPTER SEVEN

Present Day

Northern Gulf of Mexico

"AG Base, do you read, do you copy? Come in. Polo to base, come in . . . Still nothing, Jack. I don't think it's getting through."

"Turn it off then, and pull down the slackline antenna, too. We gotta move, they may have already gotten a fix on the transmitter."

He and his crew had been ducking in and out of inlets and small coves all day trying to avoid the open sea. The four men on the recently acquired and renamed *Marco Polo* had been making pretty meager trade stops down the coast to Louisiana. The thirty-five-foot Hike Workboat was a beast, a real find for the gang in Harris Springs. Bartos had spent two months retrofitting the craft to be less conspicuous. While it no longer looked like the coastal patrol boat it was, it certainly didn't look like a shrimp or fishing boat, either. The man originally called to preach was now more of a merchant, trading goods from the AG up and down the coast.

With no working radar, they usually stayed moored in shallow harbors at night. That changed two nights ago, though, when they saw running lights from both the east and south heading directly for where they were anchored. They had fled into the labyrinth of rivers and bayous. They knew pirates, or whatever they wanted to be called these days, were beginning to work the coastal regions. They had heard about them mainly operating between Houston and New Orleans; the pickings over this way were pretty slim: no big towns or ports until you got to Mobile, which was under Naval control.

The cargo hold of the *Marco Polo* was stocked with food, bourbon, sugar and other supplies they had been trading for. One more stop down the coast for seafood, rice and ammo, and they would be done. Jack looked at his marine pilot. "Scoots, what's your call?"

The young man removed his ball cap and wiped the top of his bald head. "I think we're fucked either way. Dem launches dey was usin' had to be high-speed cigarette racers or something, no way we can outrun 'em. Most likely have a mother ship out there farther back, too. Soon as we poke our head out, dey gonna close the noose on it."

That was the problem with the end of the world. Yeah, food, fuel and porn were scarce, but you pretty much had your pick of boats, cars, houses . . . more stuff than anyone could ever have use for. "Keep us as close to shore as possible," Jack replied. "If they have radar, I want us to look like just another sandbar. Slow drift us when you can, but let's keep heading west."

"West? You don't wanna try for home, Preacher?"

"Nope, we got one more stop to make, and I'm counting on them having exactly what we need to make it back to Harris Springs Marina in one piece."

"Roger that," Scoots dropped the idling motor into gear and began to nudge her out into the channel.

"All eyes on the horizon," Jack yelled. "We need as much warning as possible if they spot us."

While they spotted reflections on the horizon several times, somehow, they seemed to escape detection. By late afternoon, they were feeling more confident and running full throttle toward their next destination. Jack was troubled, though; he knew the only way home was right back through the noose. If Todd had been there, they would have just taken the boat out to deep water and gone around that mess. But none of the crew were real sailors, and even Jack preferred to stay in sight of land at all times. Todd had his hands full trying to keep the *AG* and what was left of Harris Springs functioning, as well as looking out for DeVonte, whom he'd taken in after the boy's family was murdered over near Mobile.

At nightfall, they anchored several miles up the Old Pearl River, which was also the state boundary between Mississippi and Louisiana. Slidell, their next stop, was still several hours farther west. As Jack studied the maps, Scoots came over to offer a suggestion. "Once we make dis last pickup, we could head straight out the Rigolets and across Lake Borgne to Bay Boudreau. Then we could leapfrog much of our way back using all those little islands for cover."

Jack had already considered just such a move and dismissed it.

"Don't think so, that lake is a wide stretch of open ocean, probably ten miles at least. I'm not sure why they even call it a lake, it's just a big bay. The islands are a maze . . . the boat will be too heavy for the shallows. I don't think we could refloat her if we got stuck, which means if we ran her aground, we'd be dead men. I also don't think we can take on enough fuel to make it that way, assuming our friends over in Slidell still have some to trade."

The real truth was Jack would rather face pirates than the possibility of being stranded in the open ocean. No one would ever know they were there, much less come looking, if that happened. Scoots nodded and headed aft toward his small sleeping berth.

Jack went back on deck to enjoy the cool air. The biting little black flies were back, but that was common this time of year. The night was clear for a change, and he took a moment to pray. He knew that they would need all the help they could get tomorrow.

~

They motored quietly into Slidell just after dawn. The three men on the dock were all familiar to Jack. He had known one of them since childhood. They had been friends in the nearby town of Pass Christian.

"Bill," he smiled as he shook his friend's hand, "glad to see you're still hanging out with the living."

The weather-beaten man pulled him into a hug. "You're a lifesaver, Jack. I can't tell you how happy we were to hear your message."

Jack knew they needed the supplies, but he was touched by the man's show of emotion. "Glad to help. We have to look out for one another these days."

"Amen to that, brother, amen to that," Bill laughed and invited the guys up to see the goods they'd brought to trade.

The deal was quickly finalized. Sacks and crates came out of the hold of the *Marco Polo* and were replaced by the goods from the Slidell group. Jack asked his friend what they knew about possible pirates nearby.

"Yep, we know about 'em. They came through here a few weeks back, but we blasted away at 'em 'n' they got the message. Seems to be, they's hittin' the smaller towns and watching for any stragglers out on the water. All they have is small arms . . . think they may've come up from New Orleans."

"Any idea how many there are?" Scoots asked.

"Can't rightly say. Guess we saw 'bout sixteen or seventeen? There were four boats, comin' in, shootin' up the place. Another larger one about a mile out seemed to be with 'em. It was a big one, had to be a seventy-footer."

Jack nodded. "Probably where they're basing out of. I was afraid of that. We have to get around them to get back home."

"Your boat's an old patrol boat, ain't it?" one of the men asked.

"Yeah, Canadian Coastal Patrol. It was down in dry dock being retrofitted when the sun cooked us," Jack replied.

"Hmmm . . . got something that might help—if it still has the fittings, that is," he smiled as the idea dawned. "Yes, we may have something that'll work." The man whispered something to Bill, then left.

Bill looked up and grinned. "You gonna like this, friend."

CHAPTER EIGHT

While the men were working to install the new toys on the *Marco Polo*, Bill showed Preacher Jack where the town's remaining church was. Walking into the little building alone, Jack was struck by how enthusiastically the priest came out from behind the makeshift vestibule.

Father Ernesto was a short man in his late fifties. "Come in, come in, my son," the priest said. His beatific face and the singsong rhythm of his voice put Jack immediately at ease.

"Thank you, brother," Jack said as he introduced himself.

"You are the man bringing the supplies and medicines?"

"Yes," Jack answered, looking worried. "There's not much medicine to spare, but we included what we could. How many survivors are you supporting here?"

"Survivors," the peaceful little man seemed to mull the word over for several long moments. "You are a man of God, too, no?"

Jack nodded.

"We are being tested, brother. The Lord, he is not so merciful these days. He has allowed us to descend into this pit. None of us are survivors. *Dios mio!* I am so sorry. Our church was destroyed . . . most of my parishioners are gone. We had at least 25,000 people on that day. Now, I would be surprised if the entire parish is more than a few thousand pitiful, starving souls."

Jack knew there were volumes of unspoken sadness behind those words. "Father Ernesto, what do you know about the people calling themselves the Messengers?"

The priest's eyes went cold. "They are an abomination."

"Have you or any of your flock had contact with them?"

"*Si*, I have seen them. I have seen what they can do. It was they who burned my church. They said I had failed my flock and that I had been judged and found guilty. They made me watch while they set fire to the sanctuary."

"I'm sorry, Father. But buildings can be replaced—"

"*NO!*" the man said, cutting him off with undisguised fury. "No . . . you do not understand. My church was not empty! It was full! Full of my people, God's children. I heard their screams, and I could do *nothing* to help them. I tried so hard to get free and go to them, but they bound me to a post in front of my church. I could feel the heat, I—I could smell the burning flesh." The poor man sobbed at the memory.

It took a long time for the priest to speak again. Jack laid a hand on the man's shoulders and said a quiet prayer for the alleviation of his suffering. Eventually, he looked up at Jack with a pleading look and said, "The Messengers said not to fear. That they were being born anew into the house of the Lord. Do you think that is true?"

Jack wasn't sure how to answer. He, too, had seen unspeakable horrors since this nightmare began, but nothing like the scene the priest described. "I am sure it is true—they are home in the arms of the Father now," he soothed, "but they didn't deserve to be murdered. I hate to ask, but can you tell me what happened, from beginning to end?"

Father Ernesto looked into the flickering candles. "They burned many of the other churches and all of the mosques and synagogues. They say they are Christian, but they are a cancer, spreading hate and judgment. They say God turned his back on us because we abandoned Him. But there is no love, no tolerance, no forgiveness in them."

Father Ernesto was a broken man, on the verge of losing his faith if the look in his eyes was anything to go on. Jack didn't think he was the one to pull him back from that edge. He decided to change the conversation. "Padre, I have been reaching out to other religious leaders since this all took place. Just to see if we could help organize our groups, be willing to help others . . . spread some message of hope. I don't worry too much about doctrine at this point—I feel sure most people who come to my services have at least a slightly different belief system, but we're all praying to the same God. The church has to take on a new role, or maybe it's an old role that we need to rediscover. It's not about the building or the ceremony . . . but something much more basic."

The priest gave a feeble smile. "The church I attended while growing up in Mexico was the center of our village. Everything happened around the church. It was our school, it was our meeting hall and it was often our shelter. Even with the drug lords running everything around us, the church was our refuge and our strength."

Jack could see the man was about to drift back in his mind to what he had lost, and so he responded hastily. "Exactly. I think that is our mission again. I don't know how to combat these terrorists, these extremists, but we must have faith. We must follow the path the Lord has laid for us."

The two men talked for some time and agreed to talk with each other again when they could. Jack was rising to leave when Ernesto asked him, "What will you do when they come for your people? Will you turn the other cheek?"

Jack couldn't help himself and laughed a deep, full laugh. "I'm not that kind of preacher, friend. I'll kill the bastards. Send the demons straight to hell before they can harm anyone else."

His new friend was obviously a pacifist, but the smile on his face seemed pleased nonetheless. "We all serve in our own way. Right now, I like your way better than my own. Good luck, my son."

CHAPTER NINE

Scoots met Jack before he made it back to the dock. He was clearly excited. "You are gonna *love* this shit. Oh fuck, man, this is awesome."

Jack smiled, "Scoots, I haven't seen you this happy since you discovered those girlie magazines in the toilet. What has you so fired up?"

The two men rounded the corner and Jack saw for himself. Bill and two of his guys were just stepping off the *Marco Polo*. Mounted both bow and stern were what looked to be twin .50 caliber machine guns. The belt-fed guns rested on swivel pads and included a deflector shield to protect the gunner.

Bill smiled as Jack stepped onto the boat to take a closer look at the weapons. "Jeezus, Bill! I'm speechless."

Bill pointed to one of his buddies, "It was all his idea. He's a—*was*—a machinist working with a local armorer. Thought these would fit your mounts, didn't you, Frank?"

Frank smiled at Jack and raised his hand in a small gesture of greeting. "We were working on these for the DEA's river patrol," he called up to the preacher. "They were s'posed to be mounted on a Shallow Water

Interceptor, but when the shit went down, no one came for 'em. Thought maybe you guys could make good use of 'em. They'll throw out 900 rounds per minute, so go light on the trigger. We dropped in all the fifty-cal ammo we had."

Jack was still searching for words to express his thanks. "I don't know how to repay you for this, boys," he smiled with relief. "It—it means we actually have a chance to get back home. This may literally save our lives."

"You are welcome, Preacher," smiled his friend in return, "but it's not a completely selfless act . . . we don't have anything that can take on those pirates out there—now you do. We need to keep tradin' to survive, not just with you, but the few others who're struggling to hang on round here. What with the Messengers wreaking havoc to the north, we have to do that by sea. What I'm asking is for you to take the fight to them. Take care o' the patrol boats, at least. If you can take out the big ship, course, that'd really help."

Jack was shaking his head now in concern. This was not a deal he'd bargained for. "We're not soldiers, Bill, not even good sailors. I'm okay with fighting to get through their lines, but I would have no way of knowing how to beat them in a battle." He sighed as he reckoned the situation. "You'd probably be better off just keeping the guns."

Jack could see his crew shaking their heads at his response; they liked the new firepower—that much was clear. Overhead, the sun was finally breaking through and erasing the morning chill. A light hint of fog rose from the river. Bill looked around at the gathered men. "Jack, I've known you a long time. I would never ask you to sacrifice yourself for us. Just be prepared. If you get attacked, don't run, turn and fight. Sink who you can. If we send a strong enough message, they'll move on down the coast to easier pickins. Radio us back and let us know. If you or your guys can come up with a way to take out the mother ship, we would be very indebted. I think it's in all our best interest that we keep the coastal routes clear."

Jack had joined Bill back on land and nodded and grasped his friend by the shoulders. "We can do that." Turning to his crew, he yelled, "Load up, let's get to open water."

Bill leaned in close. "One other thing. We got a fella who could probably help if you don't mind an extra passenger." Bill motioned to one of the young guys who had been loading ammo cans to come over. "Jack, this here is Abraham. He was a gunner with the Marines and part of our auxiliary river patrol. Grew up near here, family ran a fleet o' shrimp boats out of Houma . . . He knows the swamps, rivers and ocean—an' more important, he knows how to use them guns."

Jack looked at the mountain of a man who seemed to be in his mid-twenties. The boy had a body that looked to be nothing but muscle. Jack held out an open hand. "Nice to meet you, Abraham."

"Just call me Abe," he replied, taking Jack's hand in his bear-like grip, "everyone does."

The preacher thought it over. He was not eager to let anyone unknown on their boat, much less take them back to Harris Springs and the *Aquatic Goddess*. "Abe, I appreciate your willingness to go, but know it will most likely be a one-way trip. Not sure when you might get back."

Bill intervened, speaking in low tones, "Jack you spoke with the Padre, so you know what happened at the church. Abe's family was Catholic . . ." The rest of the statement remained unspoken. Jack could see Abe's eyes begin to glisten with tears. "He's a good kid . . . eats a lot, but he needs a fresh start somewhere else, somewhere safe. He'll be an asset to you, I promise that."

This went against the loose rules he and the council had established, but Jack reached his own decision and nodded his head.

"Welcome aboard, son. Get your gear. We'll leave as soon as you get back."

Abe smiled and walked up the gangplank empty-handed to the boat. Scoots tossed him a duffle bag that had already been loaded, and Jack realized his crew had already made the decision for him.

"Mutinous bastards," he said with a wicked laugh. Shaking hands with the men from Slidell and embracing his old friend one last time, he boarded the souped-up boat, and the *Polo* eased out into the main channel and throttled up.

CHAPTER TEN

The new guy was up in the wheelhouse directing Scoots as to the best route back to open water. They each assumed the pirates' patrol boats would have the mouth of the river under surveillance. Abe felt sure he knew where at least one of those pirate boats would be. The plan was to launch a sneak attack on that one, then head directly east as fast as they could. They would watch for pursuers and engage each one singularly with the help of their new mounted guns. That was the plan. And like most battle plans, it fell apart on first contact with the enemy.

The *Marco Polo* came out of the small tributary thirty yards from where Abe expected the pirate craft to be stationed. He had moved to the lead gunner position, and one of Jack's crewmen, a guy they called Ginger, was on the aft gun. Tensions were high, and everyone was sweating despite the relatively cool temperature. As they reached the relatively open water, fingers on triggers and ready to unleash a torrent of hot lead down each barrel, they saw . . . absolutely nothing.

"Well, fuck," remarked Abe. "This is the only smart place to be if they just have small arms."

"How far from the lake?" Jack asked, referring to the arm of the ocean called Lake Borgne.

"It opens up in about five hundred yards, sir." Abe replied.

Abe had navigated them down the river called The Rigolets into increasingly narrower channels so that they would not be coming into the ocean from the exact direction of Slidell.

"Scoots, take us out very slowly. All eyes on lookout. Weapons hot, guys."

They entered the bay and still saw nothing. Jack knew it was decision time. The enemy was out there somewhere, but where?

"Abe—ideas?"

Walking over he pointed down at the charts. "Sir, my guess is that they're patrolling the Old Pearl River, probably the mouth of it. The mother ship is likely over the horizon there, maybe near Grand Island. If we head due east, we'll go right between them and probably right into their trap. That's a lot of water for them to cover though . . . we might get lucky."

"Or—?" Jack asked, waiting for a better option.

Abe nodded, "We go south, out into open ocean. Sometime around nightfall we cruise past Grand Island. If we spot the mother ship, we decide what to do then."

"If they have radar we'll be spotted immediately," Scoots voiced.

"If they have radar we'll be spotted no matter what," Abe replied. "Based on what you said you encountered on the way over, I think we can rule that out. Most likely they're just using lookouts." Abe looked to Jack for a decision.

Jack hated the idea of taking the little boat farther out to sea but nodded to Scoots. "Take us south until Abe gives the signal, then make a gradual turn east. Half throttle. We don't want to get there before dark."

~

It was just after 9:00 pm when Scoots first spotted the low-lying island. Its few scrub trees and grass gave the only sign that anything but ocean was there. They were running at a low idle, almost silent as they watched and, more importantly, listened; sound travels well over open water. So far, they had noticed nothing unusual. They had taken their time approaching the island, certain the mother ship was nearby.

Abe was the first to spot anything. Out of the corner of his eye, he thought he saw a spark of light in the darkness. When he turned to look in that direction, he saw nothing. Still, he motioned for the other men to scan the area while he trained one of the .50 cals in that direction.

Jack trusted the man's younger eyes; all he could see were different shades of dark. The trust was rewarded moments later when Abe suddenly unleashed a long volley of rounds a hundred yards downrange. The light of the machine guns illuminated a speedboat lying in wait behind a clump of seagrass. The weapon tore through bodies and fiber-glass indiscriminately. The craft jerked sideways with each round fired. As quickly as the shots began, they were silenced. Scoots opened her up, angling away from the carnage and into deep water. Everyone's ears rang.

A half-mile later they cut engines and drifted in the darkness, waiting for their hearing to return to normal. They could now hear the sounds of multiple engines converging on the previous location. "I think we caught 'em sleeping," Abe said with an air of satisfaction. Jack was just hoping it hadn't been a boatload of fishermen. He struggled with the rules of his new world; doubts like that could get you killed.

The Gulf current was quickly pulling them eastward, and even without the engine running, they were slipping past the other boats swiftly. They could hear the indistinct voices and shouts of the pirates as they reached their fallen associates. Scoots leaned over and whispered, "Ready for engines Cap'n?"

"No, let's just keep drifting for now." Jack stared intently into the inky blue darkness. "If they throttle up or turn in our direction, be ready. Otherwise, let's try and get out of earshot before we do it." This was what they had agreed upon as their contingency plan earlier in the day, but he didn't mind Scoots checking. He was anxious to get out of here as well.

~

Thirty minutes later they heard the unmistakable crackle of a radio somewhere ahead of them in the dark. Jack had been just about to give the order to crank the engines and head for home. Instead, they kept drifting—until they stopped.

The boat lurched as the front of it beached on a hidden sandbar. There were sounds of grunts and surprise as the boat came to a sudden stop. "*Shh*," came hushed commands from Jack and Abe. The tides out here changed regularly, and even though the *Marco Polo* had a shallow draft, they'd known there was a possibility of running aground on the shoals even out here, almost ten miles from land. Scoots and Abe shuffled over to Jack.

"I make out a large ship about 100 yards to stern. It has to be the mother ship," Abe whispered.

"I'm going over the bow and into the water to see if I can free us from the shoal. We may have to go to engines to reverse us out," added Scoots.

Jack whispered his okay, but suggested Scoots take a couple of the others as well. It would help lighten the load a bit, as well as provide extra muscle. "Do it quietly," he reminded him redundantly, "no talking and don't bump anything." Scoots disappeared into the dark. "Abe, what can we do about that ship?"

Abe was nothing more than a hulking shadow in the darkness. "I can't say without knowing what we are up against . . . I'll go check it out, and if you get free just anchor within earshot."

"What the fuck do you *mean* you'll go check it out?" Jack asked before realizing no one was there. Abe had vanished, and moments later he heard a gentle noise as the big man slid over the side and into the cold water.

Scoots and the others were now rocking the boat to free it, but the current kept pushing it back toward the shoal. Jack could vaguely see that the men were up to their chests, and obviously having trouble getting leverage in the shifting sand.

"Jack," came Scoots' low voice, "She's beached good, we have to lighten the front more to get her free. We gotta do it fast, too, this water's too cold to stay in."

Unsure of what else could be shifted to lighten the front, Jack began moving the heavy ammo cans to the rear while trying not to make any noise that might alert the other boat. The men who had remained on board joined him in moving cargo.

Jack looked up at the sound of a radio transmission in the darkness ahead. He made out the glow of what must have been a cigarette. Freezing mid-step, he strained to hear what was being said, but it was too faint for him to make out. Seconds later, though, the unmistakable sound of the smaller boats returning became evident behind them. Jack guessed the mother ship had recalled them from examining the wrecked boat. *Lovely,* he thought. *Now we have the bastards on all sides. What a fucking perfect plan.* Leaning over the sides, he whispered, "Ladies, you might want to get this operation moving along. We are about to have a *lot* of company."

A face Jack assumed was Scoots came close, "Preacher, bring me the emergency life raft."

"Are you abandoning ship?" Jack asked. He didn't wait for a reply but did what the man asked. Scoots was a fixer. He had been one of Bartos' shop hands and probably knew more about practical engineering solutions than anyone. He took the small bundle from Jack and slipped back beneath the water. While the men could not free the boat, they had managed to make a foot-wide tunnel in the sand beneath the keel. The emergency raft was a tight bundle with a pull cord that unleashed a CO_2 cartridge, which would inflate the rubber raft almost instantly.

With another crew member positioned on the other side to help keep the raft under the keel of the boat, Scoots popped his head above water to tell the other guys to get ready to push. Just at that moment, all the lights flared to life on the mother ship.

A large spotlight swept the water, rapidly approaching their location. Teeth chattering, Scoots whispered hoarsely to the men, "In five," and dove again.

Jack manned the aft machine gun as soon as the spotlights came on. It was an instinctual move: if the light found them, they were dead.

He considered starting the engines, but he would still have to wait for all the guys to board before pulling away, and he had no idea where Abe even was. No, it was time to fight. He spotted splashes of white surf between them and the mother ship, then heard a small pop and felt the front of his boat suddenly lurch upward. The boat quickly settled again, but Jack felt the slight backward movement as the boat was freed from the sand.

The sounds of the approaching boats were loud now; three or four of them, he guessed. Scoots slipped over the bow rail, and simultaneously he heard one of the other men hauling Abe in at the stern.

Scoots glided silently into the cockpit and started the engine, putting her in a slow reverse as Abe took over the rear gun. Jack gave Scoots a thumbs-up—"Well played, man,"—and then ran to help the others struggling to get back aboard. The cold, wet men were exhausted, though none made any complaint. As Jack returned to his gun post, Abe remarked, in an eerily calm voice, that they should head due south: the water was deeper there.

The spotlight from the mother ship found them just as the engines engaged. Rifle fire started up from the large vessel almost immediately. Jack charged the gun he was on and was about to fire when Abe told him not to. Jack looked at him in surprise. The young man was pointing behind them at the plumes of white sea spray: "Concentrate on the patrol craft," he called to his captain.

Jack was confused. The mother ship was the main target. But he trusted his old friend's assurances, and so he followed Abe's instructions. Both men held fire as the others hid below deck or behind the gunnels, and each put his ear protection on. They had to get the patrol boats in close to be able to hit them, and for that to happen, they had to keep the pirates in the dark about the weapons they had onboard.

The pirates, on the other hand, began firing as soon as they could see the *Marco Polo*. Bullets began to ping off the metal hull, and one clipped Scoots' shoulder. To his credit, he held the wheel steady. The course they were on would take them dangerously close to the large mother ship, but they couldn't risk getting beached again.

Two of the small boats caught up, one on either side. They were indeed heavily modified cigarette racing boats. The long, sleek crafts were powerful and sexy, as boats go, in their design. Each contained six or seven guys. Everyone but the driver aimed a weapon at them. Jack tried to make himself small behind the protective shield of the machine gun. Looking back, he saw Abe, pointing his at the one on the other side, glance toward him.

Both he and Abe began firing at nearly the same instant. The boat Abe was firing at suddenly listed badly as its pilot was shot and the enemy all went into the water. Jack hadn't hit anything except the ocean, but the other boat had taken notice and pulled farther away.

Jack's first belt of ammo had emptied frustratingly fast. Abe had turned his attention to the two boats coming directly from aft. He stitched a line of shots across both bows, but the boats stayed in pursuit. Finally reloaded, Jack hit the charging handle and began firing at his target again. This time he took more care to aim and follow the path of the rounds. He realized he had to elevate and lead much more than he expected. The other boat crossed in front, and Jack had to swing the gun past the bow to fire. In the darkness, it was difficult to know what part of the boat he was firing at, but as it entered a circle of light from the mother ship, his bullets found home. A round hit one of the three outboard engines, causing it to seize and to be set ablaze. The next round must have hit a fuel tank because the entire rear of the boat promptly went up in a small mushroom cloud of flame.

Jack suddenly became aware of the rounds hitting the protective metal shield in front of him. The men on the mother ship had never stopped firing, though they had been thwarted so far by the distance. Jack could see some survivors from the attack boats struggling out of the water and climbing cargo nets into the large ship. Only one boat remained in pursuit, but it was falling back quickly. Jack had no firing line on that one, so he crouched and ran to Abe who had ceased firing as well. "Why didn't you want us to go after the mother ship?" Jack spoke above the muffle of his earplugs.

"No need," Abe answered with a smile. "I jammed her anchor cable so they can't move, and I left them a present." In punctuation of that, a thunderous boom echoed across the water. The huge mother ship listed sideways, and all her lights went out.

Jack looked at the big, young man with a look of admiration. "What kind of present was that?"

"I was certified in underwater demolitions in the Marines. We included a few bricks of Semtex in our gift bags for you," Abe grinned now from ear to ear.

"You took a brick of plastic explosive with you when you swam over?" Jack laughed incredulously at the Marine's bravado. "Damn, you are handy!" The rest of the crew had begun to resurface in the wake of the explosion, curious to see what had gone on. Jack shook hands with Abe as he surveyed the scene. "Thanks, brother. I'm not even gonna ask what else you've got up your sleeve."

Jack took over the piloting duties now that the danger was behind them. The others went below to change into dry clothes and warm up. Scoots was having his wound stitched up, and a few of the others had various cuts and bumps from the brief battle. The boat itself seemed fine: a few bullet holes, but no other problems. Jack sighed a heavy sigh of relief as they made their way back towards home. *No way that should have worked that easily. Thank you, Jesus!*

CHAPTER ELEVEN

Present Day

Harris Springs, Mississippi

Bartos' dog, Solo, trailed behind the two men. He stayed in the shadows, as was his habit, while his owner spoke. "Scott, listen man, those guys are bad, like *pure evil* kinda bad. We've got to keep listening to see what they do next. We already heard them talking about taking their message to the coast. Dat be us, man."

Both friends had a lot on their plate. Since being forced to move to survival footing the previous fall, every day had been focused on the once mundane details that now meant life or death: clean water, waste disposal, food, medicine and always, *always* the other bastards who wanted to take it away.

In some ways it was getting easier; nearly all the freeloaders were gone by now. Sadly, most of the preppers were dead as well. Those people who thought you could prepare enough to survive any catastrophe had hoarded their supplies and themselves only to run out over the winter or fall into other dangers in their isolation, like repeated attacks by thieves. That was not to say that all those living were good people, far from it. Many were ruthless and survived by migrating like hordes of locusts from house to house, one town after another. Everyone was a scavenger now, picking over the bones of a once proud nation. Those who remained were tough, smart and had most likely kept out of sight of the more ruthless. Or...they were the more ruthless.

"The *AG* is on everybody's radar, Scott. Shit, you can see the damn thing from fifteen miles away," Bartos went on.

Scott looked at his Cajun friend. This man had done so much for the town, not to mention for him personally. "I'm not saying we ignore the Messengers, Bartos. Just try and keep Kaylie from listening in on their crap. We have too much other stuff to deal with right now for Kaylie to be getting caught up in the propaganda coming from that bunch."

"Not everyone thinks it's crap, man. Most of the survivors *like* the preaching, it gives them hope. Even Jack said the church services are always full these days."

"Jack and I have discussed them already. We both agreed that you must be able to separate the message from the Messengers. Bartos, you said yourself these guys are evil. They're perverting people's faith, and at some point, that will be an issue for all of us. I wouldn't blame religion for this shit. Face it, if you're so fucked you can't tell right from wrong without listening to some jackasses who call themselves prophets—or consulting some all-powerful deity or a sacred book—then what you lack is not faith but a moral compass. Compassion and intelligence.

"That's a dangerous line to be walking, Scott, especially down here in the Bible Belt."

Scott nodded in agreement. "I know. I'm not condemning anyone's personal beliefs. I honestly don't care if they worship Jesus, Buddha, Allah or the Tooth Fairy. But if that faith tells them to do harm to others, I have a big fucking issue with it. Millions, hell, probably billions of people throughout history have been killed in the name of one religion or the other. Just because you put your particular brand of God on it or drop enough Bible verses into your hate-filled rants to convince people, doesn't make your actions any more justified."

Nodding reluctantly, Bartos said, "So, how do you really feel, man?" Scott looked at the crazy bald man who was smiling cheekily at him. "Okay, okay," Bartos conceded. "I'll tell the guys to try and make sure Kaylie stays clear of those broadcasts. She's right though: they're taking over more and more of the channels. The others we were communicating with on a pretty regular basis are no longer on. The signal strength these Messengers have is amazing. They're pumping out some serious wattage."

"Does that tell us anything useful in itself?" Scott asked.

"It tells me they are organized, must be well-funded and expanding."

"Agreed . . . thanks man." Scott sat on a bench in what had been the town's only park. The view looked over a cold, gray ocean, below a granite-colored sky. "You think they could be part of the Catalyst plan? I suppose it would fit. If they brought Grayshirts into a town and started making demands or stealing shit, everybody would gun-up and start blasting. Bring a bunch of missionaries, set up a tent revival and get all the people feeling guilty, start judging their neighbors . . . " Scott let the rest of that thought trail off. "For now, we maintain radio discipline. Never broadcast anything related to our location, supplies or numbers. These guys are thugs, a gang just like others we've had to deal with; whether they have Praetor backing or not is irrelevant. Let's just try and keep track of them and be ready if they come."

Bartos agreed. "When will Jack be back?"

"Said we should expect him back in three days. Assuming he didn't get distracted," Scott said with a smile. "I'm going to go take his spot on the canal shortly and see if I can still fish and drink at the same time."

Preacher Jack had become somewhat of an ambassador to other settlements. More accurately, he was a trade representative, venturing farther out than anyone else. They had all built up the community supplies with several big hauls from a stalled freight train, from which they had acquired more of some things than they needed. Jack and a few of his friends had started contacting other groups along the coast to work out some trades for surplus items. The roads were still dangerous, so most of the time they went by boat. Jack never revealed that the supplies came from Harris Springs.

This would be the longest trip he had made so far. He was supposed to be meeting a contact over in Slidell, Louisiana, to trade flour and molasses for salt, rice, eggs and several cases of parts and ammo. These trades went a long way toward keeping the *AG* community alive. The trips had been mostly uneventful, as he never went ashore without several heavily armed members of his crew doing advance scouting on the meeting space, with one exception: at one of the meetings with a regular trader in Pass Christian last month, Jack and half his crew got hammered on local whiskey and nearly wrecked the boat trying to leave the dock . . ..

Bartos looked over at the dog. He was standing still watching a squirrel that was getting a little too close to the ground. Solo was not above taking one as a light snack. "It still surprises me. I assumed food, water and shelter would be the most important things after the shit hit the fan. But most people we see want information first."

"Knowing what's going on in the world around us matters. That shared need is part of what makes up a society. It's a large part of what connects us as a species," Scott mused. "If you remember, that was one of the first conversations you and I ever had—you guys wanted to know what I knew after the solar flare. It's human nature. Most of us also grew up with twenty-four-hour news channels, Internet, Facebook . . . We knew the most mundane shit about everybody, all the time, not just our friends, but total strangers' lives, too.

"Right now, we know it's bad everywhere. We have more clues as to what's going on than most in the world . . . but when's the big stuff gonna hit us? I mean, it's a big world out there, and there's a lot of chaos that could come our way. Many have it worse . . . maybe some have it better. But what do we need to do, not just to survive, but to start rebuilding? Face it, getting any credible information these days is hard. People are starved for contact, for entertainment, hell . . . for anything hopeful. These Messengers are using that desperation to spread hate and fear."

"So, you're saying the planet is fucked?" Bartos asked.

"As a great man once said, 'The planet is fine, the people are fucked.'"

"Oh Lord, you're quoting Carlin again," Bartos chuckled at his eccentric friend.

Scott looked genuinely perplexed. "George Carlin was arguably the brightest mind the human race ever produced."

"Really? Was that before or after the drugs and booze?"

"Like you would even know genius if it sat down on the bench next to you," Scott said with a wink.

CHAPTER TWELVE

Angel was chopping vegetables as Scott walked in. Scott looked around for DeVonte as the boy seemed to be her ever-present shadow lately. Kaylie had spoken highly of Angel, and Scott had not taken that praise lightly. He had gotten to know her a little and was similarly impressed by her intellect and abilities. She was a natural organizer, and he had taken to dealing directly with her on matters dealing with the kitchen or food supplies.

"Afternoon, Angel."

Without the subtlest of glances in his direction, she replied, "Hey, Scott. Are you just going to stare at my ass, or did you need something?" She turned and looked at him closely, then eyed the bag in his hand and grinned. "What varmints you bringing me today?"

Her distinctive rapid-fire speech pattern was a fresh distraction from the slower southern drawls he heard most days. He laughed, a little sheepishly, at her accusation, then raised the bag and reset his face to the more serious business. "Fish . . . catfish mostly, but I did skin and clean 'em for you." He set the mesh bag down in an empty sink and turned to face her. "Let me ask you something. How are we doing on supplies?"

"Terrible," she said.

"Can we hold out until crops come in?"

She looked him in the eyes, all business herself. "I assume you mean without getting too deep into the emergency rations—the soup and freeze-dried supplies from the train?"

Scott nodded.

They had brought in cases and pallets of dry and canned goods that they added to the other staples already on the *Aquatic Goddess*. Due to the number of residents, they had used a lot of those supplies over the winter. Even with rationing, the percentage they had set aside for long-term emergency supplies was very literally being eaten away.

"We're okay until spring as long as we can keep adding some protein several times a week like this," she pointed at the fish. She pulled a chair out at a nearby table and motioned for him to sit as well. She knew this was a serious conversation. She also was beginning to see why people looked up to Scott. He was bright, but he also had a knack for seeing the potential in people. "To be honest, we're in better shape than we estimated. Mainly . . . well, mainly due to the number of people we've lost . . . fewer mouths to feed. We do need fruits and vegetables bad—our vitamins and supplements are nearly gone. Currently, we're mostly living on carbs and what little protein we can find. Our bodies are going to suffer if we don't have more diversity. I'm not a nutritionist, but I know what scurvy and gout are."

Scott nodded solemnly. It was pretty much what he feared as well.

"So, how long are we talkin'? Aren't people just starting to plant crops? I assume it's still months before we'll be able to eat anything we've grown."

"Some crops were started early—the late fall crops we planted last year. Greens and such do well in cool weather, and our winter was pretty mild. Talking to the farmers around here, they say we should be able to start adding some veggies back into our diet soon, but I'm not sure it will be enough to feed us all." Scott looked around the mostly empty and unused galley. The cruise ship was equipped to feed thousands. Now they were sitting in the area that had been used to feed just the ship's crew. Even that was larger than the survivors needed. "Bartos mentioned that he heard rumor of an old recluse who lives up on the top of the bayou. Said he was supposed to know more about surviving off the land than anyone. I have a feeling we could find a lot to eat just foraging from the land."

"I will not be eating grass," Angel said with a warm chuckle.

He smiled at her joke. "Every modern vegetable was derived from something wild. We just have to get back to nature. I'm going to try and figure out where this guy lives and pay him a visit."

"Sounds like a damn good idea."

"One other thing, Angel."

"Yes," she responded hesitantly.

"The next time the council meets, I would like you to join us."

She was surprised. "Why? I barely know you guys . . . all I do is help cook."

It was Scott's turn to meet her eyes. "Don't bullshit me and don't play down your intelligence. My niece saw it in you instantly, and everyone else does as well. You're a leader. You're smart, and even now you play one of the most essential roles in our survival. We need you. I need you to have a voice on the council. Okay?"

She nodded but seemed unsure of what to say.

"Just sit in on the next one if you want, just listen. If you feel like adding anything, feel free. If you never want to come back, that's fine. I just hope you will consider it."

CHAPTER THIRTEEN

Jack's return home was met with the normal laughter, beer drinking and good-natured ribbing. He introduced Abe to the rest of the men on board the *Aquatic Goddess*. "Todd here is our Chief of the Boat and unofficial Mayor. The big kid in the t-shirt over there is Scott. He's the entertainment director. And Bartos here will be playing the part of the village idiot, Gopher."

Bartos snarled at Jack, "Did yo' mama mean to have such an ugly kid, or was she being punished for something?" He reached out to shake Abe's hand, "Nice to have you with us, man. Damn, you're a big one."

Preacher Jack had already relayed the story of the encounter out on the Gulf. No one had believed him until they saw how shot up the boat was. "Nice trade on the .50 cals," Todd said. "Those are a real nice addition. Take 'em down and clean 'em. Keep them stowed. The saltwater will do a number on them otherwise."

They all helped unload the new provisions into the storage hold of the cruise ship. The patrol boat was too large to maneuver inside the behemoth ship's tender garage, but several of the access hatches were designed just for taking on provisions at sea. The one they were now using led directly into one of the secure storage holds.

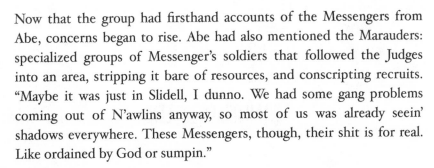

Now that the group had firsthand accounts of the Messengers from Abe, concerns began to rise. Abe had also mentioned the Marauders: specialized groups of Messenger's soldiers that followed the Judges into an area, stripping it bare of resources, and conscripting recruits. "Maybe it was just in Slidell, I dunno. We had some gang problems coming out of N'awlins anyway, so most of us was already seein' shadows everywhere. These Messengers, though, their shit is for real. Like ordained by God or sumpin."

Scoots took Abe to go get some chow and get settled into a bunk space. Todd looked at Jack, "You think they are as bad as he says?"

Jack told them what he had heard from the Catholic priest. "I think we have to take this group seriously. They're using religion as a cover to justify taking whatever they want."

"There's a problem with that kind of campaign," Scott said. "Once you rob a man and take his shit, there's nothing left. You have to move on to find more. Not like the old days. The Messengers have to keep expanding in order to have resources to survive. To keep expanding, they need to keep growing their ranks. It's a catch-22 that can't end well for them. They aren't producing anything, simply taking. Once there's nothing left to take, they'll be done. But until then, they're going to be a plague for everyone in their path."

Bartos smiled, "I think we need to get more serious about our defenses. Give dem assholes a reason to go someplace else."

"Probably a good idea. Let's hope they bypass us but have a plan if they don't." Todd paused to scratch his scruffy beard "Scott, you and your teams need to warn the farmers. They'll be the people most at risk. We keep getting reports of raiders operating farther out. We may need to deal with that problem now. Otherwise, they might become part of a bigger problem for us. If it comes down to it, I want us to have our own message to deliver."

CHAPTER FOURTEEN

DeVonte pulled ahead as the road began to decline. Scott and the young man had been taking the bikes out whenever possible to check on the farmers and several other families in the county. He was also anxious to find the man Bartos had mentioned—the forager. DeVonte had proven to be a good cyclist. Scott had adjusted his old Cervelo racing bike to better fit DeVonte.

"Hey, assflap, this isn't a race," Scott yelled.

Slowing down to let Scott catch up, DeVonte grinned, "You just slowin' down old man. Besides, I want to get back before dark. Should we go down by Ms. Lutz's house? She ain't been into town in a while."

"DeVonte, you know damn well that girl is doing just fine. She's in better shape than any of us."

"I know, but she is *fine*, she be single and . . . she likes you, Mr. Scott."

"She is not single, she's a widow. And a recent widow at that. What makes you think I need a woman anyway?"

"Shiiiit, you just a grumpy bastard right now. I was talking to Kaylie. We decided we really need to find somebody to get nekkid wit chu."

"You . . . you and Kaylie were discussing this?" Scott was embarassed and a little out of breath. "I appreciate your concern, but Ms. Lutz is not gonna be that person. I am perfectly fine and can find my own female company, thank you very much."

"It's okay, Scott, we know you ain't no playa. It ain't nuttin to be 'shamed of. We all need extra help from time to time. Not me, o' course, but mos' people."

Scott was no longer listening; something had caught his eye. They were nearing the driveway of the Thompsons' farm. Jim Thompson ran one of the bigger farms in the delta region. He and his two sons had been some of the first people Scott had started trading and working with after the collapse. The town supplied them with fuel, salt and additional labor when the Thompsons needed it; in turn, they received a share of the crops. Scott pulled to the side of the road and motioned for DeVonte to stop.

The two bodies hanging from the large oaks had clearly been there several days. They could have been Jim or his boys—there was no way of knowing. Jim had been resistant to asking for security or more help. Like most of the farmers and ranchers, he was an independent man. "Looks like another raiding party," DeVonte said bitterly.

"Yep." It was getting to be somewhat commonplace. Gangs of thieves were having more success than freelancers. What had originally been groups of highwaymen stopping travelers on major highways had evolved into raiding parties; with fuel scarce and fewer people on the roads, the thieves had to go to them.

The pair swung their rifles to the front and began walking the bikes up the dirt drive. The bodies were a cause of concern, but not necessarily a reason for alarm. Times had changed, and this may simply have been a form of frontier justice for a few chicken thieves. Just the same, Scott motioned for DeVonte to take cover as they neared the large farmhouse.

Scott took note of the eerie calm as he circled the house and headed toward the main barn. Most days the area would be a beehive of activ-

ity. The large farm was home to three families and numerous day laborers. Jim and his boys lived on the property with their wives, children
and several dogs. Today, none of them were outside.

Scott called out as he neared the barn entrance. "Hey, Jim! Randy . . .
Nick? Anyone home? It's Scott, Scott Montgomery." Getting no
response, he walked into the barn, rifle held in a low-ready position.
He moved around the edge of the solid door and stuck to the shadows
along the wall. The vast open space was filled with tools, chains,
trailers and tractors: lots of places for someone to hide, though he
didn't get the feeling anyone was here.

Twenty minutes later Scott and DeVonte were even more puzzled.
They had joined back up to search the various buildings: the barns,
houses—even down the hill to where one of the boys had parked an
RV they used as a hunting camper. No one was home. Inside the
house, there did appear to be signs of a struggle, but there was no
blood, nor any bodies. The chicken coops were empty, as were the
pigpens and rabbit hutches.

"What'cha thinking, man?"

Scott looked around the abandoned property. "Someone scared them. I
don't know, but I would say those two hanging down by the drive are
attackers, not part of Jim's brood. He probably hung them up as a
warning but wasn't gonna risk his family if they came back.

Scott sighed, eyebrows raised. "Truth is, my man, I don't have a clue.
Maybe he just got tired of it all." Scott turned to watch a lone crow
land in one of the trees in which the unknown men were hanging.
"We'll brief Todd on it and see if he or the Cajun have any thoughts
when we get back. We may want to put someone out here. Looks like
they already have crops planted."

An hour later, Scott and DeVonte were back on their bikes heading to
the next farm and hoping for a better outcome. Anything affecting the
farmers and ranchers was as much of a direct threat to the entire
community. The *AG* was the burgeoning hub in a symbiotic relationship. The farmers needed what the *AG* could supply in the way of fuel,

labor, protection and other essentials; the *AG* needed the food from the farmers, not just to eat but to trade. The system was already profoundly improving lives well beyond their community. Groups from miles away were benefiting from the arrangement as Jack used the items in trade. The farmers' side of it was production; Jack's was distribution; and in the middle? Well, that was dinner for the *AG*. If production was under threat, something was going to have to be done.

CHAPTER FIFTEEN

Scott was thinking over his previous talks with Angel. She had made him realize some problems with the path they were on. While the community was in better shape than most other groups of survivors, they were not self-sufficient; that had to change.

He began taking the time to review more of the Catalyst documents his friend Tahir had provided after the CME hit. The documents were collections of files assembled by a previously unknown organization. The downloaded computer files covered everything from the science behind the CME to how to deal with the aftermath. The Catalyst Protocols were ruthlessly efficient in their approach to saving the country: collect the best of the best into protected camps and watch while the rest of the world kills itself off.

There were also contingency plans for nearly every kind of disaster imaginable. These guys planned to survive. What puzzled Scott was the fact no one had seemed to take the danger of a solar flare seriously before it hit. NASA had made a proposal to Congress calling for a billion-dollar solar shield that would protect the US power grid if such an event were to occur. But even after the House passed it, the Senate failed to take it up for a vote.

More fucking politics. Scott shook his head in disbelief. A billion dollars, compared to this. A billion dollars compared to all the money wasted on worthless pet projects all over the country. A billion dollars compared to the 600 billion dollars they spent on defense every year. Now, none of that mattered. *Too late to shut the stable door once the horse has bolted.* How cheap that money would have been had it avoided all of this.

What he was looking for today were the planning guides. They had been invaluable in setting up a basic council form of government in Harris Springs, as well as establishing emergency food rationing and—most importantly—maintaining clean water supplies. All the things they used to take for granted were life-and-death matters now. Modern society had practically none of the skills needed to exist in a closed community. Food, power, fuel, medicines—even communication—had all been delivered from distant suppliers and massive national and global systems. Now, the *AG* community was responsible for everything it needed.

The Catalyst guides had been helpful in establishing trading groups, also. The success of the growing trade had produced a new need for some form of currency. A barter economy worked well as long as supplier and buyer had what each other needed and could agree on a simple value for each. Increasingly, though, supplier and buyer needed a third party to mediate and a more consistent manner of valuation: currency.

No one would respect paper money or even coinage unless it was of gold or silver, and there wasn't enough of that around to be widely circulated. For that reason, Scott was looking for other options. Ancestors of all cultures had resolved the problem their own ways at different times; any commodity item could be used as a basis for trade: which meant currency was less about what the item was than the perceived value it had. Bushels of corn or beaver pelts had worked in colonial times.

Scott had once been an early adopter of Bitcoin, a crypto-currency that didn't even exist anywhere in the real world. The currency was created, or 'mined', using special computers that helped control its scarcity, which in turn affected its valuation. The odd thing was that people had managed to agree on what a Bitcoin was worth, and it had flourished. In time, you could buy nearly anything with the virtual currency. Scott would have liked to talk to his friend, Tahir, and see if something like that could be done in the physical world. It would be hard to get people to trust in anything that they couldn't quickly identify as valuable, but to expand trading, something like it was going to be essential.

The documents Scott was reading on his tablet indicated that the US government had faced a similar problem after the Revolutionary War. The national government was essentially broke, with very few assets. General Washington couldn't even pay the troops that had helped save the country. Each of the thirteen states was in a similar financial state. What they did have was the advantage of being able to pass and enforce laws, so they began to coin money and passed laws that made it illegal not to accept it. The simple solution was to make coins that were backed by something tangible like gold, silver, bullets or diamonds, so that even though it might look like an abstract, worthless coin, you could bring it to the bank at any time and exchange it for gold or silver at the day's rate. In time, the coins themselves would hold the value, and the gold that backed it, sometimes referred to as the 'gold standard', would be less important.

While currency would be a good step, there was one other item that would make rebuilding civilization, at least on a small scale like the *AG*'s, much easier: electricity. The documents covered a great variety of ways to generate and even store electricity. What he read indicated that the main trouble spots that a CME would affect would most likely be the distribution channels. The Large Power Transformers, or LPTs, were the weak link in the national grid. Much of the actual power generation should be unharmed.

Scott knew there was an abandoned hydroelectric dam less than twenty miles away. The power lines still connected Harris Springs to the dam, but so far, neither Scoots nor anyone else handy with that stuff had come up with a way to engage the generators. The damn things needed electricity to operate the spillway gates, and a lot of it.

They had some solar power and lots of batteries, but nothing strong enough to get those gates moving. The *AG* itself had massive AC generators hooked directly to its behemoth diesel engines. These generators could easily produce the current, but the voltage, phasing and other issues rendered it impossible to transmit that electricity back to the dam.

There *was* a solution though, and Scott was going to keep working until he found it. If they could generate power, then in time, that would be an asset they could sell or trade as well. That would truly be a step in the right direction. Until then, they'd scavenged every large diesel and gas generator they could find, mainly from old hospitals and industrial buildings. These were being used in a variety of ways, including to break down saltwater to make chlorine bleach which they were using to sterilize the water supply. Simply running an electrical current through normal water would produce hydrogen and oxygen, which eventually might also be useful. The geek side of Scott loved this stuff, and for the thousandth time since the blackout, he wished he had become an electrical engineer or something more practical than his job as a computer security analyst had been.

Many of the items in the Catalyst documents and related texts had been lifesavers. Thank God someone had contributed a complete set of the Foxfire series of eBooks on an old iPad that still worked. These collected relics from Appalachia were used by the community at large; the knowledge of how to survive without electricity had not been totally lost after all. Angel encouraged several people to learn how to make soap and candles from rendered fat and boiled wood ash. Kaylie and others from the medical team were re-learning valuable first-aid and diagnosis from hundred-year-old manuals. Others learned how to raise chickens and did the preserving and canning.

There was so much they still didn't know, so much they needed. But they had turned a corner. Scott knew that the town of Harris Springs would not have survived if he and his friends had not reacted as fast as they did in the initial days of the crisis. They had secured food, seeds and medical supplies, collected fuel, weapons and ammo and then gone out on recovery missions to clean out stalled trucks, train cars and abandoned homes. All of this had been locked down for the community's benefit. Soon after, they had fought with their lives to defend it. They had set up a system of latrines to keep the water supply mostly clean and later, secured the cruise ship and settled it as a sanctuary. They did all this because they had understood quickly that this was the new world. No one was coming to make it all better.

Now, all of this was under new threats. Scott was under no illusions; there would always be people out there who would prefer to take rather than to contribute. There would always be some form of threat, and there would be losses. He may not even be around to benefit from what they were trying to rebuild, but someone would. Maybe Kaylie, or Angel, or DeVonte and hopefully, many others in the community. Catalyst protocols, for all the good they contained, wrote all these people off. They were good people, unexceptional to the state. Theirs were valuable lives that Todd, Bartos, Jack and himself had vowed to protect. *But can we do enough?* he wondered.

CHAPTER SIXTEEN

September, the previous year

Pakistan

Skybox and Genghis had been overruled by Praetor Command. As ground commander, Skybox had failed to come up with a military option, so Praetor had made the call. They dropped the thermobaric bombs from an extremely high altitude. The massive bombs made the napalm bombs of the Vietnam War look like toys: the new, precision-guided volumetric weapons worked by dispersing an explosive element or fuel to create an enormous aerosolized cloud on impact. The weapon's explosive then ignited the cloud, producing a powerful shock-wave and high temperatures. The heat and pressure of the blast were felt to be the best way to eliminate the pathogen they had named Chimera.

Talon Battlegroup was over seventy-five kilometers from the site already, but the scenes of destruction were still a horrific sight. Skybox had moved the unit twice in the last week to comply with the evac orders. Even from here, they could see the flames and feel the heat.

The sky itself seemed to be on fire. All Skybox could think about as he watched the devastation was the legion microscopic pathogens being blasted high into the atmosphere where the wind would drive them far beyond the current hot zone. He knew Genghis had been right; what had been a problem for a remote part of Pakistan would now become a global issue.

Those idiots have killed us all.

~

Skybox heard shouts followed by the unmistakable sound of the big man, Hooch, yelling orders: "They're out, they . . . *weapons!*" The last word was a screech.

Then the gunfire started, tentative at first, but quickly gaining in intensity. Pulling on his boots, Skybox raced from the tent, grabbing his M4 as he did so.

"Oh shit—" His remaining forces were setting up a defensive perimeter while firing at their fellow soldiers: guys they had bunked with, eaten meals with only days earlier. The infected troops had broken out of Q-hut and were now loosed on the rest of the camp. Most ran erratically in hospital gowns, trailing IV lines behind them. Skybox could tell his men were aiming to wound rather than kill. Some seemed to be intentionally missing.

Skybox yelled orders loudly as he stepped to the firing line. "Shoot to kill. These are not our brothers. End them now. That is an order!"

The shots grew more accurate, but the dozen or so infected ignored all but most brutal of shots. In a bid to stave off the fast approaching attackers, Diesel, Sky's second-in-command, yelled: "Headshots only!" The infected soldiers were moving so fast—too damn fast. Skybox could see they were already close to breaking through the firing line. Immediately in front of Diesel and coming fast were two of the infected, whom he recognized as close friends of the man. Skybox, still firing at his own targets, watched horrified as Diesel recognized them, hesitating only briefly before firing.

It was a second he couldn't afford to take. He went down under the weight of both of the infected. They tore at his skin with bloody hands and bit at his throat. Hooch dropped both with headshots before they could do more harm. All the infected were down within minutes, but it had seemed like an eternity.

The men were in shock. Skybox watched as one soldier looked down at the bite marks on his arms. Slowly, he removed his sidearm and fired a bullet into his brain. As Skybox ran to the fallen man, several others followed suit. There was no way to stop the wave of soldiers each dropping by their own hand. He could not blame them. He would likely have done the same.

Hooch walked over to Diesel who lay moaning softly. "I'm sorry, brother." His hands shook as he fired a single shot into the man's bloody and battered head.

CHAPTER SEVENTEEN

November, the previous year

Pakistan

The days and the failures since that day had all run together. Genghis never came up with an explanation of how the Q-hut breach had occurred, nor did he learn else about Chimera. Skybox looked up into the bright blue sky. No passenger jets had flown since the solar flare three months earlier, yet curiously, those contrails still crisscrossed the sky. He laughed, knowing that the 'chemtrails', as they had been named, were often not the exhaust gasses of commercial jets but more clandestine atmosphere dispersal systems. Mostly they were used for benign purposes such as inoculating an unwitting and possibly unwilling populous. The chemicals could be delivered by drones, ultra-high spy planes . . . even satellites in low orbit.

At "The Ranch," a remote training ground in Nevada for Praetor commanders, much had been discussed about the spray. What they were releasing in the skies above him now was the latest pesticide: an aerosolized antibiotic designed to limit the spread of the plague. It wasn't working. Just like the bomb had not worked, nor the suits, nor the inoculations, nor any-fucking-thing-else they had tried.

Most of his men were gone. Talon Battlegroup was no more. Comm links with P-Command had been severed, and his last orders had been unclear. The man that stumbled across the desert toward the truck in the distance was a shadow of the man who'd been known as Skybox.

He read the text again just to make sure he hadn't missed some important part of the message. Praetor Asia Station was reporting that the United States, as well as Russia, Great Britain, Japan and a dozen other former world powers, had now been officially declared 'failed states.' Without functioning governments, working economies or domestic or even border security, the countries had effectively ceased to exist. He had been in failed states before, lots of them: Somalia, Libya, Syria, Afghanistan. But those countries were not like his country, his America. Failed states were weak countries, countries that could no longer perform the basic functions of governing their people.

Who the fuck am I fighting for now?

Tommy was over there, as well as nearly everyone he had ever known or served with. Skybox looked around the arid desert landscape. The cluster-fuck this mission had turned into was likely being duplicated back home, just in different ways. Skybox laughed grimly at the irony: simply losing electricity had been all it took to set the US into a downward spiral.

Here in the sandbox, where electricity was far less common and nonessential, the CME had not been a real problem to civilians' daily lives; not to most villages, anyway. But it had set in motion the catastrophe that would now destroy the lives of every person on this part of the globe.

Most of Skybox's squad had been American, and those still alive would all have gotten copied on the broadcast. Command structure in

Praetor did not compartmentalize information in that way, other than for mission briefings with sensitive intel. He was unsure how they would react, unsure of his own reaction, still. What was the mission? What were they protecting now? Everyone knew: Asia was lost; Europe would be next. The mission was a failure, and there was nothing they could do now but run.

CHAPTER EIGHTEEN

December, the previous year

Pakistan

He looked down at the dust covered combat patch. The gray scorpion insignia was barely visible on the black patch. He added a few more shovels of dirt to the hole, and the patch and the man were erased from the miserable view. Skybox thought he should say a few words, but the gesture would be meaningless. The dust was in his eyes, his nose and his mouth. It was everywhere. It wasn't just dust either; the plague was there, hitching rides on tiny microbes. It was in him, too.

The airburst had vaporized the valley and everything within ten klicks had been obliterated, but it had been pointless. The pathogen had already been outside the containment zone. As feared, the bombs had effectively dispersed it farther and launched it higher into the atmosphere. Some of the Chimera organism was likely picked up by the jet stream and pushed onward to new homes and new host bodies in distant lands.

Hooch stood to the side at a respectable distance. Skybox eventually raised his eyes from the grave and acknowledged the man. "Sir, the survivors are loaded and prepped for evac. All other troops are already on station." The man's deep southern drawl was very out of place in this land.

'Survivors' was a loose term. Every member of the remains of Talon Battlegroup was infected, but a small percentage, including him and Hooch, seemed to be asymptomatic. While that did not necessarily mean they couldn't be infectious, so far, they weren't. As Genghis had said, a small percentage would not be significantly affected. Genghis . . . the man with the brilliant mind now lay under the sand beneath his feet. He had known he was dying, but he kept working on trying to find a solution to the problem right up until the very end when he went berserk and clawed the eyeballs from the other remaining med tech before trying to eat him.

"Mount em up, Hooch. Let's get the fuck out of this sandbox." Hooch was only level 3, but now he was Sky's second-in-command. He hurried off to give the signal. The convoy headed due south. They were to reposition 100 kilometers downrange, near the Pashtun village of Kohat. Skybox and the forty-seven remaining men and women of Talon knew it would not be far enough.

"Chief," Hooch said, "Reaper said there are zero contacts ahead."

Not zero hostiles, but zero contacts. Skybox knew what that meant: the Chimera Pox had already arrived. The village ahead would be the sixth one they had gone through with no remaining signs of life. Four more of his company had died in the last six hours. It seemed that most of those who had been given the original antiviral injection had succumbed quickly. The latest rounds of inoculations seemed to be holding the disease in stasis at least. Some of those were near death with respiratory distress, multiple organ failures and the fever, but so far without the rage. Something had changed, some were indeed hanging on.

Skybox had been reviewing the last of Genghis' notes. Before he died, he had mentioned that he'd discovered something, but Skybox had not been able to meet with him to learn more before they were attacked by infected. By the time the last skirmish was quelled, Genghis was already fevered and delirious.

Reading the medical notes was a nearly pointless task. The language and the science they referenced far exceeded his understanding. The bouncing vehicle and the hot, dry air filled with sand added to his general fatigue and increasing feeling of hopelessness. He closed the folder and set it aside. "Hooch, let's pull over when you find a good defensible spot. I want to get those bodies buried. We'll make a cold camp until midnight and move out again."

"Hooah, sir," Hooch drove on for a few minutes then pulled the heavily modified Joint Light Tactical Vehicle to a stop.

CHAPTER NINETEEN
Present Day

Little Rock, Arkansas

He passed by house after house sporting crudely painted signs. Sometimes the pleas were on the house itself. 'Send Help!' 'Please help.' 'Pray for us,' they said. The houses were all empty now. He had seen many of the people killed. They had been his neighbors, people he saw at church and ball games. Sometimes they would get together for a cookout or a birthday party. Now they were gone; all of them likely dead.

The smell was not as bad as he had feared, but even after all this time, it was still unpleasant. The battered motorcycle he was on picked this moment to die. He suspected that the fuel had been bad: it had sputtered since he had borrowed it. He dropped the old Harley unceremoniously and began walking. These streets were so familiar and yet so damn alien to him. He was uncertain, confused, lost even . . . every step he took seemed to take him deeper into his own darkness. He knew his mind was mostly gone; in its place was cold-rage and bitter hatred.

The man knew that coming back here was not smart; he had done so much to get away, to bugout. His plans had been well thought out. Not that it mattered one fucking bit. It hadn't made a difference; his wife was dead, lying in a shallow grave, forty miles back in the hill country. Ahead was his house—or more accurately, the structure that used to be his house. The useless, burned-out hulk of his near-new Ford pickup was sitting right where he left it. It hadn't moved since the day of the Big fucking Crunch.

He looked at the burnt and ragged sign still clinging to the door of the truck. ONTGOM CONTRA NG was all he could make out. Smiling slightly at better memories, the thin, bearded man ignored his old house and headed for the backyard. He had to get something, something he knew would still be there.

CHAPTER TWENTY

Harris Springs, Mississippi

Kaylie looked down the beach towards what looked like a person standing in the gray mist. It was not even 6:00 am, but the night sky above the ocean was giving way to orange and blue on the horizon. She jogged in the figure's direction but saw nothing when she got there save for a large branch of driftwood. The girl turned and looked out to sea. The normally breezy, white-capped ocean was calm. The salty smell of decay seemed commonplace to her now. Her toes dug into the sand and the coolness they found transported her to another time, a happier time. A gull shrieked as it flew overhead, shattering the fleeting memory. Finished with her morning run, she began making her way back to the house, her feet squeaking in the damp sand as she walked.

She was excited and nervous. Today she would talk to her boyfriend, DJ. She had not seen him since leaving him at the college last August. Todd and her uncle had managed to get the big radios on the *AG* working, and now she could speak to him. They had set up a new schedule, and so far, they had managed to keep it. Today would be the fifth time they spoke. Two weeks ago, he had sounded nervous, said something was up with the paramilitary group, the Praetor 5 or whatever, that had shown up on campus so soon after the CME.

That didn't surprise her; she did not trust them at all. The Praetor teams were a paranoid, brutal bunch, but DJ had chosen to keep helping them. The engineered virus someone had concocted had evolved and taken over much of Europe and Asia DJ had informed her. He was a brilliant researcher trying to help them find a cure, or at the very least some treatment to slow it down.

She was aware from her uncle that the remnants of the US Navy had been waging a limited war on Praetor units. No one seemed to know how large either force was, but the Navy appeared to have the upper hand, at least in the coastal areas. They had all also heard about the Protected Zones, also referred to as Reserves: pockets of civilization that still had power, water and food. Supposedly, this was where the brain trust of the US was deposited after the solar flare: engineers, doctors, scientists and surprisingly, even artists. She also assumed lots of politicians. It was all speculation, but they knew it had been the plan. Uncle Scott had a document with the possible locations of some of the planned reserves. Occasional radio reports also came in: someone seeing an armed convoy on a highway or even a jet flying in the direction of one of the camps' likely locations.

"Morning, pops." Her uncle was struggling to get the coffee going in the large kitchen. He finally got the pot together and on the small camp stove.

"How was your run?"

"Fine," she mumbled. "Still a little chilly but looks to be a nice day. Thought I saw someone on the beach, but it turned out to be nothing."

"Cool," he said, distracted with his task. "I'm tired of all the rain. You had your gun, right?"

"Of course, never leave home without it."

Scott looked over at his niece and smiled knowing that she was not a naïve little girl any longer; they had been through too much. "Todd wants to talk to DJ tonight when he calls. Can you give him a couple of minutes?"

Puzzled, she nodded. "Sure, what's up?"

"I really don't know. I assume his Navy connection wants him to find out something, or maybe he's just satisfying his own curiosity. Don't worry though, he won't put DJ in any danger."

They had strict rules on radio discipline. DJ moved to a different secluded location for each broadcast; channels were switched multiple times each call, and the calls themselves were limited to just a few minutes each. Todd seemed convinced Praetor had the equipment to triangulate and locate radio signals. They all feared the consequences if DJ was ever discovered. The kid was bright, though, and so far, seemed to have avoided detection.

The radio calls were always late at night when the signal range was better, and hopefully, fewer people would be trying to listen in. No actual names or locations were ever used, but the communications were not all in code. That was too impractical. Information was passed back and forth mostly in the clear. The location of FSU was 'The Campus,' Harris Springs was 'Pitstop,' and other terms were substituted as needed. It was not a solid plan, but a more complex one would have made the personal calls between Kaylie and DJ even more difficult. While the boy was a source of intel, he was first and foremost her boyfriend.

Todd sat at the lone chair in the radio room of the *Aquatic Goddess*. Kaylie was behind him, tears running down her face. The calendar on the stark, white wall showed a beautiful scene of the Greek island of Santorini. The calendar was for the prior year, but no one had taken it down.

"WhizKid, listen to me, don't do anything stupid. Try and lay low and out of danger until things settle down."

"Skipper," DJ answered quickly, "The drones have been taken out, the Grays are fucking pissed, and I can't even get back into my labs. It seems your friends have decided to take us out. Rumor is they're about to attack in force. I'm not sure how long we'll be here, but the Grays are packing equipment into trucks right now. They are bugging out. And I . . . I want to get the hell outta Dodge."

"I don't blame you, kid," Todd responded. "But you and the doctor are the most prized assets they have. They will protect you, and they're not going to let you just sneak away. You are right, the Navy is attacking, and I am sorry, but they want to end this. I do have some new information for you from them, though." Todd passed along the information Commander Garret had given him. DJ was to set his radio to repeater mode using a channel very far out of the normal broadcast range. The Navy drones would lock in on the signal and not fire on that location. "It offers a twenty-yard exclusion zone. Just don't leave the radio, keep it with you at all times. And stay close to the doctor as well."

They could hear DJ sigh on the line. "Okay. I mean, um . . . Roger that, Skipper," the young man said nervously. "What if the Grays find the radio? You always told me to keep it hidden."

"I know, change of protocol. Stay safe but understand that radio is your safety net. Leave the radio, and you are unprotected—we won't know how to find you. Here is your girl back . . . you guys have—" he glanced at his Omega dive watch, "—just over ninety seconds before we have to end this call."

Kaylie was still rattled as she took the handset and began speaking softly to her boyfriend. Todd stepped out the door and let them have their privacy and to think. He knew he had been partially responsible for putting DJ in danger, but Garret had said they would do all they could to avoid injuring him or destroying the lab. Although small, the FSU protectorate was apparently the only known Catalyst-protected zone near a coast. It was one the Navy could reach, and it was strategically important to them.

Todd had not been briefed on the attack but assumed the drones had been sent in to first recon the campus and then probably unleash air-to-ground rockets on the hard targets. Once defenses were weakened, they would drop assault teams in. The elite Praetor troops were about to have an unpleasant day in Tallahassee.

CHAPTER TWENTY-ONE

December, the previous year

Pakistan – Persian Gulf

Skybox could feel the danger. The village was so small it didn't even get a name on the map he was holding. He, Hooch and the handful of soldiers that made up his remaining squad could see the road leading to the coast—leading to home—but ISIS had controlled this stretch of road for months. It was the last stopping port before the coast.

"Put the birds up."

"Yes, Commander," came the immediate response. Hooch walked briskly toward the technical truck to get the recon drones launched into the early morning sky. It was no secret that the Chimera epidemic had crippled ISIS terribly, but they continued to attack nonetheless. For a fighting force whose ideology had no issue with throwing away lives on suicide missions, the use of the infected had given them a new, even more macabre tactic. Just before the infection reached the rage stage, they would equip their recruits with hand weapons—knives, swords and such—and attach to each a backpack filled with nails, rocks, ball bearings, and explosives. The infected warriors, once they entered into the rage, were brainless, fearless and filled with hatred for anyone in their path. The fact that the entire organization was being infected in the process of using the infected as weapons did not seem to bother them; as long as their enemy suffered as much as they did, it was a success.

Earlier in the day, Skybox had been on a secure video call with command, giving them a full sitrep. *Fucked-up beyond belief* was how he had wanted to describe it to his superiors. *Why aren't you getting us the fuck out of here?* HE wanted to scream at them.

He addressed the commander as "Sir," even though the person he was speaking to was female. "I see no way to continue to pursue even secondary MOs."

"I understand, Commander Skybox, but perhaps you don't fully appreciate the consequences of failing to delay the spread of the contagion." The commander looked weary and glanced off camera numerous times. "The US homeland is in shambles . . . we have a nearly lawless, grid-down, worst-case-scenario of our own here. We are implementing Wildfire protocol. Most of the allied powers have already done the same."

Skybox was stunned, "Catalyst is active?"

"Yes, regrettably so." She paused, looked away from the camera for a moment then continued in a much quieter tone. "Look," she confided, "the collapse of the country is imminent. Leadership—the government, is nonexistent, major cities are burning and the death toll is well above the threshold for these protocols to be put in motion. Teams are rounding up the names on the resource list and opening up safe-zone facilities."

Skybox sat on the side of the truck looking out at the expanse of desert and rock. *Shit.* He had no idea who this woman was or where in the world she was located. He trusted her, though. Praetor teams were a family, and openness was a key part of the command structure. Every member of the team would know what the others knew. It was part of what had driven him into the elite service so many years ago; that, and the amazing hardware they had at their disposal.

He watched as a dozen of the mini-drones, each the size of a sparrow, took flight from the rear of the tech truck. Skybox was never sure where all the funding came from. It was off the books for sure. But sometimes he wasn't even sure it was government-funded since some of the mission parameters made that seem highly unlikely. The missions within Praetor were always big picture strategic moves, not the tactical, headline-grabbing battles covered on the news channels.

He had always had the respect of his commanders, but in all his years, never had one been so candid as this woman had just been. The situation must be as bad as everyone feared. "Sir," he responded at his nameless commander. "Are you aware of the conditions at the Ranch?"

The Ranch was essentially his home base (if he could call anywhere home), located in a remote corner of Nevada. Much of his training had been done there as well. Praetor troops did not routinely know of other base locations, other than by codename. He and a few of his squad were from the Ranch. Some were from a place in Canada called Jackknife, and others from a spot in the South at a place they referred to either as the Swamp, or, more often, Mosquito Heaven. They also had a few rapid response teams on roving stations around the world, often embedded in the regular Army or Marine bases. Everyone generally assumed they were CIA, but those kinds of questions were never answered. Praetor commanders were the badasses, the killers. That much was understood. Other soldiers knew it instantly; you didn't fuck with their kind. You did not want to know their story.

"The Ranch is still secure, Commander," his command replied. "Its location certainly helped ensure that. They lost electricity for a time, but it is back up and running. Your friend is doing well there, though we do have a contingency plan for him and the others if the need arises."

"Thank you," he said, relief evident in his voice. The conversation went on for several more minutes as they discussed alternate mission plans and reviewed updates on efforts to develop a more effective treatment for the Chimera virus. Despite the mission failure and loss of most of his troops, command seemed neither surprised nor upset. It could be that they just had bigger problems right now.

"Commander, you need to see this," Hooch called out to him. Skybox signed off and walked back to the tech truck to view the monitors. The drones were over the road ahead and sending back images of who was there—or what was there.

"God damn," Skybox muttered, his eyes wide with alarm. The scene on the screens showed hundreds—probably thousands—of infected being pushed forward by militants using trucks and even long prods to keep the infected moving forward, toward what remained of Talon. They had faced smaller skirmishes in which the same tactic had been used, but nothing on this scale. The approaching sounds of the brigade of infected could now be heard with their own ears. Even to the elite soldiers, the effect was horrifying.

"Hooch, get four rifles on overwatch, the rest set-up a perimeter. Lay out extra mags and ammo cans for the fifties."

"We're going to fight . . . that?"

"We have no choice, we have to get through. We lead!"

"Yes, sir."

Those would be the last words he and Hooch ever spoke to each other.

CHAPTER TWENTY-TWO

Present Day

Harris Springs, Mississippi

What were you doing when the world ended? Scott Montgomery had been asked that question once or twice. It seemed that as the time passed, it was something people could speak of with a little less pain. He thought back to that previous August. It had taken him a while to fully recall the bike ride he'd been on when the massive solar flare hit. While most memories from those days were dark, muddy recollections, he clearly remembered the bright Northern Lights that followed the flare's strike. What a strange phrase to be true: when the world ended. Not something his father or grandfather had ever had to deal with, though the threat of it had loomed in numerous forms. But while life, at least a fraction of it, survived, the world as he knew it had indeed ended, along with the lives of millions—or more accurately per the Navy— billions of people worldwide.

They estimated upwards of a fifty percent mortality rate so far across the globe. That meant that as a species, then, the human population was down to 3.5 billion in rough numbers. As bad as that was, it was not a terrible number: nowhere near extinction levels. Had they been an animal monitored by mankind, humans would not have yet made it to the threatened species list, much less the endangered list. But it was far from over. They were just six months into this new world. Some still had resources stockpiled from before the flare. When those ran out, what would the numbers look like then? Preacher Jack was speaking to the council about his most recent adventure to Slidell. Scott's mind had wandered, as it had a habit of doing more and more, recently.

Jack continued, "It's pretty much as we feared. Pirates and raiders have moved out to sea, partly because the Messengers have made it unprofitable and unsafe for them to operate on land. You either convert and join their movement, or they kill you."

"So, do we have any idea of the numbers of these Messengers?" Bartos asked the question that was on all their minds.

"Yeah . . . well, we can estimate. The best guess is a fighting force of between 8,000 and 11,000. Any more than that and there's no way they could scavenge enough resources to keep themselves fed," Todd answered.

"How the hell are they even feeding that many?" Scott asked with genuine curiosity. "We're struggling to feed a fraction of that number."

"They keep expanding, only way possible," Todd replied. "They've been successful in finding large caches of food—distribution centers like they had for restaurants and grocery stores. They're usually located in industrial parks . . . not on the radar of those earlier looters who mainly hit the restaurants and grocery stores." Todd looked out the large window at the building gray clouds. "That path is not sustainable, though. It's a one-way trip. Once that food is gone, they'll begin to suffer. Ironic, but they're like a plague of locusts descending on a farm, devouring everything before moving on. When there are no more farms—they will die."

Bartos looked up, nodding, "Only problem with that is, when the food is gone, we die too."

Other heads nodded in agreement around the long table.

Jack leaned back. "Unfortunately, there's more. Other groups are copy-catting the Messengers—banding together and attacking en masse. Some have a similar ideology, some have none. In particular, we're hearing about a group coming out of Jackson, just up the road from here. They seem to be parroting Messengers' lines and tactics, maybe to resist recognition. Certainly, to take advantage of the intimidation factor in their raids. Pretty sure that will be the first group we're likely to see."

Todd looked at Scott. "Ideas?"

Scott stood and paced the room. "I think one of those groups is already hitting some of the farms. Jim Thompson's place sure looked like it could have been hit by one of them. We all know we're a big freaking target on this boat. While we've done well to keep it quiet, I'm sure the word is beginning to get out about us. We have weapons and can easily hold off a small group, but 8,000 . . . no fucking way. I assume the Navy won't supply us with any heavy arms," he looked at Todd, whose face remained serious but neutral. They had refused before; it was unlikely to be different now. He continued, "Our options seem to be: defend the ship, abandon the ship or . . . or move the ship."

The discussion ran late into the evening as each of the three choices was discussed. Todd had assigned teams to explore each option. "I just want the feasibility of each idea: time, complexity, pros and cons." The *Aquatic Goddess* was still a functioning ship, but steering, navigation, and many other major subsystems would never fully come back online. Getting her moving would not be a problem, but not bumping into shit would. Further, taking to sea would limit their ability to access the sorely needed fresh produce that would soon be coming from the farms. Abandoning the ship seemed to everyone like a desperate move. Truthfully, it was, but for the safety of everyone, it had to be considered; how could it be done and where could they all go? Defending the ship brought up some interesting possibilities. One of these involved using the firefighting water cannons onboard to blast any oncoming raiders. At best that was a deterrent, though.

Chances were, they would stay moored and fight all but the largest of forces. Few thought it likely that the main group of Messengers would head toward them. Jack and a few of his men volunteered to do reconnaissance and hopefully expand trade routes in the process. They would leave lookouts posted at roads and towns as far as the radios would reach. If they spotted potential attackers, they would radio back, hopefully giving the *AG* a few days to prepare.

Scott felt uneasy and exhausted, as he did most days. The role he had taken on covered a lot of areas, and the responsibility for all these people was never far from his mind. Most of all, he worried about his brother, Bobby, and his wife, Jess. They were in Little Rock when the flare hit, and he hadn't spoken to them since shortly after. They might have gotten up to Bobby's bugout location in the Ozarks, or maybe they tried to get down here to make sure Kaylie was safe. The not knowing was the hardest part.

At this point, trying to get here from Little Rock would be a near-impossible journey. The distance wasn't the issue; the people between here and there were. The people that were left were hard; they were survivors. Society was gone and had been replaced by something far more primal. A person either recognized another and accepted them as part of the tribe or considered them an outsider. Outsiders were not often accepted, and many people just killed them outright and took their usually meager possessions. It was safer than trusting someone these days. Common courtesy among strangers was a lost behavior . . . one that might never be seen again.

CHAPTER TWENTY-THREE

DeVonte tried again, but the engine simply would not start. They had drained the fuel tank and purged the lines. Bartos looked up from the raised covering and smiled. "Hold on, think I have it. May not've been bad gas after all." He held something up: a black and greasy round object with a wire on one side.

DeVonte had no clue what it was. If they didn't get this tractor going, it was going to be a very long day. He watched as Bartos disappeared into the gaping maw of the dark barn. Solo lay in the shadows near a hay bale. DeVonte gave an involuntary shudder. He knew the dog was not a threat to him personally, but he'd seen what the animal could do, and it unnerved him on a purely instinctual level.

"Yes!" Bartos came out looking triumphant with a new looking doozy-whutzit grasped tightly in his hand. Within minutes, he was giving DeVonte the signal to try again. This time the green tractor coughed only once before it caught and came up to a smooth idle. Bartos nodded and gave a thumbs-up. DeVonte deftly backed the tractor up to a spiked pole, and Bartos had the three-point hitch attached quickly.

Bartos and Scott had been bringing DeVonte out to help on the farms more and more, and the boy had to admit, he really liked it. Fishing, in fact just being on the water, wasn't enjoyable to him, but this, he had decided, was not too bad.

Using the spike pole, he speared a round hay bale, lifted it clear of the ground, and headed down to the cattle field. The winter grazing had left the herd looking a bit lean, and the additional hay would help keep them going until the spring rains came. He had three more to bring down, and then they would hook up a plow: it was time to start breaking up the ground for planting.

There was one other reason he had wanted to come to the farm today. He waved to Angel as she gathered eggs from the coop. Damn, that girl was fine! So far, she'd been polite, nothing more, but he was always an optimist. The strikingly beautiful girl looked his way and gave a slight nod of acknowledgment.

His focus remained on her until he realized that the tractor was taking out a long section of fencing. He had let the machine ease from the two-track path, and it had begun clipping fence poles as he watched his muse disappear into the farmhouse.

Bartos was yelling for him to shut off the tractor. "Goddammit, DeVonte, what in the hell are you doing? Never mind, I know what you were doing . . . I hope she's worth it, you got eight . . . no, nine fencepost holes to dig and about seventy feet o' barbed wire to rehang. That should take you 'til sunset. I'll get someone else started on the plowing. Love is blind kid—remember dat next time you behind that wheel."

Grinning, DeVonte yelled to Bartos as he untangled wire and post from beneath the tractor. "Jesus loves you Bartos!" and, only slightly lower through his grin, "The rest of us think you're jus' an asshole."

Bartos lifted a middle finger into the sky and kept walking away.

◠

The day had faded to inky blackness, and almost everyone was back on the ship. Solo lay behind the pile of muddy and broken fence posts, still as stone, watching the man, whose eyes darted sideways and behind. He could smell the wrongness on the stranger: fresh sweat and nerves. The dog had had him pegged as soon as he snuck onto the property. Solo was a Kuvasz–German Shepherd mix: keen senses and hyper-aggression were ingrained in his genetic code. His muzzle still rested on the cool ground; only his eyes moved, watching the figure that crept cautiously toward the small house. Solo had already noticed the weapon on the man's back. To him, it was a clumsy tool, but something he would need to avoid when he decided to end the human's life.

Solo also knew the man was not alone. He had left two friends back in the woods. This man was the scout, looking for what he could steal. Many people had walked the roads and camped in the woods in the weeks after the cars stopped working; few still did so now. Solo had been told to leave strangers alone unless they came close. He would sometimes investigate as he picked up all manner of smells and sounds. Many were sick or suffering, so he left them alone; they were no threat to his human. This one was not one of those. He was a thief, thin and malnourished, but a thief nonetheless.

The big, white dog watched as the man ran over to a boat tied off at the edge of the estuary by the farmstead. He had a thought, or perhaps it was instinct. He was a dog, after all. Either way, it caused his tail to thump just once before he regained control of his excitement. Time to go to work.

The thief didn't hear the dog slipping up behind him. He was reaching to untie the boat when Solo hit him from behind, just below his knees. The man went down hard, and the back of his head cracked off the hard wood of the dock. Seeing stars, he leaned up groggily and reached for his weapon. Solo's teeth were around the man's thin neck before he could scream. The gun clattered into the water as the dog's powerful jaws tightened and the cracking sounds of breaking bones began. Solo watched as his victim's legs shuffled up and down in a little dance. Then they were still. He pulled the body to the end of the dock and used his head to push the body into the estuary.

Solo went to make sure the man's friends hadn't been alerted. He picked up their scent immediately and found them still in the makeshift hobo camp where they'd been for some time. This was off-limits for a kill according to the loose rules Bartos forced him to obey, so he wandered back toward his favorite bush to lie down. Then he froze. His eyes watched for movement, his ears listened for threats. He sniffed . . . nothing. He raised his head higher, then lower, but still nothing. The dog's rigid calm belied what was going through its brain. Something else was here, though. The dog could feel eyes watching him. Whatever it was, it was dangerous: a hunter, a predator.

Near the dock, an alligator snapped and began tugging and tearing on the remains of the thief. The sound of the gator diverted Solo's attention for just an instant. The dead body, along with the feeling of being watched, was gone. Solo heard nothing still, but instinctually he knew he had not been alone. Uneasy, he slid into the deep shadows cast by the thick limbs of the trees and lay down, his eyes constantly roving over the surroundings.

Bartos sipped his morning coffee with its usual shot of bourbon. The morning air was still, and the day showed promise of rain. Babysitting the farm had been his idea, but so far no one threatening had been by. Perhaps Scott was wrong; no other farms had been attacked.

Few others liked staying overnight at the abandoned farms, but Bartos preferred solitude and a fishing pole to a cruise ship full of people; a gun and his dog were plenty of company. His bond with the beautiful, white dog had grown exponentially in the past few months. He now felt, more than saw, Solo resting nearby. Glancing around, he caught a glimpse of the dog under the bough of a young cypress, nearly hidden in shadow. Setting his coffee on the railing, he walked down to the edge of the bayou to check his crawfish and turtle traps.

His realized almost immediately that something was off. There were signs of a struggle and animal tracks: dog, gator and something else. He looked up to where Solo was lying. The dog's tail was thumping now.

"What have you been up to, Solo?" he asked, trying to sound stern. In answer, the beautiful dog stopped the wagging and stood. "Oh shit, you have that look again. Is that a smile?"

Bartos walked out on the dock, newly painted with gore and bloody paw prints, and began pulling in the first trap when he noticed the torn remnants of a man's shirt. It was not one of his.

Solo moved closer to the water. Puzzled, Bartos began noticing other items strewn about the overgrown shoreline: a shoe; a bit of ball cap; what he had first taken for a stick but was now clearly part of a rifle. He felt the dog brush against his leg, then lean in heavily and sit, his usual morning greeting, a combined *"Good morning"* and *"I'm hungry."* Looking down, he noticed the dog's white muzzle was stained a dark brownish-crimson.

Bartos squatted and leaned his forehead to softly meet Solo's. It was as much physical contact as either seemed comfortable with. "Did you have fun last night, boy?"

Solo's tail began thumping again, even more furiously. He had, he really had.

CHAPTER TWENTY-FOUR

Arkansas

Michael Swain had come to the church by a somewhat less-than-holy route. He had been twenty-three, a graduate student and teaching intern at a parochial school. He had enjoyed that job more than anything in his life. Not so much the teaching, but being around the young girls, so sexy in their matching uniforms. He had been there only eight months when one of the girls had made a complaint about him. When the authorities questioned him, they took his phone and found the pictures. Lots and lots of pictures. Most were only suggestively inappropriate, but a few obviously indicated that he was stepping into forbidden territory. One picture, in particular, had cost him his career.

The headmaster had given him only one choice: go into the seminary to be a priest or go to jail. The school and the DA had decided to pursue a criminal case if he chose to ignore God's will. He had not made it as a priest in the order, but he did get a degree, and with that, preaching jobs had been easy to find back home in Texas. Soon after, he had begun to garner attention for some of his more extreme right-wing sermons, as well as some of the protests his church sponsored. The ones outside abortion clinics and veterans' funerals had been the most controversial, and by his measure, the most successful. Still, when confronted by a schoolgirl, his body reacted . . . He smiled as he felt his hardness grow. Looking next to him he saw the girl was still there. They had brought her to him the night before.

Michael liked this new world; he liked his place in it. He wanted more. He slid his naked body up against the girl. Her body stiffened, and he thought he heard a small whimper as he pulled her close. Was she crying? They often did. No matter. He wanted more.

A line of dark clouds indicated the morning raids would be a messy affair. Michael, the Prophet to his followers, came out of his RV camper still buttoning his pants. The morning glow on his face was often mistaken for something divine. To be honest, it was more accurately a combination of sex, liquor and pills.

"Are they ready?" He could hear the music playing and people singing.

"Yes, Your Holiness," came the immediate response. Michael liked the Holiness part. He had borrowed it from the Pope, but big deal. The Pope was dead now. And Michael just fucking hated Catholics. It was all so much of a show: all those rules, rituals and costumes. And the outfits they made those girls wear at their schools—what a fucking joke. It was what got him in trouble, and damned if he was the only one who noticed that. He guessed they made the girls look so good just to try and keep the priests from going after the boys. *Fuckin' faggots.* He still felt boiling anger when he thought back.

He walked towards the huge congregation, up the few steps to the flatbed truck they used as a stage. Hawley, his personal aide, driver and enforcer, handed him the microphone.

"Brothers and sisters in Christ. Good morning! Who are we?"

In unison, the crowd yelled, "The Messengers!"

He nodded, smiled and continued in his laid-back baritone, "And what is the mission of the Messengers?"

"To vanquish sinners and spread the Word!" Yep, he loved this new world, and he absolutely loved his place in it.

"Today, we move eastward, into the rising sun! Onto the glory road, where our enemies will perish before us! Do you know why? Because we have God on our side! We carry the Word into the darkness of this wretched world. We carry it like the sword of God. Our Word will smite down all those who would stand against it, all the wicked, all the sinners and yes, all those misled by false religions. We carry the message. We carry the message!" His volume increased with his fervor. "We carry . . . " the crowd had picked it up now. Chanting in unison, over and over. He picked up the small trumpet that had become his trademark symbol and held it high. He felt the chant of the crowd rush through him.

"We carry the Message! We carry the Message!"

Some of his flock had their hands waving in the air; others stood on the verge of tears or hysteria. For the Prophet, it was intoxicating. Again, he felt his body responding. Smiling, he turned to Hawley and covered the microphone with a hand, "Get everyone moving. Deal with the new, um," searching briefly for the right word, "converts, and let me know when the Judges report back in. I'll be in my bus," he paused again and smiled wickedly, "praying."

Even though he knew Michael would not be praying, Hawley was convinced his illicit activities were sanctioned by a higher power. He had been with Michael from the early days, back when the movement was only a few hundred strong. Michael was a born orator, and Hawley was impressed that the man could preach for hours and never open his Bible. It was as if he were simply a vessel, and the words and divine wisdom just flowed out of him. Hawley was a true believer and proud to help His Holiness, the Prophet, in his quest to spread the Word.

Hawley and two of his disciple-brothers went to the holding pens. The stink and filth of the occupants reeked. The fetid mass of humanity inside the fencing was all male, all miserable, and all terrified of what was coming. They had seen it happen almost every day since being captured.

"Who's ready to be judged?" Hawley called out loudly. None of the men moved, nor looked up. "Come on, come on, it's time to get on your knees and confess. Release your burden as His Holiness has instructed." A few of the men cautiously moved farther back in the crowd. Looking to the other two men, Hawley said in a lower voice, "Go on and get us the first twelve, we need to get this done quickly today."

The twelve men selected were gathered and knelt in a row facing the compound. The other prisoners watched in horror. They were at once thankful that they had not been chosen and assured their time would also come. Hawley faced the large group of prisoners still in the holding pens again, "It is time to make right with your Lord. You were allowed to live this long simply thanks to our leader's abundant compassion. The Judges who found you must have felt you *could* be worthy. They allowed you to continue to live and struggle here on Earth, so you could be redeemed. You could help spread the Message of God's love with us.

"The Prophet has graciously allowed me to give you a choice. You can convert from your wickedness and help us in our mission, or you can confess your sins and meet the Lord . . . or, you can choose not to confess and go straight to fiery Hell this very morning. These twelve here kneeling before you are going on ahead to help prepare a place for us in heaven. Bow your heads in silent prayer as they make peace."

As most of the heads bowed, the sounds of axes hitting meat began to echo off the surrounding buildings. The spray of blood spattered many of those closest to the front of the pen. Hawley and his fellow Messengers watched as the effects of the gruesome deaths washed over the cowering men. The bodies tumbled forward, the ruined remnants of heads still attached tenuously to a few.

"Now you miserable sinners, who would like to come forward and convert this morning? Come on, we have room at the altar. Hold on, Pete, get those bodies out of here so we uh . . . we can have room at the altar." Hawley smiled.

The line to convert formed instantly and Hawley's men began taking names and inking the mark on the back of the hands of the new recruits. Michael always wanted more; he would be very pleased today. "You are now the very hands of God on this Earth. You are His Messengers. You will serve the Prophet, and you will obey me."

CHAPTER TWENTY-FIVE

Harris Springs, Mississippi

From the top deck, Scott could see the ocean, the town, the edge of the bayou and much of the surrounding land. An early spring was settling in, and just after sunrise, the temperature was already very comfortable. He sipped his coffee from a cup with the fancy *Aquatic Goddess* logo on it. He was not a man at peace; his mind was running. Even simple errors now could be fatal. Who can you trust, is the water safe, is that a cough or the beginning of something worse? As a man used to being alone, the responsibility for so many weighed him down.

He wanted desperately to get on his racing bicycle and take a ride; just park his brain and enjoy the open road. That might not be something he would be able to do much longer, even if he had the time. Every day brought new dangers now. Every turn of the road could be the one that ended him. When he rode now, it was rarely alone, he was always armed and he was working; fun was much less a part of his routine these days. He smiled. Who was he kidding? It still gave him a thrill to clip in and start pedaling. The gun and the extra ammo were just part of his normal outfit now.

Thankfully, he had only had to kill one other person since the day of the Waterworks Battle, as many referred to it. He had surprised a man attempting to steal his Jeep. It had just been loaded up with supplies. Even though Scott was well within his rights to simply kill the man, he hesitated—he had recognized the thief. That brief pause of recognition was all the man needed to raise his weapon. Scott's shot was faster, and the aim was true. The man he'd only known as Richard, or maybe Rich, lay dead. Scott knew the family: a wife, a son and a daughter. He would not be coming back home to them. Richard had been one of the business owners in the town, not a druggie, not a common thief. He was just a man trying to survive and feed his family. Now he was dead, and his family would starve unless they came to the *AG* and could offer some contribution to the group.

He had remembered Richard voicing a mild protest when the town council said that everybody would have to work. He didn't feel his wife should work. Her job was to stay home and raise the children. While that was a concept more relevant to the 1950s than the current era, he was not alone in that attitude. Many of the men in these parts had been traditionalists. Scott felt his demand was demeaning to women and had been the one to tell him so. If Richard came to the ship, he and his wife would work to help the group, as would his children when they reached an appropriate age. "Your archaic societal rules be damned. This is not the same world anymore."

That man's death had not weighed on Scott as he had expected. Something inside of him had gone dark and cold. He did ask Jack to check in on the family, and eventually, he had heard that they had made it to a nearby farm and were eking out an existence as day laborers. Choices. Everything in life came down to choices. It always had, but in the old world, there were safety nets to protect us somewhat. Now your life depended on every one of them—on making the right choices. In Scott's case, many lives depended on it. Right now, he had decisions to help make, but he didn't have sufficient information on which to base those decisions.

He needed to know where the Messengers were heading. He wanted to know what was up with the Praetor forces. What could he and his community do to ensure their safety? The large ship they called home was a decent enough fortress, but it gave people a false sense of security. Those on the council all knew it: the ship had many vulnerabilities. While it made a good castle, castles often fell under siege. Someone could cut off the fresh water supply, and they would be dead in a week. Explosives placed strategically on the hull near the diesel intakes could turn the entire ship into a roaring inferno in minutes.

Scott wanted to be able to move the ship out to sea, but that would be incredibly difficult. It would also be pointless if the Messengers were not coming. If he was honest with himself, he still wasn't convinced they were even real. They could just as simply be an urban legend or, at the very best, someone else's problem. America was big. This little speck on the coast couldn't be worth the effort to reach and to attack.

But if they were real, they would need to keep feeding and expanding. Like a plague of locusts, they would eventually consume everything around them.

Bartos had said little when he came urgently to find Scott. Entering the communications room, Scott could hear his niece's plaintive voice. Kaylie was right: the voice on the radio *did* sound like Scott's brother, Bobby's. Both were listening in to the faint broadcast. "Dad? Dad, are you there? It's Kaylie!" Her voice was desperate and heartbreaking. Radio discipline was forgotten as they tried to talk to the man. Unlike the handheld radios they used for local communication, the high-end system in the *AG*'s communications room had a tremendous range. You could also talk and listen at the same time. While Kaylie was transmitting, Scott could hear the man's voice. But the man could not hear them.

"Stop, Kaylie, just stop. He's out of range of us. Let's just listen to what he's saying for a moment." She reluctantly lowered the microphone and leaned toward the speaker. Scott clicked a button on the computer screen to record. The man's voice sounded so much like his brother, but it faded in and out, and many of the words were mere fragments. It sounded like someone giving a news report or a weather forecast.

Then they clearly heard: "Front coming," and something else that sounded like "God's army," and then faintly, an almost unbelievable sound. "Kaylie?"

Kaylie reached again for the microphone, but Scott was already responding. "Bobby is that you, bro?" they waited, but there was no response. "Scott and Kaylie for Bobby. Do you read?"

The voice on the other end said, "Hello . . . is someone there? Hello?"

Kaylie grabbed the mic from her uncle's trembling hands. "Daddy . . . Daddy, please talk, please respond. It's me! It's Kaylie!"

Scott was trying to get a fix on the signal, but the system was not designed to triangulate over land. He could tell the direction, though: just west of due north. The man's voice picked up an echo, then bits of another broadcast cut over, nothing legible, then a stronger signal—probably someone on a nearby frequency—drowned it out entirely.

Tears were pouring down Kaylie's face. She desperately wanted to talk to the man; she knew it was her dad, but she could tell her uncle was still not fully convinced. "Dad, can you hear me?" she tried once more.

The silence stretched out to eternity, then the background noise faded. "I hear you, Kaylie, I am here."

Scott and Kaylie looked at each other in disbelief. They knew his voice, and that last bit was clear and strong. It was Bobby. "Where are you, Dad? How is Mom?"

The signal faded and returned. "Thank God you guys are alive. I am still . . . near home. Things are really bad. Your mother . . ." The signal faded out. " . . . try to get to you . . . void roads."

Scott picked up the handset to talk to his brother. "Bobby, your signal is weak, not getting everything, but try and get here. If you can make regular contact, I can meet you somewhere. Do you copy?" The channel was silent. "Bobby? Bobby?"

Kaylie leaned over and closed her uncle's fingers around the transmit key. "I love you, Dad. Tell Mom I love her. We are doing well, but . . . we need you."

Scott saw there was no longer an incoming signal. He began to make notes of the direction, time and weather conditions. He would later be able to take a bearing, and when conditions were similar, maybe they could make contact again. It was him. They still had family. Kaylie still had parents.

He pulled his niece in for a tight embrace. They clung to each other as they both cried. "They're alive," she kept saying. Scott nodded. Bobby was still alive, but they had not heard him say the same about Jess. Scott elected not to mention it to his niece.

CHAPTER TWENTY-SIX

Todd looked grim. "I have some news from Naval command. I won't lie, it's not good. As we assumed based on the intel from DJ, a few days ago Commander Garret launched a mission to take control of the campus and labs at FSU. They sent in drones ahead of four tactical teams. When the troops went in, they found nothing. No labs, no soldiers . . . nothing, but students."

The three faces looking back at him were unsure what the news meant. Kaylie spoke before anyone else. "What about DJ, was he there? Is he okay? Where did they go?"

Scott was wondering much of the same. "DJ said something was up. They must have known the attack was coming."

Todd answered, "It seems likely they were warned or caught wind of it somehow." He looked over at Kaylie and in an apologetic tone said, "Kaylie, I'm sorry, but there was no sign of DJ or the doctor or any of the other people from the labs. Hell, the labs themselves were gone. No sign that Praetor was ever there." He paused and looked around the table. "One other thing, the SEAL team searched DJ's dorm room and found his clothes and the handheld radio we left him. Wherever they took him, we have no way of getting in touch."

"Well, fuuuuuuck," Bartos exhaled. "The kid could be anywhere now."

Kaylie was nodding as she struggled to hold back the flood of tears. Her voice was tiny when she finally found the words. "He was there as a volunteer, not . . . not a prisoner. They trusted him—they need him. They wouldn't have hurt him . . . right?"

Todd was standing near her and placed a reassuring hand on her shoulder. "I sincerely believe you are right. They have no reason to wish him harm. Most likely they transported him to a more secure location. Maybe they have another lab somewhere else.

"The Navy guys are tearing that campus apart looking for clues. As soon as they know something, they will get in touch. You can't have a logistical move of that size and not leave some clue as to where you went."

Kaylie looked at Todd, a man she had tremendous love and respect for, but right now doubt and suspicion infused her words. "Did you know your friends were attacking?" Standing, she walked to the large window and looked out toward the Gulf. "Did you know the Navy was sending in SEALs and drones and not bother to tell us or warn DJ?"

"Kaylie . . ."

"Did you?" Her tone was unflinching, and her eyes were wide and bright.

Todd sat. "I warned him about the drones. I gave him strict instructions. But no, I promise you, I did not know about the rest. Mission security would have prevented them from broadcasting that, much less telling a civilian like me. I will admit, though, that I have known for some time that the option was on the table." His voice had cracked, and he knew he had not convinced her.

"Why didn't you tell someone then?" Kaylie said, her voice filled with hurt. Scott wanted to calm his niece, but he was getting upset as well.

Todd looked at them both. "The truth is, I know Scott feels differently about what the Praetor unit is up to. Kaylie, I think . . . I know you are too personally involved to be unbiased. I had sketchy information, nothing conclusive. I thought they were going in for a quick recon with the drones... nothing more. I felt that mentioning it, even as a possibility, could have put DJ in even more danger."

Bartos spoke up, "I know it sounds fucking ridiculous for me to be the voice of reason, but isn't the real issue where did they bugout to? None of this other stuff helps us right now. Unless the Navy can come up with clues, we may have to wait and hope he makes contact."

Kaylie got up and left the room without further comment. Scott looked at Todd and said, "Bartos is right. Whatever your reasons, I don't disagree with you. You did the right thing. Please keep pushing for any information they have, though. We need to know what Praetor is up to. And try to keep DJ safe."

"'Of course, Scott, you know I am."

Scott looked even more fatigued. "Why does surviving this shit just keep getting more complicated? We have disappearing farmers, pirates along the coast, too little food, some disease outbreak overseas and a bunch of Bible-thumping crazies declaring a fucking holy war. Did I leave anything out?"

Bartos raised his eyebrows, "I've been a bit constipated lately. I mean . . . if you're making a list or something."

The three men were silent for a few seconds until Todd started shaking his head and they all three burst into laughter.

"Constipation, huh? Geeze. My problem's gas. If I don't get something other than dried beans to eat soon, I'm going to explode," said Todd.

CHAPTER TWENTY-SEVEN

Little Rock, Arkansas

Bobby gripped the small radio tighter, hoping to pick up the signal again by sheer will power. *Kaylie was okay.* That thought alone was enough to get his feet moving again. His brother had indeed reached her and kept her safe. Scott had been mostly lost in his own world the last few years—a world of pain and hurt and self-doubt. He was a good man, but Bobby had not been sure he could rely on him until he heard both their voices.

He switched the radio off and slipped it into his pack. From the hole in the ground, he removed several other items that he had stored there over the previous years. Jess had thought he was nuts; he had more gear and equipment for surviving "The Big Crunch" than any of his crazy-ass prepper friends. *A lot of good it's done me*, he thought bitterly. What was left in the small hidey-hole were just the bare essentials. A true emergency-only bugout bag that held a small Japanese-made dual-band radio, a water purification kit, a pistol and ammo, a portable solar charger, a FireSteel, batteries, a flashlight, a knife, a small fishing kit and several freeze-dried meal kits in a small, sealed plastic bucket.

He had loaded the old pickup with his real supplies when he and Jess fled to the mountain cabin—his primary bugout location. The cabin

itself was a hidden fortress, and he had spent years stocking and modifying it to be almost completely self-contained. It had a spring-fed
natural water source and a soundproofed generator room with a dual-
fuel generator and a large but well-camouflaged solar array: power,
water—it even had satellite TV. Everything worked great for the first
few months. They worried about Kaylie but hunkered down in the
cabin on the side of a hill, convincing themselves that Scott had been
able to reach her. They had all they needed.

Bobby repacked the backpack and lowered the now-loaded 9mm
Heckler & Koch VP9 into his CrossBreed IWB holster. Shouldering
the pack, he walked back to where the motorcycle lay and pulled a few
items from the saddlebags. Then he headed off toward the shelter of a
nearby forest.

He took shelter under a large elm tree. A cold, steady rainfall matched
his mood. He would not try to reach Scott again today. The little radio
had good battery life, but the rated range was only about 100 miles. He
got lucky reaching them at all today; the storm clouds may have helped
boost the signal. He was almost 600 miles from the Gulf Coast.
Thinking more clearly now, he felt stupid for his lack of radio discipline. He had just been so happy to hear from his family. He would
have to move south and stick to high ground to reach them again and
keep his emotions in check while he was at it. It was a bad idea to risk
giving away locations over an open channel.

The ham radio he'd had in the house had been state-of-the-art. He
could talk to others around the world. The radio room itself was
isolated and grounded so even the CME hadn't affected it. They'd had
no time to take it when the shit hit the fan, though. At first, Little
Rock looked like it was going to be fine. Then the rioting started.

Then, the power went off for good, and it was every man for himself.
They had just managed to get word to his brother, Scott, asking him to
please go to Tallahassee to get Kaylie. Then they were on the run. All
his mechanical tools had to be left behind, along with the nice ham

radio and hundreds of other things. He and Jess had taken his dad's old pick-up. It was old, and he'd been restoring it. It was one of the few vehicles that still ran. The three-speed transmission was on its last leg, though, and they barely made it into the valley near the cabin when it went out completely. But, they had gotten out, and they were alive.

Bobby ignored the rain as he finished off the cold MRE. He had no idea what it was he had just eaten; he didn't give a shit. He felt marginally better for getting some protein into his body and much better for hearing his brother's and daughter's voices. He had to keep moving, though. The Judges would be looking for him. The Messengers were relentless. They did not let people go willingly, and he knew they had a special desire to see him dead. Looking down, even in the darkness, he could see the outline of the tattoo on the back of his hand.

CHAPTER TWENTY-EIGHT

December, the previous year

Karachi, Pakistan, Gulf of Oman

The captain of the boat was a small Asian man with fierce eyes. With one look, Skybox knew this man had faced many demons of his own. As he approached, Skybox scanned for weapons and potential exits.

In heavily-accented English, the man spoke. "I am Wei Xiou. You are the commander, no?" Skybox nodded. "You lost your entire platoon?"

It was a company, not a platoon, but that mattered little now. He was unsure what the official role of the man or this ship was to P-Group, but they had been there waiting for him when he reached the port city. The ship seemed to be falling apart: rust flaked from every metal surface, and you could not tell from any of the occasional patches of paint what the ship's original color may have been. But looks could be deceiving. Deception was always the first weapon of choice for Praetor. Even as he thought that, he felt the big, diesel marine engines come to life and start hammering away several decks below.

Chances were that Wei Xiou was just a contractor, not an operative. That meant he would have the barest of information from Praetor or about Talon Battlegroup. Skybox's eyes fell once more on the diminutive man. "Thank you, Captain, I am grateful for the pick-up. I am unaware of your level, but you are not incorrect. Things went badly out there . . . very badly. Can I ask, where are we headed?"

Wei Xiou looked at the tall man. He knew much, but debriefing the commander was not his job. "You infected?"

Skybox looked perplexed, but gave the safer answer, "No, of course not . . . I would be dead. Your entire ship would be dead by now."

The Captain nodded and gave an almost-imperceptible smile. "Of course, of course, but must ask. We are to give you physical exam. We then rendezvous with command vessel out at sea. They will transport you stateside."

So, is was just a feeder vessel, Skybox thought. Used normally for gun running or smuggling tactical gear and assault teams into unfriendly regions. Non-western ships and crews were usually best for such roles. "Thanks, Wei. Tell me, do you have a vidcon link to the ship or Control? I need to speak with them about the situation on the ground."

Wei Xiou smiled, revealing an unpleasant array of crooked and stained teeth. "We have no links to P-Command other than for basic tasking. The EMP took out much of our ship's electronics. We were not hardened to those attacks like the more official Praetor vessels. We have not even had much news of the outside world ourselves since the blast."

That was frustrating, but not unexpected. "Your English is impeccable, Captain. Would you, in fact, be American?"

Wei's smile disappeared, but he knew better than to answer. No one answered those kinds of questions. "The doctor will be in shortly to retrieve you and begin the exam. We are ninety-six hours until rendezvous." He turned abruptly for the door and was gone.

∽

The doctor was an older woman. An anomaly on the crew, she was tall, blonde, slightly heavyset, and very Australian. She also appeared to be very competent in her job. She took a seat and for the first hour did nothing but ask him questions. She questioned everything having to do with his physical health. Nothing was off limits. Her questions ranged from what he had eaten for breakfast to the last time he had masturbated. As any good soldier would, he assumed there were reasons for the interrogation, but she was not going to let on as to what they might be.

"Look, I get it," he said at one point. "You want to know how it is that I'm not infected. My medic said I was asymptomatic, immune."

She never even looked up. "Commander, would you say your sleep pattern has been worse or the same in the last few weeks?"

"Ugh," he gave up and continued to answer. "The same." The unnamed doctor would not be answering any of his questions. She had her orders. Once the interview session was over, the exam began. If anything, it was even more in-depth and intrusive than the interview. No part of his body was overlooked. Vial after vial of blood was taken; X-rays, hair samples, and stool samples were extracted. He did not care to dwell on how they got those. Many of the procedures he endured he could not even fathom the purpose of.

After several more hours of being poked and prodded everywhere, his patience was exhausted. He reached to put on his clothes and stand up. The doctor looked at him in mild amusement, then he saw what was in her hand. The Taser barbs punctured his bare chest, and immediately every muscle in his body contracted. Two men, orderlies who had been helping the doctor during the exam, picked Skybox up and placed him face down on the exam table. He felt something fastening him tight to the table.

The blonde doctor held up a large needle, and Skybox realized she was going to stab him in the back with it. He struggled to get free, but the assistants had bound him to the table tightly with restraints. He felt the doctor's fingers in the center of his back, almost as if she were looking for something. Then the prick of the thick needle entered his spinal column. The pain was intense and then, almost immediately, numbness took over.

She removed the syringe, now full of a milky fluid, and took it back to her work counter with the other samples. One of the assistants removed the restraints, but Skybox still could not move. *What in the fuck is happening?* He could kill the two orderlies, but the doctor might have training; she looked imposing. Also, he couldn't fucking feel the bottom half of his body. That, he decided, was going to be a severe hindrance to any escape plan.

He looked up just as she approached the table again and gave an involuntary shudder. "Now, Commander, you can get dressed. You will likely have a rather intense headache from the spinal tap. You will find pain relievers in your room."

With that, the exam was over, and she was gone. At least he didn't have to try and kill her now. At this point, he'd had severe doubts about the likelihood of success. The orderlies waited silently while the numbness faded.

He reached down to his pile of clothes, but a massive headache and wave of nausea hit him. He wretched and lay back in agonizing pain. Clutching the sides of his pounding head, he vaguely noticed that one of the men was holding out a wet towel. The other was retrieving his clothes.

It took a while, but the combined effort of all three men finally succeeded in getting him dressed. He stumbled down the corridor to the cabin he had been assigned. Seeing the two pills and a bottle of water on the nightstand, he threw them in his mouth, downed the water and collapsed onto the mattress.

When he came to, he could see light, but his eyes had crusted shut. Other parts of his body seemed unresponsive now. He had no idea how much time had passed, but he knew he was hungry. Skybox attempted to rub the sleep from his eyes, but once they were open, everything remained blurry.

After several minutes the room began to come into focus. Sunlight was streaming in the small porthole. Across the cabin, Wei Xiou sat on a stool watching him. The captain said, "I see you survived the exam. The doctor is quite gifted, isn't she?"

"Yeah . . . I'm guessing she trained under Josef Mengele."

Wei looked briefly puzzled while he placed the reference and smiled. "Ahh, yes, the infamous Angel of Death. She's just doing her job." The captain held out a cup of coffee and two more pain pills. Skybox accepted the coffee but shook his head to the meds. Shaking his head made the pain unbearable, though, and he weakly reached his hand back out to accept the pills.

CHAPTER TWENTY-NINE

Near Monticello, Mississippi

The temperature had climbed into the upper seventies, signaling that spring had officially arrived. The day was spectacular with a light breeze, a cloudless sky and the earthy smell of freshly tilled soil. Scott Montgomery sat on the ground against the wheel of his Jeep Wrangler. The useful 4x4 had essentially become community property in the months following the solar flare. Bartos and his buddies had made some modifications to it over time, including a reserve fuel tank mounted in the back, run-flat tires and steel armor shielding in critical areas. His old enclosed motorcycle trailer now sported solar panels across its roof, along with several long radio antennae. Inside the trailer, changes were more dramatic. A small cookstove, water purification system, impressive medical station and a weapons locker had been added. The county tags had been removed from both as well. The Jeep and trailer were now primarily used for recon and supply collections. Today, Scott was using it to reach out to a group almost a hundred miles from Harris Springs.

They had stopped five miles short of the group's base camp. Bartos and the big man-boy, Abe, had been with him until a half-hour ago. The value of the Jeep, trailer and contents were such that they would be irresistible to any road gang. Now, when they went into potentially hostile territory, they did so with sniper cover. Scott scanned the small field and the road ahead, waiting for the signal that his overwatch was in place. He took a sip of lukewarm water and thought back to how simple life had once been. *Okay, it wasn't that simple, but it was easy. You didn't have to worry about being killed when you went to find food . . .* They had been through a lot, but they had survived the winter, and now the new normal was settling in.

Angel had told Scott about this group: a farming community looking to trade crops for fuel, medicine and likely nearly anything else.

Scott remembered a large commercial grower that used to be in this area. Along with a large public farmer's market, the farms supplied everything from fruits and vegetables to flowers and sod to retailers and grocery stores across the country. Angel had heard them broadcasting one night and made first contact. This small initial trade of fuel for an early crop of tomatoes, corn and beans would hopefully be the first of a long relationship.

The radio in his hand emitted a small chirp. The kid was already in place. Several minutes later, two chirps were heard. That was Bartos. There was no sign of trouble, or they would have broken radio silence and told him immediately. Scott climbed back behind the wheel and headed onto the road toward the contact point.

For once, things went according to plan. The six drums of diesel fuel were rolled out of the trailer, and in their place, boxes and crates of fresh vegetables were loaded. The farmers were wary and lean looking but seemed eager to trust. Their primary concern was ensuring Scott wasn't one of the Messengers. They knew the group's crusade was heading eastward. While they were also not very forthcoming about where they were from, Scott assured the group that he and his people were no threat and would even like to set up something more permanent in the way of a trade relationship.

The farms here were in the heart of rich floodplains but too remote to be a useful trading partner to most surviving groups. Scott's eyes had noticed a set of old railroad tracks heading south, and he again thought of the abandoned train and railcars they had been using for supplies. In

time, this farm could be a remarkable addition to their trading partners. Angel deserved a lot of credit for persuading them to venture out
this far.

Scott asked the man if he would be willing to trade for seeds. "We
probably have enough for this year's crops, but after that, we'll be in
trouble. Nearly everything we have is hybrid stuff, GMO seeds, and
from what I understand, you can't use the seeds from those crops as
they won't produce the same crop when replanted.

The old farmer laughed, "Yeah, we got plenty o' seed. A percentage of
all our harvest is set aside as seed crop. If you tell us what area you're
in or what crops grow best, we can set y'up . . . as long as you keep
trading with us, that is."

Scott agreed enthusiastically, "We will," he smiled. "Our soil is more
sand than clay. Corn doesn't do well, nor any of the cereal grains, but
beans, tomatoes, peppers, potatoes and peanuts all do great."

"So, you must live over near the coast," the old farmer said.

Scott smiled. "No comment. Are your crops based on
non-GMO seeds?"

"Hell, son, everything we grow is genetically modified, most has been
for centuries. We call it hybridization. Without it, corn would still be
just a weed growing on the riverbanks o' South America. GMO's taken
on a bad rep. Yeah, some o' the science lab shit with the patented
frankenplants is a bit much. They go in n'air modifying and manipu-
lating them genes o' parent plants, and who knows what other crap
they affect? But look, every farmer cross-pollinates and develops
strains o' crops to give the best yield. At its core, that's what farming's
all about. Potatoes and tomatoes were poisonous in their 'riginal state!
Without creating hybrids, we wouldn't be able to safely eat much of
what we do today.

"We got drought-tolerant and pest-tolerant varieties, so yes, our seeds
are technically hybrids and may or may not be able to reproduce
exactly that same variety year after year, but they *are* what you want.
Otherwise, you'll be losing more and more o' your harvest to disease,

pests and other problems. Tell us what you want, and we'll have it ready by late summer . . . assuming we're still here, that is."

Pushing in the crate with the last of the produce, they closed the doors, and the farmer extended his hand. "Thanks, Scott. Hope to be seeing a lot more o' you guys. You can tell your spotters to come on down and meet you now. No need to make 'em hike back so far."

Scott laughed nervously, "So you knew I brought company?"

"Hell, son," the old man laughed. "We woulda thought you were a complete fool if you hadn't. My guys tell me the one with the dog . . . well, he must look like a boxful of serious, and how in the hell do you feed that other one? They say he's huge. No way you could hide him." The man patted Scott on the shoulder with a kind smile as Scott got in and cranked the Jeep. As he turned around for the return trip, he keyed the radio. "Overwatch, you have eyes on?"

"Yeah, we see you. All looked good."

"Agreed. Good people, but, my secret Ninjas, they had you both spotted long ago. Ya'll head on back toward the small rise just ahead. I'm gonna pull over and see if I can reach anyone on the radio."

"Roger that."

The afternoon was slipping toward dusk, and the light was beginning to fade as the men regrouped. Abe had opened the trailer and was marveling at the stacks of food while Scott tried repeatedly to reach his brother, Bobby. He had thought that since he was a hundred miles closer to where Bobby was, he might get lucky. Part of the reason he was on this trip instead of Jack was so he could spend some time listening out for his brother with the stronger radio in the Jeep's trailer. He had spent weeks analyzing the signal direction and knew this outpost was in Bobby's general direction.

Bartos walked over. "I noticed a commercial antenna on a hill several miles back. Why don't we head there and camp for the night? You can hook the radio into the aerial. With that, you should be able to hear the hair growing on my balls."

Scott nodded, "Lead on, Mr. Ballsack."

"That's Mr. Hairy Ballsack to you, bud," Bartos growled.

It took Scott a while to connect the ham radio in the trailer to the large antenna towering above them. Bartos and Abe got busy making supper and securing the campsite. They all felt like sitting ducks on top of this hill, but Scott wanted to chance it. Fewer and fewer gangs seemed to be around lately. The winter had killed off large numbers, and there just wasn't that much left to steal in such a sparsely populated place as this. Everyone assumed that most of the stragglers and scavengers had signed on with the Messengers. The occasional highwaymen remained a problem, but Bartos and his recovery crews had devised some rather successful tactics to deal with them.

"Any luck?"

Scott looked at the Cajun and shook his head. "Reached the *AG* easily, everything's fine there. They said the signal was great, five by five in fact."

"Nothing from Bobby, though?" Bartos asked.

"Not yet, but this is the right frequency—same one we heard him on before. I'll keep signaling every thirty minutes. If you think it's safe to do so."

Bartos thought about it. "Hmmm," he said as he scratched a mosquito bite. "We purty sure dem fucks monitor certain common channels, but that one ain't common. I would doubt they would have the equipment to triangulate on this signal either. My guess is they're just opportunistic and take over any broadcasting radios in areas they invade rather than seeking them out. I think we're okay for now, but don't go for more than a few hours and let's bugout from this place before sunrise. Give it a break for now and eat. Me and the ox here have set up a watch for later. Solo's already patrolling the perimeter. You get to take over from me at midnight."

The meal consisted of boiled corn, fresh tomatoes, red potatoes and a small pork chop. It was divine. Scott thought about what the fresh food would mean to the community. Not only would it lift their spirits, but it would also help replace some much-needed vitamins and nutrients. "Guys, this was worth the risks. This food is so worth it. If we can keep extending the trade out and supporting groups like this, I think we can remain strong."

The other men agreed.

Bartos spoke between mouthfuls, "How can we protect them if the Messengers head this way? Or if the Catalyst planners decide they need more supplies for the protected camps?"

Abe looked up quickly. He had not been privy to the information regarding the Catalyst protocols, though he'd heard rumors since he arrived. "What are the protected camps?" he asked.

The big kid spoke so seldom that Scott and Bartos were taken by surprise. Bartos put his fork down and looked quickly to Scott who slowly answered. "According to some early intel that I uncovered after the CME, the um, cabal we call Catalyst has protected a bunch of people they consider essential to secure camps—reservations— around the country. They have power, food and resources to sustain those camps long-term. The contingency plan had been on the drawing board for some time, and the camps were regularly upgraded to be ready for several potential disaster scenarios."

"So, the government set up these reserves as a kind of lifeboat for us to get through this? Why don't we just head toward the closest one then? Fuck all this survival bullshit and horse-trading for food."

Scott shook his head. "You don't quite get it, Abe. They are not for us. We're not what anyone in that realm would consider essential. The list was filled with doctors, scientists, teachers, engineers . . . people with knowledge or skills that would be hard to replace and essential for rebuilding society. Not just any of those types even, but the best of the best. The camps are not very large, so they couldn't handle really high numbers of occupants. Also, none are located nearby. The map I saw showed nearly none in the lower southeast of the country, but we understand that the outpost in Tallahassee was converted into one, albeit a temporary one."

Abe dropped his head and looked at his nearly empty plate. "So, they really did just write us all off? Most of us, I mean. They decided to save a handful and let the rest of America collapse?"

Bartos nodded, the light from the small campfire casting his face into pitted shadows. "That is certainly one way to look at it. It is not inaccurate."

"What fucking other way is there?" Abe asked.

"They did what they could do," Bartos responded slowly. "It isn't right, but keep in mind nothing the government could have done would have made much of a difference. The numbers were too large, the logistics almost impossible. Someone decided that if you could only save, say ten percent, you might want to make sure that that ten percent was made of the right kind of people to save."

Abe got up, shouldered his rifle, and spit into the fire. "That's bull." He stood for a moment, obviously fuming and finally muttered, "I am going on patrol." The big man headed quickly into the darkness.

"He took that well, didn't he?" Bartos said sullenly.

"Keep in mind our reaction when we first heard it," Scott said.

"It is pretty fucked up, though, Scott, you have to admit. I know you see it as justified, but I tend to side with Todd that it was just a power play: the Catalyst group was opportunistic. It's been pulling strings for years to get the outcomes they want."

Scott looked up into the dark sky and took a long moment before answering. "I don't agree with it at all, Bartos. The truth is, our government did nothing. These guys were the only ones with any plan for survival. For that, we have to give them credit. It was intelligent, well-funded and executed with precision. Cold, logical precision. If you'll consider that they are trying to save the human species, then yes . . . I suppose I'm willing to accept even their levels of secrecy and brutality."

Bartos just growled, "If the Grayshirts are so committed to our survival, what's the deal with the virus DJ's working on? To me, that sounds like some Doomsday, Final Solution, Nazi bullshit."

"I admit that has me baffled as well. I just don't know, friend."

Scott stood, stretched and headed back up to the radio tower to try once more to reach his brother.

CHAPTER THIRTY

Outside Little Rock, Arkansas

Bobby Montgomery listened as his little brother's voice came again over the radio. As glad as he was to hear Scott and to know he was still alive, he didn't respond. In his muddled mind, he just couldn't think of any response that wouldn't put Scott at more risk. He wanted desperately to speak freely but would not take the chance. He had stupidly been broadcasting in the clear for all to hear for days until he had heard Kaylie's voice. Now he knew he had been acting foolishly—suicidally even.

The Messengers monitored radio broadcasts: they planned raids simply based on triangulating signals. Now he knew Scott and his daughter were okay. He could assume that they were in Harris Springs and that it had held out better than most places. The last thing he wanted was to draw attention to them from anyone who might be listening in—especially the Judges.

Scott's voice was pleading. The signal was strong; he must be closer than before. Bobby keyed the talk switch then thought better and released it. Scott paused when he heard the click. "Hey bro, is that you?"

Bobby considered a moment, then keyed the button once.

Scott's voice came back in a quieter tone, "Okay, understood."

Sitting in the dark beneath the bridge, Bobby smiled. His brother always figured things out quicker than most. Bobby knew his brother would resume good radio discipline now. Scott would assume Bobby was unable or unwilling to broadcast for his own good reasons. This would limit the amount of information they could exchange, but it was not as bad as some might assume.

Scott came back on again. "Big Ugly, are you okay and able to travel?"

Bobby smiled weakly and clicked a single key response. Big Ugly had been a call sign he and Bobby used when they were teenagers back on the farm. *Smart, kid brother . . . keep going.*

"Things have been challenging, but we are okay. Our twenty is probably the best place for you. Someone misses you, any chance she will see you soon?"

Bobby was unsure how to answer, he wanted to head south to Harris Springs, but only if he could do it safely. He keyed the talk, button twice.

"Ok, not soon, but eventually?"

A single click for yes.

"Ugly, I . . . I, um, am assuming the better half will not be with you?"

Bobby's eyes filled with tears. Trembling, he gave the button a sustained click.

"I am so sorry," Scott's voice was thick with emotion. He sighed. "Shit . . . Okay, I'm going to keep that to myself for now. We are aware of the approaching storm. It hasn't reached us, but we stay on alert for those spreading the word. We do have some general ideas about how far east it has moved. Suggest you get ahead of that storm before heading toward us. The Sandman's place should be far enough."

Bobby had to think about that one. The Sandman . . . he knew that phrase. His mind was still elsewhere, but damn, *he knew this.* Think, think—yes, he remembered! Old Man Sanderson had been one of his dad's friends. Scott had always called him Sandman. He had a farm about forty-five miles southeast of his current location.

Bobby gave a single key click.

Scott's voice came back with an edge of excitement. "I assume you are on foot and not wanting to head straight to us. My suggestion then... is to get to the Sandman and then just go with the flow for a while. Obviously stay off major roads until the storm passes. Do you understand?"

Bobby clicked once; he had understood most of what Scott meant.

"Need to get off the line, but good luck. Get somewhere safe, and we will come to meet you. Be smart and don't take chances. Love you, Ugly!"

Bobby turned the little unit off and repacked it in the waterproof bag. He felt better after hearing from Scott, no matter how awkward the communication was. He had no idea how he could get to the Sanderson place but trusted Scott knew more than he did. That was a plan at least. It beat the shit out of indulging in his suicidal thoughts to just go back for revenge.

CHAPTER THIRTY-ONE

The day had warmed up, and Bobby crawled out from his hiding place to relieve himself on a nearby shrub. Turning on his portable Garmin GPS unit, he sat back waiting for it to lock in on the satellites—assuming the satellites were still functioning, that is.

It took a little longer than he remembered, but it had been a few years since he had used the little device. It was an older version, and he had added it to his emergency bucket once he had gotten a better one to use when hunting. Now, he was counting on it getting him to his destination.

Once he had entered the coordinates, the screen lit up with a solid line reading 38.2 miles. A 'Set Waypoints' menu blinked in one corner. He bypassed the waypoints screen and zoomed in on the route. He would be navigating by night, so he wanted to know in advance every highway and piece of open ground he would need to cross. The trail indicated he would be heading for the small woodlands and hills just beyond. The elevation would be up and down for most of the journey. He realized that he would be lucky to make ten miles a day. He would also need to find food and fresh water along the way, as he had very little left, and he needed to avoid getting injured – difficult at night in rough terrain.

He looked down at the hand holding the GPS. On the bottom of his thumb was the top of the black cross tattoo. Not a Christian cross, but a crude version similar to the Iron Cross used by the Nazis. The Messengers called it the Knight's Cross, relating themselves as they always did to something noble.

Bobby had agreed to convert when the alternative was to be killed. Often since then, he had wished he'd chosen death on that day. Now the tattoo would mean death no matter who found him. The Messengers hunted down those that left the flock and made examples of them to help discourage others who may be "losing their faith." Anyone else who saw it would kill him for being part of that despised horde. In short, the mark ensured that he would find no safe haven anywhere. His only hope was to get far, far away from the radicals, if that was even possible. Maybe the people of Harris Springs would be unfamiliar with the foreboding brand. Or perhaps they could forgive him.`

Looking at the small map on the screen again, he marked the last known Messengers camp, less than fifteen miles to the west. He had been with the group for four months and knew the normal patrol assignments: they would already have advance patrols out this far— others besides the group he had encountered the day before. While they mostly stuck to the major roads, they were opportunists. If they learned of possible supplies or encampments, they would divert and head in those directions while reporting back to base what they found. Other than the farms, churches, schools and stores, he needed to identify all their potential targets as well as the routes they might use.

After nearly forty minutes he powered down the unit and stowed it in the pack. It seemed hopeless. While this area was not overly developed, it was not rural either. He could not avoid all the paths as it would take too long, and the Messengers would overtake him. He could not allow that to happen. With thousands, maybe even tens of thousands in multiple camps combing every inch of the countryside to gain favor with the Prophet, he would almost certainly be caught. He needed to move faster. *I need a horse, or hell, even a freakin' bike,* he thought. Scott would love hearing that after all the shit his big brother had given him over the years. The slightest hint of a smile crept across his hardened face before the dark pall of futility erased it and regained control of his mind. He pulled himself back into the shadows to rest and wait for nightfall.

CHAPTER THIRTY-TWO

Five miles to the east, three men on motorcycles converged at a small farmhouse. The home had been an upscale suburban mini-farm, part of an eco-development. The quaint community was an attempt to develop a somewhat self-sustaining neighborhood. The overpriced homes were built with green products and eliminated such crudeness as green lawns in favor of recycled rubber mulch and pine chips. All the homes surrounded the community farm, although none of the homeowners ever actually helped with the farming. The development had gotten tremendous press coverage and seduced several well-known investors.

One of the men stepped from the motorcycle and strolled confidently to the open door of the farmhouse. The sounds of a woman sobbing could be clearly heard. Just as the man reached the door, a new sound could be heard from the rear of the house. A door slammed, and a small boy, probably no more than ten, began sprinting from the house in the direction of a barn. The man on the porch signaled with a finger to his partners.

With slow and deliberate motions, the man on the far right, known as Lynx, unsheathed a long rifle and placed it, pointing in the direction of the running boy, on his handlebars. He glanced up at his partner who gave a small nod. Just as the boy was reaching the safety of the barn, a single shot rang out. The large caliber shell neatly cleaved the child's head from the rest of his small body. As the body fell into the dust, the head traveled on for several feet, hitting the door of the barn with a bloody thunk. The shooter gave the briefest of smiles as he re-sheathed his weapon in the long side-mount holster.

His accomplice stepped over the threshold and into the house. The sound of sobbing turned into screams before they suddenly quieted. The other men patiently waited their turn outside.

CHAPTER THIRTY-THREE

Southern Mississippi

The sound of the tires crunching on gravel was the only noise they heard as Bartos maneuvered the Jeep cautiously down from the hilltop. Bartos eyed the heavily laden trailer with a worried expression. He knew they had secured everything tightly, but still . . .

"It'll be fine," Scott said.

Bartos glanced at his friend. The man had been nearly silent all morning.

"I know, just get a little anxious, ya know?"

Scott nodded, looking back at Abe in the rear seat: shotgun at the ready and Solo's head peering over the seat next to him. They had taken out the hinge screws and removed the rear doors in case they encountered trouble on the ride back. Getting stuck inside the 4x4 would not be a good defensive position.

Bartos swung the vehicle onto the paved road at the bottom of the hill and the swaying trailer stabilized at once. "We done good, brother. Got the produce, made some new friends and you reached your brother, no?"

Scott had said they had talked, sort of. Bartos wasn't sure what that meant, but apparently, it was not all good news. He knew Scott would talk when he felt like it and not before. Things in that head always had to be worked out before sharing. Bartos had grown accustomed to his friend's retreats into silence and no longer took them personally.

They had made plans to return via a different route. This was partially to mislead anyone trying to guess where they came from or were heading to. The more important reason was to map out alternate routes to get to the farm in the future. Bartos was concerned, knowing they would be getting close to several larger towns, including Hatties-burg, on this route. He, Todd and Scott had gone over the maps in detail before they made the trip and marked numerous likely ambush points. Once they were closer to Harris Springs, the roads would be clear, but up here they had to stay on guard. They avoided major high-ways, blind turns, any roads that had overpass bridges and stuck mainly to highways through the more open farmland. When they got to the numerous wooded sections, the group was on high alert. Forest meant concealment, and anyone wanting to do them harm would likely do so from concealment.

The months of going out on these types of ops had drilled into them a much more highly attuned sense of situational awareness. They kept the maps updated constantly to record threats. From every person they traded with or spoke with on the radio, they learned a bit more about the roads and waterways, and the highwaymen, obstacles and dangers on them. While the number of road gangs was less now, the ones that remained were smarter and tougher.

The morning was beginning to warm up, and for now, the ride felt more like an enjoyable weekend road trip than what it really was.

"Scott, what day of the week is it?"

Scott shrugged. "No idea, Bartos. Maybe Tuesday . . . could be Sunday."

No one seemed quite sure anymore; calendars and days of the week were mostly mysteries. Relics of a nearly forgotten time when shit like that mattered. They knew the approximate day of the month, and that was good enough. "It feels like a Sunday morning to me," Bartos said with a grin. "Right, Abraham? It's a Sunday, right?"

The big man looked back from the passing scenery and nodded. "Kinda does, yeah, I guess."

"Yeah . . . Sunday. I like Sundays," Bartos said to no one in particular. "Coffee, pancakes, maybe a little N'awlins jazz on the radio. This . . . this is definitely a Sunday."

They all fell silent, each thinking back to Sundays they had once spent with friends, family and in the luxuries of that life that were gone. The next hour or so passed in relative peace as they tried to enjoy the ride. Scott couldn't help but think of his brother. He knew he must be in bad shape. He had no idea how he could help get Bobby down to the coast. He looked at the road map and saw that Bartos had again updated the estimated position of the Messengers. The red shaded area was well past Little Rock and not far from the farm he had told Bobby to go to. The location of the so-called Lord's Army was just a guess, but Todd and Bartos had gotten good at assimilating data and extrapolating where the advancing edge was. They even had several ideas regarding the location of the group's current base camp.

To Scott, the shaded territory controlled by the Messengers looked like a crude red dagger, stabbing from west to east, deep into Arkansas. Tendrils streaked north and south all along the dagger shape. These would be the raiders and advance scouts—maybe the ones Abe referred to as Judges and Marauders. Scott knew that everything they had was more guesswork than proof—most of the facts were reported by someone who had survived an encounter. There were very few, but the Judges were known to leave at least one survivor in most locations. Apparently, they liked having a living witness to help spread "The Word of Judgment."

Scott took notice of a sign coming up and checked the map. "Bartos, we got a marked spot about two miles ahead." This would be the fifth such spot they had encountered. None of the others had amounted to anything. The Jeep continued on, but slower, with the engine nearly silent as Bartos coaxed it closer to the pinch point in the trees. "Abe, take the high ground, again," he said.

Abe groaned, but hopped out the door opening and exchanged the shotgun for the large .50 caliber M107A1 long-range rifle. The Jeep never stopped rolling as he grabbed a handle on the trailer and easily swung his large frame onto the shooting platform that had been added to the roof. He had to position himself behind the small steel plate with the built-in gun mount and between the rows of small solar panels. Once settled in, he pushed a foam insert into each ear, racked a shell into the chamber, eased the barrel to rest on the padded frame and sighted down the road.

Scott picked up the M16 and readied himself. As the Jeep neared the short rise, Bartos motioned over his shoulder to Solo. The dog was instantly alert. Solo slipped silently out of the still-moving Jeep and disappeared into the tall grass. As the wooded section ahead came into view, they saw the makeshift roadblock.

"Well, guess our lucky streak on this trip had to come to an end at some point. So much for a quiet Sunday morning," Bartos lamented with a sigh.

Scott nodded slowly. "Yep. I see five shooters. Four vehicles."

"Four?" the Cajun asked. "I only see three. Two blocking the road and the rental truck off in the trees."

"There's another. Looks to be a chase car farther down the road. Dark blue. I assume if we made it through the barrier, it's there to pursue us," Scott said.

"Pretty smart," Bartos replied. "Do you see a driver in that car?"

Scott was now using a ranging scope to glass the area. "Windows are tinted dark, but I suppose we should assume there is one. So that makes six bandits possible, five for sure." He held his hands out the window to indicate six to Abe.

"Prolly so, my friend. You see anything of real value, anything we might not want to damage other than the cube truck?" He was referring to the small box truck painted with the rental company's instantly recognizable logo.

"Not really. These guys look pretty sad. The chase car might be good if we can take it without damage. Looks like an early seventies GTO. My brother drove a similar one back in high school. Awful gas mileage, but man, they've got power!"

Bartos checked the distance and slowed the car to a stop. "Maybe they'll let you take it for a test drive before you fully commit to it. Don't want to make a snap decision based on emotions, you know."

Still looking through the scope, Scott gave a small grin. "Range is good, 110 yards."

While still technically within range of the armed highwaymen, this distance would be a tough shot for most. It was the ideal range for Abe up on the roof, though. The rifle and scope he was using had been sighted in at 100 yards just for this purpose. He had seen Scott's fingers telling him six. He, too, had spotted the navy-blue muscle car farther down the road, but he saw no one sitting in it.

He could also see the occasional movement where Solo was scouting, just inside the line of the woods, and approaching the gang. The dog was stealthy, but suddenly froze about thirty yards from the roadblock. Abe noticed he was facing away, back into the deeper trees. He moved the rifle to follow the dog's gaze. A barrel protruded from the top of a brush pile. Someone else was there, and well hidden. The shooter's hide was good, but Abe could just make out the top of a head behind the downed limbs of dead pine needles.

"Here they come," Bartos growled as one of the men stepped from behind the old car and pointed his gun at them. "He seems to want us to come closer." They could see the man yelling at them, but the sound didn't travel this far. Eventually, he dropped to a knee, and they saw the flare as the gun fired. Both men flinched, but they had been expecting it. An immediate response was the booming report of Abe's .50 caliber. The kneeling assailant's upper body nearly disintegrated with the impact of the large round. The booming report came again, and Scott saw an explosion of limbs and red mist as the sniper shell hit someone concealed to the left of the roadblock.

Bartos put the Jeep in gear and began advancing toward the now bewildered-looking bandits. "I guess they're figuring out that this isn't our first rodeo."

Two of the figures seemed to regain their senses and began firing in their general direction. A blur of white streaked from the forest, and the first man disappeared from sight. A moment later they watched as the dog leaped over one of the car's hoods and clamped his jaws around the second shooter's neck dragging him to the ground. No more shots were heard.

Bartos pulled the Jeep up to the blockade, avoiding the ruined corpse of the first shooter, and slowed to a stop. Scott was instantly out circling to the right as Bartos shut off the Jeep and went left. "I have two down—three counting the first one," Scott yelled.

Bartos was also out, "I have one in the trees. That leaves one or two unaccounted for. They heard Solo growling and watched as an unnaturally skinny middle-aged man and a dirty, slightly overweight teenage girl stumbled out of the trees, followed by the blood-covered dog. Both the man and the girl looked like they were living through their own personal horror story.

Scott knew that Abe would have the two in his sights, so he was not worried. Between Solo and Abe, they were well protected. Nonetheless, he and Bartos kept some space between themselves and the two rough looking survivors.

"Anyone else out here?" Bartos asked calmly. The two shook their heads. "Don't lie to me, my dog doesn't like dishonest people," he continued.

The man stuttered and said," W-w-we sw-swear mm-ister."

"Good. Now listen. You guys attempted to rob us, as you have no doubt been doing to others for months. Unfortunately, it didn't work out for you this time. My friends and I like to discourage people from pursuing this particular line of work. Do you understand what I'm saying?"

Both of the strangers looked at one another with a look of bewilderment. They shook their heads, then, clearly thinking that maybe that was the wrong answer, the girl nodded her head in the affirmative.

"Seems to be some confusion," Bartos sighed. "Let me see if we can clear this up. You see, in order for would-be thieves to actually choose a new career we've learned that stealing has to get either unprofitable . . . or unpleasant. Your associates have gone the route of . . ." he looked back over at the ruined bodies, ". . . unpleasant. You still have the chance to make a choice and have a future, but it will sadly be very, um, unprofitable. Now, drop your weapons, then your clothes, and the keys for these cars." The girl started to protest, but Bartos gave Solo a signal and the dog bumped her leg. Both began to comply immediately.

Bartos used plastic zip ties to tie both thieves' hands together as Scott and Abe collected the weapons and keys. They stowed anything of value in the nearly empty rental truck, siphoned off all the fuel in the two blocking cars, and pushed them out of the way. Bartos further disabled each car so they would not move again.

Scott took the girl to one side as Abe began talking with the older man. They had learned to collect information every time they encountered road crews. What were their names and where did they live? What were the names of the dead associates? Were they family? Most importantly, what other gangs were in the area? Where did they set up ambushes, and where did they live? All the specific information went into a notebook and was also used to update the maps. Interestingly, most thieves seemed to have the best intel on others in the same line of work. After about fifteen minutes they were done.

Abe had fueled the rental truck and now pulled it out of the trees and onto the road. Scott pulled the Jeep up just behind. Bartos gave a final admonishment to the two sitting in their underwear on the side of the road. "You chose well. In appreciation, you get to live. We will be using this road again. If we encounter any more problems from anyone on this stretch, we will be coming to your homes. We will not give you another chance."

The girl whose name they had learned was Rhonda was crying now. "Please don't leave us like this, we'll die."

Bartos set his mouth in a grim line. "I'm sorry, that's not our problem. This is a consequence of your own actions. Look around. You guys are the lucky ones today." He dropped two water bottles in the dirt near the pair then slid into the passenger's seat beside Scott. "Gimme a lift down to my new ride, would ya?"

"Your ride?" Scott said with a laugh.

They pulled up to the dusty but beautifully restored Pontiac GTO. Bartos twirled the key he had removed from the body in the trees. "You can't handle classics, Scott. Remember what you did to my Bronco last year?"

Scott laughed. "Hey, Ballsack, you're an asshole. Enjoy your goat," he added, remembering the old nickname for GTOs. Solo decided to keep riding in the Jeep with Scott. He didn't seem to care for the sound of his owner's new ride. Scott used a towel to clean some of the blood from the handsome beast's face, after which the dog promptly curled up in the passenger's seat and closed his eyes.

The rich, throaty exhaust sounds are impressive, thought Scott as the dark car pulled in behind the trailer. It was not a bad acquisition. Scott saw the figures in the mirror kneeling beside the road. He still struggled with the brutality of this world, and truly hoped the rest of the trip would be less eventful.

CHAPTER THIRTY-FOUR

Arkansas Southeast of Little Rock

Bobby had been sleeping fitfully, but the sound of a gunshot brought him to full alertness. Listening to the echo heading down the valley, he made an educated guess of where the shooter was. It had not been close, so he was clearly not the target. Unfortunately, it was ahead: in the general direction that he needed to go—the next valley over, he was relatively sure.

He was uncertain of what to do. Maybe Scott had been wrong, and the Messengers were already this far out. He geared up, applied more camo paint to his face and moved, cautiously skirting the tree line into the nearby hills.

It took almost an hour to get to the summit of the hill. He paused to drink a bottle of water and double-check his bearings. The surroundings reminded him of the camp that he and Jess had used as a bugout location. He had planned it out for years, and it had gone to shit so quickly. When the Messengers found him, they had not killed him but knocked him unconscious. He was taken to a camp with hundreds of other captives. He didn't know where they'd taken his wife, or if she had even survived the attack. Within the first hours of his capture, he witnessed countless men, women and even children put to death at the hands of the Messengers.

The killing was not indiscriminate; it had a purpose. An evil, dark purpose. Anyone who looked over sixty was useless and killed immediately, as were kids under nine—unless they were female and cute . . . a few of those were kept alive. In essence, you weren't worth the food or the trouble if you couldn't serve the Lord's Army. Men were given a chance to repent and convert and become a probationary Messenger. Those who didn't were killed in the most expeditious and, it appeared, macabrely entertaining ways possible. Bobby converted on day two, and his first assignment after getting the tattoo was to help drag the mountain of dead bodies off to the burn pit. He forced the memories away; they were vile and disturbing on a visceral level, yet any time his mind drifted, it seemed to return to those moments. Those, or Jess' last.

The sun was beginning to set. He needed to find more water and food to sate the gnawing hunger in his belly. He was still curious about the gunshot. He hadn't heard anything more, although that did not necessarily bode well. *Could just be someone hunting.* Although the sound indicated a large caliber gun.

He could see what seemed to be a small meadow opening up a short way down the hill. From there, he might be able to see who was out there. Just as he reached the clearing, the full valley below came into view. Neat and expensive homesteads were scattered around a lake: a subdivision of mini-farms in an eco-community. His construction company had built several eco-neighborhoods just like this one.

He had heard the sound of motorcycles before and now saw them in front of one of the farmhouses. His heart sank. The Judges usually rode motorcycles and always traveled in threes. He despised the Judges more than all the other Messengers combined. They represented the darkest aspects of the terrorist organization. Quickly ducking back into the cover of trees, he watched the riders as they sped away on the small two-lane road that wound through the valley. Off to their next assignment—their next Mission, as it was called in the group. They would have marked the houses if there was anything for the recovery crews to collect . . . Using the small binoculars in his pack, he saw the Judges' spray-painted Iron cross on each of the buildings. He knew it would be too late to help anyone down there; they had already been judged.

From the clearing, he counted several houses, barns and outbuildings. No signs of life came from any of them. The once pristine little farmsteads had been laid out in a radial pattern around the lake. The raised planting beds in the gardens, expensively built urban chicken coops and absence of sheds or outbuildings on each lot spoke volumes: these residents had not been farmers. For one thing, farmers could have survived this. Judging by the many rectangles of fresh dirt in the still-green sod lawns, these people hadn't managed well after the actual farm hands had stopped coming to work. He saw no chickens, no livestock of any sort. Then he saw the spray of fresh blood and the small body lying prone near the barn.

Just the knowledge of the dead child caused rage to blossom in him yet again. With no further analysis of the situation, Bobby Montgomery began walking in the direction of the farms—then abruptly stopped. *What am I doing?* he wondered. The fact that the Judges had already been here was enough to tell him to avoid the area altogether: if there were resources, they would be returning; if there weren't, there was no reason to go himself. There could be survivors in hiding, but that was not something he could do anything about either. He hadn't even been able to save his wife, and he had had to ask his brother to save his daughter. Bobby couldn't see his assistance being a help to anyone. He needed water and would need food soon; there was no way he had enough to get to the Sanderson place, but theoretically, food was all around him, and he could find water elsewhere. Perhaps he could take care of himself, but that was all. He pulled the GPS unit out and adjusted his course to bypass the valley.

CHAPTER THIRTY-FIVE

Harris Springs, Mississippi

"Hey, kid!" Scott yelled as he parked the Jeep. Abe had exited the cube truck and raised his eyes in acknowledgment. "Look, I just wanted to say thanks for what you did today. That was some damn fine shooting. You saved our asses. Just wanted to make sure you were . . . were okay?"

Abe just shrugged and nodded. "Yes sir, I'm alright. I don't much like the killin', but it's necessary. I know that."

Scott placed his hand on the young man's arm. "It sadly is, and when it stops bothering us is when we become the problem." Solo was busying himself marking each of the new vehicle's wheels as his property while Bartos was opening up the doors to the trailer.

Scott turned to see Angel's grinning face as she came down the ramp from the *AG*'s large storage space. "I told you, Scott," she declared as she casually pointed to the cases of vegetables being unloaded. "I knew those people were on the up-and-up."

He gave her a quick hug. "You were right, they're good people, and they were desperate for a trading partner. I think they'll be a good ally."

"So, no trouble on the roads?" she asked, looking at the new vehicles and Solo's still bloodstained face which was now drinking deeply from a bucket of water.

"No real trouble. We should be able to easily keep the route clear."

Still smiling, Angel walked over to the growing stack of crates. "Oh, my God, I smell cantaloupes! But it's too early in the season for that."

"They have greenhouses and tented fields that trap heat, so their growing seasons are extended," Scott said as he opened the case to show her the pale melons.

Taking one, Angel lifted it to her nose, mesmerized by the fresh, sweet aroma. "Oh, shit," her eyes widened at the memory. "Almost forgot. Chief wants to see both of you at once. Something's up. You run on, and I'll get my galley crew to finish unloading this stuff."

Bartos and Scott looked at one another in concern. They headed up to the control room to find Todd.

~

Things between Todd and Scott had been somewhat strained of late. In fact, distant was a more accurate descriptor. The two men genuinely liked each other. Both had now saved each other's life more than once. Some of the problems undoubtedly arose from the fact that Todd was grieving the loss of his wife. Scott knew his friend struggled with that loss and depression on a nearly constant basis. The distance between the two men was not as easily quantifiable. At its heart seemed to be Todd's unwavering support for the Navy's aggressive response to the Catalyst protocols. Scott liked the Navy and helped them often, but ideologically he felt he was probably more aligned with the Catalyst plan than Todd liked.

To be honest, Todd didn't want to save everyone but didn't like someone else deciding who lived or died. Scott was more pragmatic and agreed that on some levels, it did make sense to save only those who deserved it, or who mattered the most in terms of survival and rebuilding. It shouldn't have been an issue between them, and the divide was not that wide, but still, Scott felt the ideological differences bubble up with increasing regularity. As he and Bartos entered the command bridge, he wondered if this would be another of those times. Todd smiled and waved them into the briefing room. Jack was there already, sipping on what appeared to be a cold beer. "Preacher . . . you bring enough for the whole class?" Bartos quipped.

"Sorry, boys . . . only one." Jack grinned before sliding a small cooler toward them.

Todd wasted no time getting to the matter at hand. "Guys, I hear the trip went well, and judging by the crates being unloaded, we should be eating well for a while. I do want to hear all about it. Scott, I'm also really anxious to hear if you made contact with your brother, but that needs to wait.

"Listen up. The Navy has been tracking some movement. They now believe that the lab at the university was moved somewhere out into the Gulf of Mexico."

"On the surface, that would seem to be a very unintelligent move," Scott said.

"Go on," Todd said, nodding.

"Well, that would put them in the Navy's playground. No matter how well-equipped the Grayshirts are, the Navy must have the superior force at sea. It would also be much harder to supply and maintain communications with a facility that remote. Moving it there would increase the level of difficulty and risk in nearly every aspect." Scott said thoughtfully.

"I don't disagree," Todd replied. "But let your mind work the problem from another way. What would they gain by doing this? Why would they feel it was necessary? Finally, what if the move wasn't connected to the looming Naval attack at the college at all? We now have reason to think the two could be unrelated."

Scott sat back to digest that new information and the possibilities it presented. "Does Garret have an idea of where they are? I mean, is it an island, a ship, an undersea bunker . . . what? Commander Garret was the top Navy man in the Gulf and a close ally of Todd and the local community.

"He is going under the primary assumption that it is most likely an abandoned oil rig. While it could be a ship, for some reason they don't think so. Also, no islands out there, it's a pretty deep part of the Gulf."

Scott leaned back contemplating the little they knew. "Hmmm, okay, just brainstorming here... I'm pretty sure the research team didn't suddenly have a breakthrough into the cure for the pandemic overseas. But based on some of the things DJ has said, I would guess that for them to make that move on their own would mean . . ." He looked at the ceiling while his mind worked. "They must have something that's too dangerous to work on in Tallahassee. They need an actual bio-lab or containment facility. DJ would have mentioned any concrete discovery, but maybe Praetor finally provided them some live viral samples to work on or something."

DJ had mentioned the outbreak many times, and they all knew it was spreading across Asia and now Europe. One good thing about this happening now was the lack of modern transportation. In the age of global travel, a disease could easily be spread vast distances by unknowingly infected travelers. The distance from the outbreak now offered a level of comfort, but Scott felt a cold shiver run up his spine. Nothing could be considered 'good' about a bioweapon unleashed on the planet.

Todd nodded, seeming to agree with this line of thought. "Perhaps they're now part of the labs charged with directly working on a cure. Didn't DJ say that his team was working on just one part of the beast?"

"Yeah," Scott nodded, "it seemed to be something relatively minor in the scheme of things, but perhaps that turned out to be a key after all."

Todd scratched at his chin before responding. "We have some ideas on how deadly this thing is. I would hope they wouldn't have any of it back stateside, but maybe they are desperate. Surely, they have better equipped, more secure facilities to do the heavier lifting. Not some improvised lab on an old oil rig."

"That's been our assumption all along," Scott frowned in thought, "but I don't think we can trust that anymore. Several things may have happened. There could have been a breach or an accident at one of the other labs which increased DJ's group's value to the overall project. Or it might be that they now realize what was going on at FSU was really the most promising solution, and so elevated that team to the starting squad. My bet is that DJ and the professor—what's his name?"

"*Her* name. Dr. Colton," Todd read from some notes.

Scott looked puzzled for a moment. "Okay, yeah, well, my bet is that they discovered something—something important enough for Praetor to elevate their research to the next level. Maybe not a cure, but something promising that meant that working with inert material in Florida was no longer viable, so they moved them to a remote station to continue. I don't know, but that seems to make the most sense to me."

Bartos looked up from the chart map he had been studying. "Todd, what does this have to do with us? I mean, aside from Kaylie wanting her boyfriend back, why is this any of our problem?"

"For several reasons, my friends." Todd sat down and stretched his arms wide before crossing them behind his head. "Commander Garret wants our take on it. Specifically, he wants Scott's opinion, since he was the person that first brought the virus to the Navy's attention. Second, we can identify at least one of the members of that research team by sight . . . if they find the new location, we may be called on to do just that. Speaking bluntly, separating the friendlies from the bad guys may not be possible without us. Lastly, he asked if Scott, and maybe even Kaylie, since she has some related knowledge, could give an amateur assessment of how risky it might be to launch an attack on the lab. That is, if they can find it, of course.

"Assuming you are right," Todd continued, looking at Scott, "and they have the pathogen there, how easily could it be released in the attack? Would it kill everyone on the rig or on the ships if they're successful? What if it gets into the ocean . . . could it make it back to land? Garret knows we don't know much, but he trusts we know more than any of his people do. The intel we provided from our talks with DJ was their main source, and now, obviously, that's closed to them as well as us. Keep in mind the Navy is cut off from nearly everyone. It's not like it was before. He can't just call up command for help. Naval intelligence is in the dark on the details, and Garret's surviving chain of command are back in the field, many helping drive the ships out there. He has to make the decision on how to move forward."

Scott looked around the table before responding, then blew out a breath he realized he'd been holding for a while. "Wow, no pressure. I can't say this idea of going after them is smart, but I can do my best to get you answers. I had a friend in college that was a med tech, and Kaylie knew some of what DJ was doing. If we mention this to her, though, she's going to get upset. You saw how she was after the attack at FSU. I'm not sure if it would give her some optimism or just dash whatever fragments of hope she has left for DJ that she's managing to hold on to."

"Thanks, Scott, and I understand. We've all grown to love Kaylie. I don't want to cause her pain, but yeah, we need to know." Todd looked troubled but continued. "One other thing Garret wanted me to ask. Do you think you could access the servers in DC and cross-reference some coordinates? They want to know if anything was mentioned in the Catalyst protocol files that might help them identify the exact location. I thought your friend in DC might be some help."

"Tahir? I haven't been able to raise him recently. Honestly, though, I've only had time to try the ship's Internet service occasionally. It's satellite-based, and I can only get a weak signal . . . not much left out there, though. Very few servers connected to the Internet still have a viable power supply. The DHS servers were still up last time I tried, so I can probably leave him a message if nothing else. But I'm not even sure he's survived . . . DC must have been a difficult place the last few months. I've honestly been dreading checking on him." Scott stood and paced before looking at his friend. "Todd, there's something else, and we may as well discuss it now."

Todd looked up, tensing in case Scott was taking the Catalyst side again.

"I'm not sure I agree that Naval action is the best thing. Even if the Catalyst people created this superbug as a weapon, they still must be the best equipped to find a cure. If we help the Navy destroy that lab, we may also be helping destroy mankind's last chance at survival. We could all be doomed."

Jack and Bartos both chimed in with a "Yeah," and "For real," respectively.

"Goddammit, Scott, don't you think I realize that? I am not ignorant to the possibility, but these Praetor asshats can't keep playing God. Someone has to stop this madness. You don't even know if they *are* working on a cure. They could be creating the next, more aggressive version—an even more lethal strain. You know these people have no moral compass. Mankind's fate is secondary to their own ambitions, their own plans."

"Todd, they are used to power and control, but I have yet to see them exercise any desire to condemn our species. You seem to overlook the fact that they were the only ones to have a plan in place for this contingency. While everyone else sat on their asses, they had facilities built, supplies provisioned, and real plans put in place to deal with the aftermath. Whatever hand they had in creating the virus is unclear to me, but I'm convinced they are honestly trying to stop it. DJ has made that abundantly clear."

Scott could see Todd's face turning red but continued. "The protocol discusses all of the possibilities: the cycle of destruction. Even they said we could survive one or two national disasters, but beyond that, who knows? First was the solar flare, which took out most of the world's power grid. The government, leadership, social order all collapsed. That's two. The economy's collapsed, not just the US, but worldwide. Three. Anarchy, lawlessness, lack of food, medicine and clean water—let's bunch all that fun under four. Now comes number five: a global fucking pandemic. This is a downward cycle. Each catastrophe has been the catalyst for the next. The US is not going to survive this, nor your precious Navy. At this point, I'm more concerned about the human species surviving than any particular side."

Scott was still speaking softly but was struggling to keep the lid on a growing anger.

"Jesus, Scott!"

"Todd," Jack spoke up, "the man has a valid point."

"Fuck . . . I knew this wouldn't go over," Todd stood up so quickly the chair tipped over. He walked to the window and peered out.

"Cap," Bartos said, "you already knew all this, didn't you? You've worked this shit out and come to the same place. You were just hoping Scott would see something different."

Scott looked over at the Cajun, who was nodding supportively to the room. Scott eased up and walked over to his friend. "Todd . . . I don't like it, but I'll give them my honest assessment, and if I can get a location, I will supply that as well. But, if I do that, we—you and I—both need to get them to understand that their interference would likely be the tipping point. If DJ and the doctor are close to finding a treatment, and the Navy inadvertently stops that research—even causes the dispersal of the thing—then it may be game over for all of us. This may not be the right time for a military solution, and they must fully consider that."

"Thank you, Scott." Todd looked tired. "I know it's not what you want —not what you feel is best. We can try and convince them, but I believe they will go through with it with or without us . . . At least if they include us, we have a chance to influence the tactics, if not the strategy, and try and save that boy.

CHAPTER THIRTY-SIX

Southeast of Little Rock, Arkansas

The hills were slowing his pace considerably, and traveling at night was proving to be a challenge. Bobby knew the terrain would even out the closer he got to Sanderson's place, but at this rate, it was going to take several more days. While he had been traveling in the dark to help avoid detection, today he kept moving late into the morning. He would start again well before sunset. It was a risk, but he needed to reach the farm as soon as possible. Getting caught by them again was not something he could allow himself. If it came to that, well... he just wouldn't let it.

He felt oddly good watching the sun rise over the hilltops. Briefly, he felt as though Jess was there with him. If things had gone according to plan, they would have been sitting on the patio watching the sunrise together. She had been the one to insist that the patio go on the eastern side of the house instead of the backyard. She had never been traditional, and Kaylie was just like her mom in that sense.

He came back to himself in a moment and felt the distinction of his place in the world now. He was, in fact, a mere shadow of his former self. His clothes hung off his thin frame like a scarecrow's. He had no idea how much weight he had lost in the last six months, how much of everything he had lost, but right now, he was fighting to hold on to the positive mood for just a few more minutes. One of his snares had caught a squirrel. He had eaten it raw, not wanting to risk a fire. It was gross, but his gnawing hunger was too strong to be ignored. The protein had reenergized him. Thankfully, water had also been relatively easy to find, as several streams fell from the steeper inclines. The water was fresh and cold. From the GPS he knew he was still over twenty miles from the farm. Somehow, he had to pick up the pace.

As he watched the sun climb higher, something glittering caught his eye on an adjacent hill. Bobby ducked into cover, assuming it was someone using a rifle scope. The telltale reflection was all he needed to realize he was in trouble. If he was lucky, it was just a hunter, but it could just as easy be the Messengers or their ruthless thugs, the Judges. The reflection did not move, however; it barely varied, in fact. Bobby didn't move either, although he was beginning to wonder if maybe it was something else, not a reflection from a scope.

As the sun climbed and the shadows faded, he could see more of what it was: definitely not a person. He moved to his right several hundred yards to get a better view. He let out a breath. It was not exactly good news, but he had seen several of these in the past few months. The reflection was coming off a charred vertical wing with a red and white striped logo: the tail section, he believed, of a crashed passenger jet. American Airlines, he guessed.

The wreck would have crashed last August. Chances were, no one had even noticed it yet; this part of Arkansas was pretty remote. Any food or bodies would have been lost to the scavengers by now. He really felt he should check it out—he needed clothes and supplies, as well as food, decent boots and socks. Maybe some luggage was still intact at the very least.

Bobby realized he was talking himself into doing something catastrophically stupid. *Stop and think, you idiot,* he chided himself. He needed to find a place to sleep for a few hours. He would move closer to the wreck site and hunker down. He would rest, but also watch for any signs of people. If this was a trap, he wanted to know well in advance.

Cautiously, he wound his way across and up the hillside. Well before he was close to the crash, he began seeing clues of what lay ahead: a plastic bag with the airline insignia, a tattered diaper and then a shred of a thin blanket. Animals, he assumed, had strewn the remnants of the plane and occupants all over this hill. The side of the hill was blackened for hundreds of yards around the wreckage in all directions. Bobby slowed his pace, then stopped a few hundred yards from the edge of the burned land. He could not see the actual crash from here but eased sideways until a depression in the forest gave him an unobstructed view. He stopped and listened, and listened. For almost an hour that was all he did. Then he cautiously moved deeper into shadows, covered himself with some blackened limbs, closed his eyes, and immediately fell asleep.

When he awoke several hours later, he remained still and took a moment to assess his surroundings. The sunlight filtering through the branches was softer now. The angle of the sun let him know it was midafternoon. There was a slight smell of smoke and decay, but it was not strong. He struggled to focus his hearing, paying attention to the forest sounds. Was anyone out there, waiting nearby to ambush him? He heard songbirds and squirrels chattering nearby. He felt a slight breeze and in it heard the small tinkling sounds of metal on metal from the direction of the wreckage. It was so distinct that he conjured up a picture in his head: a seatbelt hanging over the side of the seat frame; the wind knocking it against the seat every few minutes. He imagined the many times he had sat in tree stands hunting deer or in duck blinds waiting on game birds. He had used the same skills then, but now *his* life depended on being good at it.

He lay there, frozen until he was confident of every smell and every sound. Cautiously, he lifted his hands and began quietly moving the charred, skeleton-like limbs that had covered him. As soon as he could see out, he stopped and swept the entire hillside with his eyes, processing every item. Confident he was the only one there, he extracted himself from the hide and began walking in the direction of the American Airlines aircraft: just one of thousands that had fallen from the sky that fateful day.

The Boeing 737 had taken off from Dallas on its way to Charlotte that fateful August morning. The 115 passengers on board had mostly been business travelers used to flying. They were 75 miles southwest of Little Rock when the lights had flickered, and the engines suddenly went silent. Cruising at 32,000 feet, most quickly realized the horror that awaited them. The captain of the doomed flight, a thirty-six-year-old ex-Air Force pilot named Ward, and his co-pilot had fought to keep the bird in the air as long as possible. With avionics out, engines silent and no radio, they were flying blind. More accurately, they were gliding blind to the extent that you could glide a 100-ton piece of metal.

The 737 had a glide ratio of around 17-1, which meant that, even unpowered, it should move forward through the air seventeen miles for every mile it dropped. From six miles up, the jet theoretically could glide almost a hundred miles. If Captain Ward had any control over his craft, they potentially had time to turn and reach an airstrip. Several were within the almost 100-mile glide path. Sadly, the beautifully-engineered and reliable jet ignored all the crew's frantic attempts to steer. The fly-by-wire systems had replaced the older mechanical-hydraulic control systems many years prior. While the older systems had manual options for a total failure, the newer model's backup was also electronic. Flight 1403 with Captain Ward at the useless control wheel had stayed in the air an amazing forty-three minutes before crashing into the side of the unnamed and unremarkable hill. 1403 was just one of thousands of flights lost that day.

Bobby's boots crunched upon the charred ground. It took him a moment to assess the flight's angle on impact. The largest remaining piece of the fuselage was the vertical tail, which canted over at a sharp angle. It was farther down the hill. He deduced that he was looking at the cockpit now, but very little else was recognizable. There were no seats intact, though he could see their springs and frames. He saw no bodies, only numerous charred lumps from which blackened bones stuck out. The sound of the seatbelt tinging off the metal frame got his attention, and he saw it at the far side of the jet. Walking gingerly in that direction, he noticed part of a seat frame with the blue vinyl seat mostly intact. The ratchet mechanism for the seatbelt was indeed hitting the frame below. His eyes were drawn down to the skeletal remains of a human hand resting near a singed but recognizable book.

He picked up the Bible and noticed a slip of paper folded inside the cover. He unfolded the charred and brittle note. The penmanship was shaky and rushed, but it was still legible. As he read, he dropped to his knees.

To Thomas, My Love,

I hate writing this, but I now know this will be my last act in this life. I don't know what happened, but the engines on the flight cut out, and the lights. We've been descending for the last half hour, and I can see the ground getting closer and closer.

The crews have been telling us to stay calm and in crash positions, but after this long, we can't. The plane's hot, it feels like there's not enough air. The sounds are awful. The wind outside, people are crying and shouting. No cell phones either. I tried. I wanted to talk to you and the girls once more.

The Captain just came out, said we should prepare for the worst. I always thought a plane crash would be quick. I'm sorry, I know you always hated all the travel. You were right. I was an idiot, a selfish idiot and now I'm dead.

If this note survives and finds you somehow, please tell Alice and Bree I'm so sorry. Make sure they know I love them and was thinking of them at this moment. I'm sorry to be leaving you as well, honey, but you've always been the better parent. Love them enough for both of us.

The trees are so green here, it won't be a terrible place to stop.

I love you, Tess

Bobby folded the note and put it back in the Bible. Noticing something in the ashes below the skeletal fingers, he reached down. The delicate, silver wedding ring had a small dent just below the impressive diamond. His eyes were filled with tears as he slipped the ring back onto the bony finger of the severed hand.

"I'm sorry for you Tess," he whispered. Looking at the Bible, he remembered the comfort and compassion it once had brought to him as well. Instantly, he also felt the rage at what the Messengers had turned the book into, for him and thousands of others. They had made it a symbol of hatred, oppression and death. Pushing back against the anger in his own mind, he gently replaced the weathered book underneath the woman's skeletal hand. This was her grave; he would not desecrate it further.

Moving through what was left of the fuselage he found several travel bags that had survived the crash. He began making a pile of the bags inside the tree line. Once he had collected them all, he would go through them to see if there was anything he could use. He also discovered a crushed galley cabinet. Several of the metal carts they filled with drinks and snacks were still wedged inside. It took Bobby considerable time to free them from the blackened frame, but inside was a bonanza of trays with packets of pretzels, cookies, small liquor bottles and bottled water.

Finding a rough-looking and rather smelly backpack nearby, he crammed everything he found into it. After searching for almost another hour, he gave up. This seemed to be all the site had to offer. Retreating to the small luggage pile, he went methodically through each of the bags. It was amazing to him the items that people packed. He saw the normal clothes and toiletries, but also truly bizarre items, including a football and what appeared to be an urn full of ashes. The more useful items were less common. There were not a lot of clothes or shoes that would do him much good. He removed the laces from many of the shoes, and he finally found a pair of expensive hiking boots in his size. Also, there were several rain jackets and a pair of jeans.

Tugging open a well-used leather duffel, he hit the jackpot. "This had to belong to a Sky Marshall!" he thought out loud. Inside were multiple pairs of 5.11 brand tactical pants and shirts—the kind favored by police and military. The technical fabrics were lightweight but tough. Also in the bag were a woven tactical belt and several pairs of good quality hiking socks. The pants and shirts were sizes well below what he normally wore, but he quickly recalled that he was now much smaller than the last time he had bought clothes. Stripping out of the filthy rags he'd been wearing for so long, he was pleased to find the new pants and shirt were an almost perfect fit. They were a bit stiff from the weather, but otherwise very comfortable. Inside the leather bag was also a small black plastic case adorned with the Taser company logo. He opened it to confirm its contents, then slipped that into his backpack along with several other items.

As darkness began to fall, Bobby finished off another of the tiny packs of peanuts and slung on his backpack. The detour to this site had been risky and cost him several hours, but he knew it had been a godsend and well worth it. He offered a silent thank you to the lives lost here and then to no one in particular: "Rest easy, Tess," he muttered as he turned from the wreckage. He checked his GPS and began again his nightly wilderness trek.

CHAPTER THIRTY-SEVEN
Harris Springs, Mississippi

Kaylie was waiting on her uncle as soon as he exited the bridge. "Well?" she said at once.

"Nice to see you too, Bubbles, and yes, I'm fine."

"Don't be an ass, Uncle Scott, and don't play dumb—you can't pull it off. How's my mom and dad?"

Scott had been dreading this conversation and had really hoped to have more time to come up with a response. He thought back to one of their conversations soon after he and Todd had brought her back to Harris Springs. He had agreed never to lie to her about anything, and she had done the same. There were many things that he wanted to protect her from, but when she asked, he had always been straight with her. He didn't want to hurt her, and honestly, he wasn't sure her mom was truly gone.

"Kaylie, I was able to reach your dad. At least, I'm pretty sure it was him, but it was all in code. I don't think he's in a safe place. All the person I was talking to could respond with were radio clicks for yes or no. It was a quick call, but I suggested a destination that should be safer. I believe he's heading in our direction."

"Are they okay? What about Mom?"

"It was a quick call. He didn't respond with anything about your mom." Technically that was not a lie, but only part of the truth. Kaylie's face took on an expression that let him know she was processing all the ramifications of his statement.

"Oh, my God . . ." she leaned against the bulkhead.

"Don't go there, sweetie. They need you to stay strong. You are their top priority, and now they know you're okay. They know we are holding out pretty well down here. That has to be a relief to them."

"It's those fucking crazy Messengers, isn't it?"

"Language, Kaylie," he chided.

"Oh, come on, you know it is." She was becoming enraged. Scott took her by the hand and pulled her out of the corridor and into an empty stateroom. She dropped onto the bed. The spring sun was shining brightly through the tropical print drapes that framed the window.

"They're on the front edge of Messenger territory, yes. Whatever trouble they're having, whatever reason caused them to leave the house or the bugout cabin was likely to do with that group, yes. If we're right, though, even going south twenty miles should get him out of immediate harm."

Shit. Kaylie had caught that. He had said *him*, instead of *them*. The look on her face let him know. He still wanted to protect her but assumed the worst might be best for her at this point. He ignored the look and went on.

"Do you remember Mr. Sanderson's farm?"

She looked away for a second then said, "I think so, wasn't he one of Granddad's friends? All I remember are the cows and a big river."

"Yeah, that's it. It's a large farm south of Little Rock on a creek that runs into the Arkansas River. Your dad and I used to spend a lot of time there. Our dad, your granddad, loved going there. In the summer, we would help out a bit, but mostly we played in the hay barn and fished or swam in the creek."

"Is that where you sent Dad—I mean, them? You think it's out of the reach of the Messengers?"

"I think it is for now. It won't be safe there for long, but hopefully, he got the rest of what I was trying to tell him. I think they'll be there in a few days. He should try and make contact again, hopefully, and we will be able to hear him well from there. Then they'll head south. I believe we'll need to come up with a plan to go meet them when they get closer."

"Was that what you and Todd were talking about just now? It seemed pretty heated."

"Um . . . no, we didn't even get to that. Todd wants me to help find somebody else."

Her look asked the question.

"DJ. Apparently, the Navy now thinks he's somewhere out in the Gulf. They must have a hidden lab out there." He pointed out the window to the glittering water beyond. "Don't bother asking me anything else because that's all I know. I'm going to see if I can figure out some possible spots for the Navy to recon." Scott braced himself for another round of questions from his increasingly fierce niece. Instead, she stood up and hugged him.

"Thanks, Uncle Scott, you're the best. You will never know how much I appreciate you and what you do for everyone, especially for me." Her eyes were filled with tears, and Scott's were as well when she let him go and then hurried down the passageway.

CHAPTER THIRTY-EIGHT

Scott found DeVonte covertly stalking Angel as she was inventorying the last of the vegetables. "Damn, man, will you give the girl a break?"

DeVonte looked up with that million-dollar smile. "Are you kidding me, dude? She loves me. She jus' hasn't come to realize it yet."

Scott looked over at Angel who grinned and gave one of them a quick wink.

"Come on, lover boy," he smiled, "we have to go build the Internet."

"Well, shit, that actually sounds pretty cool. Right behind you, man."

Scott gave DeVonte a quick rundown of the items he needed from storage. "Meet me up in the lounge. That'll be the best place to set up as we have to place a satellite dish up top."

The young man scampered off, eager as always to be of help, and Scott went to fetch his laptop.

Scott had used his satellite-based Internet connection rarely over the past few months. The basic reason for this was that there was nothing out there. Nearly every server on the planet was offline, and most of those still online would never again be updated. Ham radio had proven much more reliable for information, and the computer connection they had with the Navy was only useful when they decided to share something. The Internet itself only existed in theory at this point. He had meant to do a more in-depth analysis to see what else was out there. All his equipment had been moved here for that purpose, but so far, he had been too busy just surviving.

Bringing the laptop and backup batteries to the lounge, he found a long table and began setting up. DeVonte showed up a minute later with the dish and other items the list had called for. It only took about thirty minutes to get everything connected and to find the correct angle for the satellite. The connection light blinked amber for what seemed like an eternity, but finally turned green and stayed steady. "Whew, that's good news. The satellite's still there and taking calls."

DeVonte looked impressed. "I don't understand how you can use a satellite to reach the Internet. I thought that was jus' for TV signals or cell phones."

Scott talked as he worked. "The Internet doesn't much care how you connect computers together . . . it can be with radio, telephone lines, cable coaxes, fiber optics or in this case, a satellite. In remote areas, satellite Internet was pretty popular.

"My contract work with the DHS gave me unique access, and my computer and server connection are pretty special, but the principles behind them are still fairly basic."

The boy watched attentively as Scott typed in a series of command lines and a screen with a DHS logo appeared. He placed his index finger on the laptop's biometric scanner and then typed a very long password that appeared to be just random numbers and symbols.

"We're in," he said finally. "Now I need to find Tahir. You don't have to stay if you don't want. I mean, I appreciate your help, but this may take a while."

"Are you kidding, I love this! You got the Internet, man. I'd like to sit and watch if you don't mind."

Scott laughed. He had forgotten briefly that his young friend was an intellectual sponge. Chances were that in a few days, he would be using this system and be better at it than Scott was. "Sit back and learn, my young Jedi." All of this, of course, was in complete violation of Scott's contract and security protocols, but that was irrelevant now. Before the flare, he would have been put in jail forever for doing anything like this, but it was not much of a risk anymore. Scott gave DeVonte a basic course in backchannel navigation, too, as he moved effortlessly through logs and file systems. To his credit, DeVonte interrupted only occasionally to clarify something he was unsure of.

"There you are," Scott said. The list before him was just dates and times as well as some other numbers.

"Someone, you know's been in the system?" DeVonte asked astutely.

"More than one person, yes, including my friend—the one I need to find. This is his ID number here." He pointed to a series of numbers on the screen.

DeVonte pulled a notepad over. "Scroll back up a bit, Scott." Watching the screen, he began making several notes. "Okay, next," Scott scrolled to the next screen and came to the bottom of the log. The last entry was his current login which was several weeks old.

Scott was catching on to what DeVonte was seeing. There was some kind of pattern to Tahir's logins, but it wasn't obvious. DeVonte was now adding columns to the page and listing the day of the week, month, hour, minute, and second of each login into individual columns. The kid was good. Scott usually recognized patterns before anyone, but DeVonte was way ahead of him on this one.

"It's twelve," DeVonte muttered

"Pretty sure the answer to life and the universe is forty-two," Scott retorted in amusement.

"No, the series." DeVonte barely smiled. "It's twelve, Scott. Then it repeats."

"Which column?"

"Umm . . . minutes," DeVonte answered.

Looking over it, Scott nodded. It took a moment for the pieces clicked in his head. "He logged in at specific times to leave me an IP address."

"Does that help?" the boy asked.

Scott nodded again, "He basically gave me his phone number. Let's see if anyone is home." He entered the IP address and clicked the enter key. His screen began to slowly fill with a single image, an image he instantly recognized. Checking again, he made sure he was indeed connected to the address listed in the code. What he was looking at was a screen capture of one of the first-person shooter video games he and Tahir played back before the sun fried everything. The futuristic armor, weaponry and alien landscapes were nostalgic.

DeVonte looked puzzled. "What is that? Looks like an advertisement for a video game."

"That's what it's supposed to look like. Tahir's a smart guy. Even though he had to leave this system running he didn't want to make it easy for anyone trying to get in."

"So, this isn't some *Call of Duty* website?"

"Wrong game entirely, but no, it's not. I'm pretty sure it's steganography."

"What the fuck kind o' dinosaur is dat?" DeVonte scoffed.

Laughing, Scott replied, "Not a dinosaur, a way of embedding information inside pictures." He clicked to download the image to his computer, then opened it up in a photo-editing program. "First, I'm going to see if he included any geotagging coordinates. That'd let me know where the photo was taken."

"Holy shit, that's wild. He can code it so that you can find that out?"

Laughing more, Scott said, "No, little brother, that's a standard feature almost all photos had embedded in them back in the day. If you had the right software, you could find the precise coordinates for any picture taken with a smartphone and lots of digital cameras. Unfortunately, Tahir covered his tracks: no tags on the photo itself." Scott opened the photo in another program that showed line after line of code. "This is the actual data that makes up the photo. *Steganography* is the Greek word for "covered writing." In other words, the information is hidden in the file. I'll likely have to try a few programs to find what's in here. My friend is one brilliantly paranoid fuck, so it may take a while."

It took far longer than Scott had expected to find the right program to discover the bit of code that did not belong. Then he struggled even longer before realizing the header information of the code looked familiar. Finally, he caught on that it was an encrypted and compressed file. Dragging it into yet another program to open the bit of code, he encountered a password field. He heard DeVonte say, "Shit," but on this Scott felt he knew. He entered one of the passwords he and Tahir had used privately many times; the file opened to reveal a simple text document.

BikerBoi, you are the only one who will be reading this. I am alive and somewhat ok. I hope you are as well. I won't go into detail re: where I am as I am sure they are looking. If you want to make contact I have set up another server. Not enough power to leave it on all the time and would not be smart. The schedule and IP are at the bottom. Use stegy images only as we need multi-levels of security to communicate. You obviously now know about Catalyst – it was all put into play after CME. Still, have access to some servers and communication protocols. Not safe to travel locally and we have food, but barely survived winter. Most water all around us is bad. My family is gone.

Sadly, much of Europe and Asia are confirmed as a wasteland. They are using high-altitude dispersal to spray something over much of the world. Unsure if it is pathogen, or hopefully a treatment. From what I have found out, I believe that most of the Catalyst reserve colonies are failing; unsure why, but the files and reports I can access seem to strongly suggest that. I know some were attacked by former military commanders turned warlords – some seemed to suggest the US Army or Navy. Seems they are moving Praetor units back to the US and into more domestic and proactive military deployments. This shit just keeps getting worse. Something else is getting ready to go down, just not sure what. Be vigilant, my friend.

Scott finished the message and let DeVonte read it as well. The boy began to talk, but Scott raised a finger. "I need to get a reply back to him while we still have a connection." He then began crafting a response, requesting Tahir's help in locating the possible lab in the Gulf of Mexico. Just as Tahir had done, Scott encrypted and compressed the message and embedded the code into a new image on his laptop: a new, tricked-out Trek—his dream bike. His friend would know it was from him. He uploaded the file to the address Tahir had supplied and then logged off.

Scott sat silently for a few minutes, then looked at DeVonte. "Let's go talk to Todd."

CHAPTER THIRTY-NINE

Southeast of Little Rock, Arkansas

Bobby was out of water. His last few bottles had been filled from a slower-moving valley stream, and now even they were gone. His mouth was dry, and he fought to spit the dust and grime from between his cracked lips.

The rolling hills had finally given way to the flatlands. Here, he was closer than ever to possible safety, but also more exposed. Checking the GPS earlier had put him back on course; he had taken a wrong turn in the darkness. It was now mid-morning, and he was still walking. Sanderson's place should be reachable by nightfall, so he wanted to push on through. In his scrambled mind, the Messengers were coming over the last hill now, and a band of Judges was just ahead. Bobby had come to realize he was not feeling well. Possibly it was something he had eaten or, more likely, bad water. His mind was not sharp. Something was attacking his weakened body. His steps were scuffing clumsily, and he felt alternately hot then chilled. Worst of all were the increasingly regular bouts of diarrhea and vomiting. His abdomen ached, and he was unbelievably tired.

Still, the note from the woman at the crash site kept echoing in his memory. Why was his misery any worse than hers—theirs? The thousands—no, millions—of other victims of that awful day, and the count-less awful days since. Why was he alive when so many were not? When his sweet Jessie was not. His body shook. He had killed her; his hands had plunged the knife into her dying body. Had he done it simply to be kind, or had a part of him feared that the pained sounds she made would alert those searching for them? His body had no water for the tears that tried to form. Maybe he should have left her with them, with God's Army. They would have continued to beat her, rape her . . . but she might still be alive if he had. Which was worse?

After his capture, he had worked for weeks to get assigned to the camp where Jess was taken. It was the fourth camp he had tried. The other three were so large it had taken days of cautious searching to make sure she was not there before he moved on to the next. Bobby had hoped Jess might be assigned to the food tents, or laundry, even in the ammunition reloading trailers, but deep down, he knew she'd be some-body's bedmate by now.

His eyes stung, and he wiped them to no avail. She was so beautiful. Jess was always a woman that other men looked at. He had been lucky to ever have gotten her attention, much less eventually marry her. Never, in their twenty-odd years together, had he ever looked at another woman with desire. He knew who he wanted, who he needed. The afternoon that he found her, she had been in the thrall of a filthy pig of a man.

He could still see his dark-stained teeth and grizzled beard as the man smiled and winked when Bobby entered the room. Inside the industrial warehouse, hundreds of cots and mattresses had been set aside for recreational sex with the newly-converted females. Any of the men were allowed occasional visits, and none of the women were ever allowed to leave. Seeing what that animal was doing to his beloved wife was more than Bobby's mind could handle.

With no weapons, he stepped close to the man, intent on strangling him. The ugly fuck swatted him aside. "Wait your turn, idiot. This li'l whore is mine."

So little did Bobby's presence bother the brute as he stood above, that he didn't even pause in his rhythm, his pleasure as he enjoyed her body. Jess' eyes never rose to meet Bobby's. He wondered if she were drugged, she surely wasn't fully there, an understandable retreat from reality while this man raped her. A year earlier, ripping this creature apart with his bare hands would not have been a problem for Bobby. He had been robust, strong and well fed. Since being captured, though, he had eaten little and been horrendously sick on several occasions. His body was withering away. Jess probably would not have recognized her husband had she even looked.

Indeed, even after Bobby had found an abandoned piece of steel rod and used it to club the man to death, Jess showed no signs of recognition. She simply obeyed as he dressed her in a coarse gown he found and guided her out of the building. He had no plan; he just wanted to see his wife one more time before he was likely killed. Luck had played more of a role in their escape than talent or heroics. A fight had broken out in another area of the brothel just as Bobby attacked, and the security guards had turned from him to go intervene. Apparently, fights over the women were common; males battled to get their favored conquests. Bobby saw a gap in the security cordon and hustled Jess through the loose wire and into the tall grass beyond. Briefly, he thought they might get away clean, but then the alarms sounded.

They had avoided the patrols and the dogs for two days by hiding in river mud and then lying in a hog pen in hopes of hiding their scents from the trackers. Unfortunately, one of the canines had stayed on their trail. Jess had just started to come around, and when she recognized Bobby, he had held her muddy face and kissed her. She had jerked back reflexively. He wondered just how long it would take her to recover enough to let him love her. Deep down he knew the trauma would never go away. It was a stain that would forever touch everything in their lives. If they even survived.

Neither had heard anything when the dog attacked. It went for Jess first, clamping its jaws around her neck from behind and dragging her quickly to the ground. Bobby had turned around and swung at the beast, but it just pulled back on her now limp body. Seeing his wife lying there, being ravaged by one more animal, flipped a switch in Bobby's mind. He leapt on the dog and drove his hands deep into the soft underbelly. As the skin parted and Bobby tore at its internal organs, its jaws released their hold on Jess and turned to bite at whatever parts of his attacker he could reach. Bobby ignored the bites and continued to rip away vital parts of the animal's insides until its shrieks of pain weakened, and it finally succumbed.

In the sudden quiet, he heard more men and dogs approaching, drawn to the sounds of the fight. Jess was lying in a darkening circle. The amount of blood leaking from the bite wounds to her neck and chest was too much. Bobby struggled to scoop her up and carry her away from the carnage, his own wounds also leaving an easy trail for his pursuers to follow. Up ahead, he saw something in the break of trees. Heading for it, he just barely made out what it was. His ravaged brain didn't register the danger until it was nearly too late.

The sound of a crow overhead snapped Bobby back to the present. Stumbling, then ducking clumsily, he scanned the scrubland in all directions. He was trying to stay focused, but the memories, the hatred, kept intruding. His dark eyes watched as the large black bird flew on out of sight. Something here did not feel right, and it wasn't just the shrieking of the raven. He felt dizzy, exposed and stupid for moving so erratically in daylight. Why was he suddenly making dumb decisions? He was too stupid to still be alive. Scott was the smart one; Bobby was just tough. Now, look at him: a broken wreck of a man. He wanted to see Kaylie again, but deep down he felt she was probably better off with her uncle. Again, his mind spiraled off into memory. *There's danger here, man—will you fucking focus!* His mind screamed at him to pay attention.

There—a sound. He heard something, faintly, off in the distance. He glanced up at the sun to verify that he had not wandered off course again; no, he was still on track for Sanderson's. He stopped and crouched down. His stomach growled, and he knew something inside him was about to let loose. Another small sound. He twisted his head around trying to get a fix on the direction it was coming from. Instead, he heard the unmistakable click of a gun being cocked. "That's far enough," came a voice from behind him. "Stand up with your hands on your head."

Turning back, he saw a fierce but attractive face. The woman standing there was holding a large shotgun. She must have been hiding in the tall scrub brush just behind him. "Do not look at me," she said with conviction. "What do you have?"

"I, uh, I have a knife and a pistol," he said, deciding honesty was as good a response as any.

"Well, I'm not blind. I can see that. In the pack—what do you have in the pack? Any other weapons? Food?"

The words from the woman confused him. "Ummm, no, no other weapons. Look, I don't want any trouble, I'm just passing through."

She laughed slightly: a laugh devoid of mirth. "No one just passes through these parts, mister."

He glanced back at the woman only to have the gun barrel poke him viciously. "Eyes that way," she pointed with the barrel toward a stand of trees ahead. "Walk. We can discuss your innocence once we're out of this field."

He could not understand where she had come from. Why she had not made him remove his weapons. Who was she? "Do you have a name?" he asked.

The slight laugh came again. "Well, yeah, we all got names. I used to, at least, no real need for it anymore." After a brief pause she continued, "The tattoo, what does that stand for? You in some kind of biker gang?"

"No ma'am," he replied with relief: she had no idea what it signified. Why would she though? The Messengers had not yet reached this valley. "It's a mark, a kind of brand, given by an evil group when they catch you. If they don't kill you, that is."

"It looks fresh, how long ago and what group?"

"Last fall. They call themselves the Messengers. They branded me when my wife and I were captured." He heard the woman's feet stop moving. The hairs on his neck began to tingle, and he could feel the large-bore gun trained on him again. *Just do it,* he thought. *End me here.*

Instead, she poked him again and hurried their pace toward the copse of trees. Once they were in the shade of the oaks and hickory, she resumed her questioning. "How did you get away and where is your wife now?"

"We escaped, and she was killed as we fled."

He glanced around at her, and this time she did not object. Her look showed genuine sadness. "How far away are they?"

"Not sure, I saw some a few days ago—Judges—you know what they are?"

She nodded but stayed quiet.

"They were maybe ten miles back to the north. I heard sounds later, gunshots and such, that make me think the main group may be about that far now."

"That's less than a day away. And you're leading them right toward us." Her expression had been replaced once again by the angry scowl. As she inspected him, her eyes took on yet another look as if something had just occurred to her. She approached him and reached a hand to his chin, lifting it so the face might catch more light. Satisfied with whatever had occurred to her, she let it drop back and offered a small smile.

The woman began walking away, deeper into the woods. He was unsure of what to do. He was no longer a prisoner but felt no sense of safety. In fact, he felt unsteady, as if he had stepped off a curb he hadn't realized was there.

She paused and looked back, "Come on, Bobby. We don't want to be late." He had taken several stumbling steps when something occurred to him. Before he could open his mouth, blackness claimed him. He crumpled in a heap at the base of a withered oak tree.

CHAPTER FORTY

Darkness had fallen when Bobby came to. The woman was there. He pulled a dirty, wet scrap of cloth from his head.

"Where am I?"

"You passed out. You have a fever." She took the rag, wet it in the remnants of an old milk jug, and placed it back on his head. "Did you drink bad water or some other form of stupid?"

"No, I don't think so. I boiled or treated the water, 'cept what I got out of the mountain streams."

"Well, ya got something, you shit yourself as well. I tried to get you cleaned up, but I couldn't manage. If you're up to it I'll let you handle that fun li'l task now. We gotta be moving soon." With that, she moved out of his sight. Lying there, he tried to remember what had happened. He knew that several hours had passed: it was dark now. He removed the rag from his head and struggled to get up. The dizziness and the smell of his filth reached him simultaneously. His legs buckled, and he went back down to one knee.

It was several minutes before he could stand, and the cramps and dizziness made it difficult to accomplish much else. The woman was nowhere to be seen, but he assumed she was close by. Why had she let him live? He removed his new tactical pants and underwear and cleaned himself with the wet rag. His pack was nearby, and eventually, he was able to find clean clothes. She reappeared just as he was swallowing two pain pills from his first aid kit.

"Let's go."

He struggled to sling on the pack but got no help from the woman. He attempted to talk with her several times, but she remained silent. The pair walked in silence for several miles. Topping a small rise, Bobby was surprised to see they were near his destination. Mr. Sanderson's property lay just ahead, and the still familiar creek ran on the far side. He looked at the woman again and, seeing her framed in that setting, the memory came to him. "You knew my name. You're connected to this place . . . Jordan—Mr. Sanderson's niece. I remember you. You were here when we came . . . I remember you swimming with us in the river."

The woman smiled warmly. "Come on," she called as she headed in the direction of the farmhouse.

The place looked the same to Bobby; a little more rundown perhaps. The trees and the creek behind seemed much smaller than he remembered from his childhood, but in essence, it was the same. The place was so remote that no other homes could be seen. He wondered briefly if the place might even survive the crusading plague of the Lord's Army.

Jordan walked with a simple elegance across the hard-packed dirt yard. She seemed both a part of this farm and a stranger to it. Walking up to the house, she pulled at a screen door that opened with a protesting squeal. Inside, she removed her barn jacket and set the shotgun by the door. Bobby stepped in behind her, the screen door slamming shut loudly behind him. He cringed at the sound, but she seemed unbothered.

She poured two glasses of water and produced a loaf of real bread and some dried meat. Sitting at the table, she motioned for him to join her. "Think you can hold some food down?"

"Thank you," he managed to get out as he took the water. His throat ached for the liquid. "Jordan, it is you, right? I . . . I know your uncle died several years ago. I'm sorry about that. Wasn't sure who lived here now."

She finished chewing a bite of bread and handed the hard loaf to Bobby. "So, you just thought you'd come see what was left?" Her words echoed in the large room. She rescued him from replying. "My uncle never had children, so when he died he left most of this to me and my husband. We used it as a weekend getaway until the mess last summer." She paused and gave a pensive look toward the windows.

"I loved coming here as a child. Never learned much about farming, but this place was magical to me then. Especially when you and your brother came down." She smiled and looked away. "You know, I had the biggest crush on you, Bobby Montgomery. I know I was just a little kid, and you were already a teenager. Silly now, but I wanted you to look at me differently. You never did."

Bobby looked at her in surprise, remembering the pretty girl with the straw-colored hair. "I saw." He took a bite of the jerky: venison. "I didn't know you liked me," he chuckled weakly. "I was too stupid back then, and you were young, but I saw. You were too pretty for any of us, though, even back then. I knew you'd do well, fall in love with some handsome guy and live a wonderful life in a faraway place."

"See, that's why I liked you," Jordan smiled widely. "You were kind and modest. Even though you were always the strongest and fastest, you used to let me or your brother win occasionally." She sighed at the memories, sweeping them from the kitchen like crumbs from the table. "Any idea how he's doing? I heard he was up in Chicago. I imagine that would have been tough."

"Scott's doing okay; he moved out of Chicago a few years back after his marriage fell apart. He's living down on the coast now in our old family cottage. My daughter, Kaylie, is with him, and it sounds like they're doing pretty well, all things considered. He's the one who suggested I come here, in fact."

"How? I mean, why would he suggest this old place?"

"Well, he seemed to have some information about the Messengers' path. Said they seemed to be heading due east. After Little Rock, the next target looked to be Memphis. Didn't seem like they would come in this direction. The radio conversation we had didn't allow much in the way of details, but he knew I was desperate, and this was the first place that came to mind I guess."

"So, you walked from Little Rock to here?"

He nodded. "Jordan, where is your husband? Did he make it?"

She struggled to speak, the sound of her voice started and stopped like a car struggling to get over a steep hill. "No, no . . . he didn't survive. We were stopped trying to get out of Memphis—just a group of people coming off the Interstate. Someone wanted our car. Jimmy stopped, thinking he could help, but they were too desperate to talk, too scared he might say no. They stabbed him, and he died right there on the highway. They took our car and all our belongings."

"God. I'm so sorry."

Her eyes locked on his for a moment. They were icy blue and showed none of the emotion connected to her words. "Thanks. We walked for several days and managed to catch a few rides heading this direction. I wasn't sure where to even go, but my feet kept taking me this way. The trip, well, it had its own adventures, none of which were pleasant. I got a few rides, but I walked a lot and all of the last twenty miles."

Bobby was struggling to stay focused. The tiny bit of food in his system was not enough to combat the massive fatigue and weakness he was experiencing. The image of the woman before him became fuzzy and indistinct, but he fought for consciousness to stay with him a bit longer. "I, ugh, sorry, I wanted to say thank you. I don't know why you were out there or why you decided not to shoot me, but thanks."

Jordan's face softened again, and this time it remained so. "Are you a good man, Bobby Montgomery?"

His mind danced around that question, wanting to avoid it, wanting not to have to consider the answer. He sat for several minutes, bracing himself upright through sheer willpower. "I don't know," he said finally. "I like to think I am, but by my old standards, I'm not. I've not committed evil, but I have killed. I couldn't protect my family." He paused for several seconds, struggling to overcome his emotion, his exhaustion. "I'm not a bad man, Jordan, but no . . . I am not good either." The last of the words tumbled out of him like a dam breaking loose, the flood of words and emotions bringing forth tears to his eyes and sobs from his chest.

Jordan placed a hand over his in the dim kitchen. She got up and walked to a door. *To a root cellar, perhaps,* Bobby seemed to recall. Opening it, she quietly reached in and led a young boy into the kitchen. "This is my son, Jacob. He doesn't talk much anymore."

Bobby looked at the boy. How long had he been hiding there, listening, but not making a sound? He made to speak to Jacob, but the last of his strength was now gone. His limp body fell to the floor as consciousness left him. The boy cast his deep brown eyes, full of uncertainty, from the man on the floor to his mother.

CHAPTER FORTY-ONE

West of Memphis, Tennessee

Hawley appeared out of the darkness. "Your Holiness, please excuse me."

"Cut the crap, man, no one's here. What the fuck is it?"

"Sorry, Michael, the advancing party has run into resistance. It looks like what those new converts said was true. The Judges are encountering motorized brigades of uniformed troops near Memphis."

"What troops, whose troops? Army?" *That couldn't be*, Michael Swain thought. Nothing was left of the US Army; they were a remnant of a dead country. This was his world now. Who could be standing up to his own God's Army? "Were they National Guard?"

"Doesn't look like it, sir. None of the Judges recognized any of the trucks or equipment, and they said the soldiers' uniforms were a gray camo pattern."

The two men walked down the long corridor and turned into a small break room in the abandoned industrial facility. It had been converted to a map room and was used to plan and direct the various movements of the group. They were currently between Little Rock and Memphis, their next destination. Lines radiating in various directions showed the routes of the mission teams, each led by a group of three Judges. The lines extended out thirty to fifty miles in most cases, but the ones going northeast toward Memphis were abruptly shorter.

Michael looked troubled. "Hawley, are those converts still alive? The ones that told us about the survivor camps?"

The other man shook his head. "Nah, they didn't make it through the atonement ceremony."

He paused, expecting an outburst from his leader, but none came. "Pete questioned them at length, though, but I don't think we woulda gotten anything else from 'em. They said the camp, well it sounded more like a fortified town, they said it was remote and really big. Supposedly somewhere in this valley here," Hawley pointed at a spot on the large map. "It's far enough away from Memphis to have stayed hidden, but they could've used these highways to bring supplies and people in."

"Those resources are the Lord's," Michael declared haughtily. "We have to find a way to bring them into the service of his Army. They are needed to feed the hungry . . . *our* hungry," he added with a laugh. "Little Rock was a bust. Shit, we got nearly nothing here. But this, this is where we need to go," he stabbed the map with his index finger. He saw this mystery camp as a great prize. He wanted the supplies, the equipment, the guns, all of it. He always wanted more, and this was the next more. "There's no army anymore and not even any military bases anywhere nearby, so how many troops could they have? We have the numbers, and the Lord is on our side." He walked away and looked out the single long window. "We *must* take that camp."

He turned dramatically as he continued in what he felt was a suitably military delivery, "Hawley, please recall as many of the other crews as you can . . . cancel every mission that is not heading toward Memphis. We will take them through numbers and sheer, overwhelming willpower. Whoever these gray-shirted troops are, they will suffer under the might of the Messengers."

Hawley always got worried when he heard Michael getting high and mighty like this, but he agreed that if the camp existed, it was a prize too good to ignore. "Yes, Your Holiness," he bowed, leaving the man to stare at the maps. Hawley went to the radio rooms to begin summoning the Judges.

~

The next several days were barely-organized chaos as most of the Missions returned to base camp. Judges and Marauders combined with Messenger regulars and new converts. Hawley was struggling to keep Michael and the camps under control. The Judges were all pissed at being re-called; several had not even bothered to respond. Whether they had gone rogue or were simply too deep in the hilly terrain to get the call, he didn't know.

One of the Mission crews from near Memphis had brought in more prisoners: heathens that had yet to be judged or to face atonement. Hawley had so much to do. He had had to delegate, and Pete and one of the Judges known simply as Red were offering confessional to the new arrivals now. Hawley could hear their darkly threatening words as he walked by the cage on the way to another meeting. One bloody mess of a body already lay, unmoving, on the floor. He had told Pete not to waste time. Get the intel and get it fast. His Holiness was waiting for it. They wanted every scrap of information on the camp or the troops in Memphis.

So far, they had learned nothing new. Preparations to march on the mysterious camp were moving ahead, though. The objectives were to take the troops' base first, then hit Memphis with the newly captured armaments. Hawley watched as another team of Judges roared up on their motorcycles. These stragglers had been assigned to track down a couple of recent runaways. "Nice of you boys to show up . . . Lynx, did you not get the fucking message?"

"Hawley, lay off us, we've been up in the hills for two weeks looking for that jackass Montgomery," the smaller of the three men responded with unbridled irritation.

"Mr. Simpson, I would watch my tone if I were you. All I need to know —" he looked briefly over his shoulder, "—all His Holiness needs to know, is did you get them?"

"Fuck no . . . I mean, yes, we got the woman. We tracked the man over to an area near the river, but then we got the recall. What the fuck is up?"

Hawley spat a wad of tobacco at the dusty wheel of Lynx's motorcycle. He had once been a Judge and resented the trio's attitude. They were brutal thugs in his mind, rabid dogs best kept on leashes. But the Judges enjoyed Michael's protection; nothing happened to them unless he said it could. "Never mind that, you'll be briefed soon 'nuf. Sumthin' big's in the wind. But tell me, fellas. How the fuck did you let one guy slip through? Was he a ninja? Obviously, he bested you three." He could tell he had struck a nerve, and his face cracked into a knowing smile. "Get some chow and a shower, you guys fucking stink. Be in the command room at 1500."

"Shit, Hawley, we need some sleep. We haven't rested in . . ."

Hawley cut them off with a look. "Do what I said!" Then in a quieter and more menacing voice, he continued, "You boys need to understand that your good graces with our esteemed leader only go so far. Don't try pushing it with me."

Hawley turned his back on the men: a dangerous thing to do as he knew all of them would love to see him dead, but they wouldn't risk it here in the camp, not in broad daylight. Just the same, he decided to head back closer to his top lieutenant's location. He kicked a can as he passed in frustration; he couldn't get over them letting that one get away. The man Montgomery murdered in the pleasure camp had been an original member, part of Michael's inner circle. He couldn't remember the last time anyone had survived an escape. Simpson and the other two would be in the doghouse with Michael over that. He would see to it.

CHAPTER FORTY-TWO

Three Months ago

Azores, Eastern Atlantic

The smaller ship pulled away, looking even rougher from a distance. The mid-ocean transfer had been precarious. Skybox was moved to the larger Praetor vessel, along with the doctor. Both were handled only by anonymous individuals dressed in full bio-suits and were split up as soon as they were onboard the vessel. He had caught just a glimpse of Captain Xiou—looking troubled—before being brusquely escorted back into the Zodiac used to ferry them to the ship.

He didn't care for the way this new crew was treating him. As a Praetor commander, he was accustomed to a certain level of respect. His service record and approximate rank required that. Here, it did not seem to carry any weight.

He was now sitting on a thin mattress in a small sleeping berth. It looked more like a brig than a cabin. He had felt the vessel get underway soon after he boarded, but so far not one person had spoken to him. Skybox had seen no other crew since he was brought onboard. That had been several hours ago, and he was getting restless.

The escorts who had deposited him in his quarters had told him to stay put, but he had been eyeing the cabin door with interest ever since. On the other boat he had been restricted as to where he could go and what he could see; he wondered if that was also going to be the case here. He wasn't a prisoner, but he was clearly viewed as a threat to something or someone.

Missions often ended in unusual ways . . . He could never assume the people transporting him had any idea of what he had just been through. He knew the world had changed dramatically. While he had been in his own nightmarish bubble, the rest of the world had also been going to shit. He was no longer clear of his command structure, nor the mission parameters. To a soldier and a leader, this was unacceptable. He survived through discipline; by following orders. Now he was in freefall. He needed to talk to Command and find out what the fuck was going on and what his orders were. It wasn't long before he knew.

"Commander, let's be clear, the world has changed, but your mission has not. Your mission parameters were clear, and yet the pathogen is spreading unchecked. We have your debriefing files. Do you have anything else you wish to add?" The large head of the man on the video screen was irritating Skybox in ways he rarely admitted to. He struggled to keep both his voice and emotions in check. *Surely this dick isn't pinning the outbreak on me?*

"Sir, my mission file and after-action notes are complete. Also, I would like to recommend each of my men for posthumous honors. They are all heroes, sir. No one could have survived out there."

The commander cut him off, "Yes, we expected that, but someone *did* survive, Commander. You. Do you have any idea why that is?"

The question surprised him—not the fact that it had been asked, but why it had not been the first thing they wanted to know. It was what he asked himself hundreds of times every day. The shame of surviving had beaten his normal hyper-confidence into submission. "I have no idea, sir. Geng—I mean, our med tech said several of us were asymptomatic. We were all in the same AOs—similar backgrounds, same round of normal inoculations, same diet, but no signs of the disease."

The large head with no hair out of place nodded. "What happened to the others, commander? The ones who were like you?"

"It's in my report, sir," Skybox was losing his patience with this man. "Can I ask, sir, where is my normal CO?" The supposed purpose for this VidCall had been a routine follow-up with his main contact in the command structure: a woman he had only known as Midnight.

"I asked you a direct question, Commander." The man nearly shouted the retort and Skybox's training took over.

"Yes, sir, sorry sir—each of the other three remaining uninfected soldiers . . . the final three soldiers of Talon Battlegroup were KIA. The disease made the enemy crazy and unpredictable. We were fighting skirmishes all the way to the coast. The last of them, an L3, call sign Hooch, made it nearly to the Persian Gulf with me before we were overrun. He provided . . ." Skybox's voice wavered, " . . . He provided a delay for me to get away. He was an incredible officer."

"Tell us again why he felt you needed to make it." The Praetor commander looked increasingly perturbed.

"Hooch and Genghis felt that those of us who were not infected with the Chimera Pox might carry an immunity. Genghis theorized that it could be the combination of our natural genetics and the myriad of other inoculations we received over the years. He tried to isolate it in the field to see if we could offer an antidote."

"What did your man find?"

"He found that we were all infected, but in the four of us, the pathogen was having a hard time taking root. It was progressing at a much slower rate. In me, in particular, it seemed to actually be failing, dying off. He made Hooch promise to get me back to one of the labs at any cost.

"I didn't know about this until Hooch and I were within fifty klicks of the extraction site. We topped a hill to find our way was blocked—a large group pushing hundreds of infected out in front of them. Every one of my troops fought with everything they had, but it wasn't enough. In the end, we were all overrun. Hooch went into the fray and detonated a block of Semtex. He cleared an escape path for me."

The man on the screen stared at Skybox for what seemed like an eternity. Skybox could feel him judging him, his actions, his command, his lost Talon Battlegroup.

"Commander," the voice said flatly. "You've been through hell, and I am sorry to make you relive it for our formal report. I need to know you are still the man we sent out there, which you clearly are. I am also sorry for your men. The losses we are facing worldwide are staggering, but none worse than yours. You are aware . . . your former contact, Midnight, informed you that Catalyst protocols are active."

While it was more a statement than a question, Skybox replied. "Yes, sir."

The man continued. "That means resources are stretched thin—too thin. We are recalling battlegroups from nonessential locations. We have numerous crisis points developing here in the US." He pulled a paper and studied it for a moment. "It now appears Europe and Asia are beyond help. If we can't keep the pandemic away from North America, then we will fall next. Your med tech may have been correct, and we want to get you into a bio-facility as soon as possible to find out how you are surviving. Once the ship you are on is within range, we will transport you by helicopter to the closest lab, where you will give your full cooperation. Is that clear?"

"Yes sir," he responded without enthusiasm. At least he had his orders.

"Spit it out, son, what's on your mind?" Rarely did a CO give permission to speak freely. Skybox had so many questions.

"Forgive me, sir, I'm a soldier. I would rather be fighting than being a lab rat."

"No soldier will be doing more for our survival than you, Skybox."

"Sir . . . I need to know . . . did we create this disease? My tech was pretty sure it was our facility out there and that the pathogen was engineered and weaponized intentionally."

"I can't answer that, soldier."

"Can't or won't?"

While the Praetor groups had ground up command authority, he was getting dangerously close to insubordination with such a response. He knew, but he was getting beyond caring.

The CO looked suddenly much older and wearier. "Can't. At least not with any real confidence. The facility was ours, but I'm told the disease was not something we cooked up. One of our assets learned of its possible existence in an enemy facility, and we managed to acquire a small sample many years ago. I'm certain the sample was duplicated and possibly enhanced as they worked to develop countermeasures. All who worked on it are gone and the information we have on its development is incomplete. Of course, all research at the facility has been destroyed."

Skybox shook his head, "That sounds like bullshit, sir."

"It probably is," the older man paused for a moment before he continued, "that is what we are best at, after all."

Skybox realized that he was not the only one suffering disillusionment. He moved to his next question, "Sir, what is the status of the US right now?"

"Failed state," came the immediate response. "No government, no working economic or judicial system . . . no leadership including law enforcement of any kind. The military bases have mostly gone dark . . . either abandoned or mutinied. Power is off to ninety-eight percent of the population. Rough estimates are that over 85 million citizens have perished, and the number is growing daily. Many of the safe zones have collapsed, and the reserve camps we set up as survival centers are being discovered and coming under near-constant attack by outsiders.

"We have a small contingent of former military leaders, primarily Navy, that are under the impression that we're the bad guys. They keep hitting us at strategic weak points. Commander, it is a veritable shit-show, and our Catalyst plan is ready to blow. It may not survive anything else, certainly not this virus. The protocol has already shifted focus."

"What is this new focus?" Skybox asked.

"You won't like it."

Skybox nodded impatiently, urging the man to go on.

The CO sighed and continued, "We have determined that the US is no longer something we can protect as a nation, nor even as an ideal. Sadly, we're no longer committed to ensuring the survival of the democratic nation state. We are now refocusing on the survival of the human species."

"Shit—um—sorry, sir. I just didn't realize things were so bad . . . I thought those camps were fortified and could withstand attacks."

"They rely more on staying invisible, but yes, they do have solid coun-termeasures. Unfortunately, some of these rebel groups have assembled impressive numbers and are desperate enough to target military bases or, when they learn of them, our reserve camps. We have started recalling Praetor units to aid in the defense."

"What about The Ranch?"

"The Ranch . . . yes. I saw in your files that that location is important to you. The Ranch has fallen. Survivors are being evac'd as we speak. A large group of mercenaries stormed the place several nights ago."

"H-how?" Skybox stammered, stunned. "That place is one of the most secure military facilities in the world. It trains elite soldiers, for God's sake!"

"Numbers, Commander. They had them, we didn't. As I said, we are stretched *thin*. You will be happy to note that your friend was a survivor. They evacuated the hospitals prior to the breach. Magician is in one of the staging camps near Memphis. I can have him sent to whatever lab you will be undergoing your examination. You may not get to see him, but at least he will be close."

Skybox sighed in relief at this single piece of good news. "Thank you, sir. That would be very much appreciated." He was beginning to warm to the man.

"Least we can do for you. One other thing—I saw the video—the satellite and drone feed from your mission. You've been through hell, son. You and your men are heroes. Don't take those losses personally. Put that away, for now, deal with it later, if there is a later. For now, let's get you back stateside.

"Guard Command out." With that, the screen went black and the familiar circle-and-scorpion symbol appeared. The Praetor motto in Latin at the bottom read: *Non Ducor, Duco*. I am not led, I lead. Skybox gave a dry laugh at the slogan.

CHAPTER FORTY-THREE

Present Day

Harris Springs, Mississippi

"Dammit, Jack, I know. It's just frustrating." Todd's eyes flared with anger. "I trust him, I know he's loyal to us, but he's also sympathetic to the Catalyst plans. At some point, Scott is going to have to make a choice. I'm beginning to wonder which it will be."

Jack approached the big man. "Seriously, friend? All of us have been through hell and back for each other. You know you can trust him, hell, you put him in charge when you went on your . . . your vision quest. He's a good man, and despite whatever shit is between you and him, he would take a bullet for your big dumb ass, and you know it. So, what's really the matter?"

"I don't know, life . . . it just used to be so much simpler." He sat back into the cushions of the chair with an audible sigh. "The problem— well fuck, the problem is that the Catalyst plans may be right. Scott . . . probably is right. It all just seems so goddamn heartless. I just can't condone those callous bastards. Things are tough enough right now without them adding to everyone's misery."

Jack put his hand on Todd's arm. "Cap'n, look, neither of you have to be wrong for the other to be right. Most people are backed into a corner now. No one's riding in to save anybody. Even we have limits to what we can do, but Scott's made more effort than anyone to reach out, make friends, set-up trade partners, and help you keep this community afloat," Jack smiled broadly.

"Very funny," Todd said, looking out the ship's windows to the deep green waters below.

"Yeah, I just crack myself up," Jack said with a laugh, trying to clear the tension. "All I'm sayin' is, don't dismiss something the guy says just because it's coming from him. None of us have all the answers right now, so we make decisions based on our best guess. With that in mind, Scott's guesses have been spot-on more often than not. Don't forget that."

The conversation was broken up when Angel knocked. "Chief, Scott's looking for you. He heard back from his friend in DC."

"On my way," Todd replied.

～

An hour later, five of the council were in the *AG*'s chart room looking over the various maps of the Gulf of Mexico. DeVonte had circled the coordinates as Scott read them off. "Shit," Todd muttered. "Could they have picked a less accessible spot?"

"Tahir seemed pretty convinced this would be the one," Scott said. "The chatter indicated it was once a large oil rig. The platform would have to have been heavily modified to become a floating bio-facility. It's certainly big enough and isolated as you say. It's in deep water about . . . here." He looked up to meet Todd's gaze. "What?"

"How did your friend come up with this? Do you trust him?" Todd asked.

"I do trust him, but I don't know how he does what he does. I believe he has some of their encryption keys, but honestly, all he has to do is check radio traffic. No one else out there would be broadcasting, much less tapping into satellite, for web access. If it is a research facility, the bandwidth alone would probably stand out like a beacon."

"And is it stationary? Not possible that it's on a vessel?"

"Todd, it isn't moving, and yes, I suppose it could be on a ship, but look at the location."

"I know what's there, I don't need to look. It's called Devil's Tower. Up until a few years ago, it was the largest oil rig in the world. That thing is a monster. If Praetor forces took it over and converted it into a lab, it's likely home to serious defensive measures. I'm not sure even the Navy could take it out."

Todd gathered the info, intending to take it to the radio room. "Let's push this off to Garret, see what he and his Navy brains have in mind." He glanced at Scott expecting an argument, but none came. Scott had voiced his concerns, and in retrospect, they were valid. He would pass them along to Garret along with the lab location. He gave Scott a nod and left the group to make the call.

Angel sat for a few moments, then said, "Is that it? I mean is that all we needed to do on this, or is there more we need to discuss? I need to check on the galley crew and make sure the late meal is on schedule."

"Only one other matter," Bartos said. "We're beginning to pick up something on radar. Looks like an early season tropical storm down in the southern Gulf. If it heads this way, we may be getting it in the next two weeks. I suggest we recall all ocean operations and let the farmers know that the weather could get nasty."

"That's a good idea." Scott nodded. "Any chance someone will be able to forecast a directional track in the next day or two?"

"Maybe. Your radar's top-notch, and there's an onboard forecasting system, but the telemetry connection to the radar's not functioning."

Scott nodded again, his mind clearly working. "DeVonte, could you see if you can get that working, or possibly enter the basic data manually and see if you can plot a track?"

"You bet. I'm on it." The grinning boy winked at Angel as he left the room. She shook her head and smiled.

"That kid is hopelessly in love with you," Scott said fondly in his wake.

"That kid is just plain hopeless. But he is a sweetie," Angel returned Scott's smile.

CHAPTER FORTY-FOUR

Several hours later, Todd and the original group of friends were meeting again. "Garret has gotten back to us. They're already planning a raid on Devil's Tower." Scott went to say something, but Todd cut him off. "It's not an all-out attack. They know the risks and understand your concerns that the lab and the work they're doing may be concerned with finding a cure. Garret is calling in some of the Special Forces squads, SEALs I suppose, to get covertly onboard and secure the facility with as little damage as possible. He didn't share any actual details . . . they're probably still in the early stages of planning it."

"When they gonna do dis?" Bartos asked.

"No idea, sooner rather than later, I imagine, but that is still somewhat, hmmm, fluid, as they say. There's something else, though. It involves us." Todd paused and looked around at his three closest friends. "First, Scott, he wanted you to know how much he appreciates you and your friend's work in getting the coordinates. They've crosschecked them with some of their intel and are in agreement it is the most likely spot." Scott nodded slightly, still unsure of his enthusiasm for this mission.

Todd looked down at the notes he was holding before reluctantly going on "Scott . . . the commander has requested something else from you. He wants you and me to be a part of the mission." He said it in one breath like he was ripping off the bandage all at once. Scott just looked at him without understanding. The statement seemed to make no sense.

"You are the only person who can identify DJ on sight. The only person he might trust . . . other than Kaylie, but, well, we aren't even considering that."

Scott thought for a moment before accepting the logic. "Why you, then?"

"I can't let you do it alone. We're a team." Todd grinned. "We may not be on the same page with some of this stuff, but we trust each other more than we trust anyone else out there. I'll be there to watch your back, brother."

Scott smiled and met Todd's offered fist for a quick bump. "Kaylie will be thrilled to know she may be with DJ soon," he thought out loud.

Todd looked pained, "Yeah . . . about that. We're not to let any of this out of the room before we get orders to go. I'm surprised they even told us this much, but they know by now we understand operational security. Once they give us the go, we will have between twelve to twenty-four hours before we head out. We can tell her then. Until then, we have to stay close to base. We won't be going in with the SEALs, but once the facility is secure, we will be brought in to help separate the friendlies from the unknowns."

"Dat's a li'l fucked up, Cap'n. I mean, seems like they're just using us . . . using you guys," Bartos said. "Why get any of us in the middle of this fight?"

Jack nodded in agreement with his Cajun friend. "I gotta agree with the retard here," he said, motioning to Bartos, "It is a bit fucked up. I mean, we all wanna see Kaylie get her boyfriend back, but as I recall, he's the one who made the choice to stick with the Catalyst people. He felt his work was important—that was his decision."

Scott kept quiet, obviously facing this with mixed emotions, but knowing what his niece would want. Todd spoke up again. "It is fucked up, friend, I don't disagree. Despite what Garret says, it will also likely be dangerous. I think we need to be on this mission, though, as we may have a better grasp of what is really at stake than anyone else. If we can secure the lab, DJ, and the other researchers on the team, then perhaps we can help them save all of us from whatever is out there. This is happening whether we go with them or not; this way we can try to contain the damage, temper the attack with common sense and maybe get to the bottom of some things.

"Garret did offer one other enticement for our assistance . . ." Todd picked up his coffee cup and took a sip before continuing slowly. "Their intelligence says the Messengers could possibly head this way."

"What the fuck!"

"Shiiiiit . . ."

"How—"

The three men all began to talk in unison.

"Why?

"How do they know?"

"Why wouldn't you begin with that?"

Todd sipped a bit more of the strong, black brew and let his friend's frenetic questions slowly die down. "It's not definite, and nothing's for sure yet, but they have been monitoring the growth of the group the last few weeks. The front of the group has been based near Little Rock as we had expected, but it now appears they are moving on Memphis. The Navy feels confident that will not go well for them. The Messengers are about to run into an immovable object in the shape of a massing Praetor force.

"Memphis has a safe zone—Scott's original research showed the location. It is one of the largest and now seems to be the most protected. They've seen scores of aircraft and troop recalls all heading back to that location. We know how good the Praetor troops and equipment are. The Messengers have the numbers, but when you get down to it, they will be no match for an organized fighting force. Once they realize this, they will need to retreat or redirect: north, and they'll run into harsh terrain and few resources. Back the way they came will be the end of them; they already consumed everything that way. That really only leaves the south . . . toward us."

"Well, that just brightens up my whole day," Scott shook his head and jumped to the obvious question, "What is Garret offering?"

"Protection for us, the *AG*, and possibly the farms around us. They can't fight a sustained land battle, but they can offer us air support, armament and assistance should we find ourselves on the Messengers' radar. They don't have an accurate count of how large the group is, but get this. They expect upwards of 20,000 marching on Memphis."

"Jeezus," Bartos was rattled. That didn't happen often. "So, if we believe dem' Navy guys, we gonna have tens-o-thousands of very pissed off religious nut jobs comin' our way in the next few weeks."

"'Fraid so, Bartos. Well-armed religious crazies at that. I think we knew at some point we would have to face them, but none of us expected the main group to head south. Maybe the Grayshirts will wipe them out . . . who knows?" Todd scratched his beard as he thought about it. "We can't deal with those numbers, but we have to prepare for the worst. The *AG* will be too big a prize for them to ignore. They'll lay siege to us and just wait us out. We have to have support. That's really why I said yes to Garret."

Scott looked at his friend. "Good call, Cap. Tough choice, but I'm in. I do suggest we start making plans of our own for defense here immediately, though. We can't assume anything, and when the Navy gets what they want, they may just forget about us."

"Yeah, I've been thinking about that, too." Todd flipped to another page of notes. "We need to get some things in place quickly. When Scott and I are gone," he looked to Bartos and Jack, "you will be in charge. If anything happens, you need to have multiple plans for defense and possible evacuation. I have a list here. Scott needs to look it over as I'm sure I have forgotten things. This ship is going to be everyone's bugout, so we need to make room for everyone in the area, take in as many resources as possible, and get the control systems working in case we need to move it. Bartos, we need you to finish securing the stores from the train cars. Scott and DeVonte will work on the ship's systems. Preacher, I need you to start warning the farms and your trade partners about the threat. Any of them in the area may want to start thinking about bugging out temporarily, here or wherever else."

Jack nodded grimly. "Crops are just going in the ground. Many of the farmers aren't going to want to leave . . . If that storm heads this way, then maybe I can convince them to come shelter here."

Todd looked puzzled, "What storm?"

Bartos filled Todd in on the radar image of the tropical storm.

"Well, damn, this gets better and better," Todd said with a sigh. "Okay, we all have a lot to do, let's get started. Let's stay in close contact over the next few days. Scott and I will need to stay here to discuss how to get the ship best ready for attack. If you guys are out, we will get word to you when the mission is a go. Until then, we keep it quiet. Just use the storm warning as the primary reason for all our activity for now. No need to mention the Messengers until we know more."

Heads nodded in agreement as they rose to get started.

CHAPTER FORTY-FIVE

Eastern Arkansas

Hawley considered his options. Michael had mapped out the strategy to take the federal camp near Memphis, but the Messengers mostly moved on foot. Some had motorcycles, others rode horses, and a few, like him, had Humvees or Jeeps. This meant they couldn't all reach any desired destination within the same timeframe—or with the same ease. Thus, the motor convoy he was attached to was sitting here out in the open on Route 70, only fifty miles from Memphis. He spat his chew at the feet of the man giving the report.

"So, what you're saying is there's no easy way to approach the camp?"

"Yes, sir. Sorry, sir, but thass the gist of it. We don' have an exack location, but we know iss likely in the valley. From wha' we can see, theress only one road in. Tall hills block us on one side, th'other side's a li'l easier, but we'd have th'river at our back. We'd be in a shootin' box if it went down wrong, no way we cou' retreat."

"Who in the fuck said we would need to retreat? Have you ever seen us retreat? We are God's Army, soldier. We cannot lose." Hawley would have slapped the man if it didn't involve him climbing down the side of the Humvee.

"Sir, I'm juss givin' you the tactical overview. From a military perspective, is goin' a be . . . a challenge."

Hawley nodded and dismissed the man. He knew he was right, but he had a plan for dealing with that: thousands of new converts he could put into that valley to attack from the river side while his main force flanked from the west. The hills might be a challenge, but he was confident they could take this Memphis base, assuming they could find it. So far, no one had gotten close enough to see what was there. He needed eyes on the encampment before he put the entire force at risk.

Time to talk with his boss. He could see the brown and black luxury motor coach pulling up now. The Prophet's own "Jesus Bus," as he liked to refer to it. It was already past noon; Hawley figured His Holiness would be in bed; he always slept when they traveled. Hopefully, he wouldn't lose his shit when he heard how much the delays were slowing the pending attack.

The next day started badly and got worse. It was early morning when they heard the first of the attack choppers. The smoking outline of Memphis was close now, within ten miles, but they were not heading there. The deep thumping of the Cobra gunships echoed down the Mississippi Valley. The ground force, made up mostly of newly converted soldiers, was interspersed with Messenger elders to keep them all moving in the right direction. Scout teams of Judges and Marauders—their special weapons and tactics groups—were already encountering organized resistance as they made their way up into the hill country. While the Messengers had the numbers and ample weapons, they were finding this force to be formidable.

Jimmy Solts had wanted badly to be named as a Judge. He liked the swagger and reputation they held in God's Army. Instead, he was officially named Commander of one of the Messenger–Marauder crews: part of an advance team that had been covertly working their way into the deep valley. Originally from West Virginia, he knew this terrain and felt at home here. Well, the machine gun fire from the ridgeline and the gunship choppers making strafing runs at them was new.

"They must have FLIR, Jimmy, or some other kind of Thermal Imaging," the man twenty yards to his left said. Only with heat sensitive cameras could they pick the soldiers off like this in the forest. They were easy targets.

"My guess, too," Jimmy yelled back. They had fired several RPGs at the craft, but it had climbed easily out of the way and then lined up for additional firing runs. Jimmy was currently ducked low behind a line of rocks and deadfall that offered some shelter. *I haven't heard or seen anything flying in months, and when I do, it's trying to kill me,* he thought.

His Marauder crew was scattered over several hundred yards of the forest. They were pinned down by the choppers' gunfire—unable to proceed—and he was still losing more men with each pass. He looked at the edge of a stream that meandered peacefully through the open glade ahead. He had an idea.

He radioed new instructions to the squad. After the next pass from the chopper, the men broke cover and ran to the stream where they immersed themselves in the chilly water. They also soaked their dark Boonie hats and slipped down deeper into the water as the chopper made its next run.

Jimmy was freezing, but he kept his squad there until the chopper made two more passes. Seeing no new targets, the gray Cobra gunship sought new prey farther down the valley, behind the Marauders. Jimmy gave the order to move out as he climbed from the cold, wet muck of the stream.

His men double-timed it across the glade to the forest beyond. They were within fifty yards when they noticed a series of flat panels mounted on steel poles just inside the tree line. The panels appeared to be plastic or fiberglass and were colored in a forest camo pattern. The things looked like a radar dish, but they were not moving and were pointed horizontally at ground level. He took a knee, and the others did the same. Sending out two of his men to check it out, he watched and waited.

As the men got closer he felt a tingle in his ear. Then, inexplicably, his radio earpiece began to burn his ear. He reached to jerk it out and realized that his hand was itching and hot. Looking at his hand, though, nothing seemed to be wrong with it—but there was, oh God, there was! Up and down the line he saw and heard men in agony. He looked over at the Marauder next to him. "What is it, Willy?"

Willy didn't speak, but Jimmy followed his eyes. The two advance scouts were no longer standing; they were on their knees. Smoke was rising from their bodies; their uniforms were beginning to smolder and catch fire.

"WHAT IN THE FUCK IS GOING ON!" Jimmy screamed. "PULL BACK! PULL BACK!" With no working radio, he shouted at his men, who were now writhing in agony. Several of the squad began to retreat just as the very dead bodies of the front scouts boiled and ruptured in wet, red bursts.

CHAPTER FORTY-SIX

The command trailer was underneath an overpass on I-40. Hawley's ruthless lieutenant and several other officers had just been invited in and were waiting to speak. They didn't look good.

"Shit, Pete, you look like hell," Hawley sounded as shocked as they all looked. "How close are we to their base camp?"

Pete looked at the ground, "We aren't sure," he was trembling. "Best guess would be five miles, but no one's actually seen it yet. Our guys are getting hammered, though."

Hawley opened his mouth to respond but could see his leader looking up at the men, so he waited his turn.

"Where are they attacking?" Michael asked.

Pete looked to his left, and the man standing there began to report, "Your Holiness, they are mostly ignoring the ground force near the river. The gunships are targeting and wiping out the heavier technicals, mounted guns and all our crew-manned guns. Our advance force is also encountering strong resistance. The ridgeline has heavy machine gun emplacements, bunkers with clear fire lines and, apparently, a sniper nest that we have been unable to neutralize. We are losing a lot of men."

Hawley was sweating; this had been mainly his battle plan, but he hadn't been prepared for this level of resistance. Michael glared at him. He looked over at Pete before speaking. "Recommendations?"

"The pincer movement isn't working, sir. They're too prepared, and we can't match the firepower. They have a secure and entrenched location, which means we'd need overwhelming numbers in a sustained attack to defeat them. We *must* mobilize *all* guns and manpower along the most direct route. Pour everything we have into a single, rapid, frontal assault. It sounds suicidal, but it's the only way we stand a chance."

Michael sprung to his feet and paced as best he could in the confined cabin. "Who in the *fuck* are these guys?" he spat, "Have we captured anyone? Found any markings on any of the equipment?"

Pete cleared his throat nervously, "No idea, sir. No prisoners yet, no markings we've seen, other than what looked like a scorpion on the side of the Cobra copter. Everything's in dull gray camo, none of our guys recognize it. But sir—I mean—Your Holiness. Some of the stuff they're hitting us with is insane."

"Like what?" Michael asked.

"Well, one of the advance Marauder groups was immobilized by what they said was a flat-looking radar dish. They advanced to take it out, assuming it was part of the communications array, when they started feeling like they were on fire. Their skin's blistered, weapons got too hot to hold, the uniforms burst into flames. Said they felt like they were being cooked."

"Devil's fire," Michael said, looking erratically at the company around him as he took back up his character. He needed to be the Prophet more than ever.

Pete reluctantly corrected his leader: "One of the surviving Marauders said it was likely a portable microwave generator. He used something similar back when he was in the Army. They had a few units, testing for crowd dispersal. Back then they didn't do any real damage, though—just made people feel like they were getting hit by a heat cannon . . . worst they could do was cause a case of mild sunburn. Whatever this is, the wattage was turned way up. We lost 150 men from that assault, most to that weapon."

Hawley looked at Pete in amazement. "Who in the *fuck* are these people?" he demanded once more. "We're back to living in the fucking Stone Age and these guys have fucking heat rays?" He looked around, but no one met his gaze. "We need answers. Maybe they're Chinese— or Russian. We could be occupied by any number of foreign powers when you think about it. Who would have this kind of hardware?" He was starting to sound panicked; bewildered. "Look, we need to find out who we are up against. Find a way to capture a prisoner—alive. Bring them here to me when you do. Have all the regular troops pull back for now.

Michael erupted in fury: "PULL BACK? Who do you think you are questioning the Lord's will? We continue to attack, move forward. The question isn't who are we fighting, it is what are they protecting with all this? It must be something impressive. Use the converts, make the enemy stay focused on them. God has given me a vision. He has shown me that we will enjoy a great victory in this battle. Go make it happen."

Twenty miles away on a nearly abandoned stretch of airstrip, a fleet of modified drones began taxiing down the runway. The fully loaded autonomous jets were the third of five waves destined to hit the attackers: their target was the Messengers' command and control apparatus. They had identified it as a large coach style bus with numerous Humvees and armed technical trucks. The drones were all unmarked, but the AGM 114 Hellfire missiles each bore Praetor's scorpion. The drone pilots had been talking to God, too, but they had a different message to deliver.

CHAPTER FORTY-SEVEN

Southeast of Little Rock, Arkansas

Bobby awoke to the solemn face of the young boy staring down at him. He was confused; it was now daylight outside. He went to sit up, but nausea and dizziness forced his head back down onto the wood floor. He had muddied memories of the previous night—he hoped it was just last night. His body was weak, but he recalled the talk with Jordan, and the boy. What had she called him? *Jack, no something else . . . Joey . . . Jacob.*

"Jacob, my name is Bobby. I was friends with your mommy when she was about your age," he smiled weakly. He managed to sit up again. The boy remained silent, still staring. "Is your mom around? Could you get her?" Another wave of dizziness hit, and when he was able to open his eyes again the boy was gone, and the screen door across the room was slamming shut. He heard indistinct sounds from outside; something wasn't right, but the fuzziness in his head couldn't process it. He saw a pitcher of water on the counter, and the cottony feeling in his mouth overrode his desire to stay seated.

He was seated at the table and on his second glass of water when Jordan and her son walked in. "You look better, I—well, I was worried for a while. How are you feeling?"

Bobby shook more of the cobwebs free before speaking, "Like you shot me, then ran over my body several times with a truck."

She felt his forehead then walked to the sink. "The fever came back. Sorry, wasn't much I could do for you, so I let you sweat it out. This morning when you didn't wake up I began to worry. I was beginning to wonder if you were going to sleep through the entire war."

"This morning . . . what time is it? Wait—" he said, finally registering what she'd said, "What war?"

"You need to come outside. If you can, that is."

With considerable effort, Bobby made it out the door and down the few steps into the yard. What he saw made little sense to him. Numerous fighter jets flew silently above them, making a wide turn over the nearby hills. The sound followed several seconds later. In the far distance, he could hear the massive, concussive blast of bombing runs. Black smoke billowed on the horizon. "Who is fighting?" he wondered aloud.

His confusion kept increasing; no one had seen jets overhead since last summer. He hadn't seen any signs of the Army, the Air Force . . . shit, not so much as the Boy Scouts. "How long has this been going on?" Looking at the sun, he estimated the time at around five in the afternoon.

"We started hearing the bombs about lunch time. Then the jets showed up a few hours ago. They've been steady since. The sounds were farther away earlier, but they seem to be getting louder and closer now."

Bobby thought for a second, "What's in that direction?"

"Memphis," she said, with an edge of remorse. It had been her home once.

"So, they started near Memphis around five hours ago, and now they're moving this way. Whoever it is, they must be attacking the Messengers. Scott mentioned a paramilitary group, I can't remember who, but he called them "gray shirts" or something. Maybe they have the fire-power to turn the Prophet away."

Jacob was hiding behind his mother's leg watching the jets, all the while keeping a wary eye on Bobby as well. Jordan spoke, "If that's true, I hope they kill them all."

Bobby thought about it, then said, "I do, too, but I doubt it. Most are on foot, which makes them hard to target from the air. They had tens of thousands of followers last time I knew—they could be spread out over fifteen miles or more . . ." He thought for a moment. "The Mississippi River makes a natural border to the east, and if they're coming this way, they'll also have the Arkansas River blocking a westward escape. That means that even if these guys manage to wipe out most of them, we're going to have a horde of the crazy bastards heading this way in the next few days."

"Shit," she said. "We need a car."

The sounds of battle seemed to be quieting slightly, and the pounding in his head was also subsiding. He walked over to the creek he knew so well. The sunlight played across the ripples in a hypnotic pattern. The sound was soothing. He wanted badly to stay here. It was familiar, and it was comfortable.

Jordan walked up behind him, "D'you think they will find us? We aren't near anything important. Won't they just keep running south?"

All these questions. He didn't have the answers, but he knew the threat. "They will find this place, yes. They are very thorough, and they will likely be very desperate. We can't stay, and we can't hide. I've seen how they work. We won't have a chance." Something was nagging at him, though, something his brother had said. He tried to force his mind to clear. *Why did he send me to this spot anyway? It's remote, sure, previously not in the Messengers' path . . . .*

He looked out at the creek again. "Go with the flow." That was what Scott had said—go with the flow. Bobby now knew what his little brother had meant.

"Jordan, do you know if your uncle's old kayaks or canoes are still here?"

"Uh . . . yeah, they are . . . well, the canoe is anyway—it was up in the rafters of the barn. The kayaks, I believe they were stored under the house, but I haven't even looked under there. Why?"

"This creek feeds into a larger one that eventually flows into the Arkansas River. Scott, Dad, and I paddled all the way down to the big river a few times. It's around twenty miles from here."

"I've paddled the creek some too, but tree-falls block the way now in a lot of places. It would be slow going. Besides, what do we do when we get to the Arkansas River?"

"We go with the flow!" he almost laughed. "We can take that all the way down until it flows into the Mississippi River. Then, if we take that closer to the coast, we should be able to get pretty close to where Scott and my daughter Kaylie are."

"Wait, wait, wait! I'm all for getting outta Dodge, but that would have to be what—600 miles on the river? I am *not* an outdoors type, and I have a small boy. Those rivers are huge, with strong currents and—don't you think other people will be on them—bad people?"

"It's probably closer to 700 miles, but we won't take it all the way down, and the current will be pushing us. This stretch right here will probably be the hardest to navigate. We'll have to be careful but staying here is suicide."

Jordan was unconvinced, and he didn't blame her. He took her aside and shared with her some of the atrocities the Messengers were known for. It took fifteen minutes more, but when a large air burst bomb sounded down the valley, shaking the house and even the trees, she came around. They began pulling the dust-covered boats out. The kayaks were in good shape, but the brightly colored plastic on two of them stood out to Bobby. The canoe was solid but looked about as ancient and unsafe as could be imagined. He found some roofing tar and plugged a few obvious holes. In the meantime, Jordan and Jacob busily assembled supplies.

Rummaging around the old barn, Bobby found several rattle cans of dark paint. He sat the kayaks up on sawhorses and began spray painting over the brightly colored plastic. He knew it would probably scratch or flake off fairly quickly, but it didn't need to last long.

Once finished, he pulled all the boats to the edge of the creek. Jordan and Jacob began loading the supplies they had gathered. They had the large fourteen-foot canoe and three kayaks. The supplies would ride more secure in the canoe, as would Jacob. He and Jordan would take a kayak each and tow the canoe and the extra kayak behind them. Jordan had only brought what she felt was essential, but Bobby still thought it was too much. What they lacked were bags to store many of the items. It wasn't bad now, but the unstable gear would be very difficult to keep upright when they hit rapids or stronger currents. The problem was solved when Jordan produced a large roll of commercial plastic stretch wrap. They wrapped everything into bundles, including extra life jackets. They decided to completely wrap the canoe and the extra kayak into one large floating bundle.

"It isn't pretty," Bobby said with satisfaction, "but it should work."

"So, how early we going to head out?" Jordan asked.

The sun was beginning to dip lower in the sky. "How about now? We still have several hours of daylight, and I'd rather be increasing the miles between us and them right away." The sound of small arms fire from just up the valley enforced the impending threat.

For a moment she looked as if she was going to protest, but she nodded and said nothing. She fitted a life jacket onto Jacob and gave him his safety instructions. She pulled a lanyard at the boy's neck and said, "If you fall in the water, blow this whistle until we see you. You will be fine, okay?" He nodded, looking excited but nervous.

They pulled the tiny flotilla into the deep part of the gentle creek and settled into their hard seats. Swiftly, they began to paddle away from the homestead. Bobby took the lead, glancing back regularly to make sure all was good. "Bro, I hope you know what you're doing, sending us down this route . . ." he muttered to himself in a low voice.

Jordan had been right about the number of fallen trees, and in the first five miles, they were forced to stop numerous times to pull the boats over or tuck them through the limbs and walk behind them.

Now they faced a large, fallen poplar tree that blocked the route entirely. The tree was still thick with green leaves; a recent occurrence. The tree limbs were too thick to go over or through. He thought briefly about portaging the boats around but noticed the high banks on both sides. He had anticipated this and moved his kayak over to the shallows and hopped out. Going to the canoe, he gave Jacob a wink as he pulled out a large, curved, bladed bush-ax. While the ax was not designed to cut down trees, it was great with limbs up to a few inches thick. Bobby eyed the tree and determined the fewest limbs he would need to cut to get them through. He climbed onto the main trunk, walked out to the point he had eyed, and began chopping.

The task was time-consuming and noisy, but it only took around thirty minutes to get enough limbs out of the way. He was now exhausted, but he climbed back into his kayak and worked the party through the hazard and into clearer waters. The next stretch was relatively clear, and they entered the larger creek just as night was beginning to fall. Traveling at night had not been in the plan, but the lingering dusk gave them ample light for quite a while longer. The creek began to widen and pick up speed.

"We must be getting close to the Arkansas," Bobby said. "Let's pull over and find a camp spot."

The trio had not talked much since leaving, in fact, Jacob hadn't spoken at all. But they were now all close to exhaustion. The sounds of battle had faded to nothing, and all that they heard now were the sounds of the river and the forest. They made a cold camp, eating left-overs and bread before rolling out bed mats and falling to sleep.

CHAPTER FORTY-EIGHT

Arkansas River, Arkansas

Waking before sunrise, Bobby nudged Jordan as he began building a small fire to make coffee and cook some breakfast. He planned for them to stay on the river all day, so they would need the calories. He also assumed that if anyone smelled the smoke, the three of them would already be gone before the source could be located.

Forty-five minutes later they were fed, the adults' caffeine addiction was sated and they were pulling out of the mouth of the creek and into the main river. Though less well known than its neighbor to the east, the Arkansas River system was still one of the largest in the country. *If you could still call it a country,* Bobby mused.

The river, which began in the hills of Colorado, was mostly tamed by numerous dams and locks, many of which now lay between them and their destination.

One of the first things Bobby realized they needed was a more complete map of the waterways. Thankfully, he had guessed correctly that one would be available at the first lock system they came to. Since no electricity was available, the massive river locks were inoperable.

This was a challenge as the canoe, kayaks, and supplies all had to be pulled across the ground to the other side. It was still preferable to dealing with the several large reservoir dams they would also encounter along the way: the slack current in the deep lakes slowed them, and at the dams, the portage across was arduous. Often, it took most of a day just to get everything carried over to the opposite side. On the first day, they made nearly thirty-five miles. The next day they struggled to make thirty.

They were nearing the town of Pine Bluff. Bobby was nervous, as the riverbanks here were heavily developed, with little cover. He wanted to travel at night, but Jordan resisted. If Jacob fell asleep and fell out, she might never find him in the dark. It wasn't as if he would yell for help. A ten-year-old boy wouldn't have a chance.

They rested at a shady patch of the riverbank on the north side of Pine Bluff, watching the activities downstream. Fishermen were numerous, but they also heard gunshots and saw a large fire burning somewhere in the downtown area. Jordan finally agreed that night travel would be better. They pulled the boats into the brush out of sight and tried to get some sleep. The heat, the insects, and their ever-present worries made rest during the day impossible for the two grown-ups, but Jacob slept soundly against his mother.

They found themselves talking at length for the first time since leaving the farm.

"Has Jacob ever talked?"

"Some . . . never much." She picked a stem of grass and began to chew it. "He used to have a therapist who was wonderful. She ruled out several things, including mental illness. He's not a mute—he *can* talk. In fact, the first time he did it, he spoke in complete sentences."

"Is it me?" Bobby asked. "I mean, is he scared to talk since I showed up?"

She shook her head before looking down to where the boy slept. "He hasn't uttered a word since he saw his father killed. He understands most of what's going on. Don't let his silence fool you. He's intelligent, above grade level still, I imagine. I'm not sure if he will speak again, but I'm not forcing it."

"He's a good kid . . . definitely not a complainer," Bobby said with a grin.

Jordan smiled. "Thanks." She paused and looked more serious. "Bobby, I appreciate what you're doing for us. I'm sure your trip would be easier and faster without us around." He started to say something, but she cut him off. "Let me finish, please. We are not your responsibility. I'm just someone you knew in another life. I told you I had a crush on you back then, and that was true, but I don't anymore. I'm not looking for a new father for Jacob or a new man for myself. I know you're still very much in love with your wife and not even thinking about this, but . . . I just wanted to make that all clear. I've been told that I tend to be a bit blunt, but I feel it's better that, than to give you the wrong idea. You know?"

"So, not even a handjob?" he said with mock seriousness. He broke into a grin as she punched his arm hard. "Okay, okay," he conceded, feeling playful for the first time in a long time. "But you deserved that. I do understand, but I do owe you, you saved me, and well, I appreciate your determination. It couldn't have been easy surviving on your own and taking care of a child. I have no expectations, just to put your mind at ease. I just want to get us to the coast and safety . . . see my own child. You're an impressive mother and a friend, and I don't say that lightly. I appreciate you and Jacob being with me. It gives me purpose."

Jordan smiled but said nothing. She eased over to the grass and lay down, curled around her son. Bobby plugged the slackline antenna into the little two-way radio and tried to raise anyone in Harris Springs. Recently he had been doing so at least once a day.

After thirty minutes, he gave up and plugged the batteries into the solar charger, laying them out on his pack. Then he, too, fell back and finally drifted off to sleep.

~

He awoke some time later to find a small hand clamped over his mouth and another pushing his chest down. He looked up to see Jacob over him. It appeared to be early evening, and the sky was growing dark. The boy being so close surprised him, and he went to move his hand, but the boy raised it and placed one finger to his lips, shaking his head.

Bobby heard the men's voices; they were close. Jacob patted something else into his hand and silently disappeared back into the bushes. Bobby looked down to find his pistol in his hand. He ran his thumb above the handgrip to find the hammer back. Jacob had cocked it as well. *Jeeze.* The kid was smart; smarter than him—why had he not made one of them take a guard watch?

He assumed Jacob was waking his mother as well, though he heard nothing. It was already too dark to see them. Bobby rolled to his side and slowly raised his head to look in the direction of the sounds. He could just about see them: four of them, about fifty feet downstream. They appeared to be fishing, but the straight barrels of rifles were clearly visible on each man's back. They may not be a threat, but that was no longer an assumption anyone could make in this world. If the men moved any closer, they would likely spot the boats, and most definitely the people lying beside them. The best option was to simply be invisible. No sound, no movement.

Bobby lay still in the grass for what seemed like hours before the men moved farther downstream. In reality, it had been less than one hour, but the exertion of being perfectly still, combined with the adrenaline of the situation left him fatigued. He crawled back to where mother and child lay and saw both figures watching him. He reached out and hugged Jacob tightly. The boy did not resist. They waited together until they could no longer hear the men, then slowly they slid the boats back into the river and began paddling.

CHAPTER FORTY-NINE

Present Day

Devil's Tower Oil Platform, Gulf of Mexico

Skybox looked at the medical team with anger mixed with amusement. It was obvious to him they were not normal doctors. They were not used to having subjects that responded to questions, had opinions, or were, like him, fed up with being drained of more and more of the blood from his body.

"No offense, doc, but you must have gallons of the stuff by now."

Dr. Colton leaned away from the man and studied him briefly. "We do, but it's old. Our pets require fresh."

He was unsure if she was kidding. The woman was bookishly beautiful, with glasses and deep auburn hair pulled back under her surgical hat. The researchers wore full bio-suits. He did carry the Chimera virus, but in his body, for some reason, it had remained almost completely dormant. He was immune.

Skybox had been at the facility for weeks and still had not managed to develop a rapport with anyone here. He wanted to know if Tommy was also in the facility, but no one answered those questions. He had not met anyone in command, so he assumed the "staff" was mainly made up of civilian contractors. In his walled-off rooms, he had limited free-dom; he was not allowed to go outside. He had been on a stretcher in a self-contained bio-tent when he was transferred here, so he was unsure of where or even what it was. Although the air was filtered, cycled, and irradiated to kill germs, he occasionally thought he could smell salty air. He was not used to this level of secrecy. He was a commander, after all, and now he was taking instructions from a civilian and her minions.

He realized she had been speaking to him again while he fumed. "Commander, we are going to start running some different tests with you. Tests that will involve differing levels of stress, and I'm afraid, in some cases, pain. We will also be taking more blood during each phase to see if the disease shows any change in activity. It is very important for us to know exactly how stable it is within your body. Do you understand?"

He looked at her piercingly. Her eyes were amazing, he thought.

"Do you understand?"

"Huh? Oh, sure, yeah. No problem, doc." The pressure on his arm relaxed, and he saw the needle being withdrawn. Why had he not felt it going in? The thought fluttered away like a seagull on an updraft.

"Hey, doc, do you know where they located my friend? His name is Tommy, and he was supposed to have been transported here." None of the medical staff ever responded to personal questions, but it was worth a shot. This woman seemed to be the boss, so maybe she had information to share.

"No one has been brought here since you arrived," she said. "If he is an active duty soldier, I probably wouldn't be able to find out . . . none of you guys use real names, you know."

"No . . . he's not active. He was—he's disabled. Head trauma. He has to have constant care and monitoring. Last I heard he was at a camp hospital in Memphis, but my CO said they were bringing him here . . . wherever here is . . . to be with me."

"Memphis?" she said, her voice shaky.

"Yeah."

He noticed tears in her eyes. What did she know? "No one from Memphis has made it here."

Skybox watched as the doctor gathered her equipment and his blood and hurried away. Clearly, she knew something more, something that caused her great pain. How that was connected to Tommy he didn't know, but his mind was scattered from the drugs they kept pumping him with, the blood they kept extracting. He would keep asking until he understood.

But soon it became clear no one really knew much about the outside world. This was what they knew: this lab and their specimens, of which he was now one. Their world was one of proteins and bacilli and disease vectors: a brutal microscopic world now eerily mirrored by their big world.

Week after week slowly passed with little distinction for Skybox. The poking, prodding and more and more elaborate tests continued, intensified in strangeness. This morning he was greeted by one of the more likable researchers, one he had learned was called DJ. The guy was nice and smart, but he also had something of an actual personality. He even laughed at jokes. He was also the one Skybox felt sure was holding something back; it seemed the young man knew more about what was going on than he let on.

"DJ, how would you know if the virus became active? I mean, do you have sensors that go off? Alarms? Would they seal the exam room and fill it with poisonous gas?"

The kid grinned. "That would be cool, but no, nothing that sophisticated, unfortunately. We'd still have to take a blood sample to see . . . or of course, if you started presenting symptoms, we would know that way." He was busy attaching another electrode to Skybox's bare chest. "The pathogen's not typically airborne, but none of our biofilters are equipped to register something as small as the Chimera. The molecules of the disease are ridiculously tiny. We still have trouble spotting it, even now that we know what we're looking for . . . the size is one reason it's been so hard to isolate. We thought it would be easier with a live host, but . . . so far, Commander, you haven't really been that helpful." DJ smiled at Skybox.

Skybox was both amused and deflated. "Fuck," he exhaled. *All this and nothing yet.* "I think I'm offended by that." They both laughed briefly. "Tell me, DJ, where are you from? Do you have family there, a girlfriend maybe?"

"Not sure anymore," he answered sadly.

Skybox knew he had struck pay dirt. "What's her name?"

"Look, we aren't supposed to discuss stuff like this, you know that. I'm sure someone's listening to all our conversations."

"Yeah, I get it. I'm just a lab rat," Skybox ran his hands through his hair in frustration. "I've been here for weeks with no real human contact. I just thought . . . you know . . . I just wanted to feel human for a second. I thought maybe hearing about someone else's life would help me deal with not having one."

DJ looked the man over, "You have a life, man, you're a soldier. Christ, you're a Grayshirt! You guys are the best of the best, aren't you?"

Skybox couldn't decide if his tone was one of scorn or respect; something seemed a bit off about it. "Just a soldier, kid, nothing special."

DJ finished attaching the leads, plugged in the monitoring station and walked out without comment. Moments later, another suit came in. She would be administering today's test. He saw DJ's face on the other side of the glass in the observation room. He was even more convinced the kid knew something.

CHAPTER FIFTY

"Kaylie . . . I don't recall ever knowing a Kaylie. Pretty name. You think she's okay?"

"She's okay—I mean, I think she is."

Inwardly, Skybox gave himself a mental high-five. The kid had just let something important slip out. It had taken several weeks to get this far, but there it was. "So, what's everyone so excited about?"

"They think they've isolated the proteins, and we finally managed to get to the genetic core of the virus thanks to you. Dr. C. thinks we can finally see what mutations have been going on with the agent."

"I'm not sure what any of that means, but I helped?"

"Yes," DJ smiled, "you helped. Without you, we couldn't have made this leap. I mean, it's no cure, but we finally know how to slow it down at least. The DNA of this thing is, well, freakin' awesome. It's unlike anything we were considering—unlike anything anyone's ever seen, to be honest. We were assuming all along that it was based on a more traditional carrier, a tuberculosis mycobacteria, something like that, but that was a false clue. Your field team's notes from the point of origin have been very helpful. The lead scientist you had there was a genius. He was definitely on the right track. I'm sorry he didn't survive."

"So, was he right about the disease being some cutting-edge, engineered virus?" Skybox responded, testing how much the lad actually knew.

"No, that's just it—it's not new at all." DJ looked around briefly as if he was about to give out the cheat codes to his favorite video game. "No, man, it's ancient. Like, prehistoric—*predating mankind* kind of ancient. I should probably let the doc talk to you about it. She's the expert. But basically, we have—" he held up a hand and began counting off fingers, "—poisons, viruses and bacteria, each of which are very different beasts, also prions . . . anyway, Chimera, as you call it, started out as none of those, though it actually has parts of all of them. The genetic base of this pathogen could be millions of years old. Like, this might be what wiped out the dinosaurs!"

"And . . . I have it." Skybox nodded remembering a similar conversation with Genghis. "I thought a meteor took out the dinos."

"Possibly, but they lived for a really, really long time, during which there were numerous mass extinctions, and we're pretty sure disease caused several of those. The most interesting part is this: there's still some confusion over what kind of animals most dinosaurs even were. Forty years ago, they were all thought to be cold-blooded reptiles, then amphibians, maybe mammals, then early members of the bird family."

"Yeah," Skybox said. "I remember some of that. What difference does it make?"

"All the difference, man," DJ was clearly excited. The kid clearly loved science. "Do you have any idea how rare it is for diseases to jump across species? Dogs don't catch colds from their owners and so forth. Humans can and do catch diseases from birds, pigs, even primates, but it's not very common. Very few animals can catch diseases from people."

Skybox had heard much of this before from Genghis. "Okay. Not really following," he responded, mainly to engage DJ more.

"Think about the diversity of animal life back then. All types were alive—warm-blooded, cold-blooded, mammals, birds, reptiles . . . Yet something wiped *nearly all* of them out in one punch. This pathogen, or some variant of it, seems to us to be a likely candidate. It adapted to each host in a way that allowed it to survive and multiply across species. That's basically all nearly every life form wants to do at the base level: survive and multiply. And this one achieved it. It's almost beautiful in its effectiveness."

Skybox fell serious. "DJ, listen. I've seen this thing out there, out in the wild. It is in no way beautiful. In fact, it is the scariest, creepiest fucking thing I have ever seen in my life."

"I know, I know, Commander. I mean, I've seen videos. I just mean that, from a purely scientific standpoint, this is amazing. This is discovering-life-on-Mars levels of awesome."

Skybox leaned back with a sigh. He suddenly felt very, very old. "Sounds great. Tell me one thing then. Why is it not killing me?"

DJ shrugged. "We're still unsure. We finally have all your prior medical history, records of all your immunizations and illnesses since you were born. Part of the team is busy doing the genetic mapping to see if anything in your base DNA might have the answer, and another group is looking at the early antiviral treatments you were given overseas, including those dispersed in the atmosphere. The truth is, we may never know. If your man was right, and the Archaea domain is the key to this, we likely don't have the expertise or equipment to solve it."

"So why am I still here?"

"You need to speak to Dr. Colton about that. She seems to feel that synthesizing your blood chemistry might be the better step. We may not need to know *why*, as long as we know *how*—how to stop the transmission of the disease, that is, or at least how to keep the symptoms contained. You are the key to that, sir."

"Yeah, well, the doc hasn't been one for speaking to me much. I've only seen her a handful of times the last few weeks. She seems . . . preoccupied. Sad."

DJ looked left in the direction of his boss's office. "She is, she—well, we've all lost people during this mess. Her family was in an accident, all of them were killed."

Skybox groaned. He didn't like the thought of her in grief.

"Yeah, Praetor agreed to bring them down from Tennessee before they relocated us out here. Apparently, the helicopter they were on went down near the coast. Might have been the Navy guys. They seem to have a hard-on to be rid of you guys."

"Navy?" He was confused for a moment; then remembered a conversation with his CO. "I hate that that happened to her." He shook his head in empathy. He had lost so many people in his life, but none were family. Still, he could imagine how she must feel.

"Yeah," DJ nodded, "She deals with it, I know she and her husband weren't on particularly good terms when the shit went down, but she had a daughter. She's being real strong, but . . ." DJ started for the door.

Skybox thought for a second, "Hey, DJ—where in Tennessee were they coming from?'

"Memphis, sir. Why?"

CHAPTER FIFTY-ONE

Harris Springs, Mississippi

Scott saw Kaylie heading down the gangway with her friends. There was always so much to do, but some days you just had to rediscover some of what was lost. He wanted that for Kaylie, especially. She was still a kid, after all.

Today he would extend that indulgence to himself, too. He went to the tender garage. He slipped into his padded cycling gear, slung on a go-pack, checked his weapons and mounted his Trek racing bike. His head was full: thoughts of the pending rescue mission in the Gulf; Bobby's journey south; the storm; the virus; the Messengers . . . the list went on. He needed to clear some space.

He did a circuit around town then headed toward the marina where he could hop a ferry ride to the far side. The drawbridges were rarely lowered anymore unless farmers radioed ahead that they were bringing supplies, or the trade crews were heading out. Nothing as unscheduled as this bike ride warranted the risk. He told old Ben—the man who ran the ferry—that he'd be back in a few hours.

"No problem, Scott," he replied, "I'll keep an eye out for you 'til dark."

Scott doubted he'd be out that long; his riding time had been severely limited since the CME, and his endurance had suffered. The conditions of the roads were deteriorating quickly; besides the trash, downed tree limbs, leaves and pine straw now covered the roads. Grass was also beginning to reclaim the paved surfaces. There was so little traffic now, he guessed it would only be months before the land reclaimed it all, especially with spring here and summer on its way. Scott leaned down, found the right gear and hammered out a familiar pace.

He considered his route based on what seemed safest. First, he would take Hwy 50, then decide on his next move from there. Muscles that had not been recently tested began to wake up. "Fuck, that hurts," he groaned. But soon, the miles began to fly by. He knew he was supposed to stay close, but he needed this. He picked up on the familiar smells of the late spring day, along with some new ones. Turning off the main road, he took a road that was even more familiar than all the rest.

Bartos wouldn't be happy he was leaving the so-called "AG safe zone." *Tough*, he thought as the burned-out hulk of his old family cottage came into view. The sight still filled him with anger and sadness. While it was just a building, it had represented so much more to him and his family. He dreaded his brother Bobby ever seeing it like this. *It will break his heart.* Barely slowing, he pedaled on past, keeping to the road bordering the black water of the bayou.

Thinking of Bobby made him wonder how his brother was doing—where was he now, and should he tell Kaylie that he was fairly sure her mom was gone? She would hate him for keeping it from her, but he wasn't sure it was true, nor could he see any benefit to telling her at this moment. He suspected she understood the situation better than he let on.

His time on the bike had been meant to clear his mind, but today he was struggling. His eyes kept sweeping side to side, looking for dangers. He was well aware of how desperate many were now. Nearing the end of the next road, he saw a small paved lane. He had seen it countless times, but had never actually paid attention it, nor could he remember ever taking it. It was narrow and rough asphalt, about as good as all the rest now. His desire to discover overcame his caution, and he headed down the new route. The road curved through abandoned farmlands, several fallow, awaiting crops that would probably never again be planted.

As his Garmin noted twenty-two miles, he noticed the road he was on did not even show up on the little device's map. He considered turning back toward town. He stopped and downed most of a water bottle. His ears picked up the faint sound of an animal, and removing his helmet, he turned his head to hone in on the sound. It was louder now: bleating and the tinkling jingle of bells. *Someone here has goats,* he thought. He walked the bike a dozen yards and caught glimpses of the little gray and white goats frolicking near an unpainted wood house. It was more of a shed than a house, really, but Scott's attention was now on the black man sitting on the porch of the house.

"Ease yoself on ova, young fella."

Scott saw no weapon, and the man's words didn't seem threatening. He propped the bike against a fencepost, stepped out of his cycling shoes, and walked barefoot toward the man. "Afternoon," he said warmly.

"How ya doin? Name's Roosevelt, Roosevelt Jackson."

"Scott," he replied, "it's a pleasure."

The man looked ancient: dark, wrinkled skin and wispy, wild, white hair surrounded two bright and piercing eyes. *Do not underestimate this man*, Scott thought. "How'd you get so lucky to have the name of two presidents?"

"Only named for one president, the other came wit me from my pa," Roosevelt laughed deeply at that.

Scott shook the outstretched hand and took a seat on the steps leading up to the porch. "I wasn't aware anyone was still living down this road. You've been here the whole time?"

"I's been heah purt much all ma life," the man nodded, "born right ova dair in that back room. I don't get out much, need to head to town sometime soon and get some staples, but mosely I stays right chere. Just me and all the odder animals."

Scott had to tell the man that the town didn't exist anymore. "Roosevelt, are you aware the power went out worldwide, nearly a year ago?"

"Naw, suh, can't rightly say I do . . ."

Scott looked at the man with pure admiration, "I'm guessing by the lack of power lines you never even had electricity."

"Nah, no need fo it. I seen it when I wint tuh town. Seen it when I joined th'Army, sent me all over the world. I seen electricity and a whole lots mo'. Whole lots mo' . . . stuff I don't never care to see again."

"You're a veteran? A soldier?"

The old man spat something in the direction of an old coffee can beside the porch. "Nothin' special, son, lots o' boys did, lots of stupid runnin' round back din. Some on our side, some on their's. All fightin' over this li'l scrap o' sumpin or somebody else's. Killin' each otha for their insignificant li'l kingdoms. Kingdoms o' sorrow, that's all dat was. I don't talk 'bout it, not no mo'."

Roosevelt seemed pretty firm on that, so Scott let it go. "People have gotten pretty desperate out there since the power went out, lots have died. You haven't had any problems out here?"

The man laughed to show a nearly toothless grin, "Didn't say I ain't had problems. Few boys came sneakin round . . . purt sure one was escaped from a road gang. Best thang 'bout not having nuttin', ain't nobody wants to steal it."

"So, they left you alone?"

"Yeah, yeah . . . well, dat one needed a bit more encourgement, so I shot 'im and let 'im take it up with the hogs over yonda. His head prolly still in nair. The other one turned out, too. He weren't a bad guy, he was messed up a bit in da head. He don't talk none, but I gives him a li'l bit o' food ever now and again, den he leaves on his own. He leaves quick, dat one do, maybe wonring if ole' Roosevelt gonna feed *him* to the pigs, too," he chuckled at that.

"You fed one of them to the hogs? Roosevelt, remind me not to get on your bad side," Scott chuckled comfortably in return. He liked this old man.

"Naw, you fine, Mr. Scott . . . anybody comes here wearing a outfit like dat, ridin' a bike, can't be up ta too much bad. 'Sides . . . I got a feelin 'bout you. Gotta good feelin'. The good Lord gotchou workin' on sumpin' mighty important, don't he? You got de signs. Ole' Roosevelt can tell."

Scott wasn't sure what to make of the man, but looking around the homestead, he saw he seemed to have everything he needed: chickens, goats, hogs—even beehives in a neat row. A small washbasin full of greens that looked native to the area was on the table. This man lived in balance with nature. The world provided in proportion to the effort he put forth. "I suppose I am involved in something important, and I could really use your help."

The man grinned from ear to ear, "Well, come on inside, and lit's talk it over."

Several hours later, Scott patted his new friend on the shoulder, promising to come back. Roosevelt had shown him his small house and around most of the farm. It was compact in acreage but impressive in output. Scott felt this man had more practical knowledge than any farmer, hunter or fisherman he had ever met. His bushcraft skills seemed part Army Ranger and part Apache Scout. He had been married, was now widowed, had raised four children and, sadly, buried two. The other two lived elsewhere having retired from lifetimes of military service.

He had taught himself how to read, then how to write. Here was a man who was utterly self-sufficient: who calmly lived his life on the edge of survival without ever realizing it. Scott struggled to process it all; this genius had been sitting here peacefully, just a few miles away from him, all along. Scott realized that while he may be a leader in the community, Roosevelt should be king.

"Roosevelt, there may be some really bad people heading this way. If that happens, you know you can come to town and take shelter with us."

"I's don't take help easily, Mr. Scott, but if the Lord says go, I'll come knocking."

Scott nodded respectfully. "Is there anything you need, Mr. Roosevelt? Next time I come out, I can bring it."

"Naw, naw . . . dat's awful nice o' ya, but sounds like you guys ain't got much to spare. You best hang on to what you have." He started back up the rickety steps to the porch. "Course now, if you could find some of dem li'l hard lemony drop candies . . . I could prolly find a good trade for dat. I miss me some lemon candies," he grinned wide once more.

"I'll see what I can do, friend."

Scott pedaled back toward the town, struggling to reach it before dark. He knew he would be back to see Roosevelt. He had much, much more to learn.

CHAPTER FIFTY-TWO

Finally, a day off! Kaylie and DeVonte had been planning this trip to the beach all week. It wasn't a full day off, but none of the small group was complaining. With the never-ending lists of tasks each had just to help everyone stay alive, anything resembling recreation was rare and greatly appreciated.

Abe, Angel and several other of the "young ones" had joined them. Preacher Jack was even along, though he sat in the old lifeguard chair sipping a beer and reading. The ocean water was unusually clear, though still a little cooler than Kaylie preferred.

Abe kept looking at her strangely and made her glad she had the *Aquatic Goddess* t-shirt over her swimsuit. Angel and DeVonte were closer to shore. One of the other girls, Diane, was saying something to her about a ghost. Kaylie rolled her eyes to herself. "I don't believe in ghosts, that's just nonsense," she responded dismissively.

"No, Kaylie, not that kind of ghost. It's this shadow man thing people keep seeing around. He's there one minute and gone the next. Just seems to vanish."

"Right . . . does he fly off? Or just step into another dimension?"

"Fine, don't believe me." Diane pouted slightly before forging ahead. "No one seems to have gotten a good look at him, and he never speaks."

"Sounds like someone found Bartos' moonshine out there in the swamp if you ask me."

Diane nodded. "Could be . . . I don't really know. I do know people are feeling pretty freaked out. They say his head looks all messed up."

"I think maybe they're messed up, Diane," Kaylie said soberly. She looked out at the horizon and, slowly, a memory began to surface. Something Kaylie felt she should recall—the man she thought she saw on the beach? No, something else.

Just as the memory was forming, Angel came up behind her, interrupting the thought. "Hey, girl, DeVonte and I are heading back up. Didn't think you wanted to be left here with the big guy," she winked and gestured with her head towards Abe.

Kaylie knew whom she meant immediately. "He's harmless," she paused for a moment before laughing, "but yeah, I'd rather not."

"That boy has got you in his sights, girl," Angel teased.

"Kinda like DeVonte has you in his?" The two were obviously a couple now, and DeVonte overheard and grinned.

"She knew a good thing when she saw it," he laughed, then added, "Not sure yo' man DJ gonna be able to take ole' Abe in a fight, Kay. That boy is *big*. Unless your guy's been working out and stuff. What was it DJ does again?"

"He's an epidemiologist—or he will be."

DeVonte cracked a crooked smile, "And what is that again?"

"DeVonte, do you know anything?" she laughed and nudged him with her shoulder. "You do understand what the science of classifying living things is?"

"You mean racism?" He laughed at his own clever joke.

"Oh, God," Kaylie laughed too at the uncomfortable joke. She loved DeVonte in her own, sisterly way. "Biology, goober . . . all life on our planet is divided into kingdoms—classified life forms. There used to be just two: plants and animals. Now there are five or six, depending on the school of thought. They cover all forms of life, from the very simple to the very complex. DJ's work is mainly in a subphylum of bacteria. One that covers infectious disease origins. He also works with viruses and parasitic agents. Basically, he studies the origins of the life itself . . . how it evolved on its own, or in other non-human hosts." Angel and DeVonte both looked impressed. "He may not be able to defeat Abe in a fair fight, but I'm pretty sure he could out-think him," she concluded.

Abe looked up from whatever had his attention and over at the three friends. He smiled and gave a small wave.

"Okay, time to go," Angel said.

Glancing over, she saw Jack had fallen asleep in the sun. He was already beginning to turn pink. "Let me wake up the preacher, we don't want the old guy getting sun stroke," she smiled fondly in the man's direction. "I need to run something by him anyway. I'll catch up in a sec."

CHAPTER FIFTY-THREE

Mississippi River Confluence, Arkansas

It had taken four more days to get to the Mississippi River. They had lost time on one of the many switchbacks of the lower Arkansas River when it narrowed and split into multiple tributaries. They had pulled the boats up onto a wide sandbar. Bobby was showing Jacob how to fish with a handline, and Jordan was using the radio as Bobby had shown her. She scanned the channels, listening to various reports from and about the Messengers who were now heading south along the Mississippi River. The broadcasts were heart-wrenching: chaotic and ghastly in their detail. If Jordan had had any remaining doubts about fleeing her home, they were now gone.

With the help of the broadcasts, she was piecing together where the Messengers may be and marking spots on the river map. Jacob dropped two fish in the sand in front of her. The large catfish flopped about, desperate to be back in the water. The boy was beaming from ear to ear. "Did you catch those?" she asked with a broad smile.

He held up one finger.

"Which one?"

He pointed to the larger of the fish. She hugged her son excitedly and praised him. Looking over at Bobby, she mouthed a silent thank-you.

She deftly cleaned and filleted the fish, cooking them on hot rocks by the river. As they ate, she showed Bobby the map. "They're somewhere near the White River which runs parallel to the Arkansas for a good while, then joins the Mississippi. Basically, they're not far from where we are."

Bobby shoved the last bit of fish into his mouth before responding. "Let's hope they are on the north side of it. That way, we're divided by both rivers *and* the land in between. Otherwise, they may be right on our heels. Not many roads through here, so it'll be slow going for them, and no towns to speak of in that stretch. It's pure wilderness, so water and food will be a problem for them."

"Some of the reports are coming from people on the other side of the river," she said pointing to spots she had marked.

"Those areas have highways and roads. If I had to guess, I'd say they got split up during the Memphis attacks. Any vehicles remaining probably crossed the river to the east side closer to Memphis, then headed south."

"I thought we were crossing the river, too. What if they're already ahead of us?"

"It's possible, but this is not a developed area, on either side, and we can go south on the Mississippi much faster than what we've been doing so far. I'm not sure it will be fast enough . . . Scott suggested the idea, but it is slow. He could probably do five times what we can on his damn bike."

Her eyes met his, "What are you saying?"

"I think we need help. We can stay on the river, but we won't be gaining much time on those already on the other side. It'll also take us way too long to get to the coast. Besides, the river goes through some rough areas and ends in New Orleans, which is definitely not where we want to show up. We need to go south as fast as possible, maybe to

Vicksburg, then head inland and find another way to get to Harris Springs. If possible, ahead of the Messengers."

She looked at the man's trembling hand with its black cross tattoo. "Vicksburg must be a hundred or more miles away. You think we can stay ahead of them for that long? It'll take us several days to go that far."

Bobby was aware that she was watching his hand, and he forcibly willed it to stop shaking. "Maybe, but the Mississippi River has a much stronger current than the Arkansas. It'll probably push us faster than we can paddle. I would say three or four days, tops—but it will also be more dangerous. That current is not something we want to fool around with."

Looking down at her map, Jordan asked, "Do we have any choice?"

"No," he sighed. "Not really."

"Well, then." She was resolute. "Jacob, finish up, we need to get going." She folded the map and was clearing their plates before the boy even looked up.

Bobby and Jacob were both in the canoe and Jordan kayaked nearby as they paddled into the Mississippi River, the Big Muddy, accompanied by a flock of red-winged migratory birds that dove and scattered in the bright afternoon sky. All three now wore life jackets, and new rules had been laid out as to what to do if they were caught in the current, went overboard or got separated.

The confluence of the two rivers was intimidating. The rolling waves, several feet high, indicated the difference in current between the rivers. As they got into the deeper channel, the water smoothed out, and soon they were zipping downstream at a steady pace. Bobby took the time to show them how to use the paddles as a rudder for steering and how to look for eddies in the current where they could pull to a bank and rest. Despite the risks of the river and the dangers just behind them, they were having fun; this was an adventure. Occasionally catching the eyes of the boy sitting ahead of him, he knew Jacob was feeling the same.

The joyous side of the trip was short-lived. The riverbanks pinched in places, and the current got more anxious in its mad dash to the sea. The noise of the water was constant, and at several points, an incessant ringing became noticeable. The source of the sound soon became clear. Signs gave dire warnings that no vessels should enter: *EXTREME DANGER!* they read. The ominous sound of the flood control gates was warning enough to get the boat to the opposite side of the waterway.

For the most part, the sides of the river were barren. No towns, no bridges, no people. Bobby knew the Mississippi floodplain extended many miles in each direction, which meant very little development would have been allowed there. But on the river, it was a different story. Old docks, ships and boats of every size were littered up and down the shoals and banks. Remembering its history in a calmer moment, he said, "Jacob, we are on the largest river in the country. The Mississippi gathers water from almost forty states. The map we have is already nearly useless, as the river constantly reshapes itself. These riverboats probably got stranded after the power went out. With no radar or depth gauges—maybe even no engines—they were at the mercy of the water."

Jordan was paddling close enough to hear as well. She smiled to see how Bobby spoke to her son. She liked that he talked to him like he was . . . normal. Despite her reservations, she liked this man more and more. "Wouldn't some of these wrecks have supplies?" she asked.

"Possibly. It's a good suggestion," he called above the rush of the river, "but I imagine the river folk would have stripped them bare by now. Also, I don't feel confident enough in my skills to try and pull us up to one safely. We're moving at about twenty miles an hour or better right now. We hit one of these wrecks, and we might not make it back out. Might lose our boats," he concluded, though Jordan understood that he had left out the final details for the sake of her son.

Several miles farther down, the river went into one of its many large, sweeping bends. They stayed on the inside curve where the current was not so severe, and Bobby spotted a calm pool of water coming up. He pointed it out to Jordan, and they pulled off onto the shoals to rest and get some calories into their hungry bodies.

They were making excellent time, so Bobby felt good about taking these occasional breaks. The cramps from sitting in one position and working so hard to keep the canoe straight for hours on end were nearly constant, and he was still not fully recovered from his illness and the near starvation of the past months.

After a meal of dried fish, bread and homemade pickles, they noticed Jacob was gone. Just as they rose to look for him, the nose of a beige canoe appeared around the bend, with a single person paddling gently toward them.

Bobby had no time to pull his gun as the river pushed the boat the last thirty yards in mere seconds. The person in the canoe seemed to take notice of them slowly. It was a man: an older man in the kind of large, floppy leather hat once common to people in the area. In a relaxed mood, he raised his paddle with both hands and smiled. His canoe grounded itself gently on the sandbar. "Don't want any trouble, friend, just needed to take a rest if that's okay."

Bobby's hand was close to his holster, but he was not picking up any sense of danger from this man. He saw no weapons in the boat. He walked the few steps across the coarse sand and helped pull the man's canoe farther up onto the beach. He reached a hand out to help the stranger out. "No problem, friend."

The man eyed the tattoo on the outstretched hand before taking it. "You aren't with them, are you?"

As the man stood uneasily on the dry ground, Bobby realized what the man had seen and pulled that hand back somewhat self-consciously. "No, well . . . I was captured, but I got away. Name's Bobby, and this is Jordan."

"John, John Russell," the man said, shaking both their hands. Looking around, he said, "Lot of boats for just two people."

"We like to have backups," Jordan said.

"If you feel like talking, I'll sit with you. Otherwise, I will move over to the side and throw a fishing line in and not bother you fine people."

Bobby and Jordan looked at one another briefly. "We'd like the company," Bobby affirmed, "but we need to know if you're armed first."

John pulled up the buckskin jacket he was wearing and showed a hunting knife, which he removed and threw expertly into a piece of driftwood by his canoe. The point of the knife sunk deep into the solid tree trunk. He sat down and waited for them to speak.

"Are you from around here?" Jordan asked.

"On the river, all my life. When the lights went out, I didn't even know it for a week. I run an outfitter and guide service out of Greenville." He paused briefly, "Well, I did. Had a lot of wilderness trips down the river system." Jordan got up and began fixing the man some food. "No bother, ma'am, I have my own supplies. Don't want you wasting yours on me."

"It's fine, ours is already out, and some of it needs to be eaten soon," she said, handing him the metal camping plate, now stacked with food.

He nodded his thanks and between bites said, "You folks aren't from around here." It was not a question. "So, are you running from something, or to something? Care to let me in on what would force the two of you and a child out on the most dangerous river in the country?"

Bobby smiled. The man was no fool. "Child?" he asked with a grin.

"I'm sorry, I saw the smaller life jacket, and I can see those little footprints headed up into the trees. I caught sight of you guys on the river a few times, thought I could see three people."

Jordan had already caught sight of Jacob's hiding spot. She now motioned for him to come on back down. Bobby thought the boy seemed to have a sixth sense about danger.

"We're from Little Rock," Bobby replied, "and we are running from them." He held up the tattooed hand as an explanation.

John finished the food and greeted the boy with a smile. "Little Rock, huh? Damn, that's quite a haul. But this river's dangerous, man, don't you think you and your family are safer on land now?"

"Unfortunately, no," Bobby's brow furrowed. "The Messengers tangled in battle near West Memphis. Not sure who with, but we're relatively sure they're now being driven south. If we're right, and we've been tracking them pretty closely over radio transmissions, then they may be within a day's journey behind us already."

John absorbed all this without comment for several seconds. Nodding, he then said, "That'd make sense. Several days ago, we started seeing dead bodies floating downriver, lots of 'em. In bad shape, too. Burns, missin' parts. Man, it was bad. Someone did a number on 'em. All looked like you," he pointed at Bobby's hand to clarify. "No idea who they fought?"

"Well, we have an idea, but it's a crazy one." They proceeded to tell the story Scott had relayed to Bobby. John seemed to absorb it with ease. "You don't seem too surprised or concerned," Bobby remarked when he'd finished.

John leaned back, dug a finger into the sand and watched a gray wading bird easing through the shallows. He was slow to speak. "I nearly died on this river as a kid. Me and some friends built a raft and launched it upstream. We couldn't steer it . . . didn't even think about that," he chuckled ironically at the memory. "We were dumb shits. We crashed into the side of a control tower—you know, the big lock gates with the warning signs? We all survived, but just barely. My buddies never went near the water again, but I...well, I couldn't stay away. Something about the Mississippi that just makes you feel so small, so insignificant. It's a powerful beast, the heartbeat of this country. It didn't want to kill me, so I spent the rest of my life trying to learn its secrets." He stroked his long gray goatee. "Whatever these fools are doin' upstream don't bother me. I can hide out in a thousand places they will never find. Eventually, the river'll wash the filth of this land out like a giant pissing away the toxins from its healing body."

Bobby smiled, enjoying the analogy. Eventually, the conversation turned to destinations. Bobby was reluctant to give any precise information but said they wanted to head toward Mobile. They were planning to take the river down to Vicksburg then start heading east.

"You do realize that the Vicksburg Bridge is one of the only ones south of Memphis? That bridge is a toll bridge now, the cost to pass'll likely be your life, or at least your woman. Lord, where you think those Messengers on this side are goin' to be heading? I suggest you avoid Vicksburg altogether. You need to start heading east now . . . get over to near the Pearl River and head south t'ward Biloxi. Not easy these days either, not by boat anyway." He stayed silent a few moments before seeming to reach some conclusion.

"Listen, you seem like good people. What say I help you for a couple of days in trade for say, hmm, maybe a couple of jars of those pickles?"

Bobby and Jordan made eye contact before Bobby answered. "You charge a pretty steep price, John. I can see why your outfitting business didn't make it," he smiled playfully at the old man.

"Hey, I like pickles, and these, Jordan, are a masterpiece. So, what do you say?"

They reached an agreement and made plans to head out before dawn.

CHAPTER FIFTY-FOUR
Harris Springs, Mississippi

Todd entered the hangar as Scott was putting away the bike. "Hey, man, have a good ride?" Scott nodded enthusiastically, but Todd began again before he could speak. "Hey, we need to talk. The mission is a go. We have to head out before dawn."

"Are they sending a chopper?"

Todd nodded. "Yeah, it's coming in early, so we need to let everyone know we'll be out of touch for a few days. We also need to review the plans for . . . well, you know, if shit goes sideways. Come see me after dinner, and we can work out the details."

Scott went up to his cabin, taking a moment in the communal shower to wash off with the bucket of clean water, soap and rag that were always put there. Nothing like a real bath, but it kept the smells to a minimum.

He thought about what he was about to do, and his stomach flip-flopped. He then remembered he had promised Angel he would help with the cooking tonight. He supposed he could back out of it, but that wouldn't be right either. He also had to tell Kaylie he was going with Todd. He wasn't sure what her reaction would be.

Angel was wearing a hot pink bikini covered by a chef's apron. Several inappropriate thoughts flashed through his mind. The girl was beautiful, but DeVonte had fallen for her, and as such, she was off limits. Also, she was about a zillion years younger than him, but still . . . parts of him ignored all of those facts.

She looked up at him and grinned. "You like the new uniform?

"Very fetching."

"Sorry, I stayed out at the beach longer than I realized. Got behind prepping for the late meal. Kaylie said she was going to come help as well."

Scott picked up a knife and began peeling veggies. Several other cooks were already busy in the galley. He looked at the menu on the marker board and nodded. "I can handle the entrées and salads."

"Okay, but remember to use the most perishable items first. We have to make these vegetables last as long as we can." They took a few minutes deciding on the quantities of food for the number of people on board. The work was steady, and Scott found himself again sharing a lot with the young woman. She was easy to talk to, and everyone seemed as fond of her as they were of her boyfriend.

"So, where did you go ride off to today?"

"Just out in the county . . . some of the roads I used to ride every day before all this." He waved the knife around in the air for emphasis.

"How did it look? See anything interesting?"

"Looks the same, but rougher. I did meet someone, though, someone who I would call . . . very interesting." He proceeded to tell her about Roosevelt Jackson.

"That man sounds like a treasure! He could probably help us in more ways than we can imagine. It's just amazing someone could live their whole life off the grid like that."

Scott was nodding in agreement. "He would take some special handling. He's very independent, don't know that he would come here to help us easily. That farm and those animals are his entire world, and he is very contented with that world. I wanted to ask if you would be willing to go out there with me next time."

"Sure, Scott, I'd love to. We might want to let Bartos or Jack know where he is as well, so they can keep an eye out and check in occasionally when they go on patrols. Obviously, if the storm or the crazies head this way, we can try and get him to shelter with us as well."

"Good idea," he said. "Listen, I have to leave in the morning for a few days. It's kinda hush-hush, but the guys may need to rely on you more. Todd and I both are going to be gone."

She stopped slicing potatoes and looked up, "What are you up to, Scott Montgomery? I know Kaylie doesn't know you're going anywhere. I was with her all day."

"You were in the meeting, you know what it's about."

Angel caught the serious tone and the look of concern on his face and stood up straight. "Are you all going to go do something stupid?"

"Probably, but the Navy will protect us, and it's for the good of everyone here."

"Scott, haven't you done enough? You take more on than anyone." She paused in what she was doing to turn and look at him. "Kaylie said you used to be a loner, you lived alone, never went out. I can't even imagine you being like that. You do so much for so many people here."

"How do you imagine me?" he said in a playful tone he immediately felt awkward about.

"Well, not like that," she said nearly dropping the potato in her hand. "You're just, I don't know. You're a nice guy. I mean you're in charge, you and Todd. Everyone knows this is ya'll's ship, your town. But you help out, you're interested in others, and you are always looking for ways to make life better. I just see no selfishness in you, ever. I mean, here you are helping make dinner for hundreds of people you barely know."

Scott continued to peel and dice the vegetables, "I like to cook, no matter how many it's for. I'm also, well, I'm not that good. I've had to do some bad things, Angel. Things I'll spend the rest of my life trying to make amends for."

"Maybe so, but you're a good man, and I feel sure you never did anything bad to anyone that didn't have it coming. DeVonte talks about you constantly, he looks up to you like a hero, Scott. We're lucky to have you, and you better be coming back from whatever this damn fool adventure is tomorrow. You hear me?"

"I hear you," he said. "I'll be careful. The timing of it sucks, we have so much going on and so many things here that need attention. I just feel like none of it may matter if the Navy screws this up." He laid the knife down on the wooden block. He reached over and put his hand over hers. "Angel, I am extremely glad you are part of this crew. You are a leader, and you are wise. We need you, I need you...I need you to help take on the leader's role when Todd and I are gone. I know there's a badass under that apron," they laughed conspiratorially at that, but he continued, "and you're going to need to keep that part of you close at hand. I have a feeling we are all about to be tested."

She grinned at him and nodded slowly. Scott released her hand and patted it as she gripped the knife again. "Trust yourself, Angel, and the people around you. DeVonte is a good man, smart as anyone I know, use him if you get in a bind. If you do get a chance, you can get Roosevelt's location off my bike computer, he was the farthest point in my ride today. If you go out there, take him some candy—lemon drops if you can find any. He will adore you. You and DeVonte should go out and make a day of it, take the Jeep."

She nodded and walked by him on her way to the sink. Stopping behind him, she leaned in and gave him a hug and planted a kiss on his cheek. "Just come back, we need you."

CHAPTER FIFTY-FIVE

At 4:30 am Todd was waiting for Scott by the roof deck's landing pad.

"Morning, brother," he said as Scott approached. "Did you get any sleep?"

"Not much," Scott said, slinging into his 72-hour go-bag. After he'd spoken to Kaylie, he had tried to sleep, but her worry and his concerns for the ship had kept him awake 'til well after midnight. In the distance, he could hear the familiar sound of an incoming chopper. They hadn't been told exactly where they were going, but they assumed they'd be taken to one of the command vessels.

The pilot stopped forward momentum and dropped cleanly to the small deck with an efficient and practiced motion. Several men greeted Todd and Scott and helped them load up. The helicopter rose before the cabin door was slid shut. They picked up headsets from the seats, buckled in and said good morning to the naval aircrew.

Scott spoke again into the microphone, "I guess we woke up the *AG*."

"Probably," came Todd's reply. "Although it's hard to hear much of anything from the passenger decks. I told Bartos to make an announcement if people took notice. And I told him and Angel to keep an eye on that storm."

The storm. Scott looked out over the dark sea. Everything looked calm, but somewhere several hundred miles south it was building. "So, the entire schedule is predicated on this storm?"

Todd nodded, "Yeah. It's expected to be quite a blow. Garret thinks it will help cover the insertion. Navy SEALs don't need clear skies."

"What about the *AG*? Will she be okay?"

Todd nodded, "She should be fine, even in a major hurricane. This one's just a strong tropical storm. All the same, I told the bridge crew to run the radar several times a day to keep track of it."

The trip took them several hours, and the morning sky was lightening when they first saw the gray flotilla from several miles out. The announcement came over their headsets: "Traveler two-eight, this is flight. You are clear to land on the aft deck."

The chopper was heading for the lone carrier in the small grouping of ships. They touched down gently, and the men stepped onto the busy, noisy tarmac of the floating runaway. An officer wearing a blue cap with *USS Bataan* embroidered in gold escorted them toward the bridge wing.

Commander Garret greeted them warmly. Scott thought the man had aged considerably since he'd last seen him the previous year. He liked Garret, thought he was a man with remarkable conviction and intelligence. Scott understood why Todd was so loyal to the man, and to his mission.

Once inside, the sounds from the flight deck were much less noticeable.

"Gentlemen, glad you could join us. Your help on this mission is extremely valuable to us."

"Did you change ships?" Scott asked. "Where's the rest of your fleet?"

"No, Scott, just over here for this mission. Much of our fleet is involved in another operation. *The Bataan* is a Wasp-class carrier, and beyond flight operations, it has some special attributes including the best medical facilities in the fleet. We even have full level-four containment facilities if we need them. I will be transferring back to my command flagship tomorrow or the next day."

Todd asked, "Do we have a schedule yet?"

"Not precisely. The storm is strengthening but also slowing its northern progression. We need to be ready to go when it arrives. I wanted to go ahead and get you guys out before we turn south. The *Bataan* will get within fifty miles of the platform and hold position. We don't think they can spot us that far out, but we've also located several derelict vessels drifting in the Gulf currents at about that same spot and plan to stick with that mass in case the ship is detected. Best guess on time is forty-eight to seventy-two hours from now. In that time, we'll get you guys kitted out, go over comms, talk you through the operation and, of course, introduce you to the rest of the team. For now, Ensign Patillo will escort you to your cabins." A young man took the bags from both men and led them away.

Several hours later, Garret introduced the insertion team with a minimum of formality. The nearly two-dozen men and women looked battle-hardened and very capable for the fight ahead.

Garret turned to introduce Todd and Scott. "These men are civilians with a unique perspective on the bio-lab's status and medical team. They also helped us determine the lab's actual location. While they are not combatants, you need to pay attention to what they have to say. They know the risks, and more importantly, they know the friendlies."

Todd deferred to Scott when it came to doing the talking. Scott brought the group up to speed on DJ and the research teams. The special ops battlegroup was already aware of the pathogen's lethality. Scott did not want to sugarcoat it. "Guys, listen, it will never be more serious than this. If you do not secure that lab, the samples *and* the researchers, it may be the end for all of us, I don't just mean the people in this room. Everything!" He drew the last word out for emphasis.

"I know your training and mission-op probably says treat everyone as the enemy until you know otherwise. In this case, that could be catastrophic. That research team is our only hope to find a cure for this disease—a disease that's wiping human civilization off the face of the Earth. From what our man on the inside says, none of these scientists is our enemy. In fact, it seems that for the most part, they are clueless as to what's going on outside that lab. Most believe they are still doing important work for DARPA. They are not our enemy. I know that throws a challenging element into the mission, but I can't stress this enough."

The planning of the mission had been ongoing since Todd provided Garret with the lab's location. Scott was surprised to learn that the SEALs were trained to both attack and defend oil rigs. This was good news.

"Oil platforms offer very appealing targets to terrorists," one of the SEAL commandos explained. "Not only does occupation offer the prospect for interfering with the flow of oil and the destruction of a valued asset, but there's also the potential to cause a large-scale environmental disaster. Think of the problems resulting from the Deepwater Horizon oil spill near here."

Todd whistled. "Never considered it, but it makes sense."

The Navy SEAL, whose name was Perez, continued, "Infiltrating a rig is not an easy task. Be much easier just to destroy it—launch missiles at it and watch it burn—but on most of our training missions we had to assume it was a hostage situation and, of course, be cognizant of the environmental damage that destruction would cause. These big rigs hold tens of thousands of gallons of oil and often have multiple drills and pumping lines flowing up from the seabed, as well as a pipeline transporting oil and natural gas away to pumping stations. We've worked for years on tactics for a scenario like this."

"Care to share any of it with us?" Scott asked. He and Todd were beginning to get comfortable with the men.

Perez and another man nodded, "We've been cleared to give you the basics. The problem is the approach. We must assume they have radar looking out, CCTV cameras pointing down and a tremendous sight advantage thanks to their elevation. There's really only one way that's viable."

The other man chimed in: "From above."

"Above? Won't they hear that?" Todd asked.

"Not with what we're going to use," Perez said with a grin. "We have a couple of stealth choppers that will deliver some of the crew by fast ropes to the top deck. They will be supported by other assault teams coming in from other locations."

As they got down to the actual operations, Scott had to admit it seemed plausible. As the first team dropped from the stealth choppers, another team would be approaching underwater via Swimmer Delivery Vehicle: essentially a small ride-on submarine. The last and largest force would be coming in using the Navy's M80 Stiletto—a fast attack craft designed to present little or no profile on radar—and a new, experimental Safehaven Barracuda Interceptor—a small stealth craft that was both extremely fast and resilient. These forces were to be backed up by long-range snipers placed on neighboring platforms and regular attack choppers once the offensive began.

"As you can see," Perez said, "the worsening weather is vital to masking these multiple approaches but does also present a much higher degree of difficulty."

Scott made eye contact with the man, "You guys are aware of how good the men and equipment you're going up against are, don't you?"

"Yes, sir. Praetor units were handpicked from elite branches of service all over the world. Their training is as good as ours, and their weaponry may even be better."

Scott knew that it had to be difficult for the man to admit this. "Perez, you and your men must assume they are the best. That they will not make mistakes. They believe they are right just as much as you believe you are. In their minds, they are defending civilians who are trying to save the world from a pandemic. Your plan is good . . . but is it good enough to defeat Praetor and preserve the lab and its scientists?"

The SEAL commander, a large man named Ramos, spoke up at this point. The man had remained silent thus far. "Mr. Montgomery, you make an excellent point, and as we all know from experience, no plan ever survives first contact. We will have to improvise and adapt to whatever our enemy presents us with. We may take losses. It is likely that not everyone in this room will return. My team knows the risks, but they also understand the cost of failure. We will not fail."

CHAPTER FIFTY-SIX

Grenada, Mississippi

"Pete, where in the fuck are we?"

Pete looked at Hawley's ruined face. Burned hair and blackened skin surrounded raw tissue that was struggling to heal. "I don't fucking know. Somewhere near a town called Grenada. Maybe a hundred miles down to Jackson, Mississippi."

Hawley watched Michael; the man looked much less like a prophet now—more like a pauper. The ferocity of the attacks in Memphis had taken them completely by surprise. The drone attacks took out thousands of God's Army along with most of the technical trucks and their heavier mounted guns. They'd even destroyed the Jesus Bus. Then came the jets, which had pursued them for miles, until they were deep into Mississippi. Hawley had been next to a Humvee when it was hit by a rocket, the blast from which incinerated two men near him. The Messengers had been divided by the coordinated attacks; most of the surviving ground forces were still over on the Arkansas side of the Mississippi River, but they, too, were heading south. What remained of the Messengers was the core of the movement, Michael assured them: the true followers of the Prophet. The conscripts that had been used as cannon fodder lay dead in the fields, forest and rivers around Memphis.

Hawley looked over at his leader with pity. "Michael, we aren't strong enough to hit Jackson. We lost too many men and too much equipment. I suggest we hunker down and tend to our injuries." They had been going nonstop for days with little food, no sleep and countless injuries that required more treatment than they could provide. They had been tossing out more dead and dying hour upon hour. Hawley estimated that less than 4,000 of the original 15,000 in God's Army remained alive. "We need to find food . . ." he breathed heavily, "nearly all of our supply trucks were destroyed."

Michael looked up and spoke with quiet fury in his voice. "The Lord will provide."

"Fuck that," Pete replied in anger. "We need food and water, not religion. This whole fucking crusade is a sham. Everyone knows—"

The sentence died on his lips moments before the pistol disappeared back into the folds of Michael's robe. The echo of the gunshot sounded through the forest.

"Hawley, get that out of my sight." He kicked Pete's body with the toe of his boot. "Send out patrols to find food and set us a route east of Jackson; somewhere remote . . . somewhere peaceful. Keep trying to contact the other groups and tell them where to rendezvous. Also . . ." Michael toyed with the medallion around his neck, "have we heard anything else from our friend? The one who was trying to get into the town with the cruise ship?"

Several hours later they were gathered in a small copse of trees overlooking a clearing near a large lake. "So, what in the fuck is that?" Hawley asked Michael.

"It appears to be some sort of school or camp," Michael said, lowering the field glasses. "Send in whatever Judges we have left to round 'em up first."

"Yes, sir," Hawley sighed, exhausted. He could tell the old Michael was coming back around. They had all been hit hard by the recent defeat, but Michael worst of all. He had all but dropped the role of the Prophet now and returned simply to the ruthless, bloodsucking bastard that had originally started the band of mercenaries that would become the Messengers.

The camp that they'd stumbled upon, hiding here in the deep forest of the Pearl River State Wildlife Management area, was once a Boy Scout jamboree site. Along with the Boy Scouts and the odd scout leader were numerous stragglers from the area, including over three hundred surviving grad students and their freeloading friends from the Mississippi Valley State University up in Itta Bena, Mississippi. The refuge had become a millennials' haven thanks to the Scouts' know-how and ample food supplies from the surrounding lakes, river and forest. The scenes that had played out over the last ten months resembled Orwell's *Animal Farm*. Most of the group was male; those now in charge had once been the affluent older college boys. They were also the ones who did the least work.

Matthew Baker was an Eagle Scout. He had not yet been to college. He didn't much care for the group here anymore, but he also had no idea how to get home. Home for him was just north of Charleston, South Carolina, and like all the other people here, he had no car or way out; the Scouts had all come by bus from Jackson last August. The jamboree was supposed to last two weeks. Then the lights went out, buses quit running and phones and radios died. Since then, the group of over 2,000 Scouts from all over the South had dwindled down to just a few hundred.

They had done their best once they realized they were on their own. As others found the camp, they learned more of what had gone on out in the world and had decided to stick it out where they were. They had developed a system based on skills, kept the campsite pristine, learned to purify water, and made do with the basics. Then busloads of college kids began showing up.

Matthew couldn't blame them for wanting to find a safe place of refuge, but why did it have to be here? The grounds had quickly become filthy with litter and feces. Mud had replaced grass; they had no respect for the place. If the truth be known, he'd have rather been at home playing video games, too, but he also liked Scouting and took satisfaction from being self-sufficient. Scouting had taught him more about himself than it did about bushcraft or survival.

He heard the approaching sounds of motorcycles as he was returning to the camp with fresh water. He ducked down to hide immediately, knowing the sounds did not bode well. He left the larger water containers, tightened his pack and jogged deeper into the nearby woods.

Two hours later, Michael and the remainder of the main command battalion of Messengers rolled into the clearing. The Judges had surrounded the campground and marched everyone back inside the muddy tent. "Fuck, it stinks down here," one of the men said. "They were living like pigs," echoed another.

Michael stepped down and walked to the edge of the assembled group of young men. "It smells like loneliness and masturbation. What did you do with all the girls?" All of Michael's men laughed. "Who's in charge here?" A young man with a stained and torn college sweatshirt on stepped forward and proudly said, "I am." Michael shot him in the head. "Nope... wrong answer, college-boy. One more time, who's in charge here?"

"You are," came several stuttering and frightened responses.

"Alright, you totally awesome millennial snowflakes, listen up! You're special and unique and all that horseshit. We all know you are loved and adored and missed by your families. I would absolutely love to take the time to get to know each and every one of you, but, well... honestly, I'm working through some issues right now, and I am a bit on edge. But listen...and this is really important. I need you to put away all your participation trophies and forget about updating your Face-book status because, well...all you bastards are about to die." With that he stepped back out of the circle of men and gave the signal, and the gathered Judges began firing into the crowd without mercy. Every one of the nearly 600 campers was dead within seconds. All but one; Matthew watched in horror at the carnage from his hiding place.

"Fucking millennials," said Hawley as he walked by the mass of bodies. "Burn 'em! Gather the supplies and then burn it all."

CHAPTER FIFTY-SEVEN

Hawley was in too much pain from his injuries to concentrate on his job. With Pete gone, he'd had to promote two others to help take some of the load off: Cyrus, who'd been with them since Kansas, and a tall, Nordic-looking man named Iklin. Neither man appeared that happy with the promotion and were well aware of the fate the previous man with the title had met. With considerable effort, Hawley sat up from his makeshift bed and took the report.

"You're telling me there are no reserves of food or supplies in this camp?"

"Correct, sir. It looks like just barely enough food to feed everyone a meal, two at best."

Hawley shook his head. "Can't be. How were they staying alive? Fuckin' college boys couldn't take care of themselves."

"They have lots of snares, nets and fishing gear," the large blonde man answered nervously. "Looks like they were hunting and fishing. Living off the land."

Hawley picked a large piece of dead, blackened skin from his forearm, revealing the oozing and bloody meat below. "Well, ain't that just fuckin' lovely? Cyrus, please tell me you have better news."

"Yes, sir. The others are beginning to regroup, although they're strung out all up the Arkansas line. They are making plans to cross over at Vicksburg and rejoin us. It'll take them a few days, maybe a week. I told them to look for riverboats and trucks along the way to speed up their arrival."

"Good idea," Hawley nodded with his eyes closed.

"Sir, some of the news wasn't as good. The . . . the commanders say the number of survivors is well below what we thought. Most of the injured have died or been left behind. Many more are dying on the trek south."

"So, you're telling me what? We don't even have 4,000?"

"Taking into account all the estimates, it's probably more like 2,800."

Hawley thought on this. It wasn't a big deal; new converts were easy enough to find, but it did limit the size of the targets they could overcome.

"So, we can't take any of the larger towns. Still, we need to find supplies. Even 3,000 need a shitload of food. Okay, get with the Judges and Marauders and decide what smaller towns to target next. Tell them to keep us moving south and east."

"Sir?"

"What!" Hawley demanded, his patience at an end.

"Sorry, sir, it's just that the Marauders are gone. None made it out of Memphis."

"Fuck, yeah . . . talk to the Judges then."

CHAPTER FIFTY-EIGHT

Harris Springs, Mississippi

DeVonte looked over at Angel, which was something he thoroughly enjoyed doing as often as possible. "What? Are you done?" she demanded. Grinning, he went back to work on the console. "I'm obviously distracting you," she rolled her eyes with a bright smile his way. "I'm going to go see if Solo can take my place. I'm no help with the computer stuff anyway."

He was going through the command sequence that Scott had suggested. "No, I'm almost there, and I'm gonna need you to help me operate the dish. Besides, that dog always looks at me like I'm lunch."

"Solo's a sweetie," she chided him. Her fingers stroked the length of her left leg, which was folded beneath her in the chair. It wasn't just DeVonte who was distracted; she couldn't stop thinking about the previous night. Despite her reservations about getting close to him, DeVonte had proven himself a thoughtful boyfriend and a very attentive lover. A flush of heat radiated from her groin in response to the memory. "Okay, I have to do something else." She leaned over, kissed him and walked away.

DeVonte was puzzled, but let it pass. He had to get this interface working between the radar and the ship's GPS. Accurate telemetry would allow them to track the storm, and the onboard forecasting computer would give relatively accurate predictions for the storm track, wind speeds and even potential wave height and storm surges.

He slid the office chair over to the radar controls and hit the commands to start up the dish. Then he went back to the modified laptop he was using as a replacement for the forecasting terminal. When he activated the interface port, data was coming in, but it was not corresponding to the built-in templates. He could see more of the edge of the storm on the maps now. To him, it seemed to be getting bigger, but he had no frame of reference to compare it to. He turned the dish back off and returned to the chair. Looking down at Scott's notes, he tried the next method.

Angel headed down to the gym to work off some of her energy and was not surprised to find Kaylie and Jack busy with Keysi self-defense training. It was a ritual for them every morning. She had even tried it a few times until she realized it was not simply exercise. Kaylie and Jack often both left the sessions with cuts and deep bruises.

Jack looked up at her arrival, "Hey, chief, any problems?"

"No, Preacher, and don't call me chief. DeVonte's trying to finish up the radar thing for the storm, Abe's on duty in communications, and Bartos is, well, somewhere doing whatever it is Bartos does."

"Are you planning to go see any more of the farms today?" Jack said, just before Kaylie's foot swept his legs out from under him and he fell, winded, to the floor. That girl did not play when it came to training.

Angel put her towel on the weight bench and straddled it. Looking at the man lying on his back now, she replied, "Yeah, I'm just waiting for DeVonte to finish up, I'm not supposed to go alone."

Jack was back on his feet again, blocking several kicks and elbow strikes from Kaylie. "I'll go with you if DeVonte can't. Actually, I'd like to go either way."

"Sure. Glad to have you."

~

It was late morning before DeVonte got the radar tracking system working. They now only needed to run the system a few times a day to track the storm's progress. Angel and Jack had loaded into the Jeep and headed out to the farms. Now that she had a better idea of what to expect from the storm, she could let the farmers know how bad it might be and when it would likely be hitting the coast. Most of them declined shelter on the ship; heading to the coast in a hurricane seemed counter-intuitive to them; the locals that were closer to the old town of Harris Springs agreed to come without reservations.

While early season hurricanes were rare, they did happen. The storm was not a hurricane yet, but the computer said it would be within the next few days. They would bring in the shelter seekers' extra supplies, precious farm equipment and animals. Jack knew the deck layouts better than anyone and had assigned each category its own dedicated location. Bringing the livestock on board would stink up the place, but it was far better than losing them.

Angel had been to most of the farms in the area more than once. Her familiar face and easy demeanor put everyone at ease. Jack noticed more than one of the old goats staring just a bit too long at her. She took the "sugas," "hons" and "babes" like a trooper. Her kitchens depended on these guys getting their crops planted and harvested. It was worth the price of a few lingering looks and inappropriate comments.

Everyone had crops planted, and most were doing well, but the rain from the upcoming storm was badly needed.

"Suits me fine if it just dumps all that water on us," one of the farmers said.

They still had not decided on the signal that would let everyone know to come on in, but for now, they all agreed to use DeVonte's estimates on when the storm would make landfall. Jack assured them the bridges and ferry would be ready. Bartos had worked out a modified schedule for lowering the drawbridges back into the town. "If you're moving animals, get them there well before the storm's arrival. Bring extra straw for mucking the stalls and hay for food."

Heading farther out to reach the more outlying farmers, Jack checked his sidearm and chambered a round. "Angel, this is a real test. As a town, I mean—a society. Are we going to be able to pull together and survive as a community? We went through it last year when we had to take out that gang of thugs, but that's nothing compared to this."

"It will be fine, Preacher."

The remainder of the farm visits went smoothly. None of them had run into problems with looters or gangs. The frequent patrols now coming out of Harris Springs seemed to be keeping problems to a minimum. These farmers planned to shelter in place; they were far enough inland that they were confident the storm shouldn't be a problem. As Angel turned the Jeep onto an unmarked side road, Jack looked at her, confused.

"Young lady, if you're planning to take me to a hideaway and have your way with me, I just won't stand for it. Though I will be more than happy to lie down," he said with a yawn.

"Hush, you dirty old man," she quipped. "I just want to check on a man Scott told me about." She pulled to a stop outside the coordinates she had gotten from the little cycle computer.

"I never knew anyone lived out here," Jack said. "Shit, I didn't even realize this was a road."

Getting out of the Jeep, Angel took a look around and called for the hermit gentleman. "Mr. Roosevelt? Mr. Roosevelt, I'm a friend of Scott Montgomery. Are you home?" Angel approached the house slowly with her arms raised. In one hand was a clear package with hard yellow candies inside.

A shuffling sound came from inside, then the door opened. "Mercy, child, I much rather see you than that other fella!" he beamed, "Get on up heah." Roosevelt saw Jack and motioned for him to come up as well. "I was jus' about tuh eat, come on an' I'll fix yawl good folks some. Oh, my! What's that dis pretty young thing's holdin'?"

She handed him the lemon candies, and the old man's eyes lit up like it was Christmas. "I like dat Scott," he smiled at them both. "I like him just fine. I better put dese up, for now. O'erwise I'll eat 'em all." He gave Angel a hug and shook Jack's hand. "Come on in."

He sat them down in the small kitchen. The neat table was empty save for a jar with an exquisite single orchid. He brought over small dishes of fried chicken, fresh butter beans, sliced tomatoes and two other vegetables that neither visitor could identify. "Glad yawl made it out when y'did, we gotta baaad storm comin' in a few days, ya know."

Jack and Angel exchanged an amazed glance. "Thank you, Roosevelt, we really don't want to take your food, though, times are tough," Jack said, even though his mouth was watering.

"Oh, hush up and fix a plate, you think I cooked all this jus' fuh me? Not sure what you mean about tough times neither, same as it's always been for ole' Roosevelt."

Angel and Jack thoroughly enjoyed the meal and the older man's company. They agreed with Scott's assessment that he was someone they could learn a great deal from. Angel helped clear the table, then sat back down, staring at the flower. "This is an orchid, isn't it? I've never seen one this color or this beautiful. Do you raise them?"

"No, child, no . . . the bayou does that all on its own. There's a spot deeper down inna swamp where dae grow wild. It's a hard, ugly place, tough to get to, but e'ry year a few o' dese flowers bloom there, and no one ever even sees 'em." He pulled the jar that was acting as a vase closer and smelled the blossom. "The good Lord will always put a bit o' beauty in the middle o' the ugly."

Jack read a lot into that statement and very much agreed with the man. "So, you already know about the storm. We wanted to ask you if you would be interested in taking shelter with us in town. We have a large cruise ship at anchor, and it should be fine no matter how bad it gets. Also . . . um," Jack struggled with the wording; he didn't want to alarm the kind, old man. "There may be some bad people heading this way. Scott may have mentioned them. We're preparing for a possible attack. I'm not sure if you're better off here or with us if that does happen, but we just wanted you to be aware."

"I appreciate that, Mr. Jack. Do these people coming, do they know God?"

Jack looked briefly at the worn Bible sitting on the table near the flower. "Mr. Roosevelt, they are evil people. That's about all we know about them. They claim to be doing God's work, but what they spread is in truth only hatred and death."

"They's a plague, then," the old man said in recognition. "I seen other groups use religion like dat, just to give an excuse for 'em to keep on bein' bad. I got no time for that. You make a mockery o' the Lord's word, you deserve to be punished. Remember the Amalekites!"

The discussion lasted nearly an hour longer before Angel reached over and took the old man's hand. "So, will you come with us, or at least come in before it gets bad? I need you to teach me more about how to forage and a whole lot more."

"We'll see, honey, we will see. I think I'm fine right here. I got my animals that need me, but if it's the Lord's will, I might come and stay awhile wit you good folks when the time comes."

"Please do," they both said, rising to leave.

"Thank you for the meal and the company, Roosevelt. You've a standing invitation to come in whenever you want. We will gladly return the hospitality," Jack shook his big, calloused hand.

The old man laughed and nodded. "I appreciates that, I do, yes sir, I do, and you all are welcome back at my table anytime. Friends are good to have. Always remember that. Specially friends wi' lemon candy."

CHAPTER FIFTY-NINE

Mississippi River, Mississippi

Bobby watched the silent child as he paddled the canoe downstream. John was in the lead boat and Jacob never seemed to take his eyes from the riverman. For the past two days, they had ventured farther south with the help of this man as their guide. Together they had navigated the treacherous waters of the wide Mississippi and added fish and turtles to the menu each day. Jordan kayaked just behind them, keeping an eye on the group.

She pulled her kayak up closer to talk. "My ass is killing me. It's raw from staying wet and rubbing on this hard plastic every day. How much longer are we staying in these damn things?"

This was the first complaint he could recall hearing from the woman. "I don't know, but we have to be getting near Vicksburg by now, and I know John wanted to get off the river before that. Do you want to take the canoe for a while?"

She eyed the hard, flat board that served as Bobby's seat and shook her head. "No thanks, it'd take too long to swap out anyway . . . I can manage."

In a slightly louder voice, she asked, "Jacob, you doing okay?"

The boy turned briefly to his mom and nodded yes before returning his eyes back to the canoe ahead.

It was late afternoon before John signaled a stop. He had guided them several miles up an inlet river on the Mississippi side. They had been fighting the current, but against the slower-moving tributary, it had been manageable. On land, John helped pull the boats ashore.

"Say goodbye to the Big Muddy," he said with a chuckle. "This is where we head eastward."

"Thank God," Jordan sighed with a smile. "I'm going to start us some dinner," she said, as she began to unpack the cooking gear.

Sitting down and pulling off his damp socks and shoes, Bobby asked John what the plan was.

"Well, like I said the other day, no easy way to get where you want to go from here. Lots of creek and rivers, but they're mostly flowing into the Mississippi, not in the direction you want. We're 'bout thirty miles from Vicksburg, and I'm not goin' to risk getting any closer. So, from here, well, let's just say it gets more challenging. I'll stick with you guys for maybe one more day, just to get you pointed in the right direction, but that's about it for me."

"Okay, friend, we appreciate what you've done so far and whatever additional help you can give. So . . . do we leave the boats and start on foot?"

John laughed. "No, no, not yet. We're goin' to head upstream on this creek for about half a day. Back up in the direction of Yazoo. There's a system of even smaller creeks—actually, they're just old irrigation canals. We can weave our way south and east from there. Then we'll have to portage over land over to the Big Black River. That passes close to the Pearl River. That's where I'm going to need to leave you. You can take the Pearl as far south as you want, even all the way down to the coast, although, I would suggest otherwise."

Bobby was following along, looking at the map. "That sounds like a solid plan. May not be a direct route, but at least we won't be walking hundreds of miles." He wasn't looking forward to paddling upstream that far, but the current was mild compared to what they had been on thus far.

Jordan did her best with the meal, but all were too tired to stay up afterward. With darkness fully settling, the fireflies began to light up the darkness, and they all turned in. Bobby was exhausted, but sleep refused to come. The soft sounds of Jordan's sleep reminded him of Jess; how he could lie there beside her and just listen to her breathing. His thoughts eventually took him back to his final moments with her.

The dog attack was the beginning of the end. She was bleeding out; he knew it, and so did she. As he carried her through the woods, the sounds of men and more dogs closed in behind. In the darkness, branches kept striking him, and twice he had caught his foot on exposed roots that nearly took them down. *That's all it would take*, he thought then. Who was he kidding, he wasn't getting out of this alive. No one ever got away. Suddenly, he had broken out into the clearing.

Three motorcycles stood side by side. A man was casually leaning against one of the bikes. Judges bikes. Where were the other two? He lay Jess down as quietly as possible. The other man looked at him in amusement.

"I don't think they allow you to take 'em home, brother." Bobby knew he had seen the tattoo. He could again hear the dogs.

Thinking fast he said, "She was a runaway, from the pleasure camp. Clubbed her bedmate and fled."

"Damn," the Judge said. "That's fucked up. I thought they kept 'em juiced to the gills in there?"

Bobby forced a grim laugh, "Yeah . . . guess not enough for this one. Hey, you got a smoke?"

The man searched his pockets, "Yeah. Let me find 'em."

Bobby approached the other motorcycle and saw the sheathed knife in the saddlebag. He slid it out as the man finally found the pack of ciga-

rettes. Palming the knife, he continued to move toward the unsus-
pecting man.

Holding out the pack with one cigarette extended, the man took
notice of the sounds. "Those dogs are getting closer, didn't you radio in
that you had her?"

Out of the man's sight, Bobby switched the knife to his dominant hand
and reached for the cigarette with his other.

"Wait a minute, where's your rad—" The knife blade plunged deep into
the Judge's heart and Bobby jerked it upward, cutting through organ,
bone, and muscle. The man collapsed beside his bike.

Bobby rushed back to Jess. She was very near death now. He looked at
the knife in his hands. *Please no*, he begged, looking up at the sky.

Bobby woke from his fitful sleep sweaty and panicked. Within a
moment he recalled that many days—weeks, even—had passed since
Jess had died. He worked hard to calm his breathing so as not to wake
the others. Finally, he drifted off once more, just as the birds began
to wake.

Morning brought fog and a cold breakfast of smoked fish and hard,
leftover biscuits. They had gone through much of the food they had
brought with them by now, which was both good and bad. It was good
because it would mean less weight to pack across land when they had
to leave the boats; bad because it also meant they had less variety of
things to eat. While they ate and packed up, Jacob disappeared along
the riverbank and sandbars, and in the fog, Bobby feared the boy
would get lost or hurt. They didn't have time to go looking for him.
His mother never seemed that concerned, though, and each time she
called he appeared within seconds. Bobby decided the boy had just
perfected the art of hiding. It was now his natural instinct to be wary.

"Time to get moving," John said. They had argued briefly over abandoning one of the boats; towing the extra kayak against the current for

no real reason seemed foolish. Bobby thought they could better divide up the gear and leave the extra boat. In the end, John made the decision easier. "Leave the extra gear on the spare, and I'll tow it. I'm probably the strongest on the water, I'll be glad to haul it a few more miles."

Several times Bobby lost sight of John in the fog and convinced himself the river rat had paddled off with their gear, but each time the fog would eventually diminish, and he could see the man paddling calmly up front. They paddled onto another larger river: the Yazoo. The current was not strong, but it was tiring nonetheless; the river had numerous shoals and rapids where the boats bottomed out and had to be pulled or carried. By midafternoon, the fog was long gone, and the heat was rapidly approaching unbearable.

They were in a long stretch of open land with no trees. "Floodplains," John declared. "'Riginally, the Mississippi River would flood all o' this every few years. It helped replenish the soil, and the farming here was excellent. Then, when the government decided they needed to control the river, they put in the levees and the flood control gates. Solved one problem but caused another . . . anyway, this land began to die without the regular flooding, so they started cutting in the long canals and irrigation ditches. That helped a little, but now most o' the farmin's also gone elsewhere. The canals are still around, though, if you know where to look."

A short while later they saw him turn to one side and seem to disappear into the bank of the river. As they closed the gap, they could just make out a small opening and a tiny stream of water. Paddling toward it, they were surprised to see the weed-choked entrance gave way to an open channel of water that ran straight for miles ahead.

The channels were a maze. Bobby tried tracking the number of turns they took but eventually gave up. Some were little more than drainage ditches, while others were the size of the first. Several times John beached and instructed the group to portage over several hundred yards to another canal. As darkness began to close in, they heard the sounds of a river nearby. "That'll be the Black River," John said. "The

Big Black. To be honest, it's not that big, nor is it black, but we won't be on it for long. Let's camp here tonight."

Bobby looked out over the small river; it reminded him of the one behind Sanderson's house. The banks were covered with roots and trunks of fallen trees. The muddy water was only a few feet deep. As a kid, he would have dragged his brother down every day to a place like this to fish or swim or just have adventures. Now, it was an adventure for real, but not one he much cared for any longer. This meager channel was his highway, his road to safety; at least he hoped it was. He saw Jacob up in the trees; he was also looking at the river. It seemed to bring the boy no joy now either. *What's going on in his mind?* Bobby wondered.

They were on that river for only a few miles when John signaled them to stop. "End of the road for me, troops. I'm going to ride this on down to below Vicksburg and back out to the mighty Mississippi. The Pearl River's 'bout, hmmm, ten miles east. That's going to be too far to portage your boats, but I imagine you can find more on the other side —there's a big reservoir, and they have lots o' outfitters near the recreation areas.

They left all the boats with John and about a third of the food and supplies, including his promised jars of pickles. Bobby knew they could not manage all the supplies on foot. With sadness, he wished the man well. "You've been a godsend, friend."

John nodded, climbed back in his lead boat and began paddling away. Bobby noticed Jacob visibly relax as the man went out of sight. While he and Jordan might have trusted the riverman, clearly Jacob had not.

CHAPTER SIXTY

It was mid-morning on what looked to soon be another scorching day. Each of them was covered in mud, insect bites and blisters from the constant days of travel. All three had large packs, including Jacob who had shouldered his with a willing smile. Bobby also made sure he and Jordan carried rifles, with rounds already chambered. Taking a bearing, they headed away from the river in the direction indicated on the GPS.

"How far ahead of them do you think we are?"

Bobby thought about her question. "Well, if what John said was accurate, the ones on the other side of the river are at least a day behind us, maybe more. Hopefully, they just keep heading south toward New Orleans."

Jordan moved another limb out of her and Jacob's way. "You don't expect them to do that, though, do you?"

He pulled a piece of venison jerky from a pocket and took a bite before responding. "Uhh, no, not really. They mentioned having some arrangement with the gangs around New Orleans. The Judges made some deal with one of the heavies down that way. Not sure what it is, but they're unlikely to want to go there with their tails tucked."

They walked on for several minutes before he continued, "No . . . I'm figuring they'll most likely cross over at Vicksburg, probably raid the town for anything that's still left, then start heading east again."

She paused and looked at him. "Doesn't that mean they're still heading right for us?"

He nodded as he passed her, "It does, which is why we don't stop today, we have to get to that other river. We also don't know what happened to the ones who were on this side of the river. They may be behind us or ahead. Roads are better over here. And as we get back toward more populated areas, we're going to run into locals, each of whom has their own idea of hospitality."

"Bobby, I thank you for getting us out of harm's way and all, but it seems we can't avoid the danger. I have my boy to think about. I know you want to get to Scott, but maybe Jacob and I should just head back north, try and slip by the Messengers and get back home."

"Yeah, I thought of that . . . and I wouldn't try and stop you, but . . . it's a bad idea."

"Why?" she said, more defensively than she meant.

"The Messengers don't move like a regular army: they spread wide, so they can clear every town, farm, warehouse, anything they come across. They descend on a place, and once they've taken what they want, they destroy whatever's left. If they found your place, and it's unlikely they didn't, then it's gone—burned to the ground." He was empathetic and sad to say so himself, but he needed her to know the danger she would be undertaking.

"Even if their numbers are less now, the tactics won't have changed, and they'll be even more desperate for food, fuel and water. So even if you two could slip around them without getting captured, you'd have hundreds of miles to go with no real hope of finding supplies."

Jordan was beginning to understand the scale of the danger.

Bobby took another bite of the hard, peppery meat. "You also don't know who's pursuing them—driving the Messengers south. You saw the jets, the bombs. I don't want you and Jacob being caught in the middle of that. Whoever those guys are, they scare me more than the Messengers."

As night began to fall, the thick woods thinned, and they were forced to cross fenced pastureland. They avoided the few barns and farmhouses they saw. Finding a secluded hollow, they stopped long enough to eat and rest for a few minutes. Bobby had been relying on the GPS less and less, as the battery was getting weak. He risked checking it now: it showed they were only about half a mile from a large reservoir on the Pearl River. "We're close. Another twenty minutes and we'll be at the river." He couldn't see the others' faces, but he knew they were ready for this leg of the journey to be over.

He put the GPS away and pulled out the little handheld radio, tossing the slackline antenna into the branch of a tree. The overgrowth had been so thick for so long that he had not been able to hear another broadcast, much less reach Kaylie. He hoped the Messengers were too busy surviving right now to be paying much attention to the radios. After just a few minutes of the same white noise, he switched it off and re-wound the antenna.

"Ready?"

Jordan clearly wasn't, but offered a resigned, "I guess."

They shouldered the packs—Bobby taking Jacob's the last stretch—and started eastward once again. Bobby had shown the pair how to move in the woods at night; catching a foot on a rock in the dark could end the journey for that person. They moved with hands in front of their faces to shield against limbs and shuffled their feet to encounter obstacles with a minimum of danger. While they had flashlights, they wouldn't use them unless absolutely necessary. Even a tiny light could be seen for miles, and after using one they would have to wait for their eyes to readjust to the darkness. That was time Bobby did not feel they had.

Eventually, they came to a clearing. They could just make out the useless power lines running high overhead. The slash of clearing cut through the forest, made traversing easier, but it also risked exposing them. For the few minutes remaining on the trail, however, he felt it was worth the risk.

Ten minutes later they were staring into the inky blackness of a large lake. This was the reservoir Bobby had seen on the GPS. The overhead power lines kept going in the direction of the dam. "We need to see if we can find a boathouse or a recreational area." His thoughts were interrupted by Jacob pulling on his sleeve. He could just make out the child outlined in the dark. Lowering his voice, he had come to automatically assume anything that got Jacob's attention meant danger. "What is it, Jacob?" Jacob pulled his hand in the direction he wanted Bobby to look. Far up on the other side of the lake, Bobby could now see what had the kid so alarmed. Hundreds—more like thousands—of fires were burning. Small campfires, he assumed; the wind was at his back, so they had not smelled nor seen the smoke. "Shiiiittt," he growled. "We fuckin' walked right up to them."

CHAPTER SIXTY-ONE

Harris Springs, Mississippi

Jack and Bartos sat on the steps of what had once been Castro's Sports Bar. Someone had taken the sign down, and it now hung over one of the lounges in the *Aquatic Goddess*.

"What's bothering you, Jack?"

The preacher was looking out over the town—what was left of it, at least. Most of one street had been burned down. All the buildings were showing signs of neglect. "I don't know. Just, something."

Bartos had seen his friend in all manner of moods over the years, but this was something new. "Not like you to be unsure of anything, Jack. Is it just the fact that Scott and Todd are gone?"

"Maybe, I just have a feeling we have more to worry about than just the storm. The man Angel and I talked with the other day, Roosevelt . . . Before we left he said something that . . . well, it seemed insignificant then, but now I feel like it might be important."

"I must admit I never knew anyone lived down dat road. When Scott tol' me about the old man, I didn't believe him. What was it he said, Preacher?"

"A few things. First, he talked about how the light is always pursued by the darkness and referred to the Amalekites. When we went to leave, he quoted a verse out of Matthew to me—when Jesus said, 'Think not that I am come to send peace on Earth: I came not to send peace, but a sword.'"

Bartos looked confused, "And who were the Ameckelites, is that something like Canadians?"

Jack smiled and corrected his friend. "The Amalekites were a tribe of people in the Bible . . . fierce enemies of Israel. They fought the Israelites over everything—food, water, land. They were said to 'devour the produce of the land' in the Book of Judges."

"That sounds eerily familiar . . . like dem crazy Messengers. What happened to the Camelites?" Bartos asked.

"Not fucking Camelites, you heathen bastard. Amalekites! What happened is that God told his people to go slaughter them." He took out his Bible, turned to the Book of Samuel, and quoted: "Thus saith the Lord of hosts, I remember that which Amalek did to Israel, how he laid wait for him in the way when he came up from Egypt. Now go and smite Amalek, and utterly destroy all that they have, and spare them not; but slay both man and woman, infant and suckling, ox and sheep, camel and ass."

"Jeezus," muttered the Cajun. "That's some pretty ruthless shit, Preacher. So, God said 'Wipe all these fucks out?'"

"Yes . . . it's sometimes referred to as the Amalekite genocide. It's controversial, as you can imagine."

"Gives a whole new level o' crazy to being a 'good Christian,' don't it? And this man, this Roosevelt, just said this to you? For what reason? Did he know you were a preacher?"

Jack pondered for a moment. "I don't think Angel or I ever mentioned it, we were just there to introduce ourselves and to warn him about the storm. He's an interesting fellow. I confess I've been a bit unnerved ever since." He paused, watching a seabird soaring over the shoreline.

"Mostly 'cos I think he might be right. If the Messengers do come this way, Bartos, we're sitting ducks. The ship stands out like a damn light-house. We have to come up with more of a plan—a real way of defending it. We can't just wait for Todd and Scott to come back and hope the Navy takes care of us."

Bartos nodded, looking back over his shoulder several blocks to the corner of the cruise ship that could still be seen from their spot. "We have some contingency plans, a lot of firearms, and Todd assured us the Navy would help out in an attack, but you're right. We need to do more . . . a lot more. Whether it's the Messengers or these raiders that keep hitting the ranches, or whoever, we need to be better prepared."

Jack was nodding. "We need to be smart. The fact that we've done relatively well at surviving doesn't mean we will continue to. The dark-ness is all around us, my friend."

"And now we have a mandate from God to slaughter those mother fuckers."

Jack laughed and clapped his friend on the back. "Brother, you are a savage, but I'm glad you're on our side."

CHAPTER SIXTY-TWO

Solo stopped rolling in the tall grass when he noticed his human was looking elsewhere.

The conversation with Jack had bothered Bartos more than he'd let on. He watched as his friend walked down the empty street toward his old, abandoned church. This wasn't Bartos' town, not in any real sense. Yet he felt a debt to these people, his friends. They had survived so much, yet with each day more seemed to be required. If not the Messengers, it would be the Grayshirts; if not them, some other gang of thugs. The only thing that helped was strength. They had come this far—mostly by being smart. The next chapter would require more smarts—and more brutality. Of this, he was quite certain. Luckily, he had some experience in the area.

Bartos strode to his old workshop down by the marina. He had never liked depending on others for anything, but especially not for protection. The building had been a newly built dry dock: a boat storage warehouse finished just before the CME hit the previous year. The building now held boats as well as his much-loved Bronco, a varied array of other equipment including weapons. Some of these were basic firearms, but others were assets on loan from the Navy. Still others had been taken from an abandoned National Guard base in Gulfport. The larger crew-served guns were his primary focus now; some of these could be mounted on the *Aquatic Goddess*. Walking past the guns, he came to what he and Todd had taken to calling the War Room. In it, among other things, were varying maps of the island, Harris Springs, the Intracoastal Waterway, the bayou and much of the surrounding county.

He looked over the map he'd pulled down, trying to put himself into the mindset of an attacking force. This was an exercise he performed regularly. The attack on his bugout location in the swamp the previous year had humbled him. Though he had technically won that battle, it had been a defeat for him. He was a survivalist, a prepper, yet he had been beaten that day by thugs and a treacherous opportunist. Never again, he had vowed, would he be surprised . . . never again.

He recalled a quote from Sun Tzu: "To know your enemy, you must become your enemy." While he could not be sure who might attack, he could plan for the more likely enemy. What would they want, how would they approach, what weakness might they exploit? One thing was clear: like Jack said, the *AG* was an obvious target, but to get to it, any group would need boats to transport the attacking force to the side of the canal on which the *AG* was moored, or use heavy artillery to fire on the ship from the inland side. Planning an attack on the *AG* and Harris Springs was the only way to anticipate the dangers and shore up their defenses in a meaningful way. Bartos was no strategist; his talent was tactics, what-if scenarios and contingency plans. Urban warfare required a different set of skills since military tactics wouldn't necessarily apply when fighting an unconventional enemy. *If you are going up against crazy, it helps to have one of your own.* He smiled at his inside joke.

The racks were filled with boats they'd confiscated from houses on the other side of the canal. Anything that floated that couldn't be moved had been destroyed: leave nothing for the enemy to use against you. The crew weapons, technical trucks and other heavy guns had been confiscated, more to keep them away from a potential enemy than for actual use.

Bartos looked at the shelves of guns and ammo, thinking back to another time, another life. His childhood had been chaotic, but not at all what most people would have guessed. He wasn't a Cajun from the swamp; as a child, he'd spent many years in rebel military camps in the swamps and tropical forests of Nicaragua. His father was a soldier and member of the Contra rebels. Targeted by the death squads after the Iran-Contra affair came to light in the mid-eighties, they fled to New Mexico. Bartos had been twelve then, although he did not go by that name yet.

He had not adjusted well to life in America. They never had a permanent home. Instead, they stayed with friendly Indian tribes and with the transient Mexicans, illegal aliens that camped in the desert. He was unsure of when exactly he realized that his father was a killer—a mercenary—but he recalled that it had not been a surprising fact. The man had a talent for bushcraft, weapons and warfare tactics, all of which he demanded his son master from an early age.

"Become your enemy, think as he thinks."

He could hear his father's heavily accented words repeating over and over even now. The other gift his father had bestowed on him was paranoia.

"Never give your real name, never give up anything real about yourself, or your enemies will learn how to use it."

His father had seen enemies behind every corner, and for a good reason, it turned out. It had been on a trip to New Orleans when Bartos was just seventeen that his dad, on assignment, had gotten his neck sliced open.

Bartos was pursued by his father's killers. He had led them into the bayous and then hunted them, one by one. The swamps had remained his home for most of his life since then, but he had also spent time in other areas including New York City. He had never told anyone that version of his past, and never would.

Grabbing a notepad, he looked down at the topographical map and began writing. He would know every possible way the *AG* could be breached before he left his War Room.

CHAPTER SIXTY-THREE

"Solo, what do you see?"

Solo looked back dismissively at him. *WTF dude? Am I supposed to be able to speak now?* he seemed to say.

Bartos continued to watch the dog, which behaved strangely. Here on the opposite side of the Intracoastal, he was always on guard, but there was something more today. The dog had his back, he wasn't worried, but he certainly wasn't relaxed.

He knelt in the middle of the main road that led into Harris Springs. The giant bulk of the *Aquatic Goddess* loomed ahead of him. It was a prize too large for any outsider to ignore.

Think like an enemy, become your enemy.

He walked down the trail to where the boat ramp had been. They had worked hard to conceal the road and make it look like the rest of the bank. His men had driven a row of large telephone-pole-sized dock supports across the access and used a backhoe to lay a trench on the far side. It was the only easy place to launch boats from this side into the canal, and now it was nearly impassable. Satisfied, he continued the long walk toward the swamp and lowlands several miles ahead.

For better or worse, these were ancient castle siege tactics. The enemy had to navigate over a moat to even think of gaining access. The moat in this case was the Intracoastal Waterway. The green water looked calm but belied its swift current and significant depth. It was also wide: almost 100 yards across.

Bartos was coming up with, implementing and discarding attack plans at a fever pace. While he might be a "blunt instrument," as Todd often dubbed him, "better at checkers than at chess," he was confident he was the best checker player in the bayou.

He had identified multiple ways a group could cross the water to the far side. While it could not be done in great numbers, it would be possible. Of course, they could also simply swim across; the swift current would make that challenging, but not impossible. Obstacles in the water such as alligators and a few other nasty surprises would likely deter that plan. He had come up with numerous counter-measures that would help defend them, but in the end, he and Jack had concluded that any sufficiently determined force would be able to reach the far side and therefore the base of the ship.

Assuming the ship was sealed, how much damage could an attacking force do? Could they breach the ship and get inside? Looking up at the huge vessel, that was doubtful. It would be like assaulting a high rise. All the access hatches on this side would be dogged shut from the inside and secured with chains and locks. Once everyone was sealed in, the far side access could be secured the same way, the gangways raised and mooring lines thrown off. *How long would that take?* He made another note to check that, put a drill in place for practice. The anchor lines would be all that remained . . . could those be used to climb to the deck? Was there possible access around the giant propellers?

All of this ran through Bartos' mind, giving him an increasing list of items to review. Some things he had to concede were impossible to prevent; if an enemy got across with a significant amount of explosives or cutting torches, then in time, they could find a way to enter. The hundreds of passenger cabins had windows and some balconies that would be vulnerable to small arms fire from the far side. Each of the weaknesses would need to be examined and, where possible, turned into strengths. Of course, the size of an attacking force and how well prepared they were—either for battle or a long, protracted siege—would change the plan significantly. In many castle battles, the enemy had simply waited the defenders out, sometimes for years.

This triggered a new concern. Water: that was their real vulnerability. Water would be the one resource they couldn't store significant quantities of onboard. They had large cisterns to catch rainfall and could desalinate seawater if they could run the engines, but most of the water supply for the *AG* still came from the city's deep wells. *Shit, why did we not give that more thought?*

If the enemy could get across, cutting off the water supply would be the natural first step. Doing the math in his head, he figured that without access to the wells they would have perhaps thirty days. After that, they'd be as dead as the previous occupants of the cruise ship.

Bartos whistled but did not see Solo. "Come on, boy!" The dog was his own master and loved to hunt on his own, but Bartos was relying on him today to watch his back. Several of his men would also be watching him from a deck high up on the ship. They had worked out a regular plan of sentries and patrols months ago, as well as an emergency signal that would alert all residents to return to the *AG* at once.

Bartos turned back, following the canal to the ocean side near the marina. This path was thick with mangrove and almost completely impassable, but it also had to be checked out. He caught an occasional glimpse of Solo at the edge of the trees in the distance. Briefly, he stiffened as he thought he saw the shadow of a man standing there. He moved a small limb to get a better view and this time saw nothing—nothing but the dog. Solo was staring into the woods.

Bartos raised the scoped M4 to his eye and swept the tree line. Nothing out there but the dog. But something else *was* there . . . instinctually, he was increasingly sure of it. What had him confused was why Solo had not attacked, or at least given a warning. He kneeled and watched the dog for several more minutes until the white tail began to wag. Calming his paranoia, he shouldered the carbine, filed his suspicion away and continued scouting.

CHAPTER SIXTY-FOUR

Pearl River Nature Preserve, Mississippi

Bobby was struggling again to keep Jordan in sight. He had taken a few minutes to give the taser to Jacob and shown him quickly how to use it. They had quickly given up looking for a canoe after realizing they'd stumbled right into the enemy and taken off on foot. They'd been moving ever since—all through the night—so as to put as much distance between them and the Messengers' camp as possible.

Bobby had frozen in fear when he heard approaching motorcycles. Most of the day they had stayed out of sight, but Bobby felt sure they had been spotted crossing a logging road a few miles back. He had heard shouts followed by a shot that seemed to be aimed at them.

He had thought they were being observant, but in their mad rush to go east and get to the river, they had made mistakes. He was also in bad shape, and it was affecting his decision-making. The woods and roads were crawling with Messengers: shooting game animals; netting fish; sending out patrols in every direction. He could tell there was a lot less of them now; they had been depleted and hurt in the Memphis battle, but like wounded animals, they were now even more dangerous in their vulnerable state.

Jacob was in front and Jordan behind her son; Bobby just physically couldn't keep up with them. Finally, Jordan looked back and she motioned for him to hurry up. She looked pleadingly at him, silently urging him on, but when it became clear that Bobby could not, she nodded and pushed on to join her son who was moving deeper into the forest. They disappeared into the murky valley below, where she, too, struggled to keep her son in sight.

～

Not long after they split up Bobby's luck ran out.

"Hey, stop!" He heard the sound just as he saw several men pointing guns in his direction, though not at him. Then he saw the target: a skinny boy in remnants of a khaki shirt, hiding in the trees. "You there, stand up and walk toward us!" The boy slowly rose and walked from the woods.

Bobby was standing in the open; the men could clearly see him but must have assumed he was one of the patrols. One looked in his direction, a question forming on his lips. Thinking fast, Bobby took the lead. "Chill out guys, we're all on the same team," he played it light, showing the three Judges his cross tattoo.

They turned their attention back to Matthew, the lone survivor of the Scout camp. The boy had survived most of the prior year by learning and using every lesson a Scout could know. "Well, shit, it's just another one of those kids." The Judge reached over and removed the large hunting knife from the boy's hand. He examined it briefly. "This thing is sharp," he commended the boy, who stood terrified and confused. "You did good, kid." The Judge smiled at the young man, who smiled weakly back with clear relief. In a split second, the older man's arm leapt out and sliced the length of the young Scout's neck with the knife. Matthew's hands reached up toward the deep gash that poured blood, but they never made it. He was dead already, and his body sank to the ground, where it would remain. Bobby unintentionally let out a gasp in surprise.

The men eyed him once again. "Fuck, man, where are your partners?" The guns in the men's hands rose fractionally.

"Why you carrying that pack and all that gear?" asked another. "Tryin' to slip away?"

Bobby didn't have the answers. He knew it looked strange to the men, and he had no ready response. His rifle was slung on his back and his pistol was in his pack—close, but not that close. The guns were now squarely aimed at him.

"Red . . . call it in, see if we should end this fuck right here. You, mista, drop the pack."

Bobby went to slide the straps off.

"Wait!" One of the men stepped close and shone his light in Bobby's face. "I remember you, you are one of us."

Bobby started to smile, "See guys, I—"

He raised his gun to shoot as he said Bobby's name with a sneer. "Montgomery . . . You killed a Judge, motherfucker, call it—"

The shot ended the statement. The Judge fell dead as Bobby dropped the pack revealing his hand holding the smoking pistol. He had aimed and fired in one smooth move. He was turning to fire at the next Judge when a shot tore through his side. He returned it and dropped that Judge as well.

The third was on the radio, screaming, "We got Montgomery, he's alive!" Bobby's third shot ended his communication and his life. Bobby was on his knees. He couldn't catch his breath and his vision was beginning to tunnel. He was surprised to be alive, and the blood spurting from his side let him know it wouldn't be for long. The pain was so fucking bad; it crowded everything else from his brain.

Clumsily, he rose and took the man's radio. He stepped toward the woods before remembering his pack. He needed the medical kit. Stepping back, he pulled the pack, but couldn't lift it from the ground. Supplies spilled out of it in all directions. His blood was doing much the same. He could hear voices calling for locations on the radio. His hands moved through the supplies, finally finding a t-shirt with which to pack the wound. His eyes closed, and he grimaced against the pain as he swept whatever supplies his hand touched back into the pack. He grasped what must have been his roll of tape which he used to secure the shirt. Finally, he struggled to his feet with the lighter pack and stumbled into the woods.

Consciousness became a vaporous thing: not something he could identify, much less grasp and hold on to. He vaguely recalled stopping once and pouring alcohol in the wound. He could feel the pull of duct tape on skin and remembered it was holding in a large blood-clotting bandage. Sounds went away, as did his vision; he assumed he was dead but realized slowly that he was still standing. At one point, he thought he saw Jacob running in the distance, then the image faded. He must be dead—he heard angels. No, not angels . . . the distinctive sound of a piano echoed softly down the valley. It was so out of place he could not be sure it wasn't just in his head. He struggled a few steps into a clearing. A small white building stood ahead. The little church had candles lighting the interior. The wound in his side was bleeding heavily.

Bobby stumbled toward the steps, the melodic sound of a choir starting a rich, traditional hymn of thanks. He stumbled to the open door and leaned on the doorjamb. The sanctuary was packed with a dark-faced congregation. The piano faded, and the choir let the song die in fits and whispers as the bloody, ragged man collapsed in the doorway.

He thought briefly that they were approaching to kill him: they had seen the tattoo and knew the evil it represented. "You people are out of your fucking mind . . . do you have any idea what's out there?" Consciousness was leaving him. He would never make it to Kaylie, nor see his brother ever again. He had lost Jordan and her son. Bobby saw the hands reaching for him as the floor rushed up to meet his face. "Please, put out the candles," he croaked.

CHAPTER SIXTY-FIVE

He had no idea how long he had been out, but it was still dark when he came to. He felt, more than saw, numerous people around him. A kind, clear voice spoke near his ear: "What are you running from, brother? Who hurt you?"

"The Messengers," he managed with difficulty.

A hushed whisper seemed to pass through the assembly like electricity. "Shhh, hush down, brothers and sisters. Let the man talk."

"Oh, dear Lord," came one particularly robust voice.

"Quiet, Ms. Johnson," the same voice urged. "Those heathen Messengers can't be here," the kind voice replied, "they stay up nowth."

Bobby tried to rise and found someone handing him a cup of water. He drank deeply and leaned a few inches up and to the side. "Preacher, you gotta get these people out of here. The Messengers are here . . . something up in Memphis drove them south. A huge battle . . ." His head started spinning, but he carried on. "They're camped at the reservoir . . . thousands of them."

"Day at da backwatah?"

"Sister Johnson, please," the voice urged once again. "I'm not the preacher, son, but I guess I'm as close as we got. Sister Tasha got your wound stitched up. If what you say is right, that dem animals is here, what can we do?"

Bobby felt his side for the bandage. It hurt but did seem to be sealed up. Only time would tell if he had internal damage as well. He would be dead by morning if he did. He struggled to sit up on the rough wooden pew. "You can pray, brother, but you might want to stop playing the piano, too."

"Aren't these people Christians? How can they be treating God's people dis bad?"

"Brother, they aren't Christians, they are a murdering army of devils. They captured me and my wife in Memphis. She was killed when we tried to escape. I've been running from them ever since."

The man stood up decisively. "Everyone get your stuff and head out. Service is over. May the good Lord bless and keep you all safe."

Bobby could hear feet on the hardwood floors as the small church emptied out into the night. "Tell them to hide for the next few days—not to travel, not to stay in their homes."

The man walked just outside the door and quietly passed along Bobby's advice. "Come on, you have to follow me," he said as he walked back inside. "There's flashlights up in the forest heading this way."

"I'm not sure I can. Did you hear dogs?"

"Dogs? Oh, lawd no, I don't do dogs. They got dogs?"

"They did in Memphis . . . not sure they still do. They're going to be searching for me, though. I can't go with you. Thank you, but it would just get you killed. I have to keep moving."

"I understands that, brother, and I ain't gonna stand in your path. I can help get you started, though."

The man helped Bobby back into his pack and put his arm under Bobby's shoulder to guide him down the steps. He didn't need to ask what direction; the opposite direction from the approaching men was the obvious choice.

"Thank you, mister . . . my name's Bobby. I appreciate what you and your flock did for me."

"Name's Tremaine Simpson," the man replied in a hoarse whisper, "an' I think it's us that owe you some thanks. We so out da way out here we never expects no trouble. We knew dey were sum college kids up at the lake, but dey never bothered us. Jus' assumed no one else would neither. Yes suh, I think you saved us tonight, not the other way 'round."

Bobby was getting winded and he had not even gotten out of sight of the church yet. His side was on fire, the rough stitches pulling with every step. "Tremaine, can you and your parishioners keep an eye out for a woman and a child? I, uh, I lost them in the forest today, just before I was shot."

"Dey somebody special to you?"

"She's a friend, a childhood friend actually. Her son doesn't speak, but he's a good boy."

"I'll pass the word, if dey still wit us livin' we can find her and keep 'em safe." Tremaine started slowing the pace. "Here we is."

Bobby assumed this was where they parted ways. "Thank you, brother, you have been a godsend."

"Oh, hush up and crawl up on this wagon."

It was only then that Bobby heard the snort of a horse. "I . . . I can't . . . you have to get away from me."

"Naw, sir, I ain't heard no dogs, and I can tell you ain't gonna make it half a mile in this shape. I'll get us on out of the way of dese heathens. You a good man, I aint gonna let you go jus' yet."

Bobby was too far out of it to argue, so he allowed himself to be pushed onto the deck of the wooden wagon. He heard Tremaine climb up and get the horses moving. Far off in the distance, he could hear motorcycles. *Please, God, let Jordan and Jacob get away, and protect these people who helped me tonight.* The sounds faded, and the world slipped sideways.

CHAPTER SIXTY-SIX

Sunlight was streaming in like slices. He could see dust motes and insects through the scattered rays of light. His mouth seemed glued shut, and he ached all over. How long had he been out? Days? weeks? He smelled hay and realized that was what he was lying on. Sitting up sorely, he found he was in a barn; the rough siding left wide gaps for the sun to shine through. A wagon—he assumed the same he had been riding in—was parked nearby.

He gently lifted his shirt and looked at the bullet wound. It appeared the dressing had been changed recently. A few streaks of red radiated from the area: possible infection. He had some antibiotics in his kit— if they hadn't been lost. He would need to get those started soon.

"Hello?" he called out.

There was no answer, but he realized that calling out might not be the smart thing to do anyway. The pain was still intense, and the barn swam in and out of view. It wasn't large. He was lying on a low row of hay bales that were stacked to the rafters behind him. His pack and weapons were propped nearby. He reached for and missed the pack. His lack of coordination surprised him; his body usually did what he instructed it to do, but then again, it was not used to this level of abuse. Twice more he tried before his fingers finally landed inside the strap.

"Fuck." No antibiotic. Not even any pain reliever. His supplies were mostly gone. A fuzzy memory let him know that it was his fault: he had dropped the contents of his pack himself. The other supplies in his trauma kit were scattered around him, left over from whoever had dressed his wounds. Remembering something, he pulled his spare socks from the pack. Inside was a single packet of Tylenol 3. Feebly, he tore the pack open and attempted to swallow the pills. His mouth was so dry that all he managed to do was cough them out onto the floor. He fell off the hay onto the dirt floor as he went looking for the pills.

As he found the last one, a shadow blocked out the sun and Bobby looked up to see a battered, half-full bottle of water being offered to him. His eyes would not focus beyond the water. He took it from the outstretched hand and downed it along with the dirty pain pills. Looking up, the face of the helper remained in shadow, and his vision still could not focus on any one thing. "Thank you," he said.

Who was this person? He propped himself back against the hay and moved his head so that the light coming in didn't put the face in full shadow. The person didn't appear large, but he didn't trust his eyes or his mind anymore. "Who are you? What do you want?"

The figure knelt beside him and tiny arms enveloped his neck. Jacob's tears fell down the side of his sparse beard. "Where did you come from? I'm so glad to see you."

Bobby hugged the boy as his heart broke open. He loved this precious child.

CHAPTER SIXTY-SEVEN

Bobby hobbled and stumbled out of the barn, trailing well behind the boy. "Jake . . . Jacob, hold on, slow down." Instead, the child came back, took his hand, and pulled him toward the house. The ground seemed to be tilting away from him in all directions. Infection, blood loss . . . something was still up. Whatever it was, he felt helpless to stop it at that moment. "Jacob, where is your mom? Is she inside?"

Jacob kept tugging on his arm and got him up the board steps. "Dat you, boy?" an older woman's voice sounded from inside. Jacob pushed on the unpainted wooden door and dragged Bobby into the darkened interior. "Well, it is you, and I see you done brought your friend back from the dead. Weren't sure you was gonna make it. Jus' wasn't your time I guess. Come on in."

The woman introduced herself as Mrs. Mahalia. She was Tremaine's aunt. The boy was still pulling on Bobby. "You gonna pull his arm off boy. You better go wit him, mister. He not gonna stop 'til you do."

Jacob pulled him to a side room where a window was open. The sunlight streamed in. Bobby was relieved to see Jordan lying on the bed. It was the first time he had truly noticed how lovely she was.

Lying on her back, fresh flowers in a vase near the bed, she radiated beauty. Jacob went to his mom's side. Bobby knelt beside the bed. *She must be exhausted*, he thought, as he reached for her hand.

Mrs. Mahalia leaned in the doorway. "We did all we could for da poor thing." Bobby was holding her hand now and just beginning to realize how cold it was. He looked at Jacob then turned to look back at Jordan. His confusion was obvious.

"I sorry mister. Mister . . . can't remember what my nephew said your name was."

"B-Bobby." It came out as a whisper.

"Mr. Bobby." She moved around to the side of the bed as well. "The snake got her down on her leg. Gotta be Cottonmouth. Dey bad out dere near d'river."

"But we were on the river for almost a week. How could this happen now?"

"Good Lord got his own clock. I thought she was gonna make it, I truly did. She kept asking if you was okay. Maybe she made a deal wit da Lord. Swapped her life for yours. Dat's what I think, 'cause I wouldna give ya two nickels for yo' life last night. You was a goner."

Bobby buried his head on the bed beside her. The old springs creaked under the pressure. Tremaine said the boy wanted you to see her before we . . . well, you know. Tre and dat boy got some way o' talking I ain't figured outs yet."

Bobby held his arms out to Jacob and hugged the boy again as he came close. "Thank you, thank you, both." Blackness clouded his vision again.

This time when he woke it was dark. He was on a sofa that had seen better days. Jacob was sitting on the floor, his back against the sofa. The child was breathing deeply, his tiny snores barely audible. Bobby ran a finger through the boy's wispy hair. Many years earlier, in another life, he had done the same with his daughter's hair. He knew he might never see Kaylie again, but while she was safe and old enough to take care of herself, what did this boy have? What was there for him to look forward to?

He lay there for a short while, letting his sadness overtake him: an old, familiar friend. The sound of a chair scraping on the wooden floor came from another room. Easing softly from the sofa so as not to disturb the boy, he moved in the direction of the sound.

Sitting at a table in the tiny kitchen were Tremaine, Mrs. Mahalia and another man. The three were drinking coffee and talking softly. Tremaine's aunt noticed him first.

"Come sit down, Mr. Bobby. You feel up t'eatin'?"

"Umm, I don't know, honestly. Maybe if you have anything to spare. Something smells really good.'"

"Good deal, getting yo' appetite back. You gonna be fine, jus' fine. Ain't nuttin' special, just some greens, and ham hocks, but I got a half-pan o' cornbread left. I was keeping it all hot for you, case you waked up."

As Bobby sat down, Tremaine introduced him to the other man: his brother, Wilson. "I'm sorry I had to leave today, but we needed some help. Wid da boy's mom. That jus' a shame, she a sweet woman and dat boy . . . man, he something else."

"Thank you, both, for what you did for her."

Mahalia pushed a steaming bowl and a big wedge of cornbread in front of him. The smell was intoxicating, and he dug in rudely.

She laughed, "Gave you some extra pot liquor in there if'n ya wanna sop it up wid dat bread. You want coffee? Ain't got no sugar or milk or nuttin'."

"Thanks, yes thanks. Coffee would be great . . . Mrs. Mahalia, this is fantastic."

"You jus' hongry boy," she smiled at the compliment, though. "Like I said, nuttin' special."

Bobby paused, realizing how many questions he had and how rude he was being. "I'm sorry for being a pig. Did Jacob eat?"

Wilson spoke up, "Oh, yeah, the boy ate good. Only time he left yo' side all day. Well, when we laid his momma down he came out and helped. Planted flowers out there and scratched her name in a scrap o' wood. Tre said a few words. I sure am sorry for your loss."

"Tremaine, I have to ask, where did you find them?"

"Dat boy was standing in the middle of the road not two miles from the church. He made me stop, then took me to where his mom was lying. I woulda never seen 'em in the dark if he din't have one of dose li'l glowin' sticks in his hand. I thought I was dead and some ghost had done come to fetch me. I'm jus' glad it was me and not one of the crazies."

Bobby smiled. "He wouldn't have shown himself to any of them. He knows good people. He knew you would help him."

"You sho right about dat! I noticed that he din't seem surprised to see you in the wagon neither—like he knew you'd be there. If you hadn't mentioned that the boy din't talk I would't na had a clue who he was."

"That child got da gift. He's special, he is."

"Aunt Mahalia, don't be starting somethin'. Bobby knows. I'll tell you what, though, he does know danger. Not sure how his mom got hurt wi' him 'round. He had this thing in his hand."

Bobby took the black object and saw it was the Taser. It had been fired. The wires coiled out and the bloody barbs were still attached.

"He sat on the buckboard wi' me and stopped me twice on our ride over here. Both times he put his finger to my lips, and then I see armed guys in the distance crossin' the road. He may not say nuttin', but I starts listnin' real good to him after dat."

Bobby gave a chuckle as he took another bite. "Where are they? The Messengers, I mean." He heard Mrs. Mahalia huff back over at the stove.

"They jus' thugs . . . ain't got no message 'ceptin hate. Thought dey was a myth—a boogeyman tale 'til yesterday. Jus' a damn plague, dat's what they is."

Tremaine refilled his cup from the pot. "They all out there, bunches of 'em. Thanks to you, all our people got hunkered down. I decided to come here cause it's well out da way. Don't think nobody'll come this far. We uh, we borrowed one o' your radios."

"My radios."

Wilson answered "Yeah, one on your pack kept makin' noise, and when we took it out it was dem folk. Dey was cussin' and lookin' for someone. That was you, weren't it?"

"Probably. I took it off one of the three that shot me." Bobby looked over at the older woman. She was pretending not to listen. "They had no further use for it. Yes, they were looking for me. I told your brother to leave me. It'd be dangerous to be found with me."

"Yeah, he's a stubborn one, always gotta be doing the right thing." Wilson chuckled. "From what we be hearing it don't matta, they killin' and stealin' anything they finds."

"Did you hear anything else?"

"Yeah, sounded like somethin' going on with 'em. They waitin' for more to join 'em from somewhere else. Several thousand mo'. They got a real army. The man said for all of 'em to come to the dam on the river. Thousand mo' . . . lawd."

Bobby tried to do some calculations in his foggy brain. "Means they lost two-thirds or more in the battle."

"They was that many mo' than that? Mercy," Mrs. Mahalia tutted.

Tremaine looked at his aunt. "We okay here, they heading somewhere else anyway."

"And just how you know dat?" she asked as she sat back down.

"Just what da man said. I figured they'll hit Jackson next, I know they could wipe dem gangs out down there, but dey said they're going some-place called Harris Springs."

Bobby dropped the fork. "I need the other radio and the GPS. Is my pack in here?"

CHAPTER SIXTY-EIGHT

Harris Springs, Mississippi

Bartos was trying his best to get all the information down. Bobby was talking low and steady. All thoughts of radio discipline were gone. Bobby was injured, panicked, and paranoid. He had made Bartos ask the on-duty radioman, Scoots, to leave the room and waited for Bartos to make sure and secure the door.

"She is there, though?"

"Yeah Bobby, she's here. Scott's away right now, but Kaylie is here with us, just not on the base." He didn't want to say ship, but Bobby already had several times.

"Just let her know, okay?"

"Of course, I'll go find her soon as I get off. I got your position, and we'll get a mission pulled together to head in your direction."

"You can't, man. I wish you could, I have someone I'd like my daughter to meet, but it's too dangerous. If you come up this way you'll run straight into the Messengers. They're heading out in two days, and they're coming for you. Do you understand me? They know about you, about the boat. I don't know how, or why, but you're the next target. Someone must have tipped them off."

"Bobby, listen, I get that. I don't know why they would, but I get it. That puts them a few days away depending on how many are on foot. Could be a week. We can get to you before then."

"Negative, you have to do whatever you can to keep my daughter safe, you have to move everybody on the ship to someplace safe. The motorized column and the Judges could be on that road to Har— headed your way today."

The two men talked for several more minutes and agreed to talk again in five hours. Bartos sat back, going over the details. He then reviewed the radio logs and spoke with Scoots who pulled up some recorded conversations on the laptop. What he concluded left him sick inside: he knew who the goddamn traitor was. He went to go find Abe and Kaylie. At the bottom of the gangway, he also ran into Jack.

"Where's the fire, Cajun?"

"We have a problem."

"I know, but the storm's—"

"No, we have a new problem—several actually. Follow me, I may need your help."

They ran into Kaylie first. She was overjoyed to hear that her dad was okay and had made it farther south. "When are we going to go get him?"

Bartos turned to look her in the eyes. "We did make a plan, but it didn't include you, and your dad has forbidden any of us from coming to him. The whole God's fucking army is apparently headed straight for us, and in the next day or two they'll be between us and him." Jack and Kaylie looked at one another, completely baffled. "Yes, you heard me right."

"You have to take me," Kaylie said determinedly. "I know you're going to go anyway."

"The plan is to take Solo and Abe. You have to stay here. Jack, could you please watch my back?"

Puzzled, Jack said, "Sure."

Bartos saw Abe at the boardwalk watching someone intently with a pair of binoculars. "Abe, can I have a word?" The big man turned around with the same neutral expression he always seemed to have.

"Sure, Bartos, what's up?"

"I need you for another road trip."

"Cool, when do we leave? I need to get my gear."

"Yeah, you see that's the problem. I needed you for a trip to get Kaylie's dad. Unfortunately, I'm not going to be able to take you."

He looked confused. "Why not?"

"Why don't you take a fucking guess?"

The big guy just shrugged and looked confused.

"It's really simple. You're a fucking spy for the Messengers. Solo, takedown!"

Abe went for his gun. The dog made an otherworldly growl as he leapt from the shadows where he had been crouched. The big man was fast, but the dog moved with preternatural speed. Solo had the man's gun hand disabled with a few tearing bites, after which he went directly for the big man's throat. Abe was huge, but the dog didn't care. Bartos delivered a sweeping kick that took one of Abe's legs out from under him and he crashed to the ground. Abe punched Solo with his good arm and the dog gave a yelp then went in for more.

Bartos got a hand in to remove Abe's pistol which he flung to the side. One of the man's flailing legs caught Bartos and the impact sent him sailing several feet. Give the kid credit, he wasn't going down easily. Then, Solo ripped an ear free and with it a large hanging piece of skin from his face. The pain must have been intense as Abe screamed and grabbed his face. The fight was leaving him quickly.

Jack and Kaylie watched in horrid fascination.

Since the order had been for a takedown and not a kill, Solo stopped the attack just short of a fatal bite. Bartos walked over to the enormous man, who was now down on all fours gasping for air. "We fucking trusted you, and you sold us out. *Why?*"

"It's not me,"

"Really?" Bartos was kneeling over the bloodied man, Solo's jaws still at his throat. "Care to swear on a Bible? If you're lying, it's gonna be your eternal soul, cause I'm going to kill you either way."

"Fuck you!"

"That's it? That's your final words on this Earth?" Bartos looked up to see a small crowd beginning to gather.

"You were good, Abe, you did just enough to keep us believing in you. Hell, you even saved my life more than once. Unfortunately, you were the only one on radio duty when someone made contact. And this scar on the back of your hand. What is that? It looks like a tattoo that was started but never finished. What was it going to be, a cross, maybe? Didn't make sense 'til Scott's brother told me about the mark. The mark every Messenger receives."

"Kaylie . . . Kay, uh." Abe struggled to call out, but having Solo latched onto his collar made it difficult. "Did he tell you, your whore mother is dead? She's dead, and they've known it for weeks. All you people are unworthy . . . you've been judged already . . ." Solo's jaws clamped shut with a grisly snap. Bartos could not remember giving him the hand signal, but he must have . . ..

Solo walked away from the twitching body as Kaylie walked up, drew her pistol and shot a single bullet into Abe's head. Turning around, she looked at Bartos with tears in her eyes. "Is it true?"

The pistol was still in her hand, and Bartos hoped it was empty. "I—I don't know honey, Scott didn't know, but he thought that . . . that yes, she probably was. Your dad hasn't mentioned her in any of the broadcasts." He went to Kaylie, but she turned away. Jack shook his head slightly at Bartos then eased up beside her and gently put an arm around her. He took the gun from her hand.

DeVonte and Angel slipped out of the crowd and over to Bartos. "Man, what the fuck? What did he do?"

Bartos glared at the boy. "He spoke to me without permission. Do you have permission?"

DeVonte took a step back. "You're joking, man, you love me. We all know that. What'd Abe really do?"

"He sold us out, DeVonte. He just put this whole town right in the crosshairs of those fucking Messengers."

Bartos kicked the dead body as he walked by. Solo was wallowing in the sand and yapping like a happy puppy. *Fuck, that dog even scares me*, Bartos thought, still unsure of whether he'd actually given the final kill command to the dog.

Jack was sitting with Kaylie at a picnic table when Bartos came up. He didn't sugar coat it. "I'm sorry you had to see that, Kaylie, but I think it was important that you did. He's just one of a bunch of people like that out there. They're after your dad and they're coming after us. The stupid and the lazy are all long dead. The ones left alive are smart and cunning . . . some are still good people, many more are not." He sighed heavily. "I'm going to get your dad. If you want to ride shotgun, you can."

Jack began to protest, but Bartos cut him off. "Jack, you and Angel are in charge, and you have a shitload of work to do. We have a storm about to hit, farmers coming to take shelter, and a crusading army of Christian jihadists on their way." He took a deep breath as a shadow crossed his features. "We had plans for one or two of those things, but not all at once. "

"How long are you going to be gone?"

Bartos looked at his friend. "Ten hours. If we're not back by then, we aren't coming back."

"How the hell are you going to manage that?"

Bartos took his keys out of his pocket. "Secret weapon."

CHAPTER SIXTY-NINE

Rural Mississippi

An hour later, Bartos had the Pontiac GTO near 100 on Highway 50. They were headed in the direction of Jackson. Kaylie was watching the GPS while Solo lay curled in the rear seat. It was admittedly not the most sophisticated of plans, but Bartos was counting on speed and audacity over well-planned strategy.

"We stay on this to Hattiesburg then catch 49 toward Jackson," Kaylie said.

Scott was going to kill him, and Todd too. He didn't like any of this, but he did fucking love this car, and for that, at least, he was happy for the opportunity to open her up on the highway. He had made a few improvements, all of which were subtle. The trunk was now dominated by an armor-plated spare fuel tank and the noisy headers had been fed into a sophisticated muffler system that canceled the throaty roar of the beast from within. While "the goat" was quieted, she was not tamed. The engine performance was better than ever. He had also added steel armor to the doors and over the radiator and installed steel shutters and gun ports on the windows that could be slid up as needed.

If she had an 8-track player, Bartos thought, *she would be the ultimate road warrior.*

"We have to cross near several major cities and a few interstates," he told Kaylie, wanting her to be prepared. "The good thing is we've mapped most of the roads up to within fifty miles of your dad."

"So, you think this is going to be easy?" she asked, her eyes still red.

"No, but it may be doable . . . at least the first part."

They rode in silence for several hours. The roads were clear of problems until they got nearer to the state capital. Jackson was the largest city in the state, though not large by the nation's standards. Kaylie had turned them onto numerous smaller roads to avoid some of the more obvious choke points. Still, they saw hard, angry eyes following them from every neighborhood that had survived so far. More than once Bartos noticed people running for cars or trucks, presumably to chase after them, but he was hitting speeds above 120 now. Not much was capable of catching them. They made it to Jackson in just over three hours.

"I told your dad I'd make contact again in an hour." Bartos had stopped on a rise that overlooked a large forested area ahead. "He said the Messengers are based mainly up here," he said as he pointed to the map in Kaylie's lap. "His GPS location is here." Another stab. "And we are right here." The map now had three red circles on it that Kaylie marked with each of Bartos' points. Each was about the same distance apart. Bartos estimated the time in his head. "We have about twenty minutes before we have to move. Get some food, pee, whatever else you need. We won't stop again until we get to him. Get all the guns up front with you. Chances are we'll be using them." While Kaylie got out of the car to follow instructions, he checked the weapons he had at hand and began mapping out an exit route. He did not want to go back the same way they had come.

～

An hour later they had made it deep into the woods in the direction of the GPS coordinates. There had been no response on the radio from Bobby yet. Kaylie kept calling him as they drove.

"Hey, sweetie, that you?"

"Daddy!"

"Hey, K, can't talk long. Afraid they may find us. Just wanted to hear your voice."

"Bartos said you were hurt, are you okay? How is Mom?" There was a slight delay, and she could see Bartos shaking his head. *Get his location*, he mouthed impatiently.

"I—I'm okay, hon, I'll be okay. I can't talk, I hear someone coming. They may have found us."

"Dad—Dad?" Bartos pulled the car to a stop as the pair saw movement ahead of them. Kaylie dropped the radio and she was out the door running.

"Solo! Out, patrol." Bartos grabbed his gear and flanked Kaylie as they watched several armed black men follow a haggard looking man and a small boy out of a shack.

Bobby recognized his daughter and relief melted his features for a moment before panic took hold once again. "Kaylie! What are you doing here?" he asked as she flung her arms around him. "I told Bartos to stay away, you shouldn't have come." He shook Bartos' hand, but also glared at him.

"Why?" Kaylie was clearly a little hurt at her father's reaction.

"Man, you needed a ride. We take care of our own, brother. She's one of us, you are one of us."

Bobby sighed and nodded. "Kaylie, Bartos, I want you to meet someone." Bobby looked around the yard. "Jacob, where are you?"

They looked around: the boy was holding onto Solo, hugging him and scratching his ears. The dog was clearly enjoying it. "What the fuck?" Bartos couldn't believe his eyes. "Solo doesn't do that."

Bobby laughed. "Jacob has a way about him."

Quick introductions were made between the newcomers and Bobby and Jacob's kind hosts, the Simpsons, before Bobby started grabbing his gear. Then he thought better of it. "I'm assuming my daughter's group has supplies," he said to Tremaine. "You good people keep what's left of this." He removed the food and other supplies from Jacob and Jordan's packs as well.

Bartos was rushing them through the goodbyes, but he said nothing as Bobby and Kaylie took Jacob over to his mom's grave. He watched as the boy said goodbye. Kaylie had taken the news of her mother's death as well as could be expected. He knew she would deal with it later; for now, she was focused on her dad and her new little brother's loss. Seeing them together, this was the only way Bartos would ever think of the boy: he was their family.

They were back on the road in fifteen minutes. Bobby was not looking good. He had urged Tremaine and his family to go into hiding. He was sorry they couldn't take them along.

"We not getting in that car with dat dog any ol' how," Mahalia said laughing. "You go get, we got yo radio, we can call you once the craziness be done."

They ran into the first roadblock soon after turning onto the paved road south. Three motorcycles blocked the road. Bartos slowed and opened his door slightly. "Solo, clear. Bobby, can you shoot?"

"Uh, yeah, maybe." He held up the M4 and chambered a round. "Those are Judges, man, don't take chances."

"I'm not," Bartos said as he slid the armor plating in place over the windows. Kaylie slipped her weapon out from the gun slot.

Just as Bartos had instructed, she waited on Solo to move on the rear target before she leveled the sights and took out the man closest. Bartos then floored the accelerator. The final Judge was clearly overwhelmed to see one colleague being mauled by a dog while the other's head exploded. The muscle car heading right for him didn't register until it was too late. The front bumper sheared off the man's legs at the knee. His torso and head hit the roof just behind the windshield. Bobby gasped from the backseat. He had just learned that his Kaylie was no longer a little girl. He looked over to place a reassuring hand on Jacob who was curled in a ball in the footwell beside him.

Bartos slid the GTO to a stop to let the bloody dog back in. He eased up out of the vehicle to look at the roofline, now smeared with blood. "Oh, yeah, that'll buff out." He slipped back into the driver's seat and floored it again, heading for the next turnoff.

CHAPTER SEVENTY

USS Bataan, Gulf of Mexico

Scott and Todd were kitted out in tactical gear. Both men had been issued night-black camo to go over a very thin wetsuit—just in case they wound up in the water at some point. They were also each issued dive watches, survival packs, and a very compact first aid kit. While they would not be part of the assault team, the platform could hold surprises, so they were provided with essentially the same gear as the assault team. Todd slipped the SOG Spec Elite knife into its sheath with an approving look.

"You are loving this, aren't you?" Scott asked.

"Hey, getting to play soldier again at my age? Hell, yeah!"

They had spent much of their time on the base going over basic mission protocols, call signs, hand-to-hand combat drills, and weapons practice. Scott was still sore as he eased out of the wetsuit and packed it in his gear bag. Like any survival situation, your gear was only as good as your knowledge. He and Todd had spent hours with the team reviewing every item, every detail. While they couldn't match the soldiers' years of training, they did not want to be a burden to the operation either. Besides that, as Todd had indicated, it was all pretty fucking cool.

An ensign called out for Scott to follow him to the radio room. Assuming it was an update on the assault, Scott put the headset to his ear anxiously. "Go ahead, this is Scott."

"Uncle Scott, it's Kaylie."

Eighteen hours later the Naval assault team was getting ready to depart, so Scott and Todd were headed to the hangar deck. Garret nodded as they walked in. "Captain Ramos, you want to add anything?" Ramos was the commander of the Special Warfare Group. His dark-skinned, weathered face was punctuated by a thin mustache.

"Gentlemen, the weather is worsening quickly down range. The truth is, it's now close to the limit regarding mission parameters. We're looking at a Category 1 hurricane. It is expected to reach the Devil's Tower oilfield around zero-five-thirty. That will be our go-time. We have our orders, you are familiar with the AO. Advance scouts and sniper teams are already in hides on surrounding rigs relaying intel. The force strength appears to be what we expected: around 100 hostiles. We will follow the execute plans as incoming information says the medical teams are isolated on a single floor. Once the rest of the platform is secure, only those of you in full bio-gear will enter that section. Non-lethal weapons only beyond that point. Our two civilians here," hooking a thumb over at Scott and Todd, "will be brought over once the AO is secure. They will initiate contact with the research team. Is that clear?"

"Hooah!" came the instant response from all.

"We know we can expect a fight. These guys are trained like us. Kill shots only, we can't fuck around with them. You have the insertion maps. At go-time, Alpha team will be fast-roping down while the snipers take out the first targets. Then Bravo and Delta go to work. We will deploy from and exfill back here to the *Bataan* for transport back to the fleet. They will take charge of the bio-lab and personnel once secure."

One of the SEAL team members stepped forward. "Sir, what is the abort code for today's mission?"

Ramos looked at Garret briefly. "There isn't one, Braxton. We either complete the mission, or we die out there. No one is coming to get us if it goes sideways. Is that a problem for anyone?"

"Sir, no, sir!" came the loud and unified response.

Garret stood up, "Gentlemen, good hunting, and stay safe."

The Airboss called out to them from his console, "Wheels up in ten, gentlemen. Head on out to the bird with your gear."

The 'bird' this time, was an obviously borrowed Eurocopter HH-65 Dolphin. The chopper was a garish red and white instead of the normal Navy gray. It would ferry Todd and Scott to the, hopefully secured, oil platform. Scott looked out at the angry looking sea. He felt very uncertain of flying in this weather. Todd put his hand on Scott's shoulder and smiled. The howling wind and the sounds from the chopper made any other communication impossible.

Once inside the cabin of the craft, they both donned headsets so they could speak to each other and listen in to the pilot's instructions.

"The shit you get me into, man," Scott said with a forced smile.

Todd readjusted himself to try and find a comfortable position. "Tell me about it, brother." He paused before continuing. "Scott . . . are we good?"

Scott answered immediately, "Yes, Todd, we're good. We may not always agree, but I respect you, and I trust you. I see the need to do this, though I admit it scares the shit out of me. Are we really flying out in a hurricane?"

"You'll be fine, man. These birds are used by the Coasties to fly into hurricanes for rescues all the time."

"No, Todd, I'm not scared for myself, I know these guys will take care of us. I'm scared about whatever DJ has in that lab. Are we supposed to transport a deadly pathogen in a hurricane? It doesn't sound good." Both friends were uncertain how the Navy could possibly take the platform without heavy casualties on both sides, but Ramos and his men seemed hyper-confident. Was that just bravado? Surely, they realized this enemy would be unlike any other they had faced.

Todd nodded, his face resolute. He reached over the gear bag and offered his hand to his friend. "It's crazy, that much is true. No one I would rather have by my side, Scott."

"Same here, brother."

Both men felt the volumes of history and emotion embedded within that simple statement. The battles—their losses and victories. Todd had asked his friend to save his town, and Scott had managed to do so, with his help. Their friendship was barely a year old, but the bond was as tight as family.

The pilot circled a finger in the air to someone out on the deck. The engines revved, the cabin shook and then they were going up and away from the enormous ship. The attack on Devil's Tower was underway.

"Scott, I know you weren't in the military, but you have been in battle. Put Bobby and all that other stuff somewhere else for now. Focus on this mission."

He nodded, "I know, I know."

Todd put his hand on Scott's shoulder. "Today is just one of those long, grueling bike rides you talk about. You know, when the wind is relentless, and the hills are never-ending? Just when you think it can't get worse, it does. How do you make it home on those days?"

Scott thought about it, "I . . . I focus on what's in front of me."

Todd smiled, "One mile at a time. That's what we do today, one mile at a time. We go in and identify DJ, help the team secure the facility, and get the hell out with the kid. Difficult, but not complicated. We can do this."

The chopper skimmed the tops of the mountainous waves. The craft jerked and bucked like an enraged bull. "For now, my focus will be on keeping my breakfast down," Scott said. "Those waves have to be forty feet high! I've never seen anything like it. No way those fast boats can manage through this, can they?"

"I've seen them do some amazing things, but this does look beyond the limit," Todd admitted. The whole thing was scary as hell. If the maelstrom below was anything like what was going on twenty miles ahead, it was going to be a day of epic proportions.

CHAPTER SEVENTY-ONE

Devil's Tower Oil Platform, Gulf of Mexico

"Apex Two-two this is Apex Actual." The pilot had switched their headset comms over to the tactical command channel.

"Go for Two-two," came the response.

The time on Scott's G-shock DW-6600 watch read 04:32.

"All units active, go hot on my mark. Three . . . two . . . one . . . Mark."

Scott and Todd leaned over, focusing on the sounds in their headsets. It was impossible to know who was speaking, but they followed as best they could. Some voices were very recognizable, like Ramos' and Perez's, but others they could only guess at. Even though they had only spent a few days with the men, they were already beginning to think of them as brothers.

One of the Barracuda Interceptor stealth boats had been swamped, and the crew was out of action and awaiting rescue. One of the underwater crews was having comms issues and so had only intermittent contact. Neither of those problems was felt to compromise the mission according to command.

"Apex Actual this is Andes One. Target acquired . . . target down."

Scott remembered Andes was the call sign for the snipers on over-watch. Whatever shots they were taking were at extreme range, in the dark and in the middle of a hurricane, yet listening to the sniper's tone, you might have thought he was telling his wife he was taking out the trash.

"Apex Four taking heavy fire. Light 'em up Andes."

"Apex Actual be advised Alphadog is down. Repeat, Alphadog is down."

"Apex One on the deck, beginning insertion."

The Dolphin copter was orbiting the oil field at a distance safely outside of the battle below. Scott felt helpless hearing the communications. Looking over, he saw Todd had gone rigid as he watched through the rain-soaked window. People were dying down there.

With a small break in the clouds, they got a glimpse of their destination.

The size of the Devil's Tower oil platform was staggering. Scott was not sure what he had expected, but this wasn't it. The behemoth dwarfed everything around it. Sitting on almost two miles of water, it looked more like a hotel under construction what with all the cranes and gantry. Designed to be functional, little thought had gone into its aesthetics. The whole structure sat atop a round pedestal.

They saw a small explosion on the southwest side of the rig.

"This is Apex Actual, all units are engaged. rules of engagement are in effect. Repeat, ROE are in effect."

More and more radio chatter could now be heard, and the sound of gunfire was fierce.

The command channel on their headsets was switched. The helicopter pilot keyed the mic. "Traveler Three-five for *Bataan*. We are bingo fuel in ten. Please advise."

Scott knew what that meant: in ten minutes the helicopter would no longer have sufficient fuel to get back to the ship.

"Acknowledged Three-five, maintain orbit."

The comm channel switched back. Voices belonging to soldiers in extreme pain were all they could hear now. "Apex Actual this is Two-two, base level is clear."

Over the next several minutes a few other reports came in with similar messages.

"Are the labs secure?" Scott asked. Only Todd and the helicopter crew could hear him.

Todd shrugged. "They'll let us know."

"Base, be advised we are at bingo."

There was a long pause before the voice of flight control said, "Take 'em down. The LZ Pad on Devil's Tower is clear, winds gusting to 145 plus, keep rotors hot."

As they neared the touchdown point, the pilot spoke to them, shouting above the noise of storm and battle. "The storm has really picked up since the other team went in. I'll have to keep the engines at full rev pushing us down just to keep it on the deck. It's going to blow you off the edge if you stand up into the wind. You do *not* want to go off the edge—it's a 500-foot drop to the water. Once you clear the prop wash, you still have the hurricane to deal with, and it's gusting at well over 100 miles an hour right now. Get out the door and drop to all fours. Crawl to the team member waiting there." Scott and Todd nodded as they prepared to alight. "Good luck, gentlemen."

"Thanks, good luck to you, too." Scott looked up to meet Todd's eyes. "This is it."

Todd grinned. "Fuck what they said. Weapons hot, chamber a round, safety off. Do that with your pistol as well." They both prepped their weapons. "Remember, I got your back, brother."

Scott nodded his thanks, "Same here." With a quick fist bump, they unlatched their seatbelts and swapped headsets for helmets. The touchdown on the helipad was hard, but they were holding on tight.

Todd swung the door back as he had been shown, and the full fury of the early morning weather hit them with gale force impact.

Both men struggled just to get out of the chopper. The downward force of the propeller and the crosswinds from the storm made it almost impossible. Todd managed to get most of his body out of the door and down to a strut by holding one of the landing wheels. He wrapped a hand around it and helped Scott do the same. Both men were on all fours, holding the landing gear with one hand and their compact MP5 assault rifles in the other. They knew they had to let go and crawl toward the interior edge of the pad, but it seemed there was no way to move against the wind. They were trying to align themselves to knife into the crosswind when they noticed the wheel of the enormous chopper sliding sideways toward the edge of the landing pad.

"We have to let go!" Todd yelled over the howl of the wind. He did so and flattened himself to the deck. Scott did the same. Unfortunately, the same wind that was blowing the chopper off was pushing them as well. *This is proving to be a very undignified entrance onto the battlefield,* Scott thought as their slide toward the rig's edge picked up speed. Todd had grabbed onto Scott, and together they were trying to glue themselves to the deck with what mental and physical powers they had.

The beautiful Dolphin chopper was separating from them now, and the pilot was trimming the prop to push up instead of down. The change in force allowed Todd to lean up slightly into the crosswind and it pushed him diagonally away from the edge. Scott watched in horror as the chopper tipped over the edge and was lost from sight. A horrendous wrenching of metal followed by a gut-wrenching explosion traveled up the side of the oil rig, momentarily nullifying the storm winds and allowing Todd to reach the tip of a finger through a tie-down built into the helipad surface. Scott just managed to snag a climbing rope that sailed past them and keep hold.

Looking over, they could just make out the dark-clad man holding onto the other end of the rope. They shouldered the MP5s and began to pull themselves along the ground by the rope and toward the man.

"Well, that was graceful," Perez said, giving them a hand down from the raised platform to the relative shelter below it. He spoke into his microphone. "Apex Actual, our friendlies are safe. Traveler 34 was lost, though." He motioned to them, "Come this way. The platform is mostly secure, although we can't say with certainty they don't have soldiers inside the bio-facility. The lab is undamaged, though—no casualties there, and our men are already on-station at the doors."

Inside the main deck, Scott saw numerous bodies, both friends, and foes. The rictus of death was already taking hold of the recently departed. "How bad were the losses?" Todd asked Perez. The soldier's facade cracked slightly so that they got a sense of the day's pain and loss. That was not a discussion for right now.

The bio-lab was on level 3. In fact, it was all of level 3. The three men donned the bio-suits along with two other black-clad members of the SEAL team who unlocked the door as they approached. Inside the lab, the lights were flickering, and they could hear people crying and talking in hushed voices.

Inside the bulky suits, it was impossible to get a fix on the sounds, but there were not that many places the medical staff could be. Scott saw Perez take up a firing position in one corner. He had switched to a shotgun that fired a non-lethal Taser-like charge. Several other suited commandos were also entering the facility now. Scott entered the corridor just behind the lead and stopped at the door marked 4. It appeared to be a meeting room. He knocked on the door, and the voices inside quieted.

He pushed it open with a metal rod he found nearby. No shots. That was a good sign. He entered the room in a single smooth motion with both hands held high. He was facing a group of at least twenty very frightened people. All of them were in lab coats or medical scrubs.

"We are with the US Navy," he said, but quickly realized they could not hear him through the suit. He saw Todd and Perez just outside the door, both holdings shotguns. Looking at the med staff, all in normal medical scrubs, he made a quick decision and unzipped the hooded suit from the inside. The quickly deflating suit fell away. A quick glance over revealed a wide-eyed Todd staring at him in shock.

"DJ, are you in here?"

Stepping toward the group, Scott was aware that he still looked imposing in the black tactical battle gear, backed by armed men who guarded the room's only exit. He tried again, "Is there a DJ in this group?"

"Scott?"

Scott was confused by the sound. It was not DJ, nor was it even male.

"Scott Montgomery?" A woman with red hair—a doctor—was emerging from the group.

He could only stare. "Gia?" There was no possible way. It could not be the same woman, the friend he had known in college. "Gia Colton? Dr. Colton, that...that, was you?" His head was spinning.

Todd was speaking into his earpiece. "Where is DJ?"

He took the several steps between him and Gia and hugged her tightly. He was still in shock. Gia had meant more to him than she ever knew. Now, he realized, she meant so much to the world, as well. "G, we have to get you and your team to safety. These are my friends. Most are with the Navy. They are here to help. You have an assistant named DJ, is he here with you?

Gia looked up into his face, "Scott, I can't believe . . . sorry, yes, DJ is in with our subject—behind the safety wall. He'll have to come through decon first. I can call him."

He stopped her, "First, is it safe for my men? Are any other Prae—I mean Grayshirt troops in here with you guys?"

"No, they never come back here, they're not allowed."

"Todd, Perez, did you get that?"

Perez came back over the comm. "That's good news, I'm calling it in to the *Bataan* now."

"Gia, call DJ up, tell him I'm here. He'll remember me. It's not safe to stay here. We need to get your team aboard a Navy vessel nearby. They're also set up to transport your lab. Is that going to be a problem?"

"No, not at all. Everything is modular, and none of us could stand those jackbooted Grayshirts." She looked him over again approvingly. "When did you become such a badass?"

He smiled as she made the call. Other members of the SEAL team began escorting the researchers down to the oil rig's mooring platform. As he monitored the broadcast, Scott recalled the still raging storm. Transferring all this equipment might have to wait until it subsided, but they could at least move the people now.

He introduced Gia to Todd who had also shed his bubble suit. "Gia, this is my friend, Todd Hansen."

Todd smiled, "Just call me Todd or Cap."

She hugged him as well and then gave Scott another embrace before hurrying off to get her team ready to depart.

"You make a hell of a first impression, dude. You'll have to fill me in."

Scott shook his head, "No deal, it was a college crush, and . . . it was embarrassing."

"What are the odds of her being here and the one in charge? Doesn't look like she thinks you should be embarrassed." Todd clapped Scott on the shoulder as he walked by.

Scott grinned. He was relieved at the outcome so far. "Well, the price was high, but I have to say it's looking like the op is going better than planned."

"Hooah that, man!" Todd agreed.

～

Twenty minutes later DJ exited from a reinforced lab door followed by someone in a bio-suit who sat down heavily away from the commotion. DJ ran over to Scott and Todd. "God, I am so glad to see you guys! Thank you! How is Kaylie? Does she know I'm here? Are we going there?"

"Slow down, tiger. Good to see you, too. Kaylie is fine, and yes she knows." Scott said. "Look, Gia—um, Dr. Colton—is assembling the team to move over to the Navy vessel in a few minutes. They have full bio-labs for all your supplies and samples, but we need your help coordinating that, okay?"

"Yeah, sure, sure. Glad to help. We have one live subject and a lot of blood samples, but most of the other material is in the freezer. No real danger."

Scott glanced over DJ's shoulder at the seated figure slumped in the chair. "That your subject? Is he well enough to travel?"

"Yeah, that's him. He should be fine. He's mostly asymptomatic, but we have been taking a lot of blood, so he's weak."

"Fucking vampires," Todd said.

DJ looked over, "You must be Todd. Kaylie talks about you a lot. She's very fond of you."

"Feeling's mutual, kid. We gotta get you two back in the same zip code, you got some catching up to do."

"Absolutely! Let me go help the doctor, and maybe we can speed this along." They watched as DJ moved swiftly toward the sound of his boss's voice.

The storm outside was raging. Scott shook his head, "You think we can wait for this storm to pass before doing the transfer?"

"I don't think our friends will go for that. Remember, they're assuming the Grayshirts will destroy the facility rather than letting the Navy get it. The whole rig may be wired to blow any minute."

"Right, thanks. Now I feel better."

CHAPTER SEVENTY-TWO

Scott watched as Gia came back into view. He cursed himself again for never asking DJ more about his boss. For some reason, he had always just assumed it was a man. Seeing her had flung all the battle plans from his head. Her gorgeous, yet still very innocent face, her striking red hair and her figure that still demanded attention, despite the unflattering lab coat. It all had utterly distracted him, and he retreated back to that schoolboy with a crush in an instant. Old pangs of regret sprung up from deep within the hidden recesses of those memories.

Todd walked by. "Come on, Romeo, we still got a job to do."

Scott could hear Perez on the radio. "*Bataan* is thirty minutes out. We need to have the teams at the extraction site then. The storm is still intensifying, so they'll stay 500 yards southeast and send tenders over."

Scott looked at his friend, "They're sending a small boat over in this storm? That sounds very unsafe." Todd agreed and went to the soldier to find out more.

Gia came up to Scott and pulled him into another hug. Her eyes were watering. "I'm sorry, I'm sorry, I just . . . I just didn't think I would ever see another familiar face. Much less yours." She smiled with what seemed like relief.

"I know, G. Listen, I'm—I'm sorry I didn't stay in touch over the years. It was . . . it was . . . hard."

She took his left hand and looked at it. "I know, Scott, I know."

"Is Steve—is your family here?" He had heard they had a daughter now, but he wasn't sure how old she would be, or even where she would be now. A shadow of sadness clouded her face.

"No, they—" she attempted before swallowing and shaking her head.

He knew not to press any further. Gia had always been a determined force of nature. Her focus and intensity were, at times, as fierce as the storm outside. Whatever had caused this pain in her had hit deep into her very soul. He could see she had lost a great deal.

She struggled for a moment but continued. "They didn't make it. They were on a medical transport that went down near the coast. No cause was ever given, but . . . there were no survivors. When they took me to Tallahassee, Steve kept Jennifer, our daughter. She would have been ten next month."

"I'm so sorry. I'm so very sorry."

She visibly forced herself to brighten. "What about you, everyone doing okay?"

The storm was too much to ignore. "We can talk later, we'll have plenty of time. Right now, we have to get you off this rig and over to the ship."

"In this weather?" she asked, concerned.

Todd had walked up and was speaking into his mic. "Hey, Doc, yeah. The Navy is picking up some activity from some ships nearby they had previously tagged as derelicts. Apparently, Catalyst has active assets in the area. We think they may try and take the lab out rather than let the Navy take it."

Scott's face went ashen. "Oh, shit, we have to move everyone and the lab now. We can't wait for the Navy med-techs."

"My thoughts exactly," Todd responded. Addressing Gia, he said, "Dr. Colton, can you oversee the packaging of the samples and other vital materials? We can start moving any of the non-essential members of your team and equipment in the next few minutes. We can come back for the patient and the remainder on the next trip." She nodded and went to get everyone moving.

"Todd, are we going to have time for two trips?" Scott asked, his mounting concern evident.

"The *Bataan* is nearly on-station. They are sending over multiple transports. We'll have to load them separately as the mooring point only has space for one at a time. We'll get as many of the people, samples and essential items as possible to the *Bataan*, then back off several miles. If the lab isn't attacked, we can come back in and take everything else. Either way, we need to be on those boats in ten. They're lowering the platform exit stairs now, so we can all get down to the docking point. The seas are still high, but they expect the eye of the storm to be overhead at that time, so we'll have a few minutes of relative calm to load."

Scott, Perez and another SEAL named Alvarez carried case after case down the metal stairway leading to the lower metal gridwork. The angry sea was pushing up through the grates with a churning ferocity. He saw the first of the modified Barracuda attack boats moving deftly through the waves to the extract point. They handed over the crates to the men inside the next Barracuda, moving with as much care as was possible in the hellish conditions.

DJ was coming down the stairs behind them with quite a few of the lab techs. They were ushered onto the boats along with several of the remaining SEALs, and the boat disappeared back out to sea. Perez held up five fingers, indicating the next boat would be there in five minutes. Scott was drenched, thankful now for the wetsuit beneath his clothing. His pack was still upstairs, as was Gia, so he went back up the several flights of steps to retrieve it and check on her. The second boat was just coming into view as he opened the door to enter the lab.

Todd and Gia were coming toward him, both gingerly carrying boxes with biohazard labels all over. Gia was bundled in a storm slicker. She looked at Scott's drenched uniform and shook her head.

"How bad?" Todd asked.

"Walk in the park old man. Need some help with your luggage?"

Todd gave a good-natured growl. "Nah, just give them a hand with the patient. He isn't looking too good." He motioned to the man in the bio-suit, who was getting unsteadily to his feet.

"Will do. You guys watch your step out there, it's slippery and dangerous as hell. The railing is missing on the south side as well." He walked past them, punching Todd lightly as he went by.

Gia slowed briefly and said, "Take good care of that man, Scott, he's the cure." She then kissed his cheek lightly and disappeared out the door.

Scott was somewhat euphoric as he slipped his pack back on and reached out to help the man in the orange bubble suit. He idly wondered if he should have his suit back on as well. The last of the lab techs carried the remainder of the crates behind Todd and Gia.

Scott put out a hand to the man, and slowly they, too, walked towards the door. Reaching the stairs, Scott could see the second boat attempting to tie off with increasing difficulty. The man in the suit stiffened when he saw the storm, and Scott realized he was not quite as weak as he expected. He tugged on the patient's arm and motioned for him that it was okay. Neither could hear anything the other was saying.

Scott saw a line of dark, ominous clouds approaching fast. The white-caps of the distant waves indicated that the eye wall was closing in quickly. The storm was gearing back up and the southern edge looked even worse than what they had been through so far. Todd and Gia had reached the landing, but Scott was slowed by the patient's awkward and reluctant gait. As Scott tried to coax the man down the slick metal stairs to the landing, it seemed that the gusting wind might blow them both over the edge.

Scott turned to make sure the man was okay and froze. The eyes looking back at him were not those of a helpless man. They were the eyes of a killer. It registered somewhere deep in Scott's primal self that the man had been trying hard to appear small before, because now, standing fully erect, he towered over Scott. The man's fist knocked Scott nearly off his feet. He landed with a gasp on the hard steel mesh grating of the upper deck. The ferocity of the attack was intense and unexpected: a flurry of sharp blows that Scott tried to move into, but he could not help but feel the incredible impact behind each hit. The man was in a fucking bio-suit; how could he do any of this?

Scott realized the guy was trying to get the weapon off his shoulder. The only advantage Scott had was that the bubble suit helmet prevented the patient from seeing anything except what was right in front of him. Scott struggled to shift his weight back, then brought a knee up into the side of the man's head in a Keysi move that would have made Jack proud. But what should have been a knockout blow had only a negligible impact; the man moved preternaturally fast to close the distance and neutralize the blow's impact. Scott could now hear shouts from below. He just caught sight of Todd pushing Gia into the cabin of the boat.

"Scott, what's going on?" came Todd's voice through the dangling earpiece. "Perez! Take him out! Shoot."

Scott could not let that happen. "Don't shoot! We need him alive." He struggled to say it, as his breaths were coming in ragged jerks between blows. He had no idea if they had heard him.

The fight had come to a brief lull, and both men stared at each other. Scott saw no menace in the man now, simply confidence. The patient, realizing his primary disadvantage, began unzipping his bio-suit from the inside. Without the suit, his movements would be unrestricted—

and if he was contagious, they would all be exposed. Scott lunged at the man and was deflected with a hip throw into a metal support beam. Pain lanced throughout his body.

"Skybox, no!" came a woman's shout from below. "He's *not* your enemy!"

Todd and Perez were racing up the steps now. The fight had taken Scott and Skybox perilously close to the edge of the south platform, which had suffered the explosion. Waves were once again beginning to top the lower sections of the structure. The pilot of the Barracudas had no choice but to cut the line to the mooring post. As soon as he moved into open water, he gunned the massive engine just to stay ahead of a mountainous wave. Scott leaned against the post and saw Gia looking at him desperately through a cabin window. A huge swell obscured the boat from view. The departing sounds of the engine let him know that the boat had been recalled to the *Bataan*. They were on their own.

The patient was ready when Perez came down the narrow access walk. Skybox lashed out a surprise kick with unbelievable speed and precision. The Navy SEAL's knee buckled sideways, and he went down. Perez was in agony but brought his .45 up to fire at the man. Skybox had already closed the distance and brought a fist down into the inside of Perez's forearm, shattering bones and ripping tendons. Scott charged at the same time Todd came within reach. This was quickly turning into a fight to the death and to hell with the damn pathogen— this fuck had to die. It was clear that the man had been feigning weakness the entirety of the time; just biding his time and waiting for an opportunity to attack and escape.

The hood of the man's suit prevented him from seeing Todd come up behind him. Todd was leveling a pistol and preparing to fire when Skybox bent sideways and unleashed a powerful high kick backward. The covered boot met Todd's jaw and he went down hard.

Scott prayed the blow had not broken his neck. Scott's own pistol was also out now and Skybox, allowing no time for reaction, charged headlong into him, sending both men crashing into the rail—except there was no rail. There was nothing. Just empty space.

Then, they were gone: swept away in the snarling tumult of the ocean.

CHAPTER SEVENTY-THREE

Todd had regained just enough of his vision to see his friend being propelled over the edge of the platform by the man in the bio-suit.

"Scott!" He tried to pick himself up and went down again, a wave crashing over the walkway and pummeling him into the steel grating. "Man overboard!" he croaked into his headset. "Montgomery and the subject are overboard, repeat, Montgomery and subject are in the water." He stumbled to the edge of the platform looking desperately for his friend.

"Sorry, Cap, no vessels in your vicinity. Can you affect a rescue?" came the concerned response.

"No eyes on the targets," he called over the storm, trying desperately to get his breath back. "They went over the southwest edge." Todd scanned the sea frantically. The driving rain limited visibility to only a few yards, the churning water effectively hiding everything.

The waves were over thirty feet now and continuing to increase. He recalled when Hurricane Ivan had come through in 2004; the waves had reached over 100 feet in this same region. That was a Category 4 storm—far larger than this one—but it was still an unbelievable scene.

No, no, no, Todd tried not to panic. *Scott, please, no.* He had brought his friend out here; he had been the one to ask him to bring the subject to the boat. He had just been the cause of his best friend's death.

Returning to his senses, Todd considered his options. He went back to quickly check on Perez. The man was in bad shape, but it was nothing that wouldn't eventually heal. Sitting him up against a far, dry corner, Todd rushed to the other sections of the platform to continue his search for Scott in the water below.

Nothing. Nothing but churning waves and the tempest's black-gray water. Scott's black battle uniform would be hard to spot, though the orange bio-suit on the other man should be easier to see and would probably keep the bastard afloat. Todd briefly considered going up to the helicopter pad on top to get a better view, but the driving wind and rain combined with the memory of their earlier adventure there, drove his decisions in other directions. He caught sight of something out of the corner of his eye.

"Perez, come in. Shit . . . Apex Two-two, come in."

"Go for Two-two," came the man's pained response.

"Did your men leave the other Barracuda boat?" Todd asked.

Perez was slow to answer him. "I don't know man, that wouldn't be SOP, but I don't recall anyone taking it. It would be suicide for you though, even if you could get it out there. You can't find them on your own."

"Listen, check with control. We don't have a choice. Something—a lot of somethings just came up out of the water, and they're heading our way. You and I have to get the fuck off this rig."

Perez stood weakly on one leg. Todd stopped long enough to help him fashion a metal rod as a splint around the man's knee. They wrapped duct tape and an elastic bandage tightly about it in a thick layer. Seeing that his hand was also dangling loosely from his shattered wrist, Todd bound it tight, using another piece of broken metal for support.

"Let's move." He raced down the steps nearly dragging Perez along.

Over the comm he heard the injured SEAL call control: "Roger, Apex Actual. Two-two attempting exfil now."

The Barracuda Interceptor was thankfully still moored to an out-of-the way blind spot on the oil platform. The Navy had tied it off to multiple posts so that it would rise and fall with the ocean swells. Todd could see no easy way of reaching it and knew Perez couldn't swim. Behind them, the flare of several missile launches brightened the dark sky. The impacts overhead caused the entire rig to shudder violently. The sounds surpassed even the raging storm in volume. The rain, now mixed with shards of molten glass and steel, fell hard as the entire structure gave an ominous groan: metal tearing from metal.

"Ideas?" Todd looked desperately at Perez.

"Grappling hook to the mooring rope. Once you're inside use the code we gave you in training to start the engine. Leave me. Just get away from here."

It was a good idea. Todd reached into his pack for the coil of rope and quickly attached the hook. It took several tries to snag a mooring line; the shifting winds kept carrying the hook off target. Finally, it hit home. Feeling only slightly secure, Todd leapt into the sea and was immediately pulled violently from the surface and away from the oil rig. Keeping the rope tight in his grasp, he began to work hand over hand to travel the twenty feet between the rig and the sleek boat. The surging water felt as though it wanted to tear his limbs from his torso. Never had he felt power like this from the ocean.

After what seemed an eternity, he reached the boat and climbed into the tiny enclosed cabin. He was exhausted from the effort but keyed the start sequence and leaned out to cut the mooring lines just as another round of rockets hit the upper decks.

Gunning the craft, he fought to maneuver over to the platform where Perez stood. The SEAL was shaking his head and waving him off with his good arm. Todd nosed the boat near enough for Perez to simply fall in, just before another wave rocketed the craft backward several hundred yards. He could see Perez had landed badly, but he was onboard and managed to pull himself through the cabin door.

Todd briefly released the controls to reach back and slam the water-tight cabin door shut on the injured man. It was going to be a bumpy ride. He accelerated in the direction Scott and the patient had been carried. The wind and waves would have had to push them this way . . . He was forced to learn the nuances of the small craft quickly and had managed to put more distance between him and the oil platform when a massive fireball erupted from it.

"Apex Actual for Apex Two-two, come in."

He keyed the mic. "This is Cap, Two-two is passed out."

There was a slight pause, "Roger, Cap, we have you on scope. Be advised: hostile force is believed to be autonomous drone ships, and some are in pursuit of your vessel. Use evasive maneuvers and return to base."

Todd was at his mental breaking point. Steering the unfamiliar vessel in these conditions was proving to be a tremendous challenge, and he was desperate to find his friend. The craft's unique hull profile, which made it hard to see on radar, also made it a bitch to control. He had to keep searching for Scott, but he also knew the boat didn't carry much fuel, and that he'd be in a lot more trouble if he hung around much longer. He accelerated north several more seconds in a zig-zag pattern before responding.

"Acknowledged, returning to base." He would get the Navy to start a proper search for Scott once he was back on the *Bataan*. He noticed a bundle lashed to the sidewall of the cabin labeled 'rescue'. He idled the craft, and between the massive waves, he made his way over to unlatch the large yellow bag. He opened the door and tossed it out, letting the wind carry it over a hundred yards before settling it into the mael-strom. Perhaps it would find its way to Scott. It was an admittedly weak effort, but perhaps it might reach him.

CHAPTER SEVENTY-FOUR
Central Mississippi

Hawley watched with rapt attention as Michael spoke. He still had it. He fed off the crowd, steadily transforming himself back into the Prophet.

The last couple of weeks had been challenging, but the Message still had to be delivered. Yes, Michael conceded, Satan would put obstacles in their path. Still, while they were unsure who they had been attacked by in Memphis, the Prophet would find a solution. He always did.

"Brothers and sisters, hear me. We have all suffered this past year. Why? Because *we* all were being judged. The Lord used His white-hot, purifying fire to cleanse this planet. The last time He walked among us, He sent His son to give us the chance for everlasting life. And what did the world do? It attacked Him! The people rejected Him, they crucified Him. Since then, Christians have been under attack: the media attacked us, the liberals and homosexuals attacked us, our own government tried to silence us," Hawley frowned at the logic of his Prophet's message . . . Where was he going with this? "Is it any wonder that the Lord has used another son—the Earth's sun—to deliver His new message?" Ahhh, very clever. The Messengers loved a bit of word play in their oratory. "We all have suffered because of His judgment upon the non-Christians of this world. Now those who have survived must pay the price."

Michael watched with fascination as the crowd got worked into a frenzy. He loved this part. His heart raced and his breath came hard with excitement and the rush of some of the drugs. Subtly, he gave the signal to Hawley that, yes indeed, he would be needing another young playmate for the night. He brought the microphone closer to his lips. The next lines had to be delivered with just the right tone.

"Evil has not yet been banished. We saw that in Memphis. Satan is fighting back, like a wild beast that is backed into a corner. Our crusade is sweeping the country clean of the devil's minions," his arms swept wide and his lips curled in reference to the enemy. "Those who have worshiped false gods, those who have craved riches, those who have slaughtered their unborn children . . . They will be judged. We will find them and wreak vengeance in their evil souls. I may be your leader, but alas, I am but a humble servant—a simple vessel for the Lord's message to find strength among you."

Damn, he could sell flashlights to a blind man, Hawley thought as he smiled widely in the direction of his Prophet.

"We are on the verge of a great victory! Once that victory is ours, we will have a holy fire with which to complete the purification of this planet! We will use it to propel God's message across the globe! Brothers, we let godliness slip away here in America. Not all at once, but bit by tiny bit. We stepped away from the Ten Commandments. We found excuses to not go to church. We looked at things on TV and the Internet that took root in our heart and, bit by bit, took our goodness away!

We have paid the price for that! We have lost our homes, our lifestyles, our simplicity," he paused momentarily for added effect. "We have lost loved ones who were precious to us. Don't let that be in vain. We may have lost much, but we will reclaim with conviction, and in one clear voice!

"We repent, oh Lord! We are your children, and we will do your work and loudly carry your message to the lost! We will vanquish evil in all the vile forms we find it, for you are a loving God and we are your hand here on Earth. We will minister to the ignorant and judge those that stand against us, for ours is a righteous movement!"

Holding up a weathered Bible, he went on. "Ezekiel 9:6 . . . 'Slay utterly old and young, both maids, and little children, and women: but come not near any man upon whom is the mark; and begin at my sanctuary.' Touch no one that has the mark! No one. Except for the one." The crowd fell wholly silent at this declaration.

"There is one out there—one who has murdered our own, attacked our Judges and defiled our women—one man who has injected his demonic venom into our group again and again. This man tried to lead us to our destruction in Memphis. He was a wolf, hiding amongst us lambs. While he falsely bears the mark, our beloved battle cross, he—must—be —vanquished. He must atone for what he has done to God's people!

"Brother Hawley, please pass around the picture." They had one image of Bobby Montgomery someone had taken on one of the few still working iPhones. The men studied it and frowned before passing it along to the next. "This animal is around here and must be found! He must be brought before me for judgment." He paused again and then, in a quieter voice, added, "The Messenger who does so will get his choice of women and first choice on rations for the duration of our crusade. He will also enjoy my full protection from harm."

The audience erupted into thunderous applause. With rewards like that, Hawley knew these idiots would do just about anything to bring Montgomery in. The number of Messengers was increasing daily as those who had been on the Arkansas side finally crossed the river at Vicksburg and joined up at the camp near Jackson, Mississippi. Most of them were in bad shape. Even the Prophet knew they were in no shape to launch a full assault against an enemy. The Judges were making forays into smaller towns and even the edges of Jackson to secure buses, trucks and other modes of mass transportation. But these were being done with caution.

Several school systems had donated big yellow buses to the effort—

without realizing it, of course. Fuel had been harder to come by, but if you asked the right questions, even that could be acquired. The willingness of the Judges to do whatever was required when it came to questioning people always did wonders for the group's supplies. Under their intimidating influence, those interrogated would always crack eventually. It rarely took long.

The Prophet came down from the podium and made a show of touching many of those gathered near the front. While much of it was theater, the effect was still mesmerizing . . . people wanted to believe; they wanted someone to follow. It was a shame that money no longer had any value, he thought, as it would have been a great moment to pass around the collection plates.

Seeing the young girl waiting outside his tent, Michael felt confident the night's offering would be just as pleasing as the previous.

CHAPTER SEVENTY-FIVE

"Fuck! I don't need this," Michael paced, his face livid. No matter the adoring crowds, all he could focus on was the losses.

"Your Holiness, we just lost too much at Memphis. The fuel, the food, the vehicles. The men are exhausted. Best estimates are we have about 3,500 men left in camp. We only have food for about half that each day. Even on half-rations, it's going to be tough. If you also want to keep the women fed...even less."

Michael fumed. "Bring him to me."

Leaning out the tent flap, Hawley yelled for the Judges to bring the new convert. They pulled him roughly into the tent, and a quick kick knocked him to his knees. The fresh, black ink of the tattoo mixed with the blood on the man's hand. One of the men calmly ate a pickle as he watched.

"New converts are not usually permitted to view me privately," Michael said in a papery voice. "I am granting you . . . an exemption. I want to see your eyes. I want to ensure that what you say next is truthful. Is that clear?"

The man made no move to respond. Hawley kicked him hard in the ribs and he doubled over, winded. Michael continued. "My disciples picked you out of a river near Vicksburg. They said you were towing several empty boats. My friend, I require the identities of the people who left you those boats, and to know where they are headed."

Michael walked over to the table and picked up a pair of gleaming, steel pruning shears. A small brownish stain on the blades was the only sign of wear. "If I believe you are deceiving me or withholding anything, you will be judged. I'm afraid it will not be particularly quick. Is that perfectly clear?" His final words were almost a whisper as they fell on the fearful man's ears.

Hawley met with his Judges later that day. He and Michael had gotten tired and left the heavy-duty torture to them sometime in the afternoon.

"You were right," one of the henchmen said, "he was with him. The river rat didn't know much, but he said the traitor has family down toward Mobile."

Hawley nodded, "That jives with what our other man said. Word is they have lots of supplies down there." Gingerly, he touched the raw burns on his face. "I think a beach vacation will do us all good." He smiled at the prospect. "Get some seafood, work on our tans, kill us some non-believers. A little rest and recuperation. Put the word out. We're going to start moving south in the next few days. We'll take as many as we can in the trucks and buses. The rest will be on foot until they find other transportation. They are to keep looking for the marked man. He should be heading the same way, and now he has a woman and a mute boy with him. They should be easy to find."

CHAPTER SEVENTY-SIX

USS Bataan, Gulf of Mexico

Two members of the SEAL team extracted on the first boat came back to the aid of their brothers in arms. They gently lifted the badly injured Perez out of the Barracuda. Todd had managed with great difficulty to get the small boat back to the ship and then into the tender garage. The waves were so large that he had not seen the aircraft carrier until he was nearly on top of it. The burning wreckage of the Devil's Tower had been the beacon he had used to navigate. The stored oil in the tanks there would burn for days, fanned even larger by the hurricane force winds.

He had come across two floating bodies in black fatigues: both dead SEAL team members. He had managed to recover the bodies, although it hadn't been easy. An officer helped Todd out of the stealth boat. "Lieutenant," he said shakily, "we need to launch an SAR. Can I speak with your Commanding Officer?"

"Sorry, sir." The man's patch read Garret. "The CO has his hands full right now. Someone on the rig must have sent an alert. We're now battling unmanned craft and have radar tracks on multiple incoming bogeys. Command is aware of your man and the medical subject missing, but no teams can be sent out now due to the rough seas."

"That's bullshit, Lieutenant, you—we have to get those men."

"Sir, my father is Commander Garret, I understand fully. But you just came through that storm, sir. You know it would be suicide to send more men out there right now, even if we could. This ship is not designed to weather these conditions. Sir, the CO feels we have lost enough men for today. Our returning boats dropped dye-packs with radio markers. We will track the current and drift rates and return when the storm passes. Right now, we need to get you to medical and get that chin sewn up. You're also going to need to have blood drawn."

"Fuck that," Todd was desperate. "I need a ride, Garret. I know damn well you have choppers with thermals. They can travel above the storm and we can use the infrared to look through the cloud cover. That man out there *is* the mission! And the other one is my best friend."

"Sir, I'm afraid we don't have that. None of the FLIR equipment survived the CME. The electronics were too sensitive."

"Where's Garret senior? Get him here now. He planned this mission, he asked us to be on it."

The young man placed a hand on Todd's shoulder. "As I said, he has his hands full. Trust me, sir, even if it was me out there, he would be doing the very same thing right now. Please, I have to get you over to screening."

Todd was upset but didn't object further. He was at heart a sailor and knew the protocol. Anyone who stepped foot on that rig had to be screened. Todd looked at the slowly closing bay door at the angry, gray sea beyond. *Scott, my friend . . . what have I done?*

Todd was led into the medical bay where the younger Garret turned him over to an orderly. Quietly, he began treating the wound and drawing blood, saliva and tissue samples. The ship rolled and swung as it tried to get out of the range of the attacking craft and the hurricane.

The up and down movement of the deck let him know that conditions outside were not improving.

In a nearby room, sealed off by reinforced metal and glass walls, he could see Dr. Colton and her team carefully moving equipment and supplies into place. She looked up at him, deep concern etched in her expression. Todd could not meet her eyes.

As the med tech finished up, he advised him to stay put until the test results were back. Gia approached from the lab. She was still in the same clothes and as soaking wet as he was.

"Scott?"

Todd looked straight ahead before shaking his head.

"He . . . he didn't make it?" she asked. "Is he dead?"

Still looking at the floor, Todd forced his eyes to meet hers. They were a most amazing shade of blue. "He and your patient went into the ocean." He felt as though he were under a microscope and dropped his eyes. "I tried to find them, but it was . . . it was impossible."

"Oh, God, Scott is out there? In that?"

"Yes," Todd admitted with resignation.

"No one could survive . . . could they?" Her eyes were beginning to water.

"I want to say yes, but . . . no. The current is too strong, and the waves are enormous. If they haven't drowned, hypothermia will get them." The reality of this hurt Todd to the very core. "The Navy will launch search and rescue when it's safe, but I'm afraid it will be too late by then. In that regard, they will probably only look for your patient. His body is the only one that's essential."

Tears streaked the doctor's face. "I am so sorry," she said. "We never thought of Skybox as a threat. He was so easy going and friendly. Over the weeks, we forgot that he was a soldier. He was just our patient."

"He was a Grayshirt?" Todd asked.

"What?" She remembered that was what DJ and some of the others had called them on campus. She nodded. "He was a Praetor commander."

"That man was a Praetor 5 commander?"

"No, he's in Praetor 9, which is, I don't know, a higher rank, I think? A more elite unit? All I know is that he lost his entire squad to the Chimera outbreak at the originating bio-lab. And somehow he survived."

Todd thought about that. He didn't think he had ever heard or read anything about Praetor 9. "So, he would know everything they were up to?"

"Maybe, but I don't think so," Dr. Colton considered for a moment before continuing. "I believe he had full information concerning his mission, but he seemed fairly clueless about anything else we asked him."

"What kinds of things did you ask him?"

She pursed her lips. "All kinds. We asked him what he knew of what was going on in the world, what the president was doing to solve the crises, how long it would be before things were back to normal . . ."

"Hmmm, might be better he didn't give you those answers." She looked puzzled. He continued, "So you're saying that this commander —Skybox—is immune from the disease?"

"No. Not exactly. He carries the pathogen—he is definitely infected— but he's asymptomatic. The Chimera agent is almost completely dormant in him. We were trying to find out why and how to replicate whatever's working in his immune system to possibly help slow the spread of the outbreak."

Todd processed all this silently for several moments. "He certainly didn't appear to be diminished. In fact, he seemed . . . superhuman. My jaw was nearly broken by him, and he almost killed one other SEAL. He fought three of us with ease."

The doctor looked thoughtful. "Well, some of that could possibly be symptomatic emergence. The pathogen *is* having an effect on him, just not like it does on most others. Certainly not to the level of being infectious, at least not yet. See, the last few weeks we have been attempting to jumpstart the virus in his system so that we could study it in action. That could be part of what is happening. If so, it may be that he possesses increased speed, more intense emotion, higher testosterone levels . . . but what I assumed is that he is just a typical Praetor 9 soldier. I've heard some of the other guards talk about them. They are the ultra-elite—the most intelligent and most capable."

"I see," said Todd. "Considering the normal Praetor 5 troops were apparently elite Special Forces soldiers, that would make Skybox an exceptional weapon without any enhancements. In other words," he sighed, "Scott never had a chance."

Drying her eyes with a tissue, she asked, "How long has Scott been a soldier?"

Laughing, Todd checked his watch and said, "That would be just over three days."

Her face scrunched into a slight frown. She wanted to know more but had to check on the progress with her team. Suddenly, she was completely composed and fully back in control. "Todd, I'm sorry about Scott, and I appreciate what you two did for us. But we have to find Skybox. Convince the captain. Nothing else matters—*nothing*." She walked away, her still wet bare feet leaving a trail on the hard floor.

CHAPTER SEVENTY-SEVEN

It was several anxious hours before the storm had eased enough to launch a search and rescue. Todd sat in the briefing room with the surviving SEALs. Also in attendance was the Deputy Air Wing commander, Air Intelligence Officer, Chief Medical Officer, and the CO, Commander Garret, was linked in by radio.

The AIO, a woman by the name of Howard, spoke first. "Gentlemen," she greeted the room somberly, "We had significant loss of life in today's operation, which saddens us greatly. Despite that fact, however, we were successful in all original primary mission objectives. If what Dr. Colton and Mr. Hansen say is true, though, we now need to find the missing patient. It seems the Catalyst bio-researchers were essentially at a standstill until he came along."

A young man seated at the table spoke up. "With respect, sir, there is no way anyone could survive that." He motioned to a steel bulkhead, but everyone in the room knew what the young officer meant. The massive waves, the undercurrents and the water temperature all combined to spell death to anyone caught in its grip.

Todd leaned in. He had been silent, but he decided it was time to state the obvious. "One of those people out there is one of my best friends.

He is strong, resourceful and very smart, but I'm no fool. I was out there in it, and I have no illusions. I realize this is probably a recovery mission now, not a rescue, but we have to try. The other subject is a Praetor commander. He may hold the keys to treating or curing this pandemic disease. And Scott . . . well, the Navy owes him that much."

Garret spoke up. "I echo Todd's sentiments. We lost some fine soldiers out there today. Let's not take their sacrifices lightly. In order to complete this mission, we must recover the bodies and search for survivors. As soon as flight paths clear, let's get more birds in the air."

Howard spoke again, "The civilian on the SEAL team—Scott?— wouldn't he have an active pinger?" The pingers were water-activated and sent out an emergency distress beacon.

One of the other SEALs, a man they called Ladybug for some odd reason, answered her. "Scott was kitted out the same as the rest of the team. He has on a new thin-skin drysuit, which offers some protection and flotation, but his kit did not have the active pingers. Only the swimmers routinely get those. He does have a dye pack and a UV flasher, though, which will last about twenty-four hours before the battery dies. The good thing is that the water temperature is relatively warm, so hypothermia won't be a threat yet. If he has somehow survived the storm so far, he has a chance. We have enough reason to look for him simply because the Praetor commander will likely be in the same vicinity."

The airboss gave the orders for all remaining mission sorties to launch a full search and rescue. The drift and wind coordinates had narrowed the search to a seven-by-twenty-two-mile path. That was over 154 square miles, which put the odds of finding them somewhere close to the same as winning the national lottery. Back when lotteries still existed, that is.

The massive movements of man power and equipment were impressive, especially when it came down to finding just two men. Sadly, the SAR missions were doomed to fail from the very beginning; the time span between when Scott and Skybox went into the water and the Navy released a tracer dye package was thirty-seven minutes. In that time, the direction of the storm winds and intensity had changed slightly. Despite the Navy accounting for the shift, they overestimated the intensity. The error meant the search grid's beginning was six miles farther west than it should be, and almost thirty miles off-target at the far end of the grid.

CHAPTER SEVENTY-EIGHT

Harris Springs, Mississippi

"My God!"

"Yeah, tell me about it," laughed Jack. "Who would have thought, people actually pay attention to disaster warnings now."

Angel and Jack watched the growing line of farmers, helped by the residents of Harris Springs, move various animals and belongings onto the ship.

She looked nervously out over the assembling mass. "Will we have enough space? Enough food and water?"

"We have plenty of space," he soothed her. "And they're bringing food with them. But water, we are going to need to watch. Bartos has got the pools working as cisterns and all the tanks are full of fresh water instead of salt brine. We'll be fine for a fair while."

"Let's hope that's all it is. Any word from Todd or Scott? Or Kaylie and Bartos?"

Jack scratched at the stubble under his chin before answering. "Bartos should be back in just a few hours. We got a very short message from him earlier. Still no word from the other two. DeVonte is monitoring the comms, though."

"You're worried, aren't you?" she asked.

"I'm concerned, dear, that's all. Scott's always talking about cascading failures—how one problem can lead to another and so on until everything breaks down. Essentially that's what's been happening to everything since last year. Right now, we need to be concentrating on the crops we've planted, preparing supplies for the winter, and getting crews over to the dam to continue working on power generation. Instead, we have to prepare for a major storm with flooding and wind damage, we are in the path of an attacking army and most of our leadership is AWOL. So, in answer to your question, yes, I am concerned." He paused, then added. "Ok, I'm a little worried."

Angel put her hand on Jack's shoulder. "Preacher, keep that to yourself. Everyone around here is looking for us to keep them safe. Don't give them any reason to doubt. We have the people moving in well ahead of the problems. Bartos and his guys have a good defensive plan, and with luck, Todd and the Navy will be here to help us when it comes to the crusaders. Stay positive and help these people keep the faith. It's going to be a long few days, and we're going to need everyone's help. Let's go get them started."

∾

Jack and Angel had their hands full dividing up the new arrivals into teams. Some of them secured the animals and supplies. Others went to help set up defensive measures for the storm. Everyone coming aboard knew of the pending arrival of the storm and the Messengers. Each was expected to pitch in to help prepare for one or the other.

Bartos' old shop foreman, Scoots, was just finishing connecting the hoses to water cannons. Originally, they'd been installed for firefighting on deck, but Scoots had made it so they could be directed outward—and with lethal force. Under Bartos' instructions, he had also added a secondary supply hose into which fine sand could be introduced into the jet. The sand, which they had an endless supply of, would be propelled with a tremendous force out of the small nozzle and would act as a strong abrasive to anyone unlucky enough to get caught in the blast. Much like a sand-blaster removing old paint, the water-and-sand cannons would be a painful, if not lethal, experience. As soon as he finished showing the men looking on how to do it, they went to modify the others on deck.

Another group was busy working on a recipe that amounted to home-made napalm. It was created from diesel fuel, alcohol and styrofoam broken into small pieces. The plan was that it could be dropped over the side onto any force trying to climb up the sides of the ship. Several men were busy making rack after rack of Molotov cocktails with the napalm, and some genius had improvised a PVC grenade with a kind of impact igniter. They had even gone a step further and converted a larger PVC pipe into a compressed air cannon in order to launch the improvised grenades farther away.

Drums of diesel fuel were positioned on the deck, ready to drop into the canal where they could be ignited. Trench pits were dug on the far side that would also contain explosives. Anti-truck spikes were installed, barbed wire was strung below the surface of the waterway, and heavy guns had been brought into place on multiple decks.

The hardest part so far was proving to be the shielding and reinforce-ment of the lower deck's exterior cabin windows. They would be the easiest areas to attack, and having the ship open to the elements was something they wanted to avoid.

They were unpacking the .50 caliber guns Jack had gotten in Slidell when they realized the ammo was missing. *Abe.* Jack couldn't get past his guilt at having brought that traitorous bastard to the *AG.* "I hope you rot in hell," he growled, glancing down at the blood stain still visible on the docks below.

The sheer volume of work being done was impressive. Everyone was nervous and on edge. They had passed word for everyone to take a break at six that evening to enjoy a community meal. He and Angel were going to address the group at that time. They hoped Bartos would also be back by then, so they could get an update on the problem to the north.

CHAPTER SEVENTY-NINE

"Preacher, we gonna be aight?" a haggard-looking black man asked. Angel and DeVonte were standing nearby, also looking worn out.

Jack was standing on a small platform to one side of the dining hall. He pinched the bridge of his nose trying to decide how much to tell. "We have our hands full, I'm not going to lie to you. We all have an idea of what we are up against with the Messengers. We are in for a fight. I know our defenses are good, and this ship is solid, but we can't underestimate them. On top of that, this storm coming in is going to be tough. I just got off the radio with Todd who is stuck out at sea with the Navy right now."

Jack paused, thinking back to what else Todd had said, or more accurately, not said on the radio call. "The Navy is willing to help if it comes to a fight, and that certainly seems a likelihood. While the Messengers have been having their way with most places, we are more secure and have friends with big sticks. That does not mean the Navy will come in at the first sign of trouble. Chances are we will have to fight our own battles until we know what size group we are dealing with. That's why all of us are doing our best with the defensive measures. We appreciate you being here, and rest assured it's far safer than being out there . . . but go ahead and get it in your head: you will have to fight.

"This may be your refuge from the storm, but you are going to have to work for it. I trust the good Lord to keep us safe. If each of you does your part, we will be fine." Then he repeated one of his favorite psalms: "'He is my refuge and my fortress: my God; in him will I trust. Surely, he shall deliver thee from the snare of the fowler, and from the noisome pestilence. He shall cover thee with his feathers, and under his wings shalt thou trust: his truth shall be thy shield and buckler. Thou shalt not be afraid for the terror by night; nor for the arrow that flieth by day; nor for the pestilence that walketh in darkness; nor for the destruction that wasteth at noonday. A thousand shall fall at thy side, and ten thousand at thy right hand; but it shall not come nigh thee.'

"Brothers and sisters, do not fear these people who do not serve our Lord, but only their own wickedness. We will be victorious in our battle against evil."

Numerous "Amens" rang out through the room. Truthfully, Jack had doubts, more about himself than the Lord. He trusted his faith, but through a lifetime of fighting, he'd learned to trust his sword nearly as much. If it had just been his life he was responsible for, he would have felt better, but now he worried for all these friends and neighbors. He thought back to the priest in Slidell. Father Ernesto had seen the evil, and it scared him, scarred him. Jack didn't want that to be him. He felt that the good Lord normally expected you to do your own fighting, not just sit there in prayer looking for a miracle. That was precisely what they needed, though.

While he was temporarily in charge, his fighting skills were primarily close-quarter self-defense. He knew little about military action if it came to that, and even less about the ship's systems if anything went wrong during the storm. The simple truth was that he missed his friends from both an emotional and a practical standpoint. Todd had been essential to Jack getting his life straightened out, and Bartos and Scott were like brothers now. The four of them had stepped forward at a crucial moment to help save the town and each other. They were a team.

He was sure Todd was holding something back when they talked, and now Jack couldn't get past the unvoiced implication that Scott might be gone. Together they had been united in keeping this community alive; separately they were much less effective. He said his final words and turned the platform over to Angel, who addressed individual assignments.

He walked out the glass doors to the deck rail and watched the sun setting over the Gulf. Clouds were already beginning to build, and the coming weather produced a brilliant sunset. He checked his watch; Bartos should be back anytime now. Bowing his head, Jack said a prayer for his friends and the mission that each was on. Then he asked for protection for the group entrusted to his care. "We do need your help, oh Lord."

Looking out, he remembered the opening line from the Dylan Thomas poem tacked above Scott's work desk down below: "Do not go gentle into that good night, Old age should burn and rave at close of day; Rage, rage against the dying of the light."

A rage was exactly what he had burning up from inside.

CHAPTER EIGHTY

Bartos dropped the radio and pushed the pedal, easing the red needle closer to ninety. They had all heard DeVonte give the report on things back at the *Aquatic Goddess*. He would have stayed on a few minutes longer, but they had a motorcycle pursuing them down the country road: one of the dreaded Judges. Bartos, well, he really didn't care; in the movies, a man on a motorcycle might seem like a threat, but he wasn't much of one in real life. In the battle of GTO versus motorcycle, he had no doubt who would win.

Bobby was not doing too well, but the poultice that Ms. Mahalia had kept applying to his wound was beginning to help. It smelled and looked awful, but the redness around the wound and the fever were much improved. He glanced back every now and then to check the distance between them and the lone Judge. "So, where is Scott again?"

Kaylie went through it for the third time, but Bobby just couldn't wrap his head around it: his kid brother on a special ops raid at a terrorist location? "Dad, he's not the same anymore, he—he's, I don't know . . . different."

"He's a survivor," Bartos chimed in. Looking back at him in the mirror. "Hell, we're all different now, including your little girl."

"I see that," Bobby said with a hint of sadness.

"Hey, Pops, looks like that bandage needs changing. Bartos, you got your first aid kit in the car?" Kaylie was already looking.

"Yeah, I have a first aid kit: whiskey and duct-tape. Which one you need first?"

"Don't be an ass," she said with a smirk.

"It's in the top of the go-bag. Trauma kit is to the side."

She opened the Maxpedition pack and quickly found the kit. Removing the surgical wipes and fresh gauze, she leaned into the back-seat and began peeling away the fouled bandages from the wound. "Wow, this looks pretty good considering it's so recent. Your friends knew what to do." She dabbed some antibacterial cream around it anyway and applied the new dressing. She glanced up to see her dad wince several times, but she just smiled and kept working. "I know, Dad. I'm pretty used to seeing gruesome now. I'm terribly sorry it's you, and I know it hurts, but trust me. I know what needs to be done."

"I know you do sweetheart . . ." he said through gritted teeth, "I'm . . . just very proud of you. I didn't know what shape you would be in. It's so bad out there."

"You raised her right, Bobby, and she is a fast learner," Bartos said into the mirror. "Uh-oh, here he comes again. This guy's an idiot. I'm not leading him all the way to Harris Springs. He has to go."

Bobby looked over at Jacob who was curled up asleep with one hand lying on Solo's head. "How you want to play it?"

"I would just brake-check the goofy fuck—he's doing about ninety, and since I don't have brake lights he'd be roadkill in seconds—but that would damage the trunk and bumper. That spoiler back there would be hard as hell to replace."

Kaylie just laughed, shaking her head. "It's a car, Bartos, seriously." She rolled her eyes at her dad.

"Women," Bartos shook his head. "If I remember correctly, there's a small rise coming up in a mile or two. I'm gonna put a bit more distance between us then stop just over the rise of the hill. The three of us will be armed and ready when he tops it."

"That sounds like an Uncle Scott move, like on his bike," Kaylie said

"I know. It worked for him, should work for us. Weapons hot ya'll. I am going to swing the car to give us a firing platform. Solo, ready." Bartos cleared the hill, cut speed and swung the goat partially sideways in the road. Bobby leaned awkwardly out the side window. Kaylie got out on her side and took aim over the roof with her M4. Bartos walked out to the middle of the road, his carbine at low ready. Solo hopped out by Kaylie and padded over to the ditch nearer the hilltop.

The sound of the approaching motorcycle increased in volume. As it crested the hill, a volley of shots rang out. The motorcycle went down, the driver clutching at his chest. Bartos held up a hand as he approached the figure writhing on the ground.

"Man, you picked a lousy day to try and be a hero." Bartos kicked the man's legs as he circled him. Reaching down he withdrew a large pistol from the man's shoulder holster.

"Whoa, whoa, brother, I'm one of you," he held up a hand with the black cross tattoo.

"If you're one of us, why you chasing us?" Bartos asked the fallen rider.

"I'm shot, man, I'm fucking bleeding out, help me please."

Bartos laughed, "I'm not helping you man, shit . . . I'm the one who shot you. Saving your life would be, like, counterproductive to my goals. Now answer my fucking question, or . . ." he motioned to Solo who was instantly at the man's throat with a deep growl and his teeth bared; his face showed anticipation at the opportunity for another kill.

"Whoa, whoa, please! Mister, just call him off." The man ended the plea with a wheezing cough that sent a spray of blood down his chin.

"Yeah, can't do that either. He hasn't eaten today, and he gets a might cranky when he's hungry. Looks like you got a collapsed lung . . . you're not likely to make it much longer one way or the other. I need an answer now. Why were you chasing us?"

"I, I thought you were part of the recon convoy. I was just trying to catch up! Most of the Judges and recon teams pulled out this morning heading to that place on the coast. I had to find some gas for my bike, and I got left behind."

"How many of you are there?" Bartos was dead serious now.

"I don't know, mister, honest I don't . . . thousands—maybe three hundred in the recon division and three or four thousand total. Most of them are behind us."

"So, we're behind the worst of them and ahead of the main body? Are they all using the same route?" The man closed his eyes and seemed to fade. Bartos kicked him in the ribs. "Answer me now."

The man struggled to put words together. "Huh? No, different routes, but this one should be the quickest." His eyes fluttered. "Help me, in God's name, help—"

"What else can you tell us? Who is this prophet fellow? Is he behind or ahead of us?" The man didn't answer. Bartos kicked him again. "Answer me!" he yelled.

"Bartos, I think he's dead," Kaylie said as she and Bobby approached. She checked his pulse. "Yep, you're interrogating a corpse."

Bartos looked mildly embarrassed, "Sorry, I have issues, okay?"

They checked the man's pockets quickly, finding a few items of use. Bartos was desperate for a better plan. Speed alone would no longer work. "Kaylie, you're going to have to drive the car. I'm gonna use this clown's bike to scout ahead. If you see me slowing down, you find a place to disappear. We'll probably need to take some side roads, but I know them, the Messenger's don't. Be ready for trouble. Bobby, you better ride shotgun."

CHAPTER EIGHTY-ONE

The Judges' path of destruction quickly became apparent. Houses burned, bodies hung from trees. They were within twenty miles of Harris Springs before they encountered the first group: a recon team collecting supplies.

"Dad, get ready," Kaylie whispered. Her dad looked ashen but nodded his head grimly. Up ahead she could see Bartos waving at the men. He wore a pair of leather riding gloves he had taken from the dying man.

Bartos pulled right up to the group. "Which way did they head?" He had to yell over the noise of the Harley.

One of the guys stopped what he was doing and eyed Bartos suspiciously. "Geeze, man, that bike is way too big for you." Bartos shot him in the head, making a neat hole through the man's *Jesus Saves* hat.

He eyed the next man. "Which way?"

"Sorry, sorry man, Earl didn't mean nothin'. They went down 'at road yonda, toward Highway 50."

Bartos took off, waving the car on behind him. He did not take the highway but cut through to a less direct route to Harris Springs—one that led to the ferry landing. Once they were away from the group, he slowed enough to tell Kaylie the plan. She radioed ahead to the *AG* to let them know to be ready. "Make sure the bridges are raised and have the ferry at the dock in ten minutes," she finished, accelerating to keep up with Bartos.

The GTO was fishtailing around turns trying to stay close to Bartos. Several times they glimpsed a dust cloud from the adjacent beach road, raised by the Judges that were using it to reach the main highway into town. The route they were on meant they would be stopped by the raised drawbridges. Kaylie was worried she and Bartos wouldn't make it to the ferry in time, but it was the only chance they had.

She followed Bartos as he left the side road and slowed onto the dirt trail that went back to the secluded ferry dock. He drove the bike onto the barge just ahead of Kaylie in the car. As she pulled up, Bartos placed something beneath the dock and jumped back over just as the ferry pulled away for the far shore.

"Bobby, can you help?" Bartos handed him a nylon line that ran back to the dock. "When it gets to the end, tug it. That'll arm the Claymore I planted under it."

Bobby took the line as it rapidly fed back to the dock. He wanted to be as far away as possible before tugging, just in case. Bartos was getting back on the motorcycle; the far shore was approaching fast. The massive dirt cloud from the bikers was clearly visible now, just a few hundred yards to the west. Bobby reached the end of the line and gave a sharp tug. The line briefly went tight, then slackened again as the safety key came free from the explosive mine beneath the wooden dock.

He coiled the rope and hopped back in the car with his daughter and Jacob. He noticed the dog was gone again. Before he could wonder too much about its whereabouts, the massive white cruise ship came into view. "So that's the *AG*? Wow, hell of a bugout shelter," he remarked, visibly impressed.

Kaylie whipped the car up the short ramp. The man operating the ferry had hopped on the back of Bartos' bike, and all were soon helped into the bowels of the ship.

CHAPTER EIGHTY-TWO

Harris Springs, Mississippi

Jack was waiting by the steel door when the group arrived. "I see you brought company for dinner," he smiled, holding his hand out to Bobby in welcome. Hasty introductions were made. The preacher looked genuinely happy to meet Scott's brother.

The cloud of worry Jack was feeling had thinned a little at their arrival. "Glad to see you made it, friend. Let's get you on over to medical. Jacob, I think Angel might have some sandwiches waiting for you in the dining hall." Kaylie took the boy and her father and headed off to get both taken care of. Jack walked over to Bartos and quietly asked, "Jesus Christ, friend, just how bad is it?"

"Pretty bad, Preacher. We got the worst of them gathering on the far bank right now. The Judges. Probably be a few hundred by nightfall. The rest will be coming over the next few days. It will be all we can handle."

"Well, shit, should we call the Navy for help?"

Bartos looked at his friend and shook his head. "Not yet. I guess they're still busy with the raid on Devil's Tower. Besides, if they hit them now, they'll be missing the main body of the Messengers, and the fucking beloved leader. No, we're gonna have to stand our ground 'til the rest of 'em are here. Then the Navy can come in and do some real damage."

"Those guys aren't going to just sit there, Bartos," Jack was nervous about this plan. "They're going to be trying to take this ship. That's what they do."

"I know, Jack." Bartos looked his friend in the eye. "You and Scoots finished up the defenses, didn't you?"

The preacher nodded. "Yeah, everything you wanted . . . plus we moved the ammo and guns on board."

"Good. It's time to seal the ship. Call everyone in and secure the hatches. Get the fighters in defensive positions. Keep everyone else below deck and away from the portside windows."

"Will do," Jack turned to undertake his orders, then paused and spun back to his friend. "And Bartos, damn glad to see you back. That was a crazy thing to go do, but I'm glad it worked. And I'm glad you're back."

Bartos smiled at his buddy and then walked up the darkened stairs to the bridge wing. It was several floors above the main deck and extended far out to a point almost even with the side of the ship. It was a useful vantage point for tricky docking maneuvers or tight passages. Today it gave a front row seat to the events going on below.

So far, the group looked to be about fifty riders, mostly talking and laughing, some assessing their surroundings. Bartos laughed to see the line of alligators at the near side of the ship. Angel had been dumping food scraps over the side for the last few weeks to keep them close. Now they were part of their defense and offered an effective intimidation measure. The immediate obstacles would frustrate the men for a while, but he had no doubt the attacks would soon begin in earnest. It would not be long.

CHAPTER EIGHTY-THREE

Unknown location - Gulf of Mexico

Scott Montgomery was alive. Clinging to nothing more than hope, he was still alive. He had gone through a range of emotions in the last day, from despair to anger. He kept reliving the shock of entering the roiling ocean only to be swept out of sight on the crest of a truly massive wave. The pull had been incredible, and that single wave had taken him far enough away from the oil platform that he could no longer see it. An unimaginable weight of the waves regularly plunged him back down below the churning waters. He was an athlete and a more than capable swimmer, but no one could battle this.

The patient was gone; a blur of orange was the last he had seen of the man. Scott was struggling for air, and his tactical boots were weighing him down. He struggled but finally found the Spec Elite knife at his waist, cut the bootlaces, and kicked them free. That helped only slightly, although he found he was finally able to get marginally sufficient breaths of air between some of the waves.

To call the mountain of water he was constantly riding up and over a wave was a tremendous understatement. It was hard to gauge the depth of the troughs when he was high on the crest, but when he was in the valley looking up, each one seemed massive, maybe up to a hundred feet high at times. He had only been in the water a few minutes when a fantastic flash of yellow and red blurred his vision.

He was dead already, he knew that much, but he hoped Todd had gotten off that rig before the explosion. The wind was blowing both rain and seawater sideways at speeds that made it feel like small razors against his skin. Scott gave up trying to swim. The light Navy wetsuit and waterproof pack supplied some buoyancy. He focused on hanging on and getting a breath when he could.

He was panicking, and his breathing came rapid and shallow. The situation was dire, but he had to get himself under control. His mind was racing as he tried to get a grip. Obviously, the main issues were that he was stranded in the ocean, inside a hurricane, possibly targeted by Praetor assets. *FUCK*. Even in better days, his situation would be hopeless. His teeth chattered, and another wave drove him down deep. He felt his ears pop as the current pushed and pushed down farther. The pressure built to agonizing levels, and his lungs ached to take a breath, then an up current from the next wave tossed him briefly into open air. He vomited up seawater, everything else in his stomach had come up hours earlier. The repeated wretching had his throat and sinuses worn raw. He begged for the grip of the storm to release him, but it would not. He gasped and inhaled deeply before he was hauled under again. The process repeated and repeated. Rinse and repeat, rinse...

He prayed for the moments in which the wind and waves were simply predictable. He had given up the hope for calm waters. When it was at least predictable, he could rest momentarily and ride over the huge waves. These were the seconds he greedily hungered for. These were where he marshaled his remaining drops of energy. He had already gone mentally through the items on his body and in his pack. There was nothing there that would help his immediate situation. Even with the wetsuit, the early signs of hypothermia were creeping in.

Already exhausted, he lay back and tried to float, ignoring the nightmare around him. His next thought was of his promises—to Angel, to Kaylie, to his brother . . . He considered the irony of seeing his first

love once again just before he died. He came to a cathartic understanding of life in those moments: God was one cruel bastard. The
next few hours were a blur of water, wind, fits of coughing and
wretching up seawater and an ever-increasing level of exhaustion. As
his strength began to fully ebb, the chills really set in.

He checked the watch, but something had cracked the glass, possibly
when he went overboard. In his head, he calculated it had been over
four, probably closer to five hours since he'd fallen into the water.
Finally, it seemed the storm and the waves began to calm.

The neoprene suit was beginning to irritate his skin in several places. If
he kept moving, the chaffing would turn into sores and begin to bleed.
He fought his instincts and kept his movements to a minimum. He
found a spot for his pack that produced a kind of equilibrium: he lay,
mostly submerged, but could lift his nose out of the water to breathe
with minimal effort. Somehow, he managed to doze off in this position
and didn't drown; the next thing he knew, it was nighttime.

He had never been a fan of swimming at night. The inability to see the
dangers made them seem that much worse. The fact that he knew
there were nearly two miles of cold, dark water below him did not help
ease his temptation to panic. Now that he was somewhat rested, and
the storm had abated, he turned his mind to other dangers. He was not
too concerned about sharks; locals had always told him they avoided
strong storms, though he guessed they would be back soon enough. He
had no realistic expectations of surviving much longer anyway. What
was really bothering him was failing. Failing his friends and his brother.
Not being able to keep his promise to Angelique. The friends in Harris
Springs that he had learned to love and need. Failing Gia in keeping
her patient safe. His eyes burned from the salt and now his tears added
more to the mix.

The darkness was unending; he felt as though he were in the center of
a black ball. There were no stars; there was no moon. Nothing but
endless dark. Occasionally, he imagined he saw a bit of light or some
color—perhaps some bioluminescent life-form coming to investigate
the strange creature floating on the surface of its home. His teeth were

chattering uncontrollably now, and his extremities were going numb. His fogged mind would not produce the information he requested. What was he supposed to do to fight off the chill of the water? *Think, Scott!*

Get the circulation going. He began to swim. *Put forth enough energy to warm up, then curl into a ball to conserve heat.* He wasn't sure this was right, but it felt right. He wanted to open the pack and get a drink of water, but he didn't dare try in the darkness. *Be smart, at least try to live.* The night became an exercise: rest, swim, curl and rest. The monotony offered a kind of comfort. The routine became a lifeline. What had Todd said? Just one mile at a time. This was an endurance ride: *Focus on what is in front of you, and just get over the next hill.* He didn't have to make it until morning, just until the next time he needed to swim. Swim, curl, rest, swim, curl, rest . . . the monotony was broken regularly by unseen waves and mouthfuls of seawater that causing fits of gagging and uncomfortable periods below the surface. He could sense the futility but would not simply give up. *One more mile, one more hill. Change gears, pedal, just one more mile.*

The eastern sky had just begun to blush with the hint of sunrise when he started noticing the stars. The clouds had moved out and the night sky was on full display: millions and millions of stars, suns, planets . . . many just like the Earth and the sun that had struck out at it.

He rolled with the swells, looking up at the magnificent starry night. He lay that way in a daze, for how long he didn't know, until he realized that several of the stars were moving. As he focused his eyes, coming to from his trance, he realized they were flying craft—probably helicopters—circling near the western horizon. "You're looking in the wrong place," he said.

CHAPTER EIGHTY-FOUR

Morning. Scott had lost the bet with himself—unless death looked a lot like an endless blue ocean. He had been dreaming of riding his bike, the pedal strokes as familiar as breathing. Looking down through the crystal-clear water, he could see his legs still pedaling away. *Sleep riding*, he thought. It had kept him from drowning. The fatigue, hunger and thirst were too much to ignore. The sun was climbing into the summer sky, and the heat was slowly erasing the chills he had been dealing with for the past twenty-four hours.

He very carefully pulled his pack off and opened the sealed flap well above the water level. Reaching in, he found one of the water bottles and a food packet. He drank half of the water and returned the bottle to the pack before sealing it and putting it back on. The meal was a protein wafer: tasteless, but it helped sate the gnawing hunger. From the movement of the sun, he guessed a bearing that should be northerly. He had been trying, mostly in vain, to move in that direction, for no other reason than he knew that land was north. Devil's Tower was several hundred miles south of the Gulf coast. He thought about Kaylie. The hurricane would likely be hitting them soon, maybe even now. And here he was.

A large jellyfish swam idly by, its stinging tentacles stretching feet behind its large translucent bulb. He'd already received various stings from its brethren—painful, but not significant in regard to the bigger issues at hand. He moved the backpack underneath him for a while and gently swam in broad strokes as if he were on a surfboard. The wetsuit was becoming painfully hot and uncomfortable. He wanted to take it off, but he knew he probably wouldn't be able to get it back on again if he did. Once again, he would deal with the pain. Hour after hour he floated and swam, passing the time by tracking the sun's slow passage across the sky. During the late afternoon, he noticed a slight bump along the skyline, far ahead and to the east. It was small, but no illusion. He lost sight of it each time a swell came through, but seconds later it would reappear. He began to swim, slowly, in that direction.

Swimming toward it didn't seem to bring the object any closer. His eyesight was also beginning to blur from exposure to the saltwater. It could be small and only a few hundred yards off, or something large twenty miles away. *Just another mile, Scott, one more mile, keep pedaling,* he heard Todd saying.

Nearly spent, he paused to look up, convinced his target was distant and large when he realized it was much closer—and obviously very orange. *Well, fuck.* That was perfect. Survive all this time to float right up to the asshole who had put him here. Swimming over to the semi-inflated bio-suit, he looked inside, expecting to see a dead body. The face shield was partially open and inside was a body, unconscious but very much alive.

The man's lips and eyes were swollen nearly shut. Scott wasn't sure if this was due to the disease or simply exposure. Surely, the man had been flung around in the storm as much as Scott had. The wetsuit had certainly provided him more protection, but the bio-suit had kept the patient afloat. He thought briefly of drowning the man, but he quickly dismissed that. The guy was essential to Gia's research and—despite the fact that he'd tried to kill Scott—he needed to live. Perhaps he had some answers as well. Not that it would do either of them any good, but satisfying his curiosity would be a nicer way to pass the time.

He checked the man over for injuries; he looked surprisingly good. Wrapped around his right hand was a nylon line. Puzzled, Scott began to pull and noticed a semi-submerged yellow and black packet coming nearer with each tug of the rope. *Holy shit!* He could see the edge of a tag: ESCUE USN. The lifeboat and rescue package were a gift. The man had been beaten and battered but had the good sense to grab the line when he got close. Apparently, he had not been able to inflate the boat or get in.

Scott pulled the inflator handle and the enclosed two-man raft inflated in seconds. He pitched in the rest of the package as well as his pack. He carefully removed his knife and sliced the man out of the bio-suit. If Scott was exposed to the disease now, big deal.

Without the buoyancy, Scott struggled to keep the man afloat. *This guy is huge.* He struggled with the heavy man until finally, he managed to get one of the man's legs inside the raft. Pushing with all he had, he managed to roll him over the edge and into the raft. Scott floated beside the raft for several minutes to regain his breath. He also removed the knife and the sheath and carefully laid them inside on the packs—he did not want to risk accidentally puncturing the raft. Lastly, he reached over the side rail and pulled himself up. Unfortunately, he no longer had the strength. *Shit.* He tried again; he simply could not manage to get himself high enough to climb in.

Scott floated alongside the raft for several more minutes with one arm and one leg hooked over the top of the yellow tubing. Finally, mustering everything he had, he tried once more.

Propelling himself as far up as possible with determined kicks, he reached in as far as he could and began pulling his tired body up. Unfortunately, the effort was too much; it was more than his weakened body could handle, and he began slipping back into the sea. In the panic of his last chance, it took a moment for Scott to recognize that a hand was grasping his arm and pulling him back over the edge and into safety. The patient was awake. Scott flopped to the bottom of the raft, exhausted.

He smiled and shook his head. Panting, Scott reached and patted the man's cold hand. "Thank you."

Spent with the effort, Scott slept for a while. It was nearly dark when he opened his eyes again. The man lay close by with his eyes partially open. Scott leaned up, every muscle screaming in pain. "Ohhh," he groaned, "I don't know who hurt me worse . . . you or the damn ocean." If the man understood he showed no reaction. Scott wanted to hate the man, but he didn't have the strength.

He looked him over; he was in rough shape, probably badly dehydrated. Getting the partial water bottle from his pack, he gave the man tiny sips of the precious liquid. The former patient seemed to sense more than know what was happening. He opened his mouth like a baby bird to receive the water.

"I'm Scott."

It took the man several minutes after finishing the water before he attempted to speak. When he did, it sounded more like sandpaper on rocks. "Skkk—" he paused and tried again "Skybox."

"That's not a name, that's a call sign. What's your name?"

No response came to meet his question.

"Fine. I'm gonna call you Box, for short."

Skybox smiled feebly and shrugged. "Thanks." He waved his hand around the raft and croaked, "Why?"

Scott was finally peeling off his wetsuit, revealing the chafed and bruised skin beneath. "Why save the guy that tried to kill me? I don't know, something in my wiring I guess. I'm not your enemy, I can't blame you for not wanting to go with us. Mainly, though, you are important to a friend of mine—and the world."

Skybox nodded and said, "Dr. Colton." His tone had softened with her name, and Scott looked up to assess the reason.

"Yes, she said you may hold the cure." He settled into the raft. "So, am

I infected now too?" He motioned to the remnants of the protective orange, vinyl suit.

"No, you should be fine. I'm not contagious...at least according to your friends." He paused, mustering his strength. "You two looked like you had some history. Your face lit up when she spoke to you."

"Gia? She and I were friends back in college, nothing more."

Skybox smiled and settled back into the sidewall of the raft. He seemed to be out again within seconds. The darkness was coming quick, and soon Scott was asleep again as well.

CHAPTER EIGHTY-FIVE

There had been but one true love in Scott's life. Sadly, she had never been his to love. He had met Gia while working his way through college; she had joined the research company where he was interning. Tall, with red hair, she had striking good looks and, as he learned later, a brilliant mind and a sharp wit. Though they never worked in the same areas, he constantly found reasons to be near her. In doing so, he learned that she was engaged; the wedding was to take place after her last semester at college.

Despite this fact, he and Gia became close friends. While he secretly yearned for more, he was happy simply to have such a wonderful friend. With school and work, the days were long and often exhausting, yet his heart soared whenever he saw Gia. When they could spend time together, they looked more like co-conspirators than colleagues. Many in the company assumed something more was going on between them. Nothing was, though. Scott hid his feelings as best he could and focused only on the friendship. Gia was obviously aware that Scott had feelings for her, though she never encouraged or discouraged them. A brief hug or the occasional clasp of hands was the extent of physical intimacy between them.

Scott had never been in love before, and so he wasn't sure that that was what he was feeling, but he couldn't deny the attraction. The way he felt when he was around her made him crazy—he was crazy about her. He wanted to hold her, yearned to kiss her full lips. He tried hard to keep those feelings hidden from his best friend, his only real friend.

A few months after they first met, Gia invited him to her house to meet her fiancé and join them and some other friends for a dinner party. Steve was a gregarious bear of a man, with a quick smile and an infectious laugh. He was polite, well-informed, and Scott instantly hated him. He could see the attraction and the obvious and deep love the couple shared. Scott felt guilty for wanting Gia, and for wishing Steve ill. He had felt the temptation to cause them problems . . . Gia had already made several comparisons between the two; generally, they cast her fiancé in the poorer light.

Despite this fact, Steve seemed to like Scott, and if he felt threatened by his fiancée's friendship, he never let it show. Over time, Scott became a pretty regular guest at their home. He helped Gia in the kitchen. She was a good cook but no foodie like Scott. Together they cooked some fantastic meals. It was during one of those sessions that he asked her why she never tried to fix him up with any of her friends. Her blue eyes glanced devilishly up from what she was doing, and with a wink, she said, "Because I'm keeping you to myself. None of my friends deserve a guy like you."

He wasn't completely sure how to take that, but he blushed, and inside his heart exploded with raw emotion. His eyes watered, and he was sure she noticed. To her credit, she said nothing more and went back to preparing dinner.

As the wedding day approached, Scott was in turmoil. He had helped the couple with many of the details, and Steve had even asked him to be one of the groomsmen. He politely declined. He knew Gia's family was far away, and she was handling most of the planning. He wanted to be available to help her if she asked. She relied on him, in that respect, for many things. He wasn't sure he had ever worked so hard. He helped find and organize the caterers and bar staff, plan the menu and the deejay's playlist. He was there for her, wherever and whenever he was needed. By then, they rarely had a private moment together, which was probably good, he felt, as he had by now fully realized that he was deeply and hopelessly in love with Gia.

The wedding had been a beautiful event, and Scott was speechless when he saw Gia coming down the aisle. She radiated beauty and grace, and he could tell she was happy. She caught his eye as she passed and gave him another of those little winks and a grin. Scott melted inside, but ten minutes later a part of him died as she looked into her soon-to-be husband's eyes and whispered the words that would seal each of their fates and lock Scott out forever.

Scott could not control how he felt. He guessed inwardly that he'd been hoping she would say no, run away, or even just glance his way one more time . . . he honestly had no idea what he had expected. He was lost. The rest of the service and most of the reception were a blur. He busied himself with the various details Gia had asked him to handle. The couple was headed to the Caribbean for a weeklong honeymoon as soon as the reception was over.

Scott heard the music coming from the ballroom; the pair was enjoying their first dance as a married couple. He couldn't watch. He would not flee, although that was his greatest desire at that point. He didn't want to disappoint his friend. He was helping in the kitchen a short time later when he felt a hand on his shoulder. Gia pulled him close and said, "Come dance with me." Scott's heart beat furiously, and he found himself swaying. He nodded but could not say anything.

"Where have you been hiding?" she asked as she pulled him onto the crowded dance floor.

"Sorry G, just needed to make sure things were being handled. This is your day, and I want it to go without a hitch."

She grinned, "It's all perfect, honey. You've made it so easy for me and Steve. Thank you." With that, she pulled him close into the slow dance.

Scott was glad she could not see the tear roll down his face, but he felt sure she could feel it as her face leaned against his. He prayed no one was watching but couldn't muster the strength to be sure. As the song ended, he whispered in her ear, "Gia, you are the most beautiful bride I have ever seen." Scott kissed her cheek, and as he moved apart from his friend, he noticed her eyes were wet too. She didn't say anything, but she didn't shy away from looking him in the eye. He knew then; he wasn't fooling anyone. She knew he was in love with her. He was not sure if it thrilled, repulsed or terrified her, but he knew deep down it would do no good for him to stay in her life.

He never saw her again after that night. The newlyweds left for their honeymoon, and Scott returned home to Arkansas. He accepted a job offer and moved to Chicago several weeks later. He and Gia spoke on the phone occasionally after that, but it was awkward, and he thought that she, maybe, sensed it was painful for him. Gia and Steve seemed very happy. She was accepted to a prestigious medical research school on the west coast where she could continue her graduate studies. Scott usually talked to Steve as well; it was hard to dislike the guy. Each time they spoke, they all agreed to get together soon, but neither seemed inclined to actually make it happen. The months and then years slid by, the pain, though, never faded for Scott. He was never completely sure if he missed his best friend or his first love the most.

CHAPTER EIGHTY-SIX

Southern Mississippi

The Prophet had returned to his former glory. Somehow, he had managed to recover from the unfulfilled prophecies of their certain victory in Memphis. He had even managed to shrug off the terrible loss in numbers and supplies. He explained to his people that God needed to test His followers. Only to himself did he admit that many more encounters like that would leave him with no more followers to test.

He needed a victory. His movement demanded that he be ruthless and lead the Messengers in their mission. He once more donned his robes, as much to hide the other man—that beaten, weak man—as to present the Prophet.

Hawley's throat was dry as he waited for his boss. This morning's mission was maniacal. He barely had the stomach for it. He tried to remain calm, keep his face from betraying him, and so he raised only an eyebrow as Michael emerged from the tent. There were blood spatters on his white robe. Hawley fell into step as normal, delivering an update to his boss. "No one has located the runaway yet. Most of the Judges are at the coast but have not yet taken the ship. "

"Why not?"

"They say it will take some time to get a breaching force across the canal. Apparently, the group there has done a lot to keep the town and ship cut off from the surrounding land."

The Prophet quickly turned from well-mannered to impetuous but reined his thinly disguised emotions back in check. He had much to do this morning. The two men kept walking toward the center of the little town. "That is *our* ship, brother, our ark! It must be taken, the supplies seized and the heathens inside brought forth for judgment." He turned and locked eyes with his second in command. "Am I making myself completely clear?"

Hawley felt uneasy under the man's glare. Michael was becoming more and more erratic—unhinged. He felt something leak from the burned flesh of his eye. He wanted to wipe it away before answering but didn't dare. "Yes, yes, sir—Your Holiness. I told them to make it happen. They will not let us down."

The Prophet turned away to resume his slow walk toward the pitiful excuse for a town square. One side of the town was on a hill that gently sloped away to a small river below. Early morning fog rose lazily in silver wisps. "I remember learning in school that Mississippi was the most religious state in the US. Have you ever heard that?"

Hawley did not think the man wanted an actual answer, so he remained silent.

"Look at it, Hawley, it's like a picture postcard. Smalltown, USA. Barbershop, fire department, city hall. What a laugh. Hard to imagine anyone living in this decrepit little shithole would give a damn about anything but getting away. Perhaps the next life will be better for them." Michael smiled slightly at the words. "Is this all of them?"

"Yes, Your Holiness."

"Good. How far are we from this other town, Harrisville?" he added.

"Harris Springs. We're about forty miles from there. This here is the last real town on the road before we get there."

Michael nodded.

The Prophet reached the center of the town square where his Messengers standing guard waited expectantly. Some of the others assembled stifled sobs or sniffed. The mass this morning was not jubilant, but terrified.

The man stood erect, his blood-spattered regalia glowing in the strengthening sun. He looked out at the assembled crowd. "Good morning, everyone. I hope you good people all got a lovely night's rest." The group of mostly dark-skinned men, women and kids, were surrounded by his armed men. They watched him silently. "Today is going to be an important day for us," he continued. "God has ordained it. I know this to be true as He has given me a very clear vision of it. We are taking our message to the heathens of a nearby town called Harris . . . um . . . something. In order to best prepare for this mission, we must incur a blood debt. Do any of you know what a blood debt is?"

The crowd said nothing, dared not say anything.

He continued, "Of course you don't. You do understand the concept of debt, though, yes? When you owe someone something. Our Lord and Savior, Jesus, paid a blood debt. Paid it for you, in fact. Even before you were born, you owed a debt. We call it original sin. Because Eve bit the apple, she allowed sin to enter the world. Threw paradise away just for a taste of forbidden fruit. But our Lord and Savior, Jesus, paid that debt for us. I see many of you already know this . . . good, good."

He looked pensive as he paced up and down the front line of men. He stroked his patchy beard absentmindedly. "Today's mission will incur a separate debt of blood. Lives will be lost today. Yes," he smiled reassuringly to the crowd, "many will get to see the Kingdom of Heaven in all its glory! To do so we...and by we, I mean you must pay a blood debt— a gift to offset the cruelty of this day."

"Fortunately, that's not my fate or my brothers here, we are ordained and must go out and continue to spread the message.

Thankfully, our great and merciful Lord does not require that debt to be paid by us. We are the Messengers. We have been tasked with a much greater mission, a much greater mission indeed, and our work is far from finished on this Earth. That, my friends, is where you come in," he looked out at the bewildered crowd of townspeople. "My recent vision has shown me exactly how many lives in God's Army will be lost today . . . It just so happens that it is the exact number of you gathered here this morning." The crowd tensed visibly, but remained silent, every eye watching him. "Truly prophetic, isn't it?" He took several steps over to a hastily constructed device.

"Thank you, good people, for your sacrifice today."

With that, he raised an arm in signal and a figure at the top of the hill clambered out from the cab of a massive log truck. From the back of the truck were strung hundreds of strands of barbed wire, which led back to and around the necks of every one of the assembled crowd. As the giant load began its agonizingly slow crawl down the far side of the hill, the crowd moaned and stuttered in horror to feel the wire pull them closer together in their bunches. As the wire pulled taut, it dug into flesh. Screams and gurgles sounded, neck bones snapped with a sickening crunch, windpipes collapsed and in many cases, a sudden, sickening *thwak* sounded as necks elongated and heads separated from bodies. The Prophet watched with eyes that glittered in delight as each of the more than two thousand victims fell, decapitated and dead to the ground. This was his crowning achievement.

It was over in moments; too quickly for His Holiness, in honesty. He looked down to where his robes tented out around his crotch. He chuckled at himself. *Michael, you weak, weak man. You're a pervert, but you are creative.* The driverless truck was picking up speed now, and the several hundred bodies that remained somehow attached to the wire dragged and bounced after it like a macabre collection of tin cans tied to the bumper of a wedded couple's car.

He looked over triumphantly at Hawley who had gone quite pale. "Well, that was quite efficient, wasn't it?"

"Ye...yes, sir. It was." In truth, the scene had been the most horrific thing he had witnessed in his life thus far. They had been collecting the converts since leaving Jackson, and now Michael had just executed them all. For what? He wasn't sure. He had never been a man with many morals, but even he was surprised at his boss' increasing blood-lust. He had heard the concerned whispers, the doubts about his sanity. He was no longer so sure they were entirely wrong.

"Calm down, Hawley. If God commands it, it *must* be done! While it might've been a bit gruesome, we just can't spare the bullets or the time to do it differently. Remember in Chronicles, where God helps the men of Judah kill half a million of their enemy? God will reward us for following his Word, for spreading his Word. Now, get everyone ready to move south. Bring me some company before we go. I require my own reward."

Hawley nodded, "Yes, Your Holiness."

Michael turned to walk away but stopped and looked back. "Not as old as the one last night. She had a bit too much fight in her."

Hawley eyed the tiny blood spatters on the man's white robes again before nodding ok.

CHAPTER EIGHTY-SEVEN
Harris Springs, Mississippi

From the encampment on the side of the Intracoastal Waterway, hundreds of battle-hardened Judges were busy making preparations. They saw people on the ship's decks watching them, but so far, there had been no hostile action from either side.

"Those fucks have to be shitting themselves right now," one of the burly men said with a laugh. The others chuckled, but after the fiasco in Memphis, no one made assumptions about how hard or easy the siege might be. The Judges were a brotherhood: a protected collection of ruthless men. Each was a veteran warrior whose combat skills had been honed over the past year in almost constant fighting. Most had once been police, gang members or military men, and they fought more for their brothers than the movement they represented. Few seriously believed in the Prophet, nor gave much credence to the supposed Message. What it meant to them was that they would not go hungry. That they would not be the ones to suffer. Moral codes were for the weak and the dead.

A handful of the most senior men were looking at a battered map of the local area. One, known simply as Dobbs, summarized what they were up against. "They have all the bridges raised and there's no way of getting those lowered from this side. Our priority is to get a team across the canal. We need to send our best swimmers across as soon as it's dark. I suggest we send multiple teams, each of them leaving from a different spot. These guys aren't stupid. They picked a good location and probably have some defenses beyond what we can see. Peterson, what can you tell us about alternate routes to the other side?"

A wiry-looking man standing to one side leaned over the map. "Looks like they had a ferry crossing here, down past a thick stand of mangroves." He pointed to a spot on the map. "We can see what looks to be a small pontoon craft on the far side, but no way to get there yet. When our teams get across, this will be a good secondary route for us to use. Everything east is an impassable thicket of trees, vines, ravines and mangroves. It would take us weeks to cut over to the water. That shit goes on for mile after mile, all the way over to a deep bay."

Dobbs nodded. "What about over to the west?"

"Well, that way is probably even worse. Like you said, they picked a good spot. If you go west, you start running into bayou and swampland in about a quarter mile. We went in as far as we could... wound up losing one of Clements' guys to an old bull gator. Clem had to shoot an arrow into his head. So, it's a no-go that way too. Even if we can cross the swamp on foot, I don't see how we could bring much gear and no vehicles."

"We need a solution to this. This is what we get paid to do." The atmosphere was becoming tense with the talk of so many impasses. He realized his blunder too late: none of them was ever paid. "Michael expects that boat to be ours before he shows up. That will likely be by noon tomorrow. Get the swimmers ready to go by nightfall. Chuck, you and Sanchez pick the teams. Johnson—where the fuck is Johnson?"

No one had seen the man. "Shit, someone find him and tell him to find us some boats. *Now*. We aren't going to get many of us to the other side without something that floats."

"Dobbs, they said they done looked, didn't find nar one o' dem boats," one of the other judges said in a whiney voice.

Dobbs looked over at the man with barely concealed fury. "Look, this is the fucking *beach*, we are on a *canal*, over there is a *swamp*. Every fucking house round here must've had a fucking boat. Go and find them. If these clowns thought ahead and cleared them out, go farther. Somebody call Hawley and tell them to pick up some on their way down."

"A'ight, sure, sure." The man walked off, still muttering to himself.

"Peterson, go with him and make sure he does what I said."

Another one of the Judges, an older man spoke, "What's our plan of attack once we get over there?"

Dobbs looked around the group thoughtfully. "Good question. Ideas?"

Several men spoke in succession:

"Blow the access hatches with Semtex."

"Use scuttling charges beneath the waterline to sink it. Once she's on the bottom we can enter from the deck."

"Grappling hooks over the lower cabin rails and aft deck should be pretty manageable."

"Cut off the water supply and wait for them to die?"

The conversation went on for several minutes before Dobbs put up a hand. "These are good ideas, but keep in mind we don't have days or weeks. We don't want to be standing here with our thumbs up our collective asses when the boss rolls in. Also, and this is the real pisser, we're not to damage the ship. He wants it intact. So, we can't go blowing holes in the damn thing. Which also means none of our heavy weapons."

"Well, shit man, dat rules out juss about e'rything. Dem done most o' the tricks in the bag. Force is what we always use, and it works. Whass so important 'bout dis damn boat?"

"Well, Gibson, that is a question I don't have the answer for. Take it up with the imperial master when he arrives. For now, we have a job to do. It may come to grappling hooks. You two," he motioned to a pair standing off together, "go find a way to start collecting what we need. Anything useful. Raid some of the homes and barns around here to get the stuff. The other possibility is to unlatch the doors instead of blowing them off. I don't know how a hatch on a ship like this works. Find someone who might and see what would be needed to disable the latching mechanism. Lastly, let's find an area above the waterline where the steel plating would be vulnerable to a small, focused blast—one that can be repaired, but that would allow us to access the interior, preferably near somewhere vital to them."

One of the guys spoke up, "I can tell you where that would be. I worked in a shipyard back in my Navy days. Come up here to the road and I can show you." They wandered up to where most of the other Judges were already gathered. The man pointed to a low spot near the stern as one of the ship's most vulnerable spots. High above, on the bridge wing of the *Aquatic Goddess*, Bartos spoke into his radio.

CHAPTER EIGHTY-EIGHT

Gulf of Mexico

Scott awoke to find Skybox watching him intently. The look was unnerving, especially coming from a special ops soldier.

"Did you fix coffee yet?"

"Yeah, pot's by the stove, help yourself to breakfast, too . . . looks like you could use a good meal." Skybox glanced to his right to look at the sunrise just peeking over the edge of the horizon.

Scott shook the morning cobwebs and fleeing demons from his brain. "How are you feeling?"

"Super, ready for my morning swim." With that, Skybox rose and dove over the raft's edge and into the water. With long, graceful strokes he headed toward the sunrise.

"Well, fuck," Scott said as he gingerly moved to the far side and yelled after the man. "I didn't save your dumbass just to watch you go and kill yourself." If Skybox heard, he gave no indication. *Whatever.*

Scott heard a shout and then saw splashing. The man disappeared below the surface, leaving only empty ocean in his wake. Suddenly, Scott saw him shoot past underneath the water. He had hold of a sea turtle. The turtle seemed to be winning the battle as it dove deep, but soon Scott saw the man coming back up to the surface, the front edge of the turtle's shell firmly in his grasp. He could see the grin on Skybox's face ten feet below.

He burst to the surface and flung the turtle into the raft. Blood ran from a gash in the animal's throat. "How did you—ho—"

Skybox now returned to the raft, took the knife and made quick work of butchering the turtle. He sheathed the blade and tossed it back to Scott.

"Sorry, I didn't have time to ask for it politely."

Scott was amazed at the man's recovery, and his tenacity in capturing his prey. *This man is a predator. Never forget that.* He took a strip of turtle meat from the outstretched hand. He looked at it warily before popping it into his mouth. He swallowed without chewing. The taste and texture were not as bad as he feared: somewhat metallic and a bit like undercooked veal. His raging hunger also helped him stomach the gruesome scene before him.

Skybox took several bloody, dripping pieces of meat and began chewing with a look of extreme satisfaction. Clearly, this was not the worst meal he had ever had. "It's a little gamey, but it tastes pretty good, right? Not a traditional southern breakfast, I know. Scott, tell me something. Why were you with that SEAL team?"

Scott swallowed another strip of raw meat. "How do you know I wasn't one of them?"

"I've been in the military all my life. I can spot a soldier. Even in the sandbox when tribesmen would try to trade with us or offer to sell information, I could usually pick out the ones that meant us harm. Don't get me wrong, man, you can hold your own in a fight. You moved faster and realized my weaknesses quicker than most, and you're certainly a survivor, but you're not a soldier."

Scott wasn't sure if he should feel complimented or insulted. "My . . . community has had a good working relationship with the Navy.

Despite some reservations about the mission, they wanted me to come along. I was the only person who knew one of the people in the lab."

"Oh, Gia," Skybox said, raising his eyes to Scott's.

Scott offered a small laugh before taking another bite. "Actually no. DJ. He's my niece's boyfriend. I had no idea Gia was part of it." Quickly he realized he may have said too much.

"Ahh," a look of recognition crossed Skybox's face. "Kaylie."

Scott stopped eating, "He told you about my niece?"

"He loves her, he missed her. She does sound like a great girl. I'm sorry, Scott, but I was there for a long time. I'm also trained to get information. I could see the girl was the way to get DJ talking, so I used it. I like the kid, but honestly, not all my intentions were honorable. Too many years of training and subterfuge.". He winked, still chewing loudly.

"But you guys were in the same lab. It's a Praetor facility after all. What would he know that you didn't?"

Scott watched Skybox's eyes become more alert at the mention of Praetor. Even the name must be protected information, then. He paused to take another bite and a red dribble of blood ran down his chin. "Oh, nothing really, just a habit of mine I guess. I wanted to know where they were with the Chimera virus. If they knew how bad conditions were back on the mainland. I suppose I wanted to ease my mind about how responsible The P-Guard was for all this shit."

"P-Guard?"

Skybox looked at him before answering, "Praetor. Our command doesn't often use that name. We refer to ourselves collectively as P-Guard or the Guardians."

"Like the Praetorian Guard?" Scott asked.

Skybox gave the briefest of nods. "Our organization is probably not what you think. We may stay hidden, but we're not some cabal or shadow government. We're just patriots. The group has been at work a very long time taking care of America and most democratic countries in the world." He looked like he had said more than he should have.

Scott was full and somewhat repulsed now by the meal. He decided to change the subject. "Chimera? That's what you're calling the pandemic?"

Skybox nodded, "Good as anything I guess. The doc didn't seem to think it was a virus, though, nor a bacterial agent. Said it was something in between—a chimera."

He wiped his chin and briefly seemed lost in his memories. "We—I—lost an entire battalion to the damn thing in Pakistan."

Scott didn't have fond memories of Praetor soldiers, but he didn't wish anyone harm. "Shit, I'm sorry man. So, it really is that bad?"

"Scott, it's truly terrifying. I've never feared an enemy. But that bastard disease will end us. Well, the ocean will probably end *us*, but you know."

"Skybox, do we have any chance of being rescued? I mean, do you have, like, a secret tracking device you've activated, or something?"

"Not a chance in hell, bud. I did have a tracker, but they removed it at the lab. Said it would screw up the MRI test. I've seen your Navy friends looking the last few nights, but their search grids are in the wrong direction. If my guess is accurate, the storm blew us pretty far north, and we're now drifting closer to the Gulf Coast, maybe within a hundred miles of land. I'm guessing Louisiana or Mississippi, but you may know better than me. That's not so close, but it is attainable. We could be close enough to save ourselves." The soldier eyed Scott again. "You look to be in good shape, Scott. You a runner?"

"Cyclist. It's not going to be an easy stretch to get across the pull of the North Atlantic Gyre."

"The gyre? Oh, yeah, the offshore current . . . It goes west to east out here, doesn't it?"

Scott had to think for a moment, "Yeah that sounds right, although the hurricane may have disrupted that."

"True. Well, help me get this tarp over us so we don't bake in the sun all day."

The two men worked together to attach the canopy to the raft for shade. They also rigged up a solar still they found in the raft's supplies. The device was a simple system of clear plastic pieces that used the sun's rays to evaporate seawater. The droplets of fresh water collected on the clear plastic and drained down into the now empty water bottle. During the heat of the day, it produced a few ounces per hour: just enough for them to survive. They did still have two tins of water in the survival kit, and Scott had two full Nalgene containers in his bag. Skybox cut the remaining turtle meat into long strips and lay them on the canopy to dry. "Turtle jerky," he smiled. "Hope we don't attract seagulls."

"Yum," Scott said only slightly sarcastically. "By the way, Skybox, thanks."

"For what?"

"For not killing me, for starters. You obviously could have. You're built like a freakin' tank. But thanks for saving me, for finding the raft and for being honest with me."

Skybox waved a hand nonchalantly. "No problem, man. You seem like a good guy, and to be honest, I don't remember grabbing the raft. I think I remember seeing it, or something, blow past me in the storm. I thought I saw it a few times in the distance after that, but I don't recall ever going after it." He shuffled a bit and looked uncomfortably out to sea. "I can't say I've been *completely* honest with you."

Scott laughed, "Great. So, I'm infected?"

"No, I'm just not permitted to talk about certain things. If I wasn't reasonably sure we're going to die out here, I wouldn't be telling you anything at all. I can't even tell you exactly why I fought to get away from you guys." He leaned over the edge and tried to spit but nothing came out. "Training, I guess. From what I have been hearing the Navy is the enemy and I am a soldier. Escape and evade."

Scott nodded, having pretty much assumed that.

Skybox continued, "Honestly, I have my own questions about the Guard, particularly its role in the development and outbreak of the disease. Suffice it to say I'm not at liberty, even now, to disclose everything to you or anyone. I'm still seeking answers. I'll be honest when I can but try and understand when I can't."

"I do understand. How did you get started with them? Were you a SEAL?"

"Give me that knife again, I'm gonna gut you for that slur," he joked. Scott was starting to like the soldier. He wasn't a bad guy; that much was clear. "I was Army, the only true branch of military service."

"Green Beret? Delta?"

"Delta Shadow Force. I was a Ranger, briefly, before joining Special Forces. That was before Uncle Sam decided he needed me elsewhere. You ever hear of Jawbreaker or Operation Blue Sky?"

Scott shook his head.

"Well, my buddy, Tommy, and I were paired up in a CIA operation after 9/11. We were part of a covert team of elite special forces called Jawbreaker. Our mission was to go after Bin Laden. Contrary to what the president said, there was no "dead or alive." They wanted him dead. We were choppered into the Panjshir Valley of northeastern Afghanistan. We didn't get him . . . turned out he was already in Tora Bora, or maybe Pakistan by then, but we did wipe out most of the Taliban."

"How many of you were there?"

"By the end, there were about 100 of us in Jawbreaker. The Taliban were nasty fucks. The shit they did to women and kids, anyone that believed differently, well...it was atrocious. It wasn't hard to win the hearts and minds of the locals. We used cash to buy cooperation and intel, and then we waged an unmerciful war on 'em. To be honest, we never really looked that hard for Bin Laden. His level of mischief was practically nothing on the scale of depravity we were witnessing. It was an odd time. I think the organization started to see the usefulness of a group like us. My pay started coming from the CIA instead of the Army. Over time, I received orders from a string of civilian contractors. Eventually, I was re-tasked with a different command level and given my call sign—the only name I would ever use from that point on. I was technically still military and had access, valid ID and multiple ranks to use when needed, but I was also . . . different. We—I could finally be effective."

"What about your buddy? What was his name? Tommy?"

Skybox's expression took on a troubled look. "Tommy was the most impressive soldier I ever knew. His callsign was the Magician. He couldn't shoot worth a damn, but hand-to-hand, with improvised weapons or knives, he was truly lethal. Damn, he was something."

"He didn't make it?" Scott asked.

Skybox dropped his eyes and gave a gentle shake of his head. He struggled with talking about it, especially to people who had never been there...couldn't understand. "We were wrapping an op when the Humvee we were riding in hit an IED. We had no idea about those back then. I had minor injuries, but Tommy, well he was very nearly dead. Massive head injury. He was evac'd out immediately, and the medics managed to stabilize him. Went into surgery in Germany later that day and they saved his life, but he was never the same. They keep him alive on a regiment of serious meds for the pain and brain trauma, but that's about it."

"Sorry, man, that's terrible," Scott said. "No one knows what you guys did."

Skybox shrugged. "Some do, but that's part of our code. Don't draw attention to ourselves, just do what has to be done."

Scott took the small, collapsible paddle out of the bag and began assembling the parts. "I've run into some of your fellow soldiers—Grayshirts—before. They didn't seem too helpful."

"Good idea," Skybox said, gesturing to the paddle. "And I didn't say we were helpful, I said we do what's needed. Often, it's a cold and brutal business. What's important to us is the mission. We get total information and command authority on our assignments. We may not know anything about another team's mission even a few miles away. Our command structure is siloed—purely vertical and autonomous."

"So, who do you work for?"

Skybox had been prying the shell free from the sea turtle's carcass. He looked up and paused at the statement. "We work for the government. We work for you."

"I don't think you do," Scott said with an edge to his voice.

"Why would you say that?" Skybox responded.

"I worked with the government, I have—I *had* high-level security clearance. Never once did I hear even a whisper about you guys until shit went down. You're not under any military, defense or homeland security program I'm aware of." Scott didn't want to reveal what he knew about Catalyst, but he was beginning to realize he likely knew more than Skybox did.

Skybox paused for a moment before responding with assurance. "We're not military in the strict sense of the word. When we were operating with CIA direction, we were their paramilitary division, but we outgrew that role. Our mission parameters kept expanding and the war on terrorism, in particular, gave us a more global footprint. We have a civilian command group. Within that, they have the ability to embed us into, or remove us from, almost any friendly military force in the world. I've trained with French, Israeli and British Special Forces, among others. We have great training, excellent assets and a really shitty retirement plan. Few of us make it to that age anyway. We are a tool, Scott. Nothing sinister, nothing more than that." It sounded to Scott as though he'd learned those words by heart.

"That sounds like the script for a recruitment video, Skybox." Scott was using the stubby paddle to row the raft in a northerly direction . . . he hoped. "It's bullshit. Don't get me wrong, I admire much of what you guys have done. You were the only ones with a plan when our sun fucked us, but let's face it, Catalyst isn't about winning hearts and minds or solving problems. Shit, it creates problems."

And there it was. Scott had not meant to reveal it—not that secret word—but he had. It was out there. He concentrated hard on paddling, half expecting a knife to the back. When he looked back, Skybox was using the turtle shell as a paddle on the other side. He looked up at Scott and nodded once.

CHAPTER EIGHTY-NINE

USS Bataan, Gulf of Mexico

Todd looked out over the well deck of the *USS Bataan*. Several of the search craft were returning, their reports having come in earlier: no survivors and no bodies. He was holding the side of his head, fighting off a wave of nausea. The misery he felt at losing his friend was compounded by the effects of a mild concussion from his fight with Skybox. Now he had a report from home that the Messengers had shown up and the path of the hurricane would make landfall somewhere near Harris Springs. His world was falling apart, and he was standing here unable to do a goddamn thing.

"Sir?"

Todd looked up, his pain momentarily subsiding. The taste of bitter bile still lingered in his mouth.

"Sir, are you okay? Would you like me to get you to sick bay?"

"Huh? Oh, no, no . . . I'll be fine."

"Very good. I came to let you know the CO is ready to meet with you. If you are up for it, I mean."

"Sure, finally. Please lead the way."

He was led through the confusing passageways to the war room where Commander Garret and Captain Harris were studying numerous charts. "Come on in, Todd. You wanted to see me?"

"Yes, sir, I wanted to ask you about air support for Harris Springs. We talked a few weeks ago about it. The group calling themselves the Messengers are beginning to show up. I spoke with my people back on the *AG*, they are in a defensive lockdown and expect the attacks to be imminent."

Garret's face took on a troubled look, "Ahh, yes, the infamous Messengers. You say some of them have arrived—but not all?"

"Yes, my people say that the lead group is there, the ones they call the Judges. They are supposedly the very worst of the bunch. Several hundred so far, but not the main group. Some of my team managed to rescue Scott's brother from them. He was pretty badly injured but says they were beaten back—possibly by Catalyst forces—when they marched on Memphis. Apparently, after that, they turned south, and now they are targeting Harris Springs. We have no idea how many remain alive, but the estimate is that there could be up to five thousand."

Garret motioned for Todd to sit. "Five thousand is a serious threat. I assume even the group assembled there now is a significant threat. You have some defenses, I know, but not to fight an army. Todd, there's no easy way to say this," he sighed heavily. Todd felt his stomach clench in dread as he waited for the man's next words. The commander continued. "Captain Harris and I were discussing force strength before you came in. I'm afraid we simply don't have the assets to fully protect your little group. Much of our fleet is on assignment with Operation Homefront, and the remainder is on the recovery mission for your friend and the Praetor commander. I'm not even sure how much longer we can keep that going . . . the fuel drain alone is crippling."

Todd had been barely keeping the lid on his simmering rage. Now it began to boil over. "Sir, you—"

"Now wait, Todd, listen to me. I am going to honor my commitment.

You and your people have been extremely helpful to us. You are valued allies. I just need to be as honest as I can be. If I start diverting flights over to Harris Springs now, I'll have to take them off the recovery mission for your man and the lab subject. I don't think it would be smart to do that until the enemy is fully massed there. We cannot make multiple sorties. It must be a limited engagement. So, the question is can your people hold out, hold off these Judges until the full group arrives?"

Todd took a deep breath, growing minimally calmer. He responded with all the restraint he could muster. "I don't know."

Captain Harris spoke up. "Captain, you were down in meteorology, so you know that the storm we encountered is about to arrive at that same location. That alone negates our ability to identify ground targets, let alone reach the location—you saw firsthand the challenges of flying through that weather and the cost to us in lives and more."

Both Todd and Garret nodded grimly. "One other thing, Todd," Garret added. "We are aware of this group's reputation, but do understand that we are," he searched for the right word, *"reluctant* to fire on American civilians. Praetor apparently does not have that same concern, but we operate with a more humane directive. Under normal circumstances, it would take a presidential order to move us into direct action like this, but clearly, these are not ordinary times."

"What the holy fuck!"

Both of the Naval officers looked shocked. "Excuse me?"

Todd was done with the niceties and his respect for the rank and roles represented here. "You used us, sir, and now you are pussyfooting around delivering on an agreement we made in good faith. I convinced my friend—one of my best friends and one of the most valuable members of our community—to come out here on this mission against his better judgment. It cost him his life! And now you want to sit here and give me shit about force strength and numbers and how much fuel you're using. *Fuck that!* If you insist on waiting for the full group of crazies to get to the *AG* before you attack, fine, but they need help now. Send me back with a squad of Marines or any of the SEALs that are left. When we call—and we will call—I expect you to unleash hell on these bastards. Do you understand me? You do not let them move on to the next town. If you do, you won't have a fucking America to defend in the months ahead. It has to end here. Am I clear?"

Garret pursed his lips and placed his fingertips on the tabletop. He was trying, with greater success than Todd, to control his own emotional response. "I apologize, Todd," he began with formality. "You make valid points. You value loyalty and extend it to those around you, as your service record showed. It's a fine quality, the sign of a good leader." He thought for a moment before continuing. "I will give you the men you request, but that storm—if that storm arrives at an inopportune moment, it may limit our response. We may be unable to eliminate the threat completely. You should be prepared for that."

Todd nodded, "I understand the realities. This is not a mission with the luxury of time for planning. But I still need to know you have skin in the game. That, while there may be unavoidable limitations, you will be there when we need you as we were for you in the assault on Devil's Tower."

"And how do I alleviate that concern, Todd, even if I agree with your . . . suggestions?"

Todd thought momentarily, then eyed the picture frames behind the Captain. "I want Lieutenant Garret, sir. Your son."

CHAPTER NINETY

Harris Springs, Mississippi

Dobbs and several others watched as their brother pointed out the massive ship's most vulnerable areas. One of them produced a crude drawing and marked the access hatches and the best spots to blow if they could get close.

The swimmers were about ready to start across, and the remaining Judges were preparing to storm the bridge as soon as they got it lowered. A flicker of movement caught Dobbs' eye, and he watched, stunned, as at least fifty of his men fell back amongst a spray of blood erupting from shots that seemed to come out of nowhere.

He crouched immediately as others dove for the ditch. The unlucky lay motionless; a few writhed about in pain. The shots were so well timed, they had sounded like a single shot. A single shot from countless rifles. They must have been preparing for that attack all day: one target in the scope per sniper so as not to waste ammo as the group of men scattered. *Well played.*

The remaining Judges returned fire but could make out no real targets. The swimmers were ready to go; thankfully, none of them had been hit. That fact struck Dobbs as odd . . . they were standing down front, after all, but he had no time to consider it further. The battle had begun, and for once, the target had scored first.

"Go! Go!" he shouted and motioned the men to get in the water. They were swimming against the current, but they had anticipated this. He watched in fascination as each of the teams began to struggle, then stop altogether. They were caught on something in the water. One let out a shout and disappeared underwater. A circle of red erupted all at once from the green water.

The others in the water began screaming in panic. Dobbs could see now that they were entangled in what—barbed wire, or maybe the razorblade-edged concertina wire they topped prison fences with. What they had taken for floating logs were in fact, alligators, and they were now making a path toward the hopelessly snared swimmers. As the gators got within a few yards, they disappeared below the surface. The calls of the trapped men grew louder as they watched their cohort, one by one, being pulled below the surface of the water.

"*FUCK!*" This was quickly turning into a complete disaster. *These fucks are prepared!* They were not used to anything like this. Typically, they just marched in and took whatever they wanted. The benefit of their ruthless reputation was that intimidation did most of the work for them. But first, they had to face that shit in Memphis, and now this . . . It was obvious to him that the group's easy days were in the past.

This morning they had formed up as one of the largest groupings of Judges ever. Now at least a quarter of them lay dead in the first ten minutes. He signaled desperately for everyone to fall back. Looking over, he saw a familiar face. "Linx, you and Mark take a few guys and shoot as many of those fucking gators as you can! And stay out of sight while you do."

Dobbs and the rest of the men ran stooped over in the side ditches until they were nearly a hundred yards farther back. The price of killing a Judge was normally the life of everyone in the town. Normally, they'd just burn the town to the ground and be done with it. They were valued! The most prized members of the Messengers. Now, with so many of them dead, he felt more like the bullseye on a target than an elite soldier.

The sound of gunfire could be heard coming from ground level. Linx and Mark had both been Army sharpshooters. They would thin the fucking things out or drive 'em away. He eased over to Peterson who sported a bloody gash across his upper arm. "We obviously better come up with another plan. Where's the guy who was briefing us about the ship?"

The other Judge looked at him. "I think most of him is all over the side of your jacket. They got him, man. We have to fucking get these assholes. If the Prophet shows up and sees us like this—all these dead Judges—he'll fucking feed us all to the gators himself."

"I know, I know," Dobbs tried to regain his composure.

But this was indeed fast becoming a Class-A Charlie-Foxtrot: a cluster-fuck in civilian speak. He thought for a moment. *Just send more swimmers across now that the gators are gone. Give them wire cutters, and once they're on the other side they can drop the bridges.* If that failed, they would just have to take the swamp route to the ocean and come back around to the island from the western side.

Getting volunteers to attempt the swim this time around proved much more difficult. Hawley had radioed to check up on them, and to let them know they were on the way. The Judges were out of time. Dobbs and the more senior members elected volunteers and persuaded them at gun point to make the swim. The cursing and protests were impassioned, but after Dobbs shot two of his brethren, the rest complied with reluctant desperation. They entered the water with guns out, carrying everything from driftwood logs to inflated motorcycle inner tubes to help them float.

Each of the nine swimmers encountered the submerged barbed wire obstacle at the same time. Several tried cutting through in different spots until they realized it would be smarter for one or two to cut and clear the path while the others watched their back. It then became apparent that there were multiple rows of the submerged wire; the process took quite a while. Shots were fired into the water—some by the men watching for gators and some from the ship above. Two more Judges were taken out before they got through the obstacles.

At last, the first man slipped through the last wire barricade. He was immediately swept back, into the backside of the trap, by the current. The next man through made it within twenty feet of the far shore before he was hit by a flaming bottle dropped from above. He disappeared underwater and failed to surface again. A pool of blood erupted from where he had been. The gators were still around, they had simply dropped deeper down. Gunshots, some sort of grenade and the Molotov cocktails rained down onto the swimmers.

Dobbs was sympathetic but gave the order to shoot any man that did not keep going across. As more and more of the beady sets of eyes came back up and broke the surface on the other side of the wire, several men decided they would rather be shot than eaten alive. They were promptly shot, and then later, eaten. Well, eventually; the alligators were no longer hungry, and the attacks continued simply thanks to their ancient instincts to protect their territory. The reptiles' powerful jaws clamped around arms, legs and necks, gripping their victims securely before rolling them round and down. Several of them made it to the hull of the white ship before being pulled under. One by one the group of men was jerked down deep to their deaths.

Dobbs watched the chaos unfold in horror. It took him a while to notice that three of the men had actually made it to the far side. Dobbs knew two of them personally and chalked it up to luck more than brains. *Those two are stupider than a bag of hammers.* "Get those bridges dropped!"

He watched as they scurried up the bank on the far side and went to find the controls for the drawbridges. *Finally*, he thought. He looked up at a darkening sky. Angry clouds were gathering above the white hull of the ship. Then the rain started in a deluge.

Several of the Judges were scanning the island with binoculars in an attempt to track their intrepid brothers. Dobbs also had his up and was desperately looking for any sign they were going to be successful.

The downpour made it impossible to make anything out. Suddenly, he heard something and saw a flash of white through the trees on the far shore. It disappeared at once. He pulled his poncho tight and the rain cascaded off his leather hat. "I hate fucking waiting," he said to no one in particular. *Those bastards better make it.*

CHAPTER NINETY-ONE

As the minutes ticked by, it became apparent that they had also failed.

The rain had been pouring for nearly an hour and only seemed to be getting worse. Dobbs was almost out of ideas. "Peterson, get that group moving to the west before the water gets any deeper in that marsh. Take radios and let us know when you make it."

The man looked very uncertain about entering the bayou or attempting to reach the island that way, especially in this weather. They could hear the surf echoing over the island as it hit the shore with gathering force. The storm was definitely intensifying.

"Go on, you'll be fine," Dobbs shouted above the tempest, "just lower that damn bridge when you get there." Peterson glumly walked to an assembled group of about fifteen men who immediately began gathering their packs and weapons. "Linx, you and your best spotter find a good hide. I want you to start sniping anyone up there on the deck of that ship. If you can get anyone inside the ship's bridge, even better. They'll be the ones in charge."

"Sure, Dobbs, but they have the high ground. Not going to be easy."

He nodded, well aware of the obvious, but needing to give his men something to focus on other than the rain and the failures thus far. It took another twenty minutes before Linx began firing. The rain had abated somewhat, and Dobbs could see they were aiming for the large upper windows.

Other than the initial round of enemy sniper shots that had proven so deadly, the people on the cruise ship had not shown any desire to continue their attack. Dobbs assumed they were limited on ammo. *Although,* he argued to himself, *it could also just be good weapons discipline.* Considering what he'd already seen from this group, he decided it was best to assume the latter.

Peterson and his group of Judges had made their way alongside the deep canal until the terrain dropped away into the swamp. A seawall and levee separated the bayou from the deeper canal here in many places, but mostly, it was just swamp. The water came up quickly to their waists, but far worse was the sucking mud. It grabbed at their boots and made each step incredibly difficult. The thought of more alligators beneath the black surface was also on each man's mind. The smell of rot and decay was so thick they could taste it. Overall, it was not really a pleasant experience.

The man in front of Peterson had been complaining the entire journey, "No way this fucking boat is worth this, it's just an abandoned cruise ship, for Chrissakes."

Peterson inwardly agreed with the man but offered no response. The bayou stretched out for several miles before turning into the less wooded wetlands. They heard occasional gunshots from back near the ship, but otherwise, the only sounds were of the sucking mud on the bottom of the swamp and the torrents of rain that kept coming in tropical blasts every few minutes.

The sounds of the surf were diminished here, but they could hear it occasionally pound against something solid in the distance. It took the small group nearly six hours to go just a few miles, and all were exhausted upon reaching the deeper marshland. Strangely, here in the middle of marshland, they found a small road. It cut across the marsh toward what might have been the abandoned site for a subdivision, off in the distance. The cheaply paved road was not marked on any of the maps. A decrepit, weed-covered real estate sign said *Sea Meadows: a Hansbrough Property Development.* He wondered briefly who in the hell would buy land in a swamp.

The men, glad to be back on solid land, followed the narrow, paved road back the seventy-five yards to the canal. The canal was not as wide here, and while there was no bridge, a small wood and aluminum floating dock bobbed on their side of the choppy water. Looking down the canal, they could see where it met the ocean, still a half-mile away. A rock jetty lined the channel on both sides, and huge plumes of sea spray could be seen coming off the impressive waves that crashed over the rock jetty. The wet, exhausted men dropped to the roadway and rested.

"Hey, man, I don't think I want to try crossing over near the ocean, that storm has the Gulf in an uproar."

Peterson nodded in agreement, "I don't think we're going to be doing that." He took the plastic bag with the radio out of his pack and radioed Dobbs. The other man's voice was distorted, and Peterson wasn't sure if he was happy or enraged.

"About fucking time you checked in. Are you on the island yet?"

Peterson, feeling more confident since he was not near the man, said, "Next time you bring me to the beach, make sure you get me a room with a view." He released the talk switch and watched his men break into laughter.

Dobbs' reaction on the other end made it doubly funny. The men needed a little relief.

"Sorry, man, just fucking with you. We just made it through the swamp to the lower wetlands. The ocean route is going to be a no-go, but we do have a plan." Peterson went on to fill in Dobbs and the men around him at the same time.

They would use the floating dock as a raft: it had to float with the water level here in the tidal flats. They would free it from shore and paddle across to the far side. It should be stable enough to take them all on one trip. Two of the men would stay on the raft and paddle back in the direction of the ship and the main group of Judges so that whether they got the bridges lowered or not, they could begin moving more men over with the raft if necessary.

Dobbs sounded genuinely relieved with the plan, and Peterson's men were just glad not to have to get back into the mud. Dobbs also let them know that the Prophet and the main group were just a few miles out now. Peterson knew what that meant; he was okay with leaving the implied threat unspoken.

The group made their way down to the edge of the canal and began freeing the dock from the big telephone pole sized pilings.

The dock was floating on its own thirty minutes later. It was not as stable as he had hoped, but if they kept most of their weight in the center of the rain-slicked platform, then three men could paddle it from the edge. It took several failed attempts before they got the feel of it. The paddles came from several wooden benches that they tore apart. They were heavy and unwieldy but did the job.

They got moving and were over to the island within ten minutes. *Well, shit, that actually fucking worked,* Peterson thought with relief. As most of his group snuck onto the island, two Judges struggled to get the ungainly craft heading back east toward Dobbs' group. Peterson turned and followed his men through the thick trees toward the old town. He paused for a moment when he thought he heard something—a helicopter. The driving rain made it impossible to know for sure. *Whatever.* He was being paranoid. The sounds of the storm were bizarre and ever-changing.

CHAPTER NINETY-TWO

The Sikorsky SH-60 Seahawk came in low and fast from the south, just ahead of the approaching storm front. The Navy chopper flared for a quick touch down on the landing pad of the *Aquatic Goddess*. Todd was first off, dressed in full battle gear, and quickly followed by the younger Garret and nine other Marines and Navy SEALs. Ignoring the rotor wash, the soldiers immediately fanned out, weapons up, looking for threats and targets.

Todd ducked low and ran to meet Bartos who was coming out of the bridge wing just as the huge chopper lifted and sliced quickly back out to sea.

"Shit, man, nice of you to show up," Bartos eyed the men. "Your cavalry's a bit lighter than I hoped."

Todd scowled, "Yeah, it's not what I wanted, but it's what I could get—for now. Let's use them. Where are our main threats?"

Bartos brought him up to speed on the prior attacks. Solo was still guarding the island below. "They're going to keep throwing men at that canal until they manage to get across. All we can do is keep trying to dust them off."

Todd spoke briefly to Lieutenant Garret who suggested placing most of the civilian defenders to the rear, island side of the ship. The locals had already swapped hunting rifles for carbines and close quarter arms.

Bartos followed Todd up to the bridge deck where they found Jack and Angel. Jack hugged his old friend. Angel leveled her eyes at him with a look that expressed strong disapproval. "Hey, Chief. Where's Scott?"

Todd shook his head, unable to speak, his eyes on the verge of tears. The message was clear to all.

"Well, shit," said Bartos. "Goddammit!"

Angel's worst fears were coming true. She forgot about her own fears as she thought of Scott. Her tears began to flow. "Please, no . . .."

Bartos steeled himself the only way he knew. "We have to put that away for now." Despite his brave face, the emotion was thick in his throat. "We can mourn him tomorrow. Today we have a war to fight, and we have *got* to figure this shit out."

She was weeping openly now, "Don't be an ass, Bartos, I can't—"

Jack pulled her close, "Angel, we have to. Bartos is right. We have to get through this day first. Scott would say the same."

Out the window, Todd could just make out the enemy massing. Cars and heavy trucks were pulling in by the dozens. The line of those waiting to get close stretched back for miles. Sighing heavily, he pulled himself together somewhat and looked over at the Cajun. "Remember when the tourist season used to start like this?" He shook his head. "They weren't as well armed but usually just as crazy. Better bring me up to speed. What are we facing?"

"Well, Cap, in the skirmishes so far, we figure we've taken out about seventy-five of the Judges down there. Seems like all that did was piss 'em off. They're a crafty bunch, and they don't scare easy. They may work for the crazies, but don't underestimate 'em. Bobby gave me the run-down, most Judges seem to have been military, special ops or SWAT cops." He looked out the side window. "They've already gone through a lot of our defenses. They're obviously regrouping for another try. They seem determined to take us before the main group gets here. As we know, they don't usually fail at this, although aside from Memphis, I don't think they've come up against much in the way of a fight. When they get in range, we're slinging lead at them, but no way our ammo will hold out for long at this rate."

An explosive thud rang out several hundred yards to the east. "And now we will have to rebuild the ferry dock if we survive this," Bartos gave the slimmest of grins.

"What about our people?" Todd asked.

"So far, we've lost nine, mainly to random sniper shots, although one was likely self-inflicted. We began the day with 364 souls on board, plus a shitload of cows and pigs. Angel and Jack did well getting the word out. Many of these farmers and ranchers are damn good shots. We put guns in their hands and let 'em know we expected them to fight. They're assets, but that group you brought will surely help."

Jack spoke up. "Todd, is this all the help we're getting from the Navy? What do we do when the rest of the Messengers arrive?"

"The Navy will come when we call. They just can't come until then. They are, well . . . they're busy. They may also only be able to make a couple of attack runs, so we have to make it count."

"How the fuck we gonna do that, ask them to line up like good li'l Christians?"

"Good question, Bartos. We need to be ready to draw the main group into a confined area, preferably away from the *AG*. I don't have any ideas right now, but let's get thinking on it. Do you think that Navy chopper overhead might have put some fear into them?"

Bartos looked out to sea. "They probably heard it, but I don't think any were able to see whose bird it was. I'm sure they'll be surprised to learn we have friends like that. Come on down. Let me introduce you to Bobby and his new...um, godson—and you can see Kaylie, let her know about DJ."

Todd shook his head, "I'm not quite ready for that conversation yet.

Thanks for going and rescuing him, I—that meant an awful lot to Scott, and I'm sure to Kaylie, too. That was one of the last things that he and I talked about. He hated putting you at risk, but he was very grateful. I take it Bobby's wife didn't survive?"

"No. Those bastards . . ." He shook his head no. "Bobby hasn't said much, and Kaylie has been pretty stoic about it so far."

Todd nodded, "DJ is anxious to see her—if we can secure this area, that is. They won't let him come over here until then. He's not going to take away the pain, but hopefully, he can take her mind off things somewhat. I also want to hear more about what happened with Abe. I still can't believe he was feeding intel to those guys." He shook his head in disgust.

Jack glanced at the radar screen then looked out the south side windows again. "Man, this storm is massive. Looks like it'll be a monster. It just keeps getting bigger."

Todd walked over and looked out, scowling, "Let me assure you it is, we've already met. It's at hurricane strength, and it's huge."

Bartos pointed down at the far side of the canal, "Preacher, looks like more of your Cameltights are starting to arrive." Buses, cars, trucks and motorhomes were coming into view and forming a long line behind a handful of tactical trucks and military vehicles. "Crazies to the north and a hurricane to the south. This is turning into a very bad day, guys."

Jack just stared out the window silently mouthing, "Amalekites, you idiot."

CHAPTER NINETY-THREE

Bartos and Garret rotated out all the men on watch so they could get some hot food, dry clothes and a bit of rest. The Marines and the Navy guys were reluctant to leave their posts, but they were in for the duration; it was the wiser move. The rain, which had started to fall several hours earlier, was not bad yet, but everyone on the *AG* was prepared for what was coming. The Messengers, it seemed, were clueless about the approaching weather. They set up camp alongside the canal including what looked to be a damn revival tent.

Throughout the night, they had heard calls of distress coming from the canal. Apparently, the supreme leader had no problem sending his followers to their death. More than once they also heard Solo tearing into something. His demonic growls were as intimidating as the group he was attacking.

It took several hours before Todd reluctantly went down to the sick bay, dreading his next conversation. "Oh, my God, you're back! Why didn't anyone tell me?" Kaylie had him in a ferocious hug. "I was so worried! Did you get DJ?"

"Hey, sweetie, good to see you. I assume this is your dad?" He smiled at

Bobby and then over to the small boy huddled on the far side. "And who is this little guy?"

"This is my traveling partner, Jacob. You must be Captain Todd." Bobby shook the man's hand. He saw the glimmer of despair cloud the man's face. "DJ—he's okay?"

Todd sat on the empty chair, "Yeah, yeah, DJ's great. He and his lab team are all on one of the Navy ships. He can come up after this mess here is settled. Kaylie, he misses you greatly, and he sent this." He held out a small envelope that the young man had given him before he left.

Kaylie grinned from ear to ear and took the letter, giving Todd a quick kiss on the cheek.

"Scott's not with you. Where is he?" Bobby asked.

Todd looked at his hands, slowly, so slowly. It took everything he had to make himself look at Bobby. The man did resemble his brother. More weathered, certainly, and not as fit as Scott, but the similarities were unmistakable. Kaylie had stopped opening the letter and gone to stand by her dad's bed.

"Listen . . . I'm afraid . . . I'm so sorry, but Scott . . ." the words didn't want to come. He took a deep breath as his eyes began to tear. "Scott didn't make it." His own voice sounded alien to him as he passed the terrible news to Scott's family. He looked pleadingly at each of them, hoping against logic that they would not fall apart. "He was swept out to sea trying to save the rest of us from an infected patient." He leaned back like a boxer waiting for the next blow to land. There, he had gotten it out. Now he felt like he was going to be sick.

Kaylie cried out as if wounded, while Bobby simply dropped his head, reaching over to take his daughter's hand. "Are you sure, I mean . . . you know?"

Todd couldn't look at them now; he focused on the boy instead. The child's haunted eyes seem to stare deep into his soul. "The raid happened at the peak of the hurricane . . . the waves were the size of skyscrapers. The Navy had Search and Rescue in the air and on the water for days . . . they found nothing. Then—well, then it became a recovery mission. So far, they've still found no sign of them. They finally called it off just before we landed here."

"So . . . so . . ." Kaylie struggled between tears to get the words out. "So, he could still be alive?"

"I wish I could say so, honey, I, oh God I so do, but no, he surely drowned. No one can survive the open sea that long without supplies, even in normal conditions. It was a hurricane. The ocean was a monster that night, anything but normal. I was out there with some of the SAR teams, all seasoned Navy guys, and honestly, we were all scared to death of it. The ocean took him, I'm so sorry." He looked away. "It won't give him back."

Kaylie's sobs echoed through the stark, near-empty room.

"I am so sorry, Kaylie and Bobby, it's my fault he went. I'll have to live with that, but I am sorry to you both, and to Scott. He is . . . he was a good man, a good friend, he was . . . the very best of us."

No one said anything for several long minutes. Bobby released Kaylie's hand and gently rubbed the young boy's hair. "Thank you, Todd, but he wouldn't want that. He would not want you carrying that guilt. You know Scott. He wouldn't do something unless he felt it was right." Bobby looked at his daughter and down at the tattoo on his hand. "I am only beginning to realize that I knew just a part of my little brother. He was obviously much more—a much better man than I was. He saved my daughter. He managed to help save me from 400 miles away. And from what I hear, he helped you put this town back together. In doing so, he—well, I think he found himself again.

"Much of that was thanks to you, Todd, and Jack and Bartos. You guys were the bond, and I can't thank you enough for everything you did for him—that you're still doing for him. There is a war going on outside these walls, and you came here, in the middle of it all, to tell me about my brother. Scott was right about you. You're one hell of a friend. Todd, he loved you, and my daughter loves you, and this boat needs you. If Scott is gone, I know it's not because of anything you did or didn't do. So please, don't ever blame yourself."

Todd stood and gently laid a hand on the man's arm in thanks. He turned and hugged Kaylie, unable to speak. He left them to deal with yet another loss. What was it about that family? They were such good people. *They don't deserve any of this.*

DeVonte caught him on the stairs. "We got a problem, Cap. They want you on the bridge."

CHAPTER NINETY-FOUR

The rain was coming down in torrents. The radar clearly showed that the eye of the storm had jogged east quite a bit over the last few hours, which put the eye wall on track to make landfall near Biloxi. Todd had heard the Navy meteorologist discussing it: it appeared that it would be a glancing blow to Harris Springs if the track continued to turn east; if the main storm stayed over the warm waters of the Gulf while part of it was over land, however, it would continue to feed and strengthen instead of dying off over land like most did. The predictions for the storm surge meant that if all that water were pushed onto land in front of the storm, it would cause massive flooding. He needed to confirm that the mooring lines were secure, but there was no way to safely do that now. The massive ship would act as a giant sail in the hurricane force winds. If the ship broke free, they would likely be pushed over against the far shore, right where the Messengers were waiting.

He entered the bridge to see Bartos staring back down the canal to the west. "What's up, Cajun?"

Bartos handed him the rifle scope and pointed. "Looks like I missed something when we cleared the area. They have a raft or something, I can't make it out in this rain too well. Since they're in the channel, we have to assume some of them are already on our side."

Todd held the scope and braced on the window frame, looking back over the ship. "I see it now. Doesn't look very stable. I don't think they're going to get many of them across with that thing. You have anything that could take it out?"

Bartos thought on it. "A sniper could take out the men paddling it, but the ones on land will just send someone out to retrieve it. They seem to have no problem sacrificing bodies to get what they want. If they're smart, they'll come up close to the hull. Due to the curve of the ship, we can't see all the way down to the waterline, not until they are up near the bow. No easy way to get weapons up there, but we could try one of our napalm bombs . . . might get lucky."

Todd thought on it. Bartos had filled him in on all the weapons they had, both conventional and improvised. "Let's keep those in reserve . . . we don't want them to know about those until we have more confirmed targets in our sights."

"So, we just let the raft go?" Bartos asked

"See if Garret's men can take out the men. If so, go for it, but otherwise, ignore it. I'm more concerned with those that are already on the island." Todd could see his friend did not like the plan. "Bartos, this is what we call a very dynamic and evolving scenario. The storm, the Judges, the Messengers, us. We have to make the right plays at the right time."

"I know, I know, but when can we call in the Navy?"

Todd pointed to the highway on the far side. "Not until that slows down."

Bartos looked back at the seemingly endless line of cars, horses, buses, and foot traffic joining the growing mass of Messengers on the far shore.

CHAPTER NINETY-FIVE

The Judges on the raft slipped by right alongside the *Aquatic Goddess*. They were exposed and began paddling furiously toward the far shore.

Two Navy SEALs on board had taken concealed positions on the bow with 50. caliber Barrett sniper rifles. Their synchronized shots hit both men center mass. The massive rounds carried both bodies well off the floating platform.

The reaction from the far shore was a volley of shots that hit the ship erratically and ineffectively.

The SEALs watched as the raft floated farther down the canal and was soon out of sight. Todd and Bartos had expected them to send more swimmers out to retrieve it, but none made the attempt. Over the next hour, the reason became clear as several trucks hauling large pontoon boats appeared on the far side. With no boat ramps remaining on that side, they backed the trucks as far down the bank as they could, then used their ample supply of manpower to lift the boats from the trailers and carry them down to the water.

Bartos and Todd watched as they loaded the boats with men and equipment. "Now it gets fun."

"Bartos, my friend, you have an odd sense of entertainment."

"Yeah, I know. I have to go get Solo. Keep an eye on things, will ya?"

Todd continued to watch the Messengers, wondering who was in charge and, more importantly, when he should call Commander Garret for help. After a round hit the thick glass in front of him, he decided now was probably the right time. Garret answered immediately but did not have the good news Todd was hoping for.

"The Air Boss indicates the weather right now is too bad to send attack jets for at least the next few hours. I'm sorry, Todd, but you know how limited our flight ops are in weather like this. We can fly above it, but you guys need more precision on a strike than we can deliver right now. Our only ordinance we have left is conventional, we have no infrared and no laser guidance. In other words, we would have to blind drop the damn things nearly on top of you. No telling where any of them would land with that wind you're about to get."

Todd slammed the radio back into the receiver. *Shit!* Of course, it made sense, but that fact didn't make it any easier. They could have given him more men or heavier arms—*Hell, just some crates of ammo for the .50 cals would have helped!* He had known air sorties would be scratched during the height of the storm. He had just hoped that that wouldn't be when he needed them.

Bartos enlisted the help of another man, John, and walked down the stairs to one of the outer access hatches several stories above the dock where the *AG* was moored. Immediately upon opening the hatch, they were drenched in the deluge of rain. Cautiously, Bartos brought a thin, reedy device to his lips and blew a series of sharp bursts on the whistle. He then pulled the hatch closed, and both men began rigging up the large wire basket, the top of a grocery store buggy. To this, they attached a rope that looped over a pulley system. The pulley had already been in place, undoubtedly for a different purpose . . . Moments later, they heard a single bark from outside.

Opening the hatch fully, Bartos saw Solo—or more accurately, he saw a version of the dog that appeared to have been painted by demons. Solo was covered in blood and gore, from nose to tail. John helped Bartos lower the cage. "Jesus Christ, what's all over that dog?"

"The blood of fallen Judges would be my guess," Bartos said, a hint of pride in his voice. Solo glanced up at the men but then turned his head back to the west. Bartos looked off in that direction. He saw nothing but abandoned storefronts, but he trusted the signals from his canine friend. "Come on, Solo, let someone else have this fight."

The dog jumped nimbly into the basket, just like they had practiced. The men hauled the rope in, bringing the basket with the heavy, wet, bloody dog on board. By the time the door was sealed shut Solo was rolling like a puppy on the lush carpet of the corridor. The deep blue pattern was quickly saturated with red from the animal's fur. Bartos scratched him lightly behind the ears. "Thanks, Solo, for whatever the hell you did out there, we owe ya, yet again," he smiled fondly. "Just too many coming over for you to take on by yourself now, though." He patted the dog once more, then headed to the top deck.

"Lieutenant!"

Garret emerged from a darkened entryway. "Yes, sir?"

Bartos smiled, "Shit, son, no one's ever called me sir. It's Bartos. Look, I know you've seen the boats they're loading ready to come over. And I'm pretty sure there's already a group over here to the southwest. I think the dog probably took care of some, but there are definitely more."

Garret keyed his throat mic and sent several of his men to guard that side. "Sir, I mean, Bartos, what is the plan for the others? Should we try and take out the boats?"

"We're open to suggestions, Lieutenant. If they get over here, they are probably going to first try and get the bridges lowered, then breach the ship."

Garret looked confident, "We can repel any boarders, sir, I mean—sorry. There are too many pinch points they would have to come through, and with what we have, and the IEDs you guys prepared, we should be able to hold the high ground. Battle theory indicates they will need an overwhelming force to overtake an entrenched and well-armed enemy."

Bartos appreciated the young officer's attitude but wondered how much actual fighting the young Navy man had done. He pointed over the railing. "They do seem to have an overwhelming force, Lieutenant." The lights from the line of cars stretched out of sight.

The sailor nodded and smiled, "They do indeed, sir, but they are over *there*. It's only when they get over *here* that it's a serious problem. We can send a demo team out to blow the bridges. Keep most of them over on that side."

"That won't be necessary, but thanks," Bartos replied. "My guys removed the main gears from the mechanisms. Even if they manage to get power to the motor, those bridges aren't lowering."

"Damn good thinking," Garret smiled. "We'll wait for the boats to get to our side and then take them out. Some of them may get across, but we'll make sure none of the boats goes back for more."

"Sounds like a good plan. Use my guys wherever you need them. They aren't soldiers, but they're good shots, and they will fight."

The Lieutenant nodded, "We realize that sir, in some ways they are more battle-tested than many of us. We are quickly learning how to work together."

CHAPTER NINETY-SIX

The clouds overhead were getting even darker, and the sounds of the crashing waves were deafening to those on the exposed deck of the ship. Through it all, they could still hear singing and music; the sounds of someone preaching were also discernible. "Those guys are having a camp meeting in the middle of a hurricane," Preacher Jack said as he looked at Angel and shook his head. "Something about this doesn't feel right. I think they might be trying to distract us from the people crossing over. We need to keep an eye on them."

The full force of the hurricane was bearing down on the former town of Harris Springs. They heard shouts and sporadic gunfire from the starboard side and crossed over to look out a window.

From their vantage point several decks up, they could now see a small group of men using a hydraulic jack. It had a steel wedge attached to a hose like you might see a rescue crew using on a car wreck. They had inserted the wedge into a tiny gap to pry open one of the hatches. Several of the men were supporting a steel plate above the group to shield from gunfire. The barrier was only good from directly overhead. Garret's men were fifty yards farther down and took out the four men with a few shots.

Jack didn't like that either; something felt off about the ease of these encounters. Suddenly, a large explosion went off next to where he stood: a small outer hatch had been blown inward with enough concussive force to wedge it into a wall on the other side. Jack tried to make sense of what he was seeing. He saw but could not hear what Angel was yelling. Yes, he, too, now realized the other group had been a diversion. The voices around him all sounded like they were underwater. Lips were moving, but the rest made no sense. Then he felt a hand on him—and then he was falling. Briefly, he saw Angel's look of horror as he was tossed backward out the blown hatch.

Bartos looked out from his position on the bridge wing. "Oh, fuck! That looks like Jack."

"Where?" Todd shoved him aside in his worry.

"Solo, hunt! He landed hard on the dock, may already be dead. Three tangos are carrying him off."

Todd had to keep his eye on the three boats full of men that had made it across to the far shore. They were struggling to climb the west bank. Once they reached level ground, they approached the ship without pause. Several broke away toward the drawbridge control box.

Take out the boats. Come on, guys, do it now! His whispered command didn't happen. Garret and many of the armed men of the *AG* were busy trying to reseal the hatchway and find the man who had made it inside: the same one who had thrown Jack out the blown hatch to the dock below. Angel had managed to get a shot off before ducking behind a bulkhead. She was safe and unharmed for now.

Bartos rounded a corner just as Solo rushed through the group of Garret's men. He was on a scent for someone familiar to his expert nose. Someone he had almost ended earlier in the day. "Did you guys get them, the ones that were pulling the Preacher off?"

"No, sir, Bartos, we lost them in the rain."

Angel came up breathless, "I'm sorry, I tried to get him, but he just threw Jack overboard. I shot him, I think I hit him."

Todd's voice came through the radio, "We have more on the island. A large group heading this way, and the boats are going back for more. Someone needs to take out those boats."

Garret ordered his men back to their stations. "Solo and Bartos will find the intruder. We have to set up to repel that group. You three— get back to the upper deck and take out those boats. Use the heavy guns or those air cannon grenades, but be careful. This is it, men, be smart."

The storm was raging near its peak; the wind was beginning to uproot trees and rip roofs from buildings. The air filled with debris made into daggers by the gale force winds. The Messenger's boat was being blown farther down the canal. The revival tent was down and wrapped around several of the parked cars.

Todd scratched his scruffy beard nervously as he eyed the approaching group on this side. A powerful gust blew two of them against the side of the ship where they dropped into the gap between the dock and the hull. The *AG* was straining against its mooring lines. Something that looked like the ship's tall radio antennae came crashing down against the side windows. Below, the water level was already washing over the top of the docks. *The storm-surge is beginning.*

At that moment one of the rear mooring lines snapped with a sharp twang. The stern of the ship lurched sideways several yards until the next line pulled taut, securing any further movement.

Several decks below, it had occurred to Bartos that he likely knew where the intruder was heading. He rushed to the nearby stairs and headed toward the mid-deck hatch. The man, he realized, would undoubtedly be focused on letting in others above anything else.

As he passed the next level, he paused at the open door to that space and yelled for Scoots to follow him. Off in the distance, he heard Solo in full attack mode. He could barely pull the stairwell door open to enter the lower storage hold: the pressure was too great, an outer door had to be open on this level.

Bartos swung into the darkened space with his M4 leveled at the wall where the open outer hatch was. Rain streamed through the opening and flooded the floor. The smells and sounds of scared farm animals left a ripe odor in the air. Ahead, in the shadows, he could just make out Solo, whose jaw was clamped around a man's arm. Another man's head popped into view from the other side of the open hatch, and Bartos fired off several rounds, one of which caught him between the eyes.

Without turning he yelled back. "Scoots! Call up for more men! We got a real problem down here." Bartos turned and saw his friend slip back into the relative protection of the stairwell and speak into his radio. Bartos whistled and gave a rarely used command to the dog. "Solo, KILL! KILL!" The dog looked up from the man he had been fighting with and wagged his tail. *What the fuck?* Bartos marveled with minor disgust. The dog released the man's arm and lunged directly for his throat, clamping down with one ferocious bite. Solo released and was moving toward the next target before the other man's body hit the deck.

Scoots poked his head back in, "Hey, Boss, they said to stay away from the open hatch." Solo was farther back in the darkness attacking someone else. Bartos had no idea how many of them were already aboard, but he had no problem staying away from that opening. He saw a glint of yellow and then heard a *woosh* of flame from the open hatch. His friends upstairs were tossing the homemade napalm. The screams from outside let him know the explosives had found their targets. The burning assailants, some of whom had crawled inside, cast enough light for Bartos to see more of the storage space. Solo had two men backed against a wall. One had a gun; the other was unarmed. Bartos aimed and took out the gunman. Solo looked over and growled. If dogs could be surly, he was pretty sure this one was.

"Fine, you stupid dog, I won't help you next time."

He stood up just as Scoots yelled a warning. It wasn't in time. The piece of steel pipe the man swung caught Bartos on the side of the head. He saw stars before he crashed to the steel deck. Shots rang out, and he was vaguely aware of another man lying beside him looking into his eyes. "You come here often? Not a talker, hmmm, the silent type."

Scoots was pulling him to his feet, but his feet didn't seem interested in the effort. As he was pulled away he gave a little wave to the other man, "Okay, see ya'round."

"Jesus Christ man, you gotta concussion."

Easy tugging on the shoulder, man. Scoots finally had him back on his feet.

Bartos looked at Scoots who appeared to be shooting away from him at an odd angle. "Fuck, that's weir—" He was on the deck again, this time looking at the dead man's boots. "Hey, I'm going to go sit by the fire, now." He crawled feebly toward a burning man who was lying across the hatch opening. Slowly, he began to realize he had no idea who or where he was. *Why is this filthy dog dripping blood all over me? Fuck the fire, I'm going to sleep.*

Several of Garret's commandos secured the room. They closed the hatch and helped Scoots pull Bartos back into the stairwell. Kaylie was there to help assess the wound. "Shit, Bartos, you have a cracked skull. We have to get that swelling down, now. Get him to sick bay."

"Don't worry about me, Mom, I'm going to go shoot the neighbor's cat."

"What is wrong with his voice?" Kaylie looked at the other men. "We better hurry."

CHAPTER NINETY-SEVEN

Peterson looked down at the man; he was still unconscious. Initially, he thought the man had probably died from the fall, but then he had moaned as they were dragging him back out of sight. Peterson and the other Judges that had made it across had taken refuge inside an abandoned farm supply store. The sounds of the raging storm surrounded them. Debris was hitting the storefront like shrapnel. Somewhere near, a sound of tearing metal rose above the shriek of the wind. The sides of the building pulsed in and out with the storm gusts. It felt as though the prefab metal structure could collapse at any moment. This was no normal tropical storm. Water levels were rising, the tide was already up over some of the roads nearer the ocean, and the size of the canal was increasing by the minutes.

At least they didn't have to hide from that damn dog now that it was finally back aboard the ship. They had watched them raise it up in a basket, and that had given Peterson the idea of how to slip someone aboard. He slapped the unconscious man hard to wake him up, but the man just moaned slightly.

"The Prophet is here now . . . I guess you heard the preaching," one of the others said in a flat voice.

Peterson nodded. "Call Dobbs. See what he wants us to do next. Let him know we got one man aboard ship with orders to open the lower hatches. Let him know we got a prisoner too."

The Judge had to walk up to the front of the store to get anyone on the radio. He came slowly back several minutes later staring at the silent radio. "Dobbs is dead. Hawley was the one who answered. He wants the captive. Said several more teams have made it over to this side. They're still meeting resistance, but he feels sure they will take the ship soon. Apparently, our leader has had a vision about it." His tone was mocking; they didn't give two shits about that pedophile's ridiculous visions. Those fucking visions had just gotten over five thousand men murdered back in Tennessee.

"Where do they want to meet?"

"They're bringing the next load over closer to where we crossed. It sounds like our guys are taking a lot of fire from the ship, so the goal is to move everyone to the west, out of sight. I may have heard him wrong, but it sounded like he would also be on the next boat."

Peterson sighed. "Can't say I would want to be out on that water right now, but hey, if he had a vision. God's will, you know."

Michael and Hawley both came over with the next group, just out of sight of the massive ship and its sharpshooters. Several men surrounded the Prophet like they were the president's protective detail. He had rarely been part of any actual skirmishes, and after Memphis, none of the men expected to see him anywhere near the frontline. But the Prophet's newest persona was not going to be denied. His bloodlust was supercharged and, after learning how many of the Judges had been butchered, he had been so enraged that he had brutally killed the man who had told him. Ironically, that man—Dobbs —became yet another dead Judge. The irony had seemed insignificant to His Holiness. Now Dobbs' body and severed head, respectively, were among the many caught in the rushing current of the waterway.

Reaching land, the Prophet strolled through the howling rains like a man possessed. Peterson watched his approach from the grimy storefront. "Shit, guess who's here."

"I wonder if his vision included a hurricane," his second replied bitterly.

As he entered the store, each of the Judges bowed. "Your Holiness."

Hawley approached Preacher Jack and checked his pulse. "Wake up, you shitbag." He slapped Jack like the other man had and got slightly more of a reaction. Jack's eyes remained shut, but his arm shot upwards and his hand seized the man's throat in a chokehold. Jack opened his eyes almost lazily as he drove the palm of his other hand into Hawley's nose with such force the sound of the bones breaking was for a moment as loud as the storm outside. A huge spray of blood erupted from Hawley's shocked face. Jack rolled out from under the man who was already dead. He had felt the man's bones punch through his nasal cavity and up into his brain.

Jack was in severe pain; the shadows on the wall swirled in his blurred vision. He quickly checked his chest and felt a broken rib. He also had damaged his ankle, maybe a broken leg. Not that it mattered. He assumed one of the many people now pointing guns at him would be pulling a trigger any second. But . . . no one did. No one spoke, even.

One went over to check the bloodied man; finding no pulse he shook his head at the man in white robes. Jack eyed him: he was not much to look at. Kind of short, a sparse beard, receding hairline . . . He looked like . . . maybe a used car salesman. "No, that's not quite true, maybe more like a door-to-door insurance salesman or someone you might see on a sexual predator website," he said out loud.

One of the men kicked him hard in the chest. "Do not speak until His Holiness gives you permission."

Jack doubled up, feeling the cracked rib grinding against another. Coughing, he wheezed, "Who? Oh, him . . . holy?" he let out a short little snigger. "Well, fuck me. He didn't give you permission to speak either. You might want to shut the fuck up, too."

The man kicked him again. Jack rolled and absorbed the blow but expelled a sound like all the pain in the world lived in the Judge's blow.

"Hey, your holy fuckwad, what do you want with us? You got your ass kicked in Memphis and decided to take a beach vay-kay, huh? I get it. I gotta say, you picked a lousy time. Hurricane season started early this year." Jack's vision was clearing slightly, and he quickly eyed the dark and cluttered store. He saw no way out of this. "Hey, I have an idea. Why don't you all go outside and play Hide and Go Fuck yourself."

Michael was struggling not to kill him immediately. His plan was to use this man to draw the others out, but he could not allow such disrespect to continue. "You there, um, Peters, please cut out the man's tongue."

Peterson nodded and drew his knife as he walked up behind Jack.

Jack laughed. "I can't believe you proclaim to be a man of God. I've done a lot of shit, but nothing that brazen. I actually value my eternal soul."

The Prophet knew the man was baiting him, but he allowed it to continue a few more seconds. He rarely met anyone who was not intimidated by him or the other men around him. "What would you know about our Lord and Savior, infidel?" He motioned to Peterson to stay his hand. The Judge slipped the knife back into its sheath.

Jack cocked his head, noticing more of his surroundings and taking note of his adversaries. "We've had a few conversations. I've read His book . . . and unlike you, I actually understood it. I paid attention. I didn't use it just to suit my own fucked up agenda and do the fucked up sinful shit you guys do. What the fuck happened to you, man? Did you not get enough hugs? Oh, and I know where I will spend eternity. Do you? I'd say not. You'd look a whole lot more worried if you did."

Michael grimaced, he was not one to be challenged, especially on the topic of his faith. The man amused him though. Something in Jack's relaxed manner caught him off guard. He allowed the blasphemer to continue babbling a moment longer.

CHAPTER NINETY-EIGHT

Jack had been in some tough places before, he had served time in a state prison before finding the Lord. Tough men he could understand, broken men he could empathize with, but this guy's level of crazy was seemingly beyond the reach of even his compassion. His leg and his ribs ached, his vision was constantly collapsing inward to a tunnel filled with sparks. The shadows around the dark store danced in and out of focus. *I'm sorry, Todd, I really tried.* The men were speaking to him again. He didn't care, he was talking to the Lord. In the end, the faith was all he had. Maybe that was all anyone had. He felt another kick, this time it was to his abdomen and caused the remainder of air to be pushed out of his lungs. *Shit,* the pain was becoming all combined into something else. Something he couldn't allow to win. He was a fighter. He might not have the strength to win physically, but he could still hit with his words. *Just buy some time, Jack – time to preach.*

A long strand of blood and saliva dripped slowly from Jack's mouth. His chest made a distinct rattling sound as he drew in a breath before continuing. "Man, I get it, see it all the time. You fell into preaching through the back door. Lots of us do. People need a leader, you stepped up and took the reins. The mistake you made is at some point thinking it was about you. You see, life is what we leave behind...the lives we touch. I'll leave this Earth knowing I did my best to help saves lives and souls around me. You, you're just going to fucking die. No one will remember shit about you. Not your name. Not your message. Nothing about your evil fucking existence. I will say you changed me, though. My faith, I mean. Hell, I used to be pro-life, at least until I met your sorry ass." Jack grinned a bloody smile up at the robed figure.

Michael's face went red and he looked ready to explode.

"I'm just fucking with you man. Look, believe it or not, I am also a preacher."

Michael stepped back looking at Jack with a sneer of amusement, "You lie, your words betray you."

"Oh hey, yeah...I get that a lot. I know I don't sound like one, but that doesn't change my heart. You see, I came to God by a different path. I served time, found God calling me there. Not that unusual, I know. Hey, I got a story, you wanna hear?

"What I want is to know how to get into that ship, how many people you have aboard and how well armed they are."

Jack ignored him and continued on. "Cool, ok, well, see at one point, I ministered to a prisoner who had robbed and shot a man. He told me something I found to be profound, especially seeing who spoke it. He said, 'We are remembered by the lives we touch and the love we share.' This from a convicted felon.

Think about that, man – we are remembered by the lives we touch and the love we share. That is fucking profound."

The prophet wiped the thin wet strands of hair out of his face. "Who cares? Look, I need information about that ship, or you are about to die."

Jack continued unfazed, "I promise it's relevant. This man, his name was Jason, said the man he shot did recover and had come to see him in prison. Now, that is not all that unusual, many just need that to start healing or to get some needed sense of revenge." Jack paused to spit a bloody gob of mucus and draw in a labored breath. He wasn't sure what he was trying to accomplish but felt compelled to tell the story and live a few minutes longer.

"Now, I was young and dumb back then, but I listened as I thought Jason was sharing something important. You see, I had made bad choices, blamed others, felt like the world owed me, all for no good reason. Now, Jason was about to go to death row, his final appeals were up. Now the man that visited Jason didn't do it for revenge or some other need for retribution, he did it to tell Jason a story.

"He told him how it felt to have the shotgun raised to his face when an enraged and high Jason asked where he was from and what God did he pray to.

"The man had said, 'Huh?' That was the wrong answer to Jason. He was a man filled with hate, and that man was a foreigner. Actually, he was a man of middle-eastern appearance but was, in fact, an American. Born in this country to proud immigrants.

"He then told Jason how he felt the bee stings of shells entering his face and head, then he had heard the boom of the gun.

"That he awoke after emergency surgery and a week in a medically induced coma. Many of the shells had gone into his brain. He had a promising career and family, and in the days and weeks after it was disappearing, all because of his injuries. He felt the rage, the anger, the depression....he felt the need for revenge.

"Now see, Jason had already been arrested, so the only revenge the man would likely get was with the guilty verdict. Once he did get that, he realized revenge was not what he wanted, it was not enough. More anger, more hate. The man said it took him years to realize that was not who he was, this was not the person his parents raised, this was not the path his faith demanded.

"So, the man decided to contact the would-be killer who sat in prison. He explained all this to Jason, who he was and all the things he had been through since he had pulled that trigger. Then...you know what he did? He forgave him.

"Jason said he couldn't believe it. How could this man do that? He said it felt like something just washed over him, took all the evil away. Then he apologized, he said how sorry he was and how his stepdad had helped fill his head with hate and racism from an early age. He was blinded by the stupid hate he felt for people that were different than him. Different color, different religions, different languages...anything different."

Michael was staring at Hawley's corpse seemingly unable to process it. The two had been through so much. He spoke briefly to the others, ignoring Jack, who continued on with his own message. One he felt a growing conviction to get out before he died.

"I was still going back to the prison years later as part of my ministry. You ever do that, prison ministry? Yeah, I'm gonna guess not. Anyways, the day of Jason's execution I was one of the people he asked to talk to. He said that man had called him that same day. The man who he was being put to death for trying to kill. They talked, and before hanging up, he told Jason, 'I love you, brother.'" Jack's vision was clearing, he could now clearly see the assembled group. He had regained a measure of strength and could tell they were all focused on his words again and that the Prophet was quickly losing patience with him.

"Can you get that? The man that he had tried to kill ten years earlier, told him that on the day he was to die. It was a lesson of love, a lesson of forgiveness. You see, dude, men are not born evil, they must learn it...some feel it can be unlearned. Hopefully, before it is too late. Now I know you see the relevance to our little situation here. I know you are going to kill me but think about what I am saying. You see, I have told that same story in church many times as an analogy for God's love for his people. Today I tell it from a more personal standpoint. That man had so much love for his fellow man. Way more than I will ever have. Would I be able to forgive you for what you are about to do? I don't honestly know...I don't think so. Not yet anyway, you don't deserve that. I have friends over there on that ship that I love, friends I would die for, but I'm a fighter for my friends and my faith, and sadly, all you really are is a disease. A cancerous bit of human eating away at the rest of the species. I realize now that the courage to hold on in this world is measured by who are you willing to die for.

"I said all that to say this...what if that is the true test of any faith? The love and respect for one another. Not the dogma or rituals, not who deserved to be saved or not. Not the flavor of your beliefs, but how you treat your fellow man. Why is my belief system any more valid than yours or his? Well, yours is complete horseshit, but, I mean—well you get the point. That man...he got it. You and I, probably not so much.

"Maybe some of this will get through to you, though. Maybe you could see your crimes and still repent. God will wash your soul clean, even now, and honestly, right now, I actually wish that weren't true. But hey, that's my problem...not yours. Let me ask you what are you leaving behind besides death and ruin? I know there will be judgment for you, maybe not by me, maybe not by man, but the day of reckoning comes for all of us."

The shadows just outside the edge of his vision began to move.

That was all Michael could stand. He looked at Peterson and nodded. "Do it."

Peterson reached for his knife again only to realize it was missing. Then, with a sickening sound that lasted only a split second, most of his hand was also missing. Arterial blood shot across the store aisle. There was the sound of whooshing air and a large sharp farm implement pierced out the front of Peterson's jacket. "What the—" Peterson croaked his final words and dropped to his knees, blood spewing from his mouth.

Jack looked at Michael. "It is judgment day...I'm afraid you have pissed off the demons," he said with his eyebrows raised. "Please meet the ghost of Harris Springs." Jack had thought he noticed one of the shadows moving, and he had finally realized it was a man. He was standing still as death, well out of sight of the others. Now that man, that damaged shell of a man, operating on some long-forgotten instinct, was working his way through the armed men. One moment he was there, and the next he had vanished.

The man moved with a fluid grace that was both beautiful and terrifying. So precise was each move of the attack that it was all over within seconds. Jack watched as each of the men, confused and alarmed, fell before they could do anything about the attack. In a few moments, every one of Michael's men lay dying on the dirty floor—all but the Prophet and the preacher.

Jack turned to yell, "Roosevelt, are you back there, too?"

"Oh yeah, yes, suh, there preacher man, I's here, too. Just enjoin yo stories. You tells some good 'uns, you do." The old man's clear singsong voice came from farther back in the store. The other man, the ghost, had vanished again—just another shadow.

Jack gave a pained laugh, "I thought it must have been you who brought the ninja in."

"I don't know his name, I jus calls him da Spirit! Maybe he da Holy Spirit," the old man called out merrily, "but Ghost is a good name, too. Yeah, yeah, I thinks I likes dat one even better."

Jack looked from the stunned-looking man in the robes to the growing destruction outside. He still couldn't believe he was alive. The Navy had lied; they weren't coming. The storm was in full fury, but he had an idea; maybe a way to end all of this, if the good Lord was willing. Roosevelt approached and helped Jack walk as he picked up a gun and one of the Judge's radios. He motioned with the gun for Michael to walk out in front of them, into the teeth of the storm. He called out, "Ghost! Thank you. If this asshole gets away, can you please cut him into tiny little pieces?"

Michael staggered in front of them out into the storm, like a beaten man, his arrogance and pride melting away with each fearful step. The wind drove rain and debris sideways. Roosevelt stumbled but helped support Jack as they hobbled back toward the ship together. "Will the

Ghost be okay back there, or will he come to the ship?" Jack asked the kind, old man.

Roosevelt laughed. "He'll be fine, nobody goin' a git dat boy to go inside anything like *dat*. Jus' leave him be. I'll bring him some food later."

CHAPTER NINETY-NINE

A lookout concealed on the upper-deck spotted Jack struggling to reach the ship with the other two. The lower hatch opened quickly as the trio slogged through the water rushing over the dock to reach the ship. Jack expected to see Bartos but instead found Angel, Solo, and Bobby who was beginning to look slightly better. Each had guns pointed in his direction but lowered them slightly as they took in the scene. They were elated to see him and Roosevelt, but the odd little man that accompanied them had Solo growling at once. Angel went to help Jack, but he motioned her off. He had a plan, and nothing was going to stop it. "I need this man on the top deck for all to see." Angel hugged Roosevelt and wrapped him in a poncho as they all went back inside.

Inside the dimly lit corridor, Bobby looked over at the robed man. "You are the one they call Prophet."

Michael didn't speak.

"Yeah, you're the one. You gave me this," he said, holding up his hand. "You also took my wife, you and your pigs." Bobby's hatred now had a target. Everything and everyone he had lost came rushing to the surface. He hit the pathetic man as hard as Jack had ever seen anyone get hit. Michael went down hard. Blood and broken teeth spilled from his split mouth.

"Holy shit, Bobby. I need him to be able to speak," Jack said.

"What do you have planned, Preacher?" asked Angel, looking disgustedly at the robed man with quiet rage.

"Something awful. I'm going to end this once and for all." He and Bobby pulled Michael to the upper deck, where Garret and several of his men quickly trained their guns on him. Jack motioned them farther back, out of sight. Looking out to sea and up at the sky, the preacher seemed to be waiting for something. He watched the water intently, as though timing something meticulously. Moments later, he handed Michael the radio. "Call your people. Tell them you have taken the ship. Tell them it was God's will. Give them the Message, and then you better give the most impressive and impassioned altar-call of your miserable life."

The fallen leader shook his head. Jack looked over at the dog. He only knew a few of Bartos' commands. He chose carefully. "Solo, help."

The dog went up to the man and bared his already bloody teeth with his snout mere millimeters from the man's groin.

"Tell them." He pushed the radio up to the man's bloody mouth.

Michael gave in. "My flock," he began. "This is your Prophet." His voice instantly was clear and strong and commanding. "The Lord has delivered."

Jack watched as the man's persona changed in front of him. "Now go over to the far rail and wave to them, make sure they can see you."

Michael reluctantly did as he was instructed.

"Tell them to come join you. God has delivered them an ark to ride out the storm. Tell them to get over here at once, anyway they can. Tell them the path to the west is the best route. Tell them God will keep them safe." Jack's eyes began to fill with tears at what he was doing.

Everyone around Jack looked at him like he was insane. Michael looked like he was going to protest, but Solo began to nuzzle into his robes, still growling.

Michael lifted the radio back to his lips. "Come unto me, and I will give you rest," he said. "Brothers, we have found our refuge, our Ark. Shelter from the storm and a storehouse of plenty. Our struggles and sacrifices for the Lord have been rewarded." He continued on ad-libbing for several more minutes seemingly basking in the falseness of it all.

The reaction from the far side was immediate. Guns shots were joined by shouts of victory and praises to the Lord. Jack took the radio back as he closed his eyes and said a silent prayer. He was using these people's blind faith to kill them all.

They walked the few steps out of the storm and into the main dining room. The small group gathered at the windows to watch the scene unfolding across the canal. Hundreds, then thousands of rapturous, jubilant people were attempting to cross the water at the same time as the storm surge reached its peak and a series of huge waves swept higher and higher up the banks and over the edge of the canal, consuming everything in its path.

The canal became a scene of utter chaos: the rising waters, swift currents, gators and tumbling coils of barbed wire tangled and dragged and swept the masses into a bloody mess. The tidal surge that boiled down the canal wiped out thousands as it grew to finally top the sides of the canals. Many attempted to get away by fleeing back along the road.

"Garret, have your men target the trenches with incendiaries. Bartos laid fuel traps about fifty yards in. We have drums of chlorine gas and diesel fuel as well. Drop them now."

"Will do, Jack."

The order was given, and soon the sides of the road packed with cars erupted into huge flames. Those trying to escape were now trapped between the poison gas, the fire and the flood. It was a deeply painful sight for them all, Jack in particular. There was no coming back from the genocide that he had unleashed in the name of survival. He had crossed a line. He knew he would never preach again. He felt he had traded his soul for the survival of his people.

Michael stood at the window watching his flock struggle and die with a look of calm and... enjoyment on his face. He spoke to no one in particular. "Ninety percent of people believe in some form of religion or higher power. The key is understanding how to use that belief to get them to do what you want instead of what they want."

Jack's disgust increased as he noticed it: the robes around the small man's groin betrayed his greater excitement. This man repulsed him. "Solo," he said quite quietly, "bite his dick off."

It seemed the dog understood the command. With one quick snap, a vital portion of Michael Swain's groin became a mutilated mess. Jack caught him as he fell. He was done with this piece of garbage. He would not offer him a chance to repent.

"Bobby, this man is guilty of every crime imaginable—against humanity and you personally. Would you like to carry out the sentencing?"

"Yes, I would. Gladly." Bobby had several soldiers lead the whimpering man to the rail. He took the H&K VP9 from his waistband and pointed it at the man who had destroyed so many lives. "This is for my wife, Jessie, and Jordan, and all the countless other lives you ruined."

He did not remember pulling the trigger, but the man's head erupted as the 9mm round did its job with cold precision. His robed body tumbled unceremoniously over the rail to join the growing number of dead bodies and flaming debris below.

Jack looked over the edge. "100 percent of us believe in gravity, mother fucker."

CHAPTER ONE HUNDRED

Gulf of Mexico

The passage of time had become an amorphous concept to the two men. All conversation had quelled after Scott mentioned the Catalyst protocols. The men paddled, ate turtle jerky and took tiny sips of the warm but fresh water collecting in the solar still.

"Do you think we're making any progress?" Scott asked the soldier.

"Some," Skybox responded with a shrug.

They had seen some trees floating by, as well as bits of Styrofoam and other detritus that the storm had thrown back out to sea. Every bit of terrestrial debris they saw gave them hope. The day was fading, and it looked like it would be a clear night; Skybox could hopefully do some plotting with the night sky and determine their approximate location.

Dusk brought an end to both the paddling and the silence. "You know she lost her husband and daughter?" said Skybox.

"Who?"

"Dr. Colton. That's one way the Guard ensures loyalty, they take care of your loved ones. After the collapse, they brought her family to a reserve station, kind of like a protected oasis. When they set up the lab at the college, she requested they be brought down so she could see them. The chopper went down somewhere near the coast. Her husband and her daughter were both killed."

"Fuck," Scott sighed and shook his head at the tragic news. "That hurts. Steve was a good man . . . I didn't know her daughter. Guess that explains the look she gave me when I asked about them."

"Just thought you should know. I'm pretty sure my friend, Tommy, was on the same flight, though no one would tell me. They were supposed to also be bringing him down from the same reserve as a favor to me. Just want you to know about her and that we—that the Guard—isn't all bad. They've done a lot of good."

"Thanks. I didn't mean to imply you guys were evil. You do have some rather harsh solutions, though. I mean, I see the logic in them, even in the brutality. Better to do what is necessary and save a few than do nothing and lose everyone . . ."

Skybox sighed. "Seems like that's always the dilemma. Most people want to do the right thing, even if it's suicidal. Our missions have always been about survival. If you know about the Catalyst protocols, and I have no idea how you do, you must also know it was a well-conceived plan no matter how brutal it comes across."

"I do," Scott said flatly. "But do you have any idea of what the world is like now? I mean, outside your Area of Operations, do you understand the brutality taking place, the total lack of resources, law and order?"

"Honestly, no I don't. I haven't gotten any news except a few morsels from DJ and the doc. My superiors passed along very little to me other than our country was falling apart. I was hoping you might tell me what's happened this past year."

Scott looked up at the darkening sky, remembering the Northern Lights that had appeared overhead last summer. "Wow . . . that will take some time."

Skybox gave a little snort. "Scott, I think we have plenty of that. At least until we run out of turtles, that is."

"Very true."

With that, he began to tell the man what had come to pass since the solar flare. Skybox absorbed it all in wide-eyed amazement. He could not grasp his country as the place Scott was describing.

CHAPTER ONE HUNDRED ONE

The next day the water they had been rationing ran out. They had only the supply from the solar still now. But today the sun was not cooperating; the skies had been overcast all day. Rainfall would have worked, but none fell. There were just clouds, heat and their unquenchable thirst.

"Well . . . you got any bright ideas?"

Skybox shook his head. "No," he croaked. He was a fighter and would not go down easily, but dehydration took no prisoners. "Just don't give into the thirst and drink seawater. It'll just speed up the end."

The conversation had lagged, and the men dozed uncomfortably. Scott had sores where his skin had been rubbing against the raft. They were becoming open wounds.

It was later in the afternoon when Scott felt a light bump from underneath the raft. It alarmed him, and he shouted although the sound that he made sounded nothing like his voice.

Skybox opened his eyes. "What is it?" he asked groggily.

Scott was looking out. "Sharks."

Skybox remained still. "Swell."

"No, man, you might want to take a look at this. There are *a lot* of sharks. Holy Mother of God," Scott wasn't easily afraid, but even he could hear the fear in his voice.

"Well, if you're talking blasphemy, I guess I better." Skybox looked as well. "Holy shit."

The area around the raft, in fact as far as they could see, was teeming with sharks. Most appeared uninterested in the raft; it seemed they had plenty to eat.

"What is all that?" Skybox mumbled as he rubbed his eyes.

"Debris and bodies," Scott muttered. "Judging from the condition, they look like flood victims." Mixed into this macabre tableau were basketballs, fenceposts, milk jugs, even an old television.

"My parents used to have one like that," Skybox said, pointing to the TV, "Zenith, I believe." He gave Scott a wink.

Scott leaned back laughing. "Don't, I haven't got the energy."

"Sorry, man, but let's keep looking. There might be something useful. I'm going to grab one of those fence boards for a paddle."

"Okay, but watch for nails or splinters before you bring it in. We are sitting in a leaky balloon surrounded by thousands of sharks . . ." Scott felt hysteria rising; what he'd said suddenly sounded so funny to him.

"Point taken, little buddy." They were both feeling silly.

Scott pointed. "Okay, skipper, let's check some of those milk jugs. They could have fresh water."

It was a good idea, but none held anything of the sort. Most were simply old trash. A few had lines attached and had probably been floats for a fishing line once upon a time. The sharks were not in a frenzy, but they were unpredictable, and in a mass this large anything was possible. Most of them looked to be blacktips, although he spotted the occasional spinner and bull shark in the swarm. While the spinners were normally the least dangerous, their leaps from the water to subdue their prey meant that some were landing near—and even on—the raft.

"We have to get away from this," Skybox said as he pushed the bloated back half of a dead hog away with his new paddle. Several sharks were fighting over the carcass and did not relinquish their hold even as he pushed on it.

Scott agreed, but could not see any possible way to clear what seemed like miles of floating carnage. Some of the bodies appeared to have gunshot wounds and burns. Whatever happened to these people must have been awful—more than just a hurricane. He noticed what looked like dark bruises or possibly tattoos on some of their hands. "If we go south the mass will just catch back up to us. We need to paddle north through the thickest part of it. Shouldn't be that wide."

"Agreed," said Skybox. "Start paddling but watch your hand and your paddle. Those things are biting everything that enters the water."

Scott felt incredibly weak, and his tongue was swollen and papery, but his fear of the situation and his desire to live were powerful enough motivators for now. Carefully, he dipped his paddle into the warm ocean water and the raft pulled forward several inches. Skybox was doing the same. Together they tapped into their remaining reserves of strength, and gradually their strokes became more confident.

Several times the men had to hit an overly aggressive shark in order to drive it off, but they seemed to be making progress. With no real frame of reference, all they could do was keep working together, hopeful that the effort would pay off. They were silent, muscles strained, and sweat made rivers down their faces. The chomping, tearing and snapping jaws all around them kept their pace efficient.

The debris and its accompanying sharks seemed to go on forever. After what felt like several hours of paddling, both men were well beyond exhaustion. "I can't keep going," Scott said.

"I know, I know, but it does seem to be thinning slightly."

They continued to paddle, although the strokes were getting ragged and momentum was falling away. Scott pulled his paddle in. A piece had been bitten off one side. He set it down and looked at Skybox, who pulled in his makeshift paddle, too, and sat catching his breath against the side of the raft.

He looked over at Scott and smiled weakly. "We tried."

The bumps of the sharks on the raft's bottom continued as both men fell into a sleep as deep as unconsciousness.

CHAPTER ONE HUNDRED TWO

They awoke around midday to find the raft filling with water. The lower ring of the sidewall had a large puncture in which seawater was now bubbling through. Waking slowly, Scott watched as if he were a spectator. "Bet they didn't have shows like this on that old Zenith." He could see Skybox—was that his name?—doing something, but he wasn't sure what, nor was he really interested. "I think I'm going to take a swim. I'm hot." He began to take off his shorts.

Skybox looked at him puzzled. "Hey, you can't do, do, do that. Poo—p —pool's closed. Come on, we . . . fuck. Got to fix it. I found patches."

It took the men what felt like an eternity to get the patches on the hole. Their fuzzy brains and clumsy hands lacked the motor coordination to handle the task simply. Neither could remember how the pump worked, so they left the ring flat, which caused them to sink into a funnel shape at the center of the raft. Scott managed to find an empty bottle and bail out much of the seawater, but soon they slept again, semi-submerged in the faltering lifeboat.

"Hey, drink this." Scott awoke to see Skybox holding something to his lips. It was hot but went down without a salty burn.

"Thaks," he growled in a voice that was almost gone.

Skybox nodded and took a swallow himself. "The solar-still worked all day, but we were so out of it getting away from the sharks that we never checked it. We have this and another almost full bottle of water! We could have died, and salvation would have been right there within our reach." He handed Scott the remainder of the bottle. "We can ration the next one. Right now, drink up."

The men roused themselves sluggishly to occasionally check the patches and empty the bag on the still. It was nighttime again, and cooler now. Maybe it was getting close to sunrise, as there was a slight glare to the eastern sky. The ever-present sound of the sharks moving through the water and feeding had grown quieter. There were less of them now.

The men took turns watching the horizon, mainly for something to do, but also with hope for land or something else that would aid them. Skybox had been watching the sky for a long time and shook his head. "We're starting to move south. Probably along the panhandle. We're about to be pulled down the coast of Florida."

Scott didn't feel like it mattered much so stayed silent as he took the man's watch position at the rail. Their legs ran together at the bottom of the raft. "We have to figure out how to blow that ring up tomorrow. Your legs are like hairy tree trunks. I can't sleep with a man with hairy legs."

Skybox laughed. "Funny, I like yours, smooth as glass. Damn cyclists, you guys love to manscape."

Scott stiffened. "I think—" he paused for several seconds to be sure. "I think I see something."

The other man crawled up near him, careful not to tip the raft too much. "Yeah," Skybox agreed. "I sort of see it. Man, it's dark out here. Whatever it is, it's big. It looks like it's moving past us fast— we better paddle before it gets out of sight. Might be something useful."

Scott nodded, "That's back towards deeper water, though, back to where the sharks are."

"We have to risk it, man, it's the only promising thing we've seen."

They put the paddles out and began to stroke. They paddled for hours as night gave way to day. The men could now see what they were pursuing, although the scene was somewhat surreal. Two hundred yards ahead a boat—well, actually several boats—were moored to what appeared to be part of a floating wooden dock and a shelter: a shack of some sort. The boats all had varying damage, some severe. The largest, a fishing boat like Todd's, was listing badly. A hole could clearly be seen near the water level, and the bow was flattened. A few of the smaller boats were beneath the water more than above it.

"We have to speed up," Scott said. "These must have been swept out with the storm as well." Skybox made a sound that seemed like agreement. Maybe.

It took the two weak men several more hours to make up the final distance and get close to the boats. The sun was now up in full force. Skybox dropped his paddle and uncoiled the rope that had been attached to the raft bag. "Hold this," he said, and with that, he dove over the rail and was swimming for the closest of the boats.

Scott looked over, his hand holding onto the thin rope. He yelled hoarsely in a semi-serious tone, "Sharks, don't mind him, he's super-human and would undoubtedly taste horrible. And he has legs like a freakin' gorilla."

Despite his weakened state, Skybox was determined and managed to reach the dock and get out of the water and over the gunnels of one of the boats in minutes. He pulled Scott and the raft the remainder of the way. Soon, the little raft that had pulled them through so much was tied up alongside the other decrepit craft of the small flotilla. Scott went to climb over a fantail of a boat named *Comfortably Numb* and found he was unable to walk. Looking over, he was somewhat pleased to see Skybox suffering the same affliction. "What's wrong, brother? Forget how to walk?"

The soldier flipped him off, then began crawling over each boat, inspecting every inch to see what their new home might have to keep them alive a little longer.

CHAPTER ONE HUNDRED THREE

Scott searched the fishing boat, the most intact of the vessels. Through the stained and cracked windows, he saw Skybox methodically going through the other craft. All the boats had been through hell; he couldn't believe they were still afloat. In one of the cabinets, he had found several rusty tins of sardines and some type of canned meat spread. It could have been cat food at this point; they would have eaten it. He was overjoyed to find two large collapsible, plastic containers full of water. It wasn't exactly fresh—it had an oily, plastic taste—but upon consumption, both men proclaimed it the best water ever. They also found various tools, fishing supplies, cups, a large bag of salt in a curing box and a half-full bottle of cheap bourbon.

Skybox was forced to cut away one of the mostly-submerged boats. He had already swum through it and found it to be nothing more than an empty hull, but it had suddenly lost its remaining buoyancy and was sinking quickly. It was not small, and its demise risked swamping the others as well. He scrambled across the old dock, just managing to cut the mooring line with the knife before it spiraled downward into the blue-green water and out of sight.

Skybox hit pay dirt in the most unlikely boat of all. He was rummaging through the dash of a small cabin cruiser that had most of its top hull missing when he found a portable marine radio in a watertight case. The batteries were dead, but surely there was a battery somewhere in this floating junkyard. Having collected all the random tools and supplies, the two men sat down to a meal of sardines and water.

"You think we should cut any of these others loose? Maybe the dock?"

Skybox nodded. "The one with the hole on the side could go at any moment, so definitely yes to that one. The dock seems to be floating on its own, and I like having it close for now. It gives us an easy way to move between boats. Plus, it makes us much larger on radar or visual, if anyone is out looking."

"Makes sense to me," Scott agreed happily.

Skybox opened the back of the radio. "Now, what can we do to get this thing working?"

The rechargeable battery inside was dead. They had recovered two large twelve-volt marine batteries from the boat hauls, but they were also both dead. Scott began to consider the problem. "Two possibilities I can think of. One is to come up with a way to recharge the batteries. The other is just to generate electricity."

"You make that sound so simple," Skybox added with more than a hint of sarcasm.

"Well, neither process is overly complicated, and we don't need much in the way of voltage. I could generate electricity with the wind, or even the water current. I just need a magnet and some copper wire. The problem is getting the voltage right. It would be trial and error. I don't think the radio would survive that. It needs twelve steady volts.

"We have three batteries capable of making that, so I think the smart move is to come up with a way to recharge the batteries. For that, I may still need to make a generator or . . . or perhaps I can just use salt water. That would be safer, but slower."

Scott got started assembling what he needed: screws, strips of bare metal, some plastic cups lined up in a row. He also stripped all the electrical wire from beneath the console of one of the boats. Skybox watched the process intently. "What do you need me to do?"

"Cut the wire into lengths about fifteen inches long. Strip the plastic covering back all the way and twist the wire tight so it doesn't separate. I think we'll need twenty—maybe thirty pieces of wire. Once you're done, wrap the wire around the metal screws like this." Scott held up one he had already done.

Skybox got busy while Scott went to mix the saltwater solution. The seawater would have impurities, but he couldn't bring himself to use the fresh stuff they had found. Filling up a large bucket of seawater, he added more salt from the bag until he guessed it had the right level of salinity.

He poured the salt water solution into the row of cups. He also pulled a light from the side of one of the boats, which would allow him to know when he was at or above the right voltage. Skybox had the screws prepared and draped them over the edge of the cups, one screw in each. "There is no way this will work, Scott."

"Have faith," his companion said. "Electricity is essentially just electrons moving from one spot to another. We just have to coax them along a bit." He attached two leads coming off the signal light to two primary wires that went to the cups. The little green light began to glow very faintly. "Voltage is a little low, we need a few more cups of water."

"Holy shit, that's amazing." Skybox was very impressed. In short order, they had assembled twenty-eight cups in two rows, and the light was glowing steady and bright.

Scott looked up triumphantly. "Nerds everywhere, rejoice! Okay, I just need to watch this for a bit to see how long it takes before the electrolyte—the saltwater—is neutralized. Then I'll know how often to change out the water." The light started to dim after about fifty minutes. "We have our baseline now. Let's start charging the smaller radio battery first. I'm afraid the deep cycle marine batteries will take days to charge at this speed." They refilled the cups and removed the light from the leads, replacing it with the radio battery.

"We have a few hours before it will be strong enough to test. I don't know that it will run long, but who should we try and contact?"

"You probably won't like it, but I think we should try my people. They have a lot of assets in the Gulf and a large contingent around Tampa, which is likely where we're headed."

"Yeah . . . Tampa . . . we should probably talk about that," Scott said with an edge of remorse. "Last year, right after the solar event, Todd encountered a Navy fleet heading toward Tampa. Later we learned they were firing on an area of MacDill Air Force Base where many of the Grayshirts—sorry—the P-Guard were based."

Skybox looked pale. "Shit. All of Praetor 5 is based out of there. Still, should be able to reach someone. I can't imagine them not having assets still active."

"Works for me, we'll try them first," Scott answered.

"Scott, why is the Navy doing this, why do they hate the Guard? Shelling a domestic military base, a university—man, it's fucked up! Are they trying to overthrow what's left of the country?"

Scott thought about it. He was one of the few people who knew a little about both sides of this covert war. "Honestly, Skybox, just the opposite. They think they're preventing you guys from doing exactly that. You both—I mean, the Navy and the Guard both seem to want very similar things. But they see the Guard as a military coup, a shadow government only out for themselves. They feel they have to defend the Constitution and the ideals of what is the US."

"I guess I can see that we don't present the warm and fuzzies to anyone. And if someone pokes us with a stick, we do tend to eradicate them from the face of the Earth." Skybox looked back out to sea shaking his head. "Do you have any idea how much of the Navy is left?"

"Honestly, I don't, but I'm not sure I would share that with you if I did. I know much of what's left is involved in an operation called Homefront, though I have no idea what that is. How much of the Guard is left?"

Skybox shook his head. "I imagine a lot, but probably far less than the Navy. Honestly, it's never something our command level shares. We see many of the same faces on our deployments. Platoon strength at most. I do know that in the past year we've had significant casualties. My entire Talon Battlegroup is just one example."

Scott thought about all he had heard. He reached to an overhead rack and pulled down an old fishing rod and reel. He checked the line and fastened a hook to the end. "Do you think there's any way for the two groups to ever work together, or at least leave each other alone? The Navy just seems to be concerned with protecting the people and maintaining some level of Constitutional Rights. Your P-Guard is essentially interested in saving the species by protecting the best and the brightest people. Those are not mutually exclusive goals."

Skybox mulled it over. "Maybe. Our leadership is, well...challenging to have a dialog with. We're tasked with a very specific mission: combat and remove significant physical threats against the US, emerging democracies and our aligned nations. We stay in the shadows and help take out the trash. The Navy, well, the Navy is a fiercely independent military branch, always has been, but yes, you are right, we need to end this conflict, assuming we can get out of this, that is."

CHAPTER ONE HUNDRED FOUR

It took several attempts before they got the right balance of cells and saltwater to charge the battery sufficiently. They used the time to fish using bits of turtle jerky and sardine. They managed to catch several small fish and one large dorado, which put up quite a fight.

The pair erupted into cheers when they finally got the radio to work. Scott went to build a small fire and prepare the fish while Skybox started making calls on the newly charged radio. Scott could hear him switching efficiently between frequencies and making a general mayday call.

Scott built the fire from broken off pieces of shed roof on an old metal cooktop. By rigging up the cooking rack from the small oven as a grill, he placed the fish above the flames to cook. He added the only seasoning he had: salt.

"Damn, that smells great," Skybox said walking over with a big grin.

"Mahi-mahi if you were ordering it in a restaurant," Scott said. "So, you reached someone."

The soldier broke off a slightly charred piece of the white, flaky fish and crammed it into his mouth. Between the noises of appreciation, he replied: "Yeah, I reached someone. They got my call sign and general location. Said they would confirm and call back in an hour on our backup frequency. We have time to eat."

An hour later, both men were stuffed from overeating. Their limited diet over the last week had not prepared their bodies for the day's bounty.

"Oh, my God, I am in pain," Skybox groaned.

"Tell me about it. Fuck."

Despite that, both men perked up at the recollection of the half-bottle of bourbon. "Just one," Skybox said. Scott nodded in agreement and poured. Then poured again.

At three, he capped the bottle and returned it to the shelf. "Shame I had to be adrift at sea to discover the wonderfully complex qualities of cheap whiskey."

"Amen to that, Scott."

"I would say we are three sheets to the wind, except we have no sheets . . . or wind."

"Nonsense, Scott, this fine vessel has all we need. It's a good night here on the USS *Pile-o-Junk*."

Scott grinned. "Unless your Praetor friends decide to shoot or imprison me when they rescue us."

"You'll be okay, friend, they're decent people. And they have a deep sense of honor and brotherhood. They will know you saved my life. They'll take care of you just like they did my friend Tommy. They didn't have to take such good care of him, but they chose to because it was right."

Perhaps it was the whiskey or his jubilation or the fact that the certainty of death had been briefly pushed aside, but Scott had a moment of clarity. "Skybox, this is going to sound crazy, and I have no idea why this has only just occurred to me, but Tommy is alive, and I am pretty sure I've met him."

Skybox had been reaching for the bottle again but stopped. "That's not funny, man, whatever the punch line is, keep it to yourself. I don't joke around about him, he deserves better."

"No, no, hear me out. Listen, you said he was in a chopper that crashed near the coast. A chopper that had Gia's family aboard—a little girl. That he has a head injury. It would have happened around the end of last year."

Skybox thought briefly then nodded, genuinely interested now.

Scott told the story of how he and his niece had encountered the injured vet that morning in the yard of his cottage. "He was like a statue for hours . . . he had a girl's ribbon in his hand. Could have been from Gia's daughter. Kaylie treated his wounds. He had a hospital bracelet on. We were about to take him into town—to the clinic since we had no idea what else to do for him—when the guy just up and vanished. We looked for him, but it was like he was never there."

Skybox was leaning intently toward Scott by now, and he tried to contain his emotions, but the possibility that Scott was talking about Tommy was too much for him to remain calm about. "That sounds a lot like him . . . but that was months ago . . . from what you told me, it would be unlikely that he's still around, even if he was still alive."

"That's just it, though—Kaylie talked to my friend Jack about it. She said she had glimpsed someone on the beach, and that others had been describing a mysterious man who'd been lurking around for months. She said it sounded a lot like the man we saw that day. The locals have taken to calling him the Ghost."

"The Ghost?"

"Yeah, he just appears and disappears like a ghost or something."

Skybox stood. It was time for the call. "No matter what else happens, we are both going to Harris Springs, Mississippi. I need to see for myself."

CHAPTER ONE HUNDRED FIVE

Harris Springs, Mississippi

The storm had raged for an hour longer, but finally, the winds began to ease off. Angel and Roosevelt had helped Jack to the sickbay, and she had not left his side since. Kaylie and one of the other medics tended to him carefully: they wrapped his chest tightly, put a boot splint on his broken ankle, and gave him medicine for the pain.

The other beds were all occupied, but the *AG* community had fared much better than expected. Bartos was on the next bed over from his friend, eyes open and wearing a silly grin. His head was bandaged.

Jack looked over at him when he came round. "Cajun, what happened, you bump your head?"

Bartos turned lazily to look at Jack. "Hello, Padre, didn't think you would make it over to the spa today. You're getting the mineral wrap I see. Good choice."

"What's wrong with his voice? He sounds like a New Yorker."

Kaylie laughed. "We don't know. He took a really hard blow to the head, and he's been talking crazy ever since. It should pass. In the meantime, it seems there's a lot more to Bartos than he ever let on."

Jack leaned over and patted his friend's hand. "Hang in there, brother, I think we actually won this round. It cost us, a lot, but we're still here. You did good, my friend. Everything you planned worked." He recalled something. "By the way, Kaylie, I met your ghost. In fact, he saved my life."

She looked confused. "Wait . . . so he's real? Is it the same guy Uncle Scott and I saw in the yard of the cottage last year?"

Jack nodded. "Seems like it. He's very real. I'm not sure if he's the same guy, but it sounds like he might be. He and Mr. Roosevelt here have been hanging out."

The old man gave one of his trademark chuckles. "Oh, he's aight. Sorry, miss, name's Roosevelt, Roosevelt Jackson. He comes by an' I feeds him sometime. Never speaks, not sure he can no mo', but I see's what's inside, I do. We decided we might betta come to town, dat storm looked bad. By da time we got here, dis boat was shut up tight. He didn't seem like he wanted to come inside no how. I don't think he likes to be closed in anymo'. Anyhows, me and the shadow man went on over to one da stores I use' to shop at. Jus' happ'd to be there outta da storm when dem bad men showed up. We hid at first, but Ghost sho'd dem though. Never seen a person move like dat. Nope, never have."

Jack leaned over and gave the man a hug. "Thank God y'all were there, brother."

"Oh yeah, da good Lord knows where Roosevelt need to be. He always lookin' out for dumb animals like us." With that, he gave a deep, genuine belly laugh that had all of them chuckling.

"You got that right, friend." Jack sighed and leaned back in relief.

Todd looked out at the view. There were bodies as far as he could see. Bobby and the younger Garret had joined him on the bridge. The storm was finally heading inland and diminishing in strength.

While Bobby wasn't fully healed, increasingly he was finding his strength; taking his vengeance on Michael seemed to have renewed him. "Cap, that's not the face of a man who just won the war. What's wrong?"

Todd shook his head then broke his stare from the tableau outside the windows. Scott was right; this world just kept spiraling downwards. One fucking thing after another, after another. "I'm just not sure . . . I'm just not sure it's worth it. Bobby, you look out there and see the enemy. You have a right to hate them, they took so much from you. I . . . I just see the bodies of poor misguided souls. Teachers, mechanics, truck drivers, businessmen. People so desperate to survive, so hungry that they followed a lunatic to the very ends of the Earth. That doesn't mean they were bad people. He thought back to losing Liz, so glad she was no longer around to see all this. *The fetid brokenness of who I once was is now reflected back at me in this broken place I now live.*

Bobby nodded grimly. "Todd, it's our choices and our actions that define us. They made their choices. They were bad people, Todd, trust me. Anyone in that group with any good in them at all didn't make it this far. You are a good man, but you just can't save everybody."

Todd gave a mirthless laugh. "Damn, you do sound like your brother." He turned to the other man who had remained silent. "Lieutenant, your father let me down. Correction: let *us* down. I trusted him to honor his agreement to protect us, and he didn't."

"I understand, sir. I am sorry. I do believe he would have if it had been possible. You know how much the storm limited our operations."

"Yes, I know. But he could have provided more men or firepower before then. He gave us the barest of assistance. Don't get me wrong, I thank God you and your men were here. I appreciate that, and you're welcome back anytime. I just expected more from him . . . from the Navy."

Garret gave a brief smile. "It would have been nice to have had more. A few belt-fed fifties would have been a good deterrent. But your people fought well. I'm not sure we could have come up with a better plan. That was a very unconventional force out there, not the Navy's typical battle. Also, I am not my father. I can't speak for him. I do know this other operation has much of his attention right now. Well, that and the losses we took at Devil's Tower."

"Yeah," Todd nodded. "What exactly is Operation Homefront?"

Garret looked unsure if he should answer. "I—I don't know a lot of the details, sir."

"Go on, paint it with big strokes then."

The young man thought on it for several seconds before reaching some conclusion. "It's an act of repatriation, sir. Mostly pitched as a humanitarian mission. Bringing troops and equipment from foreign soil back to the US. They're also bringing families and any expats that want to come."

Bobby spoke up. "I hear a *but* in there. What's the secondary mission, Lieutenant?"

"It's not secondary sir, it is actually the primary mission. Yes, we want to bring US troops back to America, but, well, it's no secret that the domestic military bases have been oddly silent since the CME. Many smaller bases were abandoned completely, but others, other large bases, should have been active. We know many still have full or nearly full complements of manpower and electricity, but we believe they are being directed by members of Praetor using the Catalyst protocols as a type of executive order. Could even be the president is still issuing actual executive orders we suppose. In doing this, they have at their disposal a large, standing army to back up the Praetor teams."

Todd was puzzled. "I assumed all the military would have gone back to their own families by now. But . . . so you're bringing more of them here? Wouldn't that just add more strength to the Catalyst plan?"

"The higher-ups don't think so. Everyone coming back in our ships will hear and see the full story: everything that has gone on in America and all the shit that Catalyst didn't try to prevent. Once here, they'll be based at Naval bases up and down the coast. From there, we believe they can make contact with their fellow soldiers and hopefully convince them to join in the fight to save America."

Todd eyed the carnage again. "Not sure how much there will be left to save."

Garret nodded as Bobby joined Todd at the window. "We have a massive cleanup to perform. If we don't do something with those bodies, this place will be overrun with disease and vermin."

The Lieutenant looked on. "There must be thousands of them. I still can't believe they essentially killed themselves to follow that fool. Your preacher had them pegged, that man's words killed them, not our bullets. *I guess they did get the message.* Todd, if you can get my dad on the line, I feel sure we can help. The Navy is trained for situations like this. They could bring the *Bataan* just offshore, and their medical and rescue teams will have this area cleansed within a few days."

"Thanks, I'll get DeVonte to get him on the radio once the antenna is reattached. Then I'll let you talk to him. I believe it would be best if he and I didn't speak for now."

The late afternoon sun was beginning to come out from the cloud cover, casting everything into a surreal golden glow. The amount of damage done by the storm and the battle was now fully visible. Todd called for his men to unseal the ship. "Scoots, we have to get the aft mooring lines secured to the dock. See if you can get the heavy-duty forklift down here to do that once the water level drops. We also need to lower one of the drawbridges. If you have the gears, send them up there with a generator. These locals are going to be anxious to get back and check on their farms. Get someone to help DeVonte replace that radio antennae as well."

The golden light that streamed through the bridge windows took Todd back to the previous summer. It had seemed like just a normal summer's day. It had changed everything. Bobby placed a hand on Todd's shoulder. Both men still mourned the wives they had lost. Garret left silently, passing Kaylie and DeVonte leading Jacob who had finally come out of hiding. None of the group spoke, but all of them gathered on the bridge and embraced silently.

This was their family now. They would start again. That is what surviving meant: you handled the challenges, you faced the setbacks, you came up with solutions and you sometimes, just sometimes, got to move forward.

CHAPTER ONE HUNDRED SIX

Gulf of Mexico - West of Tampa, FL

Their time aboard the *USS Pile-o-Junk* was not destined to go smoothly. Yet one more boat began to sink, pulling much of the floating dock and shed with it. The men reacted in time to cut it free, but their island of safety was shrinking alarmingly fast.

"At least we still have the trusty raft," Scott said.

They both looked at the grimy, near-flat inflatable with its bloodstains and remnants of dried turtle on the canopy. Skybox looked pale. "I think I would really rather just go ahead and drown."

When he had turned the radio back on, his people were there, ready to talk. They spoke mostly in a form of code Scott couldn't quite pin down. Since they were broadcasting on open channels, it made sense. Some of the statements were very recognizable. Skybox raised his voice a time or two, but by the end of the short transmission he was nodding and looked at Scott with a small smile.

"Well, that was interesting."

"Okay, I'll bite. What's interesting, Skybox? Did your people say they don't exist so we should just rescue ourselves?"

"In a way, yeah. They want me to turn myself over to the Navy. Apparently, your friend and that lab are the best chance of cracking the Chimera virus. They are royally pissed at losing the asset to the Navy, but more interested in the cure being found. Their only condition for giving me up is that the Navy agree to share any potential cure."

Scott scowled but nodded. "I guess that makes sense. Just unexpected. Prae—the Guard doesn't seem like the type to give up anything easily. It makes me wonder again if the two groups could be brought closer . . . to work together. So how long are they going to make us sit out here and cook in our own juices, and who is coming to get us?"

"Not long, friend, not long. P-Guard will hire a civilian craft to come get us and transport to the nearest Naval vessel. Probably just some fisherman they can buy off."

~

It was nearly twenty-four hours later before the very thin and weary pair stepped back aboard the *USS Bataan*. He and Skybox had been deposited onto a derelict ship after Scott radioed the Navy from the fishing boat that picked them off the floating junk pile. It had taken a while for the message to reach Command, but to his credit, Garret had moved heaven and hell to get the men picked up and brought back to the ship as quickly as possible.

Scott and Skybox shook hands and, to everyone's amazement, hugged before they were each led away to separate medical bays for full checkups. They had been at sea for seven days. Despite the ordeal, the medics found that Scott was in remarkably good shape. He was not overly dehydrated. He had some sores that had become infected, severe sunburn, and a persistent, mild headache, but nothing else. He had just been given the good news when Gia came rushing in.

"Scott! I just got word. I can't believe it! I'm so glad you're alive." She hugged him, holding on with a tenacious grip.

"Hey, Gia," he returned her hug as firmly as his weakened state allowed, "I didn't mean to rush off like that, just surprised to see you and all."

She laughed. "You idiot. What made you think you could take on a Special Forces soldier?"

Scott gave a slight grin and shook his head. "No one bothered to tell me he was the freakin' Terminator." He paused to take in his friend then continued. "I knew he was important to you."

She grabbed his hand, which had begun to tremble. "Scott, you are important to me."

He looked at her and trembled more. He had something that had to be said now. Ironic that he would be scared of this after all he had been through. "Gia, I . . . I love you." She looked up in surprise and he saw universes in those gorgeous eyes. His pulse raced and his mouth was dry. "Well, I used to . . . I mean, I always have. I don't know. I'm so sorry about your family—really, really, sorry. I just—I just made a promise to myself out there, that if I survived, I'd make sure I lived with no more regrets.

Gia smiled, and her eyes began to water.

"I'm not saying I want anything from you, I know—"

She stopped him with a kiss, then smiled as she put her arms around him. "Hush. Just stop talking." She kissed him again, deeper, and with tenderness. It was very close to perfect in Scott's admittedly limited experience. He hadn't been kissed in a long time. His lips were chapped, his skin burned everywhere she touched, and his head felt like it would explode. None of that mattered in the least. It may have been the happiest moment of his life. No. It definitely was.

Gia pulled back and looked at him in a way he remembered very well. In his mind, he had called it the Friendship Look. His heart began to sink. She must just have been glad to see him; felt a sudden rush of emotion that had now passed. Her mouth gave a tiny tick of a smile, her eyes sparkled and she took his hand.

"I always knew."

His head was spinning again. He looked puzzled, then hurt.

She shook her head, "Scott, I want to explain some of my actions back then to you so that maybe you can understand why I made the choices I did. I was selfish and even cruel to you. I just had my life all planned out. And then I met you.

Scott, I've been mourning the loss of my family, the loss of my world, for the past six months. What you don't know is that for *years* I mourned losing *you*, losing my best friend, and you were so much more. Then I saw you—for just a moment, coming to save me, no less!—and then you were gone again. All those feelings came rushing back at me. The timing is awful, who knows what's going on, but I really am so very happy you are alive and that you're back."

He pulled her close into an embrace they both seemed to need so badly. They stayed like that for several minutes. She pulled away from him and smiled with tears in her eyes again. "This is one very crazy world, my friend. Do you think we might have a chance? A second chance?"

"Well, G, an hour ago, you thought I was dead, and now here we are. I would say we have a chance. This seems to be my week for miracles."

CHAPTER ONE HUNDRED SEVEN

USS Bataan, Gulf of Mexico

Commander Garret looked anxious as he spoke. "We haven't heard from Todd since the hurricane passed through. Scott, we had a situation develop there. The group, the Messengers, made a move on your town."

"Fuck," Scott felt a heavy weight descend on his good mood. "Sorry, sir, but fuck. Any word from them since?"

"Last we heard they were requesting help. The group was massing, estimates were in the thousands, and they were preparing for a fight. We let them know we would stage missions to engage the group, but then the storm made landfall near there, and we weren't able to fly any of the planned sorties." Garret rubbed his eyes. Scott thought he saw the man tearing up.

"We're yet to hear from the *AG*, so we're taking the *Bataan* in close. We had a combat team on your ship. If we find survivors, we can offer whatever assistance is required. Something else you should know is that Todd was not pleased with me when he left. He called me out on my failures, not the least of which was not finding you. On that, he was very obviously right. I . . . I apologize. I know that is a feeble gesture considering everything, but we—I—am balancing very limited resources and a mission that keeps growing more uncontrollable . . . I find myself having to make the life-and-death calls far too often. You guys have been a good ally, and I do feel—no, I know—that I let you down, let him down. I made several bad calls."

Scott listened to Garret's words while hoping against all hope to find his loved ones safe and sound. The commander's words sounded muddled and distant in his distracted mind, but he got the sincerity. "Thank you, Commander. I know you did the best you could. If I could go over with the first team, I would appreciate it."

"Of course, of course. The researcher, the boy, DJ, has requested the same. I know he was one of the main reasons you came on this mission. I hope you both find your niece alive and well. I almost forgot to mention it, but Todd did say that your brother had been found and brought to the ship as well. I'm not sure that was a good thing or not, but best of luck with all of your family."

"Thank you, sir." Garret stood up to say his goodbyes and dismiss Scott from the room, but Scott stayed seated.

The commander seemed somewhat taken aback but covered it well. The man in front of him had been through quite an ordeal and now faced the possibility of even greater pain upon returning home. "Is there something else on your mind, Mr. Montgomery?"

Scott sighed. "Yes, there is something else I need to discuss. I'm not sure either of us are the right ones to bring this up, but someone needs to."

"Go on . . . I'm intrigued."

"Commander, you—and by you, I mean the Navy, and the Praetor group—you have to end this war."

"Well, there's nothing I would like more, son, but—"

Scott cut him off. "Please let me finish. I had a lot of time out there with that man from Praetor. The commander who calls himself Skybox. We were not friends going into that ocean, far from it. The man tried to kill me. Out there, though, we realized we needed each other to survive. I discovered that he is an honorable man, and in learning more about his group, the P-Guard, I realized that their goals and the Navy's are not so far apart. You have very different approaches, yes, but you're not incompatible. You don't have to work together, but you *must* stop wasting time and resources by trying to stop them. They are the ones that turned Skybox and me back over to you. Do you know why?"

Garret shook his head.

"Because now that you have Gia—Dr. Colton—and her team, they think you have the best chance of finding a cure for the Chimera virus. For her to do that she needed Skybox. Sir, I mean no disrespect, but if you continue with this pointless mission against them, you will fail. These people, the P-Guard, feel they are right every bit as much as you do. You, them...all are patriots. The difference is that they are ruthless, well-equipped and very goddamn good at what they do. Your numbers may be larger, but that will change in time. You have Skybox now. He's the key. He can talk to his leaders, whomever they are. If you will commit to an end of hostilities, he believes he can broker the same from P-Guard Command."

The Commander dropped into the guest chair alongside Scott. He rubbed his short gray beard and looked thoughtfully up to the framed picture of the last President of the United States. "You always surprise me, Scott. You have a survivor's mentality . . . someway, somehow, you are always looking for a solution."

He took a long pause again, staring at a blank spot on the wall. "We know we can't continue fighting like we have been. More ships are running out of food or fuel almost every day now. Many of our men— hell, all our men—want to get home to check on their families. This deployment shows no sign of coming to an end, but I'm not sure I can do what you ask. The atrocities that those people have committed, their lack of decency and the way they trample all over the Constitution, it leaves very little room to make peace. My commitment to you though is this: I will speak with my fellow command group, and we will open a dialog on the subject. We will allow Skybox to bring it up with his people. What happens from that point, who knows? But, I will try."

Scott nodded and stood. "Thank you, sir. If we all can't start working together, nothing else matters. We can't make it that way. Not 'we', as a country, we...as a species."

CHAPTER ONE HUNDRED EIGHT

Harris Springs, Mississippi

Scott rode the distance mostly in silence. His hand rested in Gia's who was seated between he and DJ. He couldn't keep from looking at Gia: the friend whose presence, more than anything else in this crazy new world, had kept him focused on survival since his fall into the ocean.

He looked down at the blue water below the Navy chopper. Opposite him, Skybox, too, stared out at the massive expanse of the ocean below. The man must have felt Scott's eyes on him, as he immediately looked up directly at Scott. The two men smiled and nodded at one another, acknowledging their ordeal and the unlikely friendship that had grown from the adversity in the waters below.

DJ had been briefed that the scene at Harris Springs was likely going to be a shock. Garret had reluctantly given permission for DJ, Gia and Skybox to make the trip: a huge portion of the bioresearch team to be let out of the Navy's grasp in one go, but when they let it be known they would not continue working without this break, the CO had relented. He was also anxious to get the assault team back from the *AG*. Scott discovered that Garret's son had been assigned there. Todd had managed to get the man to put some skin in the game, literally.

The pilots gave a thumbs-up: the signal that they had made contact with the Special Forces on the ship and that the landing zone was safe. The ocean suddenly turned from blue to green and then became sand as the massive chopper began its descent. Skybox was out first and directing Gia to duck low. Scott saw a line of Navy soldiers in the same black battle gear he had worn on that fateful day. DJ exited after Gia, and Scott saw Kaylie yelling and screaming from the side of the platform. His heart soared. *She's alive!*

Scott took a deep breath as the pilots shut the engine down and the rotors slowed their motion. Scott climbed from the far side door that was now open. The devastation on this side of the ship was a blow. He tried to take it in: he had never seen so many dead bodies everywhere, even in the movies. The smell of decay was noticeable already. Flocks of seagulls hopped among the debris along with vultures and other creatures feasting on the carrion.

He walked to the rear of the chopper and recovered his and Gia's duffles. He was delaying, he knew. But he was terrified to learn whom he had lost.

Coming around the front of the massive, gray helicopter he saw familiar faces: Angel, DeVonte, Solo and Kaylie. Thank God there were survivors. Kaylie and DJ were locked in an embrace. Then he saw Todd and there...there was his brother.

Bobby and Todd locked eyes on Scott at the same time and both men shared a single expression of shocked amazement. Scott gave a wave of delight as he saw that both his brother and his buddy were alive and well. He took Gia's hand and walked over to greet them. "Hey, guys, miss me?"

EPILOGUE

Manassas, Virginia

Over a thousand miles away, Tahir closed out the open debriefing file on the tablet.

Jesus Christ! What did they think they were doing? Surely no one could be that stupid. Then again, he remembered sadly, he had spent much of his career working for the US Government, so he was quite familiar with their unimaginable levels of stupidity. But this . . . this was on a whole new level entirely. He looked down; his palms were sweating, and he felt bile rising in his throat. He was used to fear and paranoia, they had been his near-constant allies for much of his life. From the near-misses with the law in his early teens to the more serious adversaries he had dealt with as a young hacker, Tahir had learned to trust his gut and normally discovered that those in power—people in general for that matter—were just as weak and deceitful as he feared.

"Okay, think . . . think. Fuck, man, you have to have a plan!" He was talking to himself again. *Never a good sign.* It was, however, part of his problem-solving ritual. *I need a Red Bull.* He remembered he had consumed the last of them the previous week. "Shit."

While most people looked for a solution in a logical, analytical and linear manner, Tahir's brain was wired differently. When he met a challenge, his cerebral systems erupted into chaos, storming over multiple pathways simultaneously. Early on, he had self-diagnosed himself as something of an autistic savant. He had become skilled at solving complex puzzles at the age of three. By six, he was routinely beating adults at games of all types. Tahir became bored very quickly and had to keep challenging himself with increasingly tougher games and tests of his abilities. When he discovered computers and, later, the Internet, his prowess really blossomed.

Tahir had worked for the government, not his choice, but more like his only option. He had been part of a very elite group for many years, doing his part to keep America safe, but more importantly, seeking out the hidden puzzles that held clues of threats to the nation. On that fateful day last August, it had all fallen apart. Now, somehow, it was continuing to do so, in ever more shitty ways.

The folder file had an innocuous sounding name, Operation Homefront. The Navy—the *fucking* US Navy!—was bringing home soldiers and expats from overseas. *The idiots!* What were they thinking? The first of the ships had docked in Baltimore several days ago, and more were on the way.

It sounded good and noble on the surface, but among those returning were any number of people infected by the Chimera Pox: the pandemic that had wiped out Europe and much of Asia and now had been delivered to American shores by the US *fucking* Navy.

Tahir was moving fast now, stowing the tablet and securing the servers for remote connections only. His location for most of the last twelve months had been an abandoned, and very covert server farm owned by one if his previous employers, the NSA. Most of the complex was located underground. He looked at the darkened rows of towering server racks and the metal cage that was his modest living quarters. The setup had been nearly ideal for him, and he was one of the few people to know of its existence and location.

But it was time to go. The infected were only hours away. It seemed that the US would now follow the rest of the world into total anni-hilation.

He shut down the lights and everything that was unnecessary. He would dearly miss having these eyes and ears on the world, so close at hand. This server farm had been an integral part of America's and his own intelligence gathering apparatus. He prayed that the systems would survive here in their hidden hole in the ground. He picked up the last bag and walked the length of the cavernous hole in the ground, equivalent to two football fields, and then up the metal steps to the access door.

He had no real plan and only one friend who might help: Scott. He had felt bad sharing the sensitive Catalyst files with him when the CME hit, but someone else had needed to know. Scott was a good man, and he possessed more common sense than most people Tahir knew.

He had mapped out Scott's location but knew it would be a nearly impossible trip even assuming the Messengers, the Navy, the Guard or whoever was throwing their weight around now would let him pass. And who knew what other obstacles he might have to face. Regardless, he had to leave the east coast behind and he had to do it now.

The access door to the outside world opened silently, and he pushed the hinged shelving unit aside. The exit was from a small metal building on the side of a private runway. It was actually a power junc-tion: a maintenance shed for the runway lights. He pushed the shelves back again to conceal the hidden door. On the opposite side of the runway was a golf course and country club, now overgrown and deeply trivial looking. Few ever realized that beneath the once exquisitely manicured greens lay one of the most sophisticated intelligence gath-ering operations in the world.

He opened the tablet to check his drone feeds once more. All clear. With that, he dashed across the runway to the hangar with the keys to the small Honda HA-420 turbojet gripped tightly in his hands. Getting his pilot's license many years earlier had been the one activity in the real world that he enjoyed immensely. He now held an A type ratings license for private jets. The rating was not even two years old, but he was a competent pilot. It had taken him a great deal of time to find a jet that was still operational and fly it here to this hangar without being discovered. The prototype jet had been at a DC area FAA hangar undergoing testing for final approval. The jet's main computer had been located in a testing lab and some of the jet's other systems seemed to have been hardened against the effects of the CME. Reinstalling the computer was all he had had to do to get the bird operational.

He pushed the large hangar doors clear and tossed the bags into the beautiful machine. He prayed to Allah that there would be a suitable runway somewhere near Harris Springs, Mississippi, for him to land. Despite his anxiety, he did a quick, but thorough, preflight check. He paid close attention to the fuel sample he extracted from the tank. Seeing no contamination, he tossed it aside and climbed in. Strapping the harness securely, he plugged in a course on the flight computer to Biloxi, Mississippi, and began the ignition sequence.

The engines started as a whisper but quickly gained in volume. The sleek, red and white jet moved slowly out of the open hangar and onto the runway. Tahir paused to look at the golf course once more, and the black smoke billowing in the distance. He pushed the throttle to full and released the brakes. The jet seemed to leap into the air, and he climbed quickly as he went into the turn required to take him south.

The ruins of DC were below him now, and to the east, nearer the Baltimore waterfront, the landscape burned, engulfed in flame. He saw planes making attack runs and remembered to stay below radar until he was well out of the area. He would be flying relatively low until he was over Kentucky—not the safest flight plan since the Appalachian Mountains were just ahead, but the jet was equipped with excellent maneuverability and radar. If he could just avoid detection, he would be on the Gulf Coast in under three hours. That was about all the fuel he had anyway. One way or another, it would be his destination.

ABOUT THE AUTHOR

Best Selling author, JK Franks world is shaped by his love of history, science and all things sci-fi. His work is most often filled with vivid characters set in dire situations only a step or so away from our normal world. His focus on gritty realism and attention to meticulous detail help transport his readers into his stories.

The first novel of his apocalyptic Catalyst series: Downward Cycle, was published in 2016. The follow-up to that, Kingdoms of Sorrow, continued the tale of a near-future apocalyptic event and a group of survivors' efforts to hang on to the remnants of a collapsing civilization. The novella American Exodus published late in 2017 takes a look at the disaster from a fresh and more personal perspective. Look for at least one more book in the series.

Always writing, JK Franks now lives in West Point, Georgia, with his wife and family. No matter where he is or what's going on, he tries his best to set aside time every day to answer emails and messages from readers. You can also visit him on the web at www.jkfranks.com. Please subscribe to his newsletter for updates, sneak peeks, promotions, and giveaways. You can also find the author on Facebook and Twitter or email him directly at media@jkfranks.com.

Please connect with the author online:
www.jkfranks.com
media@jkfranks.com

OTHER BOOKS BY JK FRANKS:
The Catalyst Series

Book 1: Downward Cycle

Life in a remote oceanfront town spirals downward after a massive solar flare causes a global blackout. But the loss of electrical power is just the first of the problems facing the survivors in the chaos that follows. Is this how the world ends?

Book 2: Kingdoms of Sorrow

With civilization in ruins, individuals band together to survive and build a new society. The threats are both grave and numerous—surely too many for a small group to weather. This is a harrowing story of survival following the collapse of the planet's electric grids.

Book 2.5: American Exodus Novella

This Amazon best selling companion story to the Catalyst series follows one man's struggle to get back home after the collapse. No supplies, no idea of the hardships to come; how can he possibly survive the journey? Even if he survives, can he adapt to this new reality?

Please click here to leave review

Connect with the Author Online:

** For a sneak peek at new novels, free stories and more, join the email list at: www.jkfranks.com/Email

Facebook: facebook.com/JKFranksAuthor

Amazon Author Page: amazon.com/-/e/B01HIZIYH0

Smashwords: smashwords.com/profile/view/kfranks22

Goodreads: goodreads.com/author/show/15395251.J_K_Franks

Website: JKFranks.com

Twitter: @jkfranks

Instagram: @jkfranks1